MERLIN

Merlin is the second book of the Pendragon Cycle: a magnificent epic set against the backcloth of Roman Britain and the legends of Arthur and Atlantis.

STEPHEN LAWHEAD has established his name among the front ranks of contemporary fantasy writers. His novels bear the hallmarks of a master storyteller – compelling narrative, gripping suspense and awesome climax. Among his dozen or more novels the Pendragon Cycle and the three books which make up his Song of Albion trilogy are the most recent and the most outstanding.

Research for his Celtic-based novels led Lawhead, an American, to move to Oxford, where he now lives and works with his wife, writer Alice Slaikeu Lawhead, and their two sons, Ross and Drake.

MERLIN

BOOK II OF THE PENDRAGON CYCLE

STEPHEN LAWHEAD

A LION BOOK

Copyright © 1988 Stephen Lawhead

Published by
Lion Publishing plc
Sandy Lane West, Oxford, England
ISBN 0 7459 1310 5

First published by Crossway Books
Published by arrangement with Good News Publishers

First UK edition 1988
20 19 18 17 16 15 14 13 12

A catalogue record for this book is available
from the British Library

Printed and bound in Great Britain
by Caledonian International Book Manufacturing, Glasgow

BRITAIN

Scale of Miles

0   20   40   60   80

PICTLAND

THE WALL

Caer Lig

Celyddon Forest

Goddeu

Eboracum

Diganhwy   Deva

Caer Seiont   Yr Widdfa

Caer Dyvi

Caer Myrddin

Caer Legionis

Londinium

MOR HAFREN

Ynys Avallach

Caer Cam

Tintagel

LLYONESSE

THE NARROW SEAS

GAUL

**DEDICATED TO
THE MEMORY OF
JAMES L. JOHNSON**

PRONUNCIATION GUIDE

While many of the old British names may look odd to modern readers, they are not as difficult to pronounce as they seem at first glance. A little effort, and the following guide, will help you enjoy the sound of these ancient words.

Consonants — as in English, but with a few exceptions:

c:	hard, as in *c*at (never soft as in *c*entury)
ch:	hard, as in Scottish Lo*ch*, or Ba*ch* (never soft, as in *ch*urch)
dd:	th as in *th*en (never as in *th*istle)
f:	v, as in o*f*
ff:	f, as in o*ff*
g:	hard, as in *g*irl (never *g*em)
ll:	a Welsh distinctive, sounded as 'tl' or 'hl' on the sides of the tongue
r:	trilled, lightly
rh:	as if hr, heavy on the 'h' sound
s:	always as in *s*ir (never hi*s*)
th:	as in *th*istle (never *th*en)

Vowels — as in English, but with the general lightness of short vowel sounds:

a:	as in f*a*ther
e:	as in m*e*t (when long, as in l*a*te)
i:	as in p*i*n (long, as in *ea*t)
o:	as in n*o*t
u:	as in p*i*n (long, as in *ea*t)
w:	a 'double-u,' as in vac*uu*m, or t*oo*l; but becomes a consonant before vowels, as in the name G*w*en
y:	as in p*i*n; or sometimes as 'u' in b*u*t (long as in *ea*t)

(As you can see, there is not much difference in i, u, and y — they are virtually identical to the beginner)

Accent — normally is on the next to last syllable, as in Di-gán-hwy
Diphthongs — each vowel is pronounced individually, so Taliesin = Tallyéssin
Atlantean — Ch=kh, so Charis is Khár-iss

Ten rings there are, and nine gold torcs
on the battlechiefs of old;
Eight princely virtues, and seven sins
for which a soul is sold;
Six is the sum of earth and sky,
of all things meek and bold;
Five is the number of ships that sailed
from Atlantis lost and cold;
Four kings of the Westerlands were saved,
three kingdoms now behold;
Two came together in love and fear,
in Llyonesse stronghold;
One world there is, one God, and one birth
the Druid stars foretold.

SRL

PROLOGUE

They were going to kill Arthur. Can you imagine? They would have killed him, too, but I put a stop to it. The arrogance! The stupidity!

Not that Uther was ever one for a scholar's cope. I expected more from Ygerna, though; she at least had the canny sense of her people. But, she was afraid. Yes, frightened of the whispered voices, frightened of her suddenly exalted position, frightened of Uther and desperate to please him. She was so young.

So Arthur had to be saved, and at no little expense to myself. I had heard about their sordid plan in the way I have, and made it my affair to confront Uther with it early on. He denied all, of course.

'Do you think me mad?' he shouted. He was always shouting. 'The child could be male,' he said, suppressing a sly smile. 'It could well be my heir we are talking about!'

Uther is a warrior and there is an honesty about that: steel does not lie. Lucky for him he was a man born to his time. He would never have made a decent magistrate, let alone governor — he is a sorry liar. As High King he ruled with a sword in one hand and a bludgeon in the other: the sword for the Saecsen, the bludgeon for the petty kings below him.

Ygerna was just as bad in her own way. She said nothing, but stood wringing those long white hands of hers, and twisting her silken mantle into knots, staring at me with those big, dark doe eyes that had trapped Uther. Her stomach had just begun to swell; she could not have been more than four or five months pregnant.

Still, she was pregnant enough to begin having second thoughts about the nasty work ahead. I do not think any mother could coldly kill her own child, or stand by and see it done. I am not so sure about Uther. . . he of the strong

11

arm and wandering eye. Pendragon of Britain. Capable of anything — which was the better half of his power where the small kings were concerned — he was not one to shrink from any course set before him.

Outside on the black rocks the waves crashed and the white gulls cried. Ygerna touched a hand to her stomach — a brushing touch with fingertips — and I knew she would listen to reason. Ygerna would be an ally.

So it did not matter what Uther said or did not say, admitted or did not admit. I would have my way. . .

My way. Was it? Was it ever *my* way? There's a thought.

Ah, but I am getting ahead of myself. I always am. This is to be Arthur's story. Yes, but there is more to Arthur than his birth. To understand him, you have to understand the land. This land, this Island of the Mighty.

And you have to understand me, for I am the man who made him.

BOOK
ONE

KING

ONE

Many years have come and gone since I awakened in this worlds-realm. Too many years of darkness and death, disease, war, and evil. Yes, very much evil.

But life was bright once, bright as sunrise on the sea and moonglow on water, bright as the fire on the hearth, bright as the red-gold torc around my grandfather Elphin's throat. Bright, I tell you, and full of every good thing.

I know that every man recalls something of the same golden sheen in life's beginning, but my memories are not less real or true for that.

Merlin. . . a curious name. Perhaps. No doubt my father would have chosen a different name for his son. But my mother can be forgiven for her lapse. Merlin — Myrddin among my father's people — suits me. Yet, every man has two names: the one he is given, and the one he wins for himself.

Emrys is the name I have won among men and it is my own.

Emrys, Immortal. . . Emrys, Divine. . . Emrys Wledig, king and prophet to his people. Ambrosius it is to the Latin speakers, and Embries to the people of southern Britain and Lloegres.

But Myrddin Emrys am I to the Cymry of the hill-bound fastness of the west. And because they were my father's people, I feel they are my own as well. Although my mother long ago taught me the folly of this belief, it comforts me — much, I suppose, as it must have comforted my father in his times of doubt.

And as there is much evil in the world, there is much doubt also. This is not the least of the Adversary's servants. And there are so many others. . .

Well, and well, get on with it, Mumbler. What treasures from your plundered store will you lay before us?

I take up my staff and stir the embers and I see again the images of my earliest memory: Ynys Avallach, the Isle of Avallach. It is the home of my grandfather, King Avallach, the Fisher King, and the first home I ever knew. It was here in these polished halls of his palace that I took my first faltering steps.

See, here are the white-blossomed apple groves, the salt marshes and mirror-smooth lake below the looming Tor, the white-washed shrine on the nearby hill. And there is the Fisher King himself: dark and heavy-browed like a summer thunderstorm, stretched on his pallet of red silk, Avallach was a fearful figure to a child of three, though kind as the heart within him would allow.

And here is my mother, Charis, tall and slim, of such regal bearing as to shame all pretenders, and possessing a grace that surpasses mere beauty. Golden-haired Daughter of Lleu-Sun, Lady of the Lake, Mistress of Avallon, Queen of the Faery — her names and titles, like my own, proliferate with time — all these and more men call her, and they are not wrong.

I was, I knew, the sole treasure of my mother's life; she was never at any pains to disguise the fact. Good Dafyd, the priest, gave me to know that I was a beloved child of the Living God, and his stories about God's Son, Jesu, kindled my soul with an early longing for paradise just as Hafgan, Chief Druid, wise and true, faithful servant in his own way, taught me the taste of knowledge, awakening a hunger I have never satisfied.

If there was want in the world, I knew nothing of it. Neither did I know fear or danger. The days of my childhood were blessed with peace and plenty. On Ynys Avallach, at least, time and the events of the wider world stood off, remote; trouble was heard merely as a muted distant murmur — soft like the wailing of the *bhean sidhe*, the Little Dark People, the Hill Folk, in the stone circles on the far hilltops; distant as the roar of a winter storm cresting mighty Yr Widdfa in the rockbound north.

Trouble there was, make no mistake. But in those sun-sweet days of my earliest remembrance we lived as the gods of an older time: aloof and unconcerned with the squabbles of the lesser beings around us. We were the Fair Folk, enchanted presences from the Westerlands living on the Glass Isle. Those who shared our waterworld of marsh and lake held us in great esteem and greater dread.

This had its uses. It served to keep strangers at a safe distance. We were not strong in the ways men respect strength, so the web of tales that grew around us served where force of arms did not.

If that sounds to you, in the age of reason and power, a weak, ineffectual thing, I tell you it was not. In that age, men's lives were hedged about with beliefs old as fear itself, and those beliefs were not easily altered, nor less easily abandoned.

Ah, but look! Here is Avallach standing before me on a dew-spangled morning, hand pressed to his side in his habitual gesture, smiling through his black beard as he would always smile when he saw me, saying, 'Come, little Hawk, the fish are calling — they are unhappy. Let us take the boat and see if we might liberate a few of them.'

And, hand-in-hand, we go down the path to the lake to fish, Avallach working the oar, little Merlin holding tight to the gunwale with both small hands. Avallach sings, he laughs, he tells me sad stories of Lost Atlantis and I listen as only a child can listen, with the whole of my heart.

The sun climbs high over the lake, and I look back towards the reedy shore and there is my mother, waiting for me. When I look she waves and calls us back, and Avallach turns the boat and rows to meet her and we return to the palace. Although she never speaks of it, I know that she grows uneasy when I am too long from her sight.

I did not know the reason for it then; I know it now.

But life to a child of three is a heady daze of pleasures spinning through a universe too impossibly rich to comprehend or experience except in frenzied snatches — not that it is *ever* comprehended or experienced in any other way — an unimaginable wealth of wonders displayed for instant plunder. Tiny vessel though I was, I dipped full and deep in the dizzy flood of sensation to collapse at the end of each day drunk with life and exhausted in each small limb.

If Ynys Avallach was all my world, I was given the freedom of it. There was no nook too small, no corner too forgotten, but that I knew it and made it my own. Stables, kitchens, audience hall, bed chambers, gallery, portico, or gardens, I wandered where I would. And if I had been king I could not have commanded more authority, for every childish whim was honoured with unthinking deference by those around me.

Thus, I came to know early the substance and use of power. Great Light, you know I have never sought it for myself! Power was offered me and I took it. Where is the wrong in that?

In those days, however, power was seen differently. Right and wrong were what men conceived in their own minds and hearts. Sometimes in truth, more often in error. There were no judges in the land, no standard men could point to and say, 'You see, this is right!' Justice was that which issued from the steel in a king's hand.

You would do well to remember this.

But these ideas of justice and right came later, much later. There was living to be done first, a foundation to be erected on which to build the man.

The Island of the Mighty, in those days, lay in a welter of confusion which is common enough now, but was seldom seen then. Kings and princes vied for position and power. Did I say kings? There were more kings than sheep, more princes than crows on a battlefield, more ambitious little men than salmon in season; and each prince and princeling, chief and king, each jumped-up official with a Roman title seeking to snatch what he could from the slavering jaws of onrushing Night, to squirrel it away, thinking that when the darkness finally came he could sit in his den and gloat and preen and gorge himself on his good fortune.

How many of those choked on it instead?

As I say, they were times of confusion, and the spirit may become as confused as the mind and heart. The central fact of my early life was the deep love and peace that enfolded me. I knew, even then, that this was extraordinary, but children accept the extraordinary with the same facile assent as the dreary commonplace.

Was I conscious of the things that set me apart from other men? Did I know I was different? An incident from those far-gone days stands out in my mind. Once, when at

18

my daily lessons with Blaise, my tutor and friend, a question occurred to me.

'Blaise,' I asked, 'why is Hafgan so old?' We were sitting in the apple grove below the Tor watching the clouds race westward. I could not have been more than five summers old myself, I think.

'You think him old?'

'He must be very old to know so much.'

'Oh, yes, Hafgan has lived long and seen much. He is very wise.'

'I want to be as wise one day.'

'Why?' he asked, cocking his head to one side.

'To know things,' I answered, 'to know about everything.'

'And once you knew about everything what would you do?'

'I would be a king and tell everyone.'

King, yes; it was in my mind even then that I would be a king. I do not think anyone had ever mentioned it to me before that time, but already I sensed the shape my early life would take.

I can still hear Blaise's reply as clearly as if he were speaking to me now: 'It is a great thing to be a king, Hawk. A very great thing, indeed. But there is authority of a kind even kings must bend to. Discover this and, whether you wear a torc of gold or beggar's rags, your name will burn for ever in men's minds.'

Of course, I understood nothing of what he told me then, but I remembered.

So it was that the subject of age was still quite fresh in my mind when, the very next day, Grandfather Elphin arrived on one of his frequent visits. The travellers were still climbing down from their saddles and calling their greetings as I marched up to the Chief Druid, who, as always, had accompanied Lord Elphin. I tugged on his robe and demanded, 'Tell me how old you are, Hafgan.'

'How old do you think me, Myrddin Bach?' I can see his smoke-grey eyes twinkling with joy, although he rarely smiled.

'Old as the oak on Shrine Hill,' I declared importantly.

He laughed then and others stopped talking to look at us. He took me by the hand and we walked a little apart. 'No,' he explained, 'I am not as old as that. But in the measure of men, I am old. Still, what is that to you? — who will live to be as old as any oak in the Island of the Mighty, if not far

19

older.' He gripped my hand tightly. 'To you is given much,' he said seriously, 'and, as Dafyd tells me from his book, much will be required.'

'Will I really be old as any oak?'

Hafgan lifted his shoulders and shook his head. 'Who can say, little one?'

It is much to Hafgan's credit that although he knew who I was, he never burdened me with that knowledge, or the expectations that surely went with it. No doubt, he had had ample experience with one like me before: I imagine my father had taught him much about nurturing a prodigy. Oh, Hafgan, if you could see me now!

After that visit, although I do not recall it as special in any way, I began to travel further from home — at least, I began to visit the Summerlands regularly and my view of the world enlarged accordingly. We called them the Summerlands because that is what my father, Taliesin, had called the land Avallach had given his people.

Grandfather Elphin and grandmother Rhonwyn were always happy to see me and devoted themselves to spoiling me on my visits, undoing months of my mother's hard work. Charis never complained, never hinted at what she thought of their indulgence, but let them have their way with me. This eventually included weapons lessons undertaken by Lord Elphin's battlechief, a crag of a man named Cuall, who strove with me and some of the younger boys, although he had a warband to look after as well.

Cuall it was who made my first sword out of ashwood; my first spear also. The sword was thin and light and no longer than my arm, but to me it was a blade invincible. With that wooden weapon he taught me thrust and counter-thrust, and the quick, back-handed chop; and with the spear, to throw accurately with either hand off either foot. He taught me how to sit a horse and guide it with my knees, and how, when need arose, to use the hapless beast as a shield.

In my sixth year, I spent all summer with grandfather Elphin — Hafgan and Cuall all but fighting over me. Between them, I saw little of anyone else all summer. My mother came and stayed for a few days, and at first I was disappointed to see her, thinking that she would take me home again. But she just wanted to see how I fared.

Once satisfied that it was right and necessary — as both Hafgan and Cuall insisted — she returned to Ynys Avallach and I stayed at Caer Cam. This began a pattern that was to continue for several years: winter at Ynys Avallach with Dafyd and Blaise, and summer at Caer Cam with Elphin and Cuall.

Lord Elphin's caer was a world apart from Avallach's palace: one bespoke the cool heights of intellectual refinement and otherworldly grace, the other the earthy reality of stone and sweat and steel. 'Brains and blood,' Cuall aptly put it one day.

'Lord?'

'Brains and blood, boy,' he repeated, 'that's what you have, and what every warrior needs.'

'Will I be a warrior?'

'If I can do anything about it, you will right enough,' he said, resting his thick forearms on the pommel of his long sword. 'Och, but you have Lleu's own way about you: quick as water, and light of foot as a cat; already you tax my craft. All you want is muscle on those bones of yours, lad, and from the look of you that will come in time.'

I was pleased with his pronouncement, and knew he was right. I *was* much quicker than the other boys; I could make good account of myself with boys twice my age, and fend off any two my own size. The ease with which my body accommodated whatever I asked of it, seemed to some uncanny, but to me only natural. That everyone could not meld and move mind and body so skilfully was something new to me. And, though it shames me to admit it, I did wear my prowess with insufferable conceit.

Humility, if it comes at all, almost always comes too late.

So, I learned two things early: I would live long, and I would be a warrior king. The third thing, Blaise's Mantle of Authority, would be discovered by me or it would not; I saw no reason to strive after it, so thought no more about it.

But I badly wanted to be a warrior. Had I possessed even the tiniest suspicion of how heavily this aspiration weighed on my mother, I might have reined in my enthusiasm somewhat, at least in her presence. I was blind and silly with it, though, and talked almost of nothing else.

No one laboured harder, or enjoyed his labours more than I. First awake among the boys in the boys' house, and out on the yard before sunrise for sword practice, or riding, or throwing, or shieldwork, or wrestling. . . I embraced it all with the ardour of a zealot. And the summer passed in a white-hot blaze of youthful passion; I prayed that it would last for ever.

Nevertheless, the summer ended and I returned to Ynys Avallach with Blaise and an escort of warriors. I remember riding through bright autumn days, passing fields ripening to harvest and small, prosperous settlements where we were greeted warmly and fed.

My mother was overjoyed to see me home at last, but I sensed a sadness in her, too. And I noticed that her eyes followed my every move, and lingered on my face. Had I changed somehow in those few months at Caer Cam?

'You are growing so fast, my little Hawk,' she told me. 'Soon you will fly this nest.'

'I will never leave here. Where would I go?' I asked, genuinely puzzled. The thought of leaving had never occurred to me.

Charis shrugged lightly, 'Oh, you will find a place somewhere and make it your own. You must, you see, if you are to be the Lord of Summer.'

So that was on her mind. 'Is it not a real place, Mother?'

She smiled a little sadly and shook her head. 'No — that is, not yet. It is up to you, my soul, to create the Kingdom of Summer.'

'I thought the Summerlands —'

'No,' she shook her head again, but the sadness had passed and I saw the light of the vision come up in her eyes, 'the Summerlands are not the Kingdom, though your father may have intended them to be. The Kingdom of Summer is wherever the Summer Lord resides. It only waits for you to claim it, Hawk.'

We talked about the Kingdom of Summer then, but our talk was different now. No longer was the Kingdom a story such as a mother might tell a child; it had changed. From that time I began to think of it as a realm that did exist in some way and only waited to be called into being. And for the first time I understood that my destiny, like my father's, was woven thread and strand into his vision of that golden land.

That autumn I resumed my studies with Dafyd, the priest at the shrine. I read from his holy texts, badly patched and faded as they were, and we discussed what I read. At the same time, I continued my lessons with Blaise who instructed me in the druid arts. I could not imagine giving up either endeavour and in the following years gave myself mind and soul to my study, as I gave body and heart to my weapons each summer at Caer Cam.

I confess it was not easy; I often felt pulled in all directions despite my various tutors' attempts to ensure that I should not. Never did a boy have more caring teachers. Still, it is inevitable, I suppose, when someone desires so much so badly. My teachers were aware of my discomfort and felt it themselves.

'You need not drive yourself so hard, Myrddin,' Blaise told me one drizzly, miserable winter evening as I sat struggling with a long recitation entitled the Battle of the Trees. 'There are other things than being a bard, you know. Look around you, not everyone is.'

'My father, Taliesin, was a bard. Hafgan says he was the greatest bard who ever lived.'

'So he believes.'

'You do not believe it?'

He laughed. 'Who could disagree with the Chief Druid?'

'You have not answered the question, Blaise.'

'Very well,' he paused and reflected long before answering. 'Yes, your father was the greatest bard among us; and more, he was my brother and friend. But,' he held up a cautionary finger, 'Taliesin was. . . ' again a long pause, and a slight lifting of the shoulders as he stepped away from saying what was in his mind, 'but it is not everyone who can be what he was, or do the things that he did.'

'I *will* be a bard. I will work harder, Blaise. I promise.'

He shook his head and sighed. 'It is not a question of working harder, Hawk.'

'What do you want me to do?' I whined. 'Just tell me.'

His dark eyes were soft with sympathy; he was trying to help me in the best way he knew. 'Your gifts are different, Merlin. You cannot be your father.'

If they did not act in me at that moment, his words would come back to me many times.

'I will be a bard, Blaise.'

I am Merlin, and I am immortal. A quirk of birth? A gift from my mother? The legacy of my father? I do not know how

23

it is but I know that it is true. Neither do I know the source of the words that fill my head and fall from my lips like firedrops onto the tinder of men's hearts.

The words, the images: what is, what was and will be. . . I have but to look. A bowl of black oak water, the glowing embers of a fire, smoke, clouds, the faces of men themselves — I have but to look and the mists grow thin and I peer a little way along the scattered paths of time.

Was there ever a time such as this?

Never! And that is both the glory and the terror of it. If men knew what it was that loomed before them, within reach of even the lowest — they would quail, they would faint, they would cover their heads and stop their mouths with their cloaks for screaming. It is their blessing and their curse that they do not know. But I know; I, Merlin, have always known.

TWO

'The boy has the eyes of a preying bird,' Maximus said, resting his hand on my head and gazing down into my face. He should know; his own eyes had something of the predator as well. 'I do not believe I have ever seen eyes of such colour in a man before — like yellow gold.' His smile was dagger sharp. 'Tell me, Merlinus, what do you see with those golden eyes of yours?'

An odd question to ask a child of seven. But an image formed itself in my mind:

A sword — not the short, broad *gladius* of the legionary, but the long, tapering length of singing lightning of the Celt. The hilt was handsome bronze wrapped in braided silver with a great amethyst of imperial purple in the pommel. The jewel was engraved with the Eagle of the Legion, fierce and proud, catching sunlight in its dark heart and smouldering with a deep and steady fire.

'I see a sword,' I said. 'The hilt is silver and bears a purple gem carved like an eagle. It is an emperor's sword.'

Both Maximus and Lord Elphin — my father's father, who stood beside me — looked on me with wonder, as though I had spoken a prophecy great and terrible in its mystery. I merely told them what I saw.

Magnus Maximus, Commander of the Legions of Britain, gazed thoughtfully at me. 'What else do you see, lad?'

I closed my eyes. 'I see a ring of kings; they are standing like stones in a stone circle. A woman kneels in their midst, and she holds the Sword of Britain in her hands. She is speaking, but no one hears her. No one listens. I see the blade rusting and forgotten.'

Although Romans were always keen for an omen, I do not think he expected such an answer from me. He stared for a moment; I felt his fingers go slack in my hair, and then he turned away abruptly. 'King Elphin! You look fit as ever. This soft land has not softened you, I see.' He and my grandfather walked off, arms linked: two old friends met and recognized as equals.

We were there at Caer Cam the morning he arrived. I was training the pony Elphin had given me, desperate to break the wily creature to the halter so that I could ride it home in a few days' time. The little black-and-white animal seemed more goat than horse and what had begun as a simple trial with a braided rope harness soon grew to an all-out war of wills with mine suffering the worst of it.

The sun was lowering and the evening mist rising in the valley. Wood pigeons were winging to their nests, and swallows swooped and dived through the still, light-filled air. Then I heard it — a sound to make me stop rock still and listen: a rhythmic drumming in the earth, a deep, resonant rumble rolling over the land.

Cuall, my grandfather's battlechief, was watching me and became concerned. 'What is it, Myrddin Bach? What is wrong?' Myrddin Bach, he called me: Little Hawk.

I did not answer, but turned my face towards the east and, dropping the braided length of leather, ran to the ramparts, calling as I ran, 'Hurry! Hurry! He is coming!'

If I had been asked who was coming, I could not have made an answer. But the instant I peered between the sharpened stakes I knew that someone very important would soon arrive, for in the distance, as we looked down along the valley, we could see the long, snaking double line of a column of men moving northwest. The rumble I had heard was the booming cadence of their marching drums and the steady plod of their feet on the old hard track.

I looked and saw the failing sunlight bright on their shields and on the eagle standards going before them. Dust trailed into the dusky sky at the rear of the column where the supply wagons came trundling on. There must have been a thousand men or more moving in those two long lines. Cuall took one look and sent one of the warband racing for Lord Elphin.

'It is Macsen,' confirmed Elphin, when he arrived.

'Thought as much,' replied Cuall cryptically.

'It has been a long time,' said my grandfather. 'We must make ready to welcome him.'

'You think he will turn aside?'

'Of course. It will soon be dark and he will need a place to sleep. I will send an escort to bring him.'

'I will see to it, lord,' offered Cuall, and he strode away across the caer. Grandfather and I returned to the survey of the valley road.

'Is he a king?' I asked, though I knew he must be for I had never known anyone to travel with such an enormous warband.

'A king? No, Myrddin Bach, he is *Dux Britanniarum* and answers only to Imperator Gratian himself.'

I searched my scant Latin. . . *dux* . . . 'Duke'?

'Like a battlechief,' Elphin explained, 'but far greater; he commands all Roman forces in the Island of the Mighty. Some say he will be Imperator himself one day, although from what I have seen of emperors a *dux* with a cohort at his back wields more power where it counts.'

Not long after Cuall and ten of Elphin's warband rode out, a party of about thirty men returned. The strangers were strange indeed to my eyes: big, thick-limbed men in hardened leather or metal breastplates, carrying short bulky swords and ugly iron-tipped javelins, their legs wrapped in red wool which was tied to mid-thigh by the straps of their heavy hob-nailed sandals.

The riders pounded up the twisting path to the gates of the caer and I ran round the ramparts to meet them. The timber gates swung open and the iron-shod horses galloped into the caer. Between two standard bearers rode Maximus, his handsome red cloak stained and dusty, his sun-darkened face brown as walnut, a short fringe of a black beard on his chin.

He reined the horse to a halt and dismounted as Elphin came to greet him. They embraced like friends long absent from one another, and I realized that my grandfather was a man of some renown. Seeing him next to the powerful stranger my heart soared. He was no longer my grandfather but a king in his own right.

As other horsemen entered the caer Elphin turned to me

and beckoned me to him. I stood at stiff attention while the Duke of Britain inspected me closely, his sharp, black eyes probing as spearpoints. 'Hail, Merlinus,' he said in a voice husky with fatigue and road dust, 'I greet you in the name of our Mother, Rome.'

Then Maximus took my hand in his, and when he withdrew it I saw a gold victory coin shining there.

That was my first introduction to Magnus Maximus, *Dux Britanniarum*. And it was before him then and there that I spoke my first prophecy.

There was feasting that night. After all, it is not every day that the Duke of Britain visits. The drinking horns circled the hall, and I was dizzy trying to keep them filled. Through a timber hall dark with the smoke of roasting meat and loud with the chatter of warriors and soldiers regaling one another with lies of their exploits on the twin fields of bed and battle, I wandered, a jar of mead in my hands to refill the empty horns, cups, and bowls. I thought myself most fortunate to be included in a warrior's feast — even if only as a serving boy.

Later, when the torches and tallow lamps burned low, Hafgan, Chief Bard to my grandfather, brought out his harp and told the tale of the Three Disastrous Plagues. This brought forth great gales of laughter. And I laughed with the rest, happy to be included with the men on this auspicious night, and not sent down to the boys' house with the others.

What a night! Rich and raucous and full, and I understood that to be a king with a great hall filled with fearless companions was the finest thing a man could achieve, and I vowed that one day this fine thing would be mine.

I did not speak to Maximus again while he stayed with Lord Elphin, though he and my grandfather talked at length the next day before the Duke departed and returned to his troops waiting in the valley. I say I did not speak to him, but when his horse was brought to him and he swung up into the saddle, Maximus saw me and raised his hand slowly, touching the back of his hand to his forehead. It is a sign of honour and respect — an unusual gesture with which to favour a child. No one else saw it, nor were they meant to.

He said farewell to my grandfather — they clasped one another's arms in the way of kinsmen — and he rode away with his commanders. From on top of the earthen bank outside the palisade I watched the column form up and move on through the Cam valley a short time later, following the Eagle standard.

I never saw Maximus again. And it was to be many, many years before I finally beheld the sword and realized that it had been his sword I had seen that day. That is why Maximus had looked at me the way he did. And that is why he saluted me.

This is where it begins:

First there is a sword, the Sword of Britain. And the sword *is* Britain.

THREE

In the spring of my eleventh year, I travelled with Blaise and Hafgan to Gwynedd and Yr Widdfa, the Region of Snows, in the mountainous north-west. It was a long journey and difficult, but necessary, for Hafgan was going home to die.

He told no one about this, as he found the prospect of leaving his people unspeakably sad. It was the leaving, not the dying he minded; Hafgan had long ago made his peace with God, and knew death to be the narrow door to another, higher life. And, though saying farewell to his kinsmen grieved him deeply, yet he yearned to see again the land of his youth before he died, so the journey became necessary.

Elphin insisted on sending an escort; if he had not done so Avallach surely would have. Given his own way, Hafgan would have forgone this honour; but he relented, since it was not for him that the warriors rode with us.

There were nine in the escort, making a total of twelve in all as we made ready to set out that day not long after Beltane, the fire festival marking the beginning of spring. Hafgan and the escort had come to Ynys Avallach where Blaise and I waited, eager to be off. On the morning of our leaving, I rose early and pulled on my tunic and trousers and ran down to the courtyard to find my mother dressed in riding garb, complete with short cloak and tall riding boots, her hair braided and bound in the white leather thong of the bull ring.

She held the reins of a mist-grey stallion and my first thought was that the horse must be for me. Hafgan stood nearby and they were talking together quietly, waiting for the others to appear. I greeted them and mentioned that I had preferred my black-and-white pony instead.

'Instead? Whatever can you mean?' Charis asked.

'Instead of the stallion, of course.' I pointed out that I was fond of the pony and planned on riding it.

My mother laughed and said, 'You are not the only person ever to master throwing a leg over the back of a horse.'

It was only then that I took in her appearance. 'You would go, too?'

'It is time I saw the place where your father grew up,' she explained, 'and besides, Hafgan has asked me and I can think of nothing I would enjoy more. We have been talking just now of stopping in Dyfed. I would like to see Maelwys and Pendaran again, and I could show you where you were born — would you like that?'

Whether I liked it or not she meant to go, and did. The imagined inconvenience to my notion of playing the warrior never materialized — my mother was more than a match for the rigours of the journey. We did not dawdle or slacken our pace because of her, and, as the familiar landscape sparked her memory with a thousand remembrances of my father, she recalled in vivid detail those first days of their life together. I listened to her and forgot all about pretending to be a fierce battlechief.

We crossed shining Mor Hafren and came to Caer Legionis, Fort of the Legions. The enormous fortress, like so many others in the land, long abandoned and falling into ruin, stood derelict and empty, shunned by the nearby town which still boasted a Magistrate. I had never seen a Roman city before and could find nothing of advantage in its straight streets and houses crowded too close to one another. Aside from the impressive spectacle of a forum and an arena, what I could see of the town inspired little hope for the improvement of life. A city is an unnatural place.

The country beyond was fair to look upon: smooth, lofty hills and winding glens with stone-edged streams and wide flats of grassland ideal for grazing herds of cattle and sheep, and the hardy, sure-footed little horses they bred and sold in horse markets as far away as Londinium and Eboracum.

At Maridunum — where my parents had fled after their marriage, and where I was born — our reception was warm and enthusiastic. King Pendaran considered himself something of a grandfather to both my mother and myself, and was overjoyed to see us. He clasped me heartily by both arms and said, 'I held you, lad, when you were no bigger than a cabbage.' His fringe of white hair feathered in the wind and he appeared in imminent danger of blowing away. Was this the fearsome Red Sword I had heard about?

Maelwys, his oldest son, ruled in Dyfed, however, and with Pendaran's clucking approval declared a feast upon our arrival and the lords under him, with their retinues, crowded his hall that night.

The lords of the Demetae and Silures were long established in the land and powerful. They had fiercely protected their independence, despite three hundred years of Roman meddling in their affairs — a feat ironically accomplished by forming early and advantageous alliances with the ruling houses of Rome itself, marrying well and wisely, and using their power to keep the Emperor and his minions at a safe distance. Like a rock in the sea, they had allowed the Empire to wash over them; but now that the tide was receding the rock stood unchanged.

Wealthy and proud of their wealth, they lacked any hint of the vanity that so often derives from riches. Simple men, adhering to the ways of their people and resisting change, they had kept alive the true Celtic spirit of their fathers. A few might live in sprawling villas of Roman design, or wear the title of Magistrate; one or another might have comfortably worn the purple, but the eyes that looked upon me in the hall that night saw the world little changed since the day of Bran the Blessed, whom they claimed had settled his tribe in these very hills.

We sat at the high table, my mother and I, surrounded by lords and chieftains, and I began to understand what my people had lost in the Great Conspiracy when the barbarians overran the Wall and attacked settlements as far south as Eboracum, and along both coasts as well. Elphin and the Cymry prospered in the Summerlands, it is true, but were a people cut off from their past — a kind of living death to the Celt. As to that, what had my mother's race lost when Atlantis was destroyed?

After a long and lively meal, Blaise sang and received a gold armband from Maelwys for his song. Then a cry went up for Hafgan to sing. He accepted the harp with diffidence and took his place in the hollow square formed by the tables, strumming the harpstrings idly.

His gaze fell on me and he stopped strumming and beckoned me. I rose and went to him and he placed the harp in my hands and I thought he meant for me to accompany him. 'What will you sing, Chief Bard?' I asked.

'Anything you like, little brother. Whatever you choose will be welcomed in this place.'

Still I thought he meant me to play for him. I fingered a chord and thought. The Birds of Rhiannon? Lleu and Levelys? 'What about the Dream of Arianrhod?' I asked.

He nodded and raised his hand, stepping away to leave me in the centre of the square. Shocked and confused, I stared after him. He merely inclined his head and returned to his place at Maelwys' left hand. What he had done was unprecedented: the Archdruid, Chief Bard of the Island of the Mighty, had relinquished his harp to me, an untried boy.

I had no time to contemplate the implications of his deed — all eyes were on me, the hall hushed. I swallowed hard and marshalled my fleeing thoughts. I could not remember a word of the tale and the pearl-inlaid harp might just as well have been an oxhide shield in my fumbling hands.

I closed my eyes, took a deep breath, forced my fingers to move over the impossibly-wooden strings, and opened my mouth, fully expecting to disgrace myself and Hafgan before the assembled lords when the words failed to come.

To my great relief and surprise the words of the song came back to me in the same instant my tongue began to move. I sang, shakily at first, but with growing confidence as I saw the song reflected on the faces of my listeners.

The tale is a long one — I would have chosen differently had I known I would be the one to sing it — but when I finished, the gathering seemed to sit an equally long time in silence. I could hear the soft flaring of the torches and the crackle of flames in the great firepit, and I was aware of all those dark Demetae and Siluri eyes on me.

I turned to my mother and saw a strange, rapt look on her face, her eyes glistening in the light. . . tears?

Slowly, the hall came back to life, as if from a sleep of enchantment. I did not dare sing again and no one asked me. Maelwys got to his feet and approached me. In full hearing of all present he said, 'No bard has ever sung so well and truly in my hearing, save one only. Once that bard came to this house and after hearing him sing I offered him my torc of gold. He did not take it, but gave me something instead — the name I

33

wear today.' He smiled, remembering. 'That bard was your father, Taliesin.'

He raised his hands to his neck and removed his torc. 'Now I offer the torc to you. Take it, if you will, for your song and for the memory of the one whose place you have taken this night.'

I did not know what to think. 'As my father did not accept your generous gift, it is not right that I should do so.'

'Then tell me what you will accept and I will give you that.' The lords of Dyfed watched me with interest.

I looked to my mother for help, thinking to see some expression or gesture to tell me what to do. But she only gazed at me with the same wonder as the others. 'Your kindness,' I began, 'to my people is worth more to me than lands or gold. As it is, I remain in your debt, Lord Maelwys.'

He smiled with great satisfaction, embraced me and returned to his place at the board. I gave the harp to Hafgan then and walked quickly from the hall, full to bursting with thoughts and emotions and straining to contain them and make sense of them.

Hafgan found me a little while later as I stood in the darkened courtyard, shivering, for the night was cold and I had forgotten my cloak. He gathered me under his robe and we stood together for a long time without speaking.

'What does it mean, Hafgan?' I said at last. 'Tell me, if you can.'

I thought he would not answer. Without turning his face from his contemplation of the star-strewn sky, Hafgan said, 'Once, when I was a young man, I stood in a circle of stones and saw a great and terrible sign in the heavens: a fall of stars like a mighty fire poured out from on high.

'Those stars were lighting your way to us, Myrddin Emrys.' He smiled at my reaction: Emrys is the divine epithet. 'Do not wonder that I call you Emrys, for from now on men will begin to recognize you.'

'*You* have done this, Hafgan,' I replied, my voice tight with accusation, for because of his words I felt the happiness of my childhood slipping away from me and tasted ashes in my mouth.

'No,' he said gently, 'I have done only what has been required of me, only what has been given me to do.'

I shivered, but not with cold now. 'I understand none of this,' I said miserably.

'Perhaps not, but soon you will. It is enough for now that you accept what I tell you.'

'What will happen, Hafgan? Do you know?'

'Only in part. But do not worry. All will become clear to you in time. Wisdom will be given when wisdom is required, courage when courage is required. All things are given in their season.' He lapsed into silence again and I studied the heavens with him, hoping to see something that would answer the storm in my soul. I saw only the cold-orbed stars swinging through their distant courses, and I heard the night wind singing around the tiled eaves of the villa and felt the emptiness of one cut off and alone.

Then we went inside and I slept in the bed where I was born.

Nothing more was said about what had taken place in Maelwys' hall — at least, not in my presence. I have no doubt others talked of it, if they talked of nothing else. It was a mercy to me not to have to answer for it.

We left Maridunum three days later. Maelwys would have accompanied us, but affairs of court prevented him. He, like some others, had once again adopted the custom of the kings of old: ringing his lands with hillforts and moving through his realm with his retinue, holding court in one hillfort after another in circuit.

He bade us farewell and would hear nothing from us but our promise to visit Maridunum on our return. Thus, we set out once more, riding north, following the old Roman track through the rising, heathered hills.

We saw eagles and red deer, wild pigs and foxes in abundance, a few wolves in the high places, and once a black bear. Several of the warband had brought hunting hounds and these were given the chase so that we did not lack for fresh meat at night. The days were getting warmer; but though the sun shone bright and there was little rain, the high country remained cool. A crackling fire kept away the night chill and a day in the saddle assured a sound sleep.

How can I describe coming into Caer Dyvi? It was not my home — certainly, I had never set eyes on those rugged hills and tree-lined valleys. But the sense of homecoming was so

35

strong in me that I sang for joy and rode fit to break my neck up the seacliff track to the ruined settlement.

We approached from the south on the sea side. Blaise had described the place to me in detail on the way, and I had heard my grandfather talk about it so often that I felt I knew the place as well as anyone born there. That was part of it; the other part may have been Hafgan's pleasure at seeing his home, though for him, as for Blaise, this was tempered with sadness.

I could feel nothing sorrowful about the place. High on the promontory overlooking the estuary and the sea to the west, and surrounded by dense woods to the east and high, rocky hills to the north, it seemed too peaceful a haven — like Ynys Avallach in its own way — to hold any sorrow, despite the unhappy events that had taken place there. Indeed, the jawless skull I saw half-buried in the long grass testified to the grim desperation of Caer Dyvi's final hours. Our warrior escort was subdued, respecting the spirits of the fallen and, after a brief inspection, returned to the horses.

The caer was uninhabited, of course, but the ribbed remains of Elphin's great hall and sections of the timber palisade above the ditch were still standing, along with the walls and foundations of some of the stone granaries. I was surprised at how small it seemed; I suppose I was used to Caer Cam and Ynys Avallach. But that it would have been a secure and comfortable settlement, I had no doubt.

Charis strolled among the grass-grown ruins, musing deeply on her private thoughts. I did not have the heart to intrude, even to ask what she was thinking. I knew that it had to do with my father. No doubt she was remembering something he had told her of his youth there, picturing him in it, feeling his presence.

Hafgan, too, wished to be alone, which was plain enough to see. So I tramped around after Blaise, inspecting this place and that, listening as he rediscovered his former home. He told me stories I had never heard before, little things concerning incidents that had happened at one place or another in the caer.

'Why did no one ever return?' I asked. The country appeared perfectly peaceful and secure.

Blaise sighed and shook his head. 'Ah, there was not a man among us who did not yearn to come back — no one more than Lord Elphin.'

'Then why not?'

'That is not easy to explain.' He paused. 'You have to understand that this whole region was overrun by the enemy. Not Caer Dyvi alone — the Wall, the garrisons at Caer Seiont, Luguvalium, Eboracum, everything. Never did men fight better or with more courage, but there were too many. It was death to stay.

'The land was not secure again for nearly two years, and by the time it was safe to return. . . well, we had begun life anew in the south. If fleeing the lands of our fathers was difficult, and it was, returning would be nigh impossible.' He gazed around the caer fondly. 'No, let the ashes rest. Someone will raise these walls one day, but not us.'

We were silent a few moments and Blaise sighed again, then turned to me. 'Would you like to see where Hafgan taught your father?' he asked, and started off before I could answer.

We walked from the caer into the wood along an old track now overgrown with burdock and nettle, and emerged in a small clearing which had been Taliesin's wooded bower. There was an oak stump in the centre of the clearing. 'Hafgan would sit here with his staff across his lap,' Blaise said, sitting down on the stump and placing his own oak staff across his lap. 'Taliesin would sit at his feet.' He offered me the place at his feet and I sat down before him.

Blaise nodded slowly, with a frown of remembrance and mouth pulled down. 'Many and many a time I came to find them so. Ah,' he sighed, 'that seems so long ago now.'

'Was this where my father had his first vision?'

'It was, and I well remember the day. Cormach was Chief Druid then, and he had come to Caer Dyvi. He knew himself to be dying and told us so — I admit I was taken aback by his bald pronouncement, but Cormach was a blunt man. He said he was dying and wanted to see the boy Taliesin one last time before he joined the Ancient Ones.' Blaise smiled quickly, and ran his hand through his long dark hair. 'He sent me off to boil cabbage for his supper.'

There was a long pause and I sat with my arms around my knees listening to the same woodland sounds my father would have heard: the chirruping of woodfinches, thrushes, jays; the little furtive rustlings in the winter-dry underbrush and light shifting of the leaves; the tick and creak of swaying branches.

'I was tending the pot when they returned,' Blaise said when he continued. 'Taliesin was unusually quiet and his movements erratic; his speech was odd, as well — as if he were creating the sound of the words anew as he spoke them. I remember feeling the same way the first time I tasted the Seeds of Wisdom. But in this, as in all else, Taliesin excelled.

'Hafgan told me that he feared Taliesin dead, so still did the boy lie when he found him. Cormach blamed himself for pressing the youngster too hard. . . ' He broke off abruptly and regarded me strangely.

'Too hard to do what?' I asked, already knowing the answer he would make.

'To walk the paths of the Otherworld.'

'To see the future, you mean.'

Again that fierce appraisal, and the slow nod of admission. 'They thought he might see something they could not see.'

'He was looking for me.'

Blaise did not look away this time. 'He was, Myrddin Bach. We all were.'

The silence of the wood crept in once more and we sat watching one another. Blaise sought guidance for what he was about to do, and I was content not to press him, but to trust his judgement. How long we sat there I do not know, but after a time he put his hand to the pouch at his belt and brought out three fire-browned hazelnuts. 'Here they are, Myrddin, if you want them.'

I regarded them and would have reached for them, but something restrained me — a cautious thought: wait, the time for visions is not yet. 'Thank you, Blaise,' I told him. 'I know you would not have offered them if you thought I was not ready. But this is not my way.'

He nodded and put the hazelnuts back in his pouch. 'Never from curiosity,' he said. 'No doubt you have chosen wisely, Hawk. I commend you.' He rose. 'Shall we go back to the caer now?'

We slept that night in the ruined caer and just before sunrise it rained, a soft pattering of falling drops, tears from a low, sorrow-laden sky. We saddled our horses and rode inland along the Dyvi river towards the druid grove at Garth Greggyn, where we meant to leave Hafgan for a few days to meet with his brother druids.

Along the way, we passed Gwyddno's salmon weir, or what was left of it, for the nets were long gone. Several of the poles remained, however; blackened nubs in the water. We paused to see the place where all our lives had, in a sense, begun.

No one spoke; it was almost as if we stood before a holy shrine. For here was the infant Taliesin fished from this very weir in a sealskin bag. The weir pool made a good ford and as we crossed the river I could not help thinking of that now-distant morning when an unsuspecting Elphin, desperate for salmon — and a change of fortune — pulled a baby from the water instead.

We crossed the Dyvi and continued on into the rough hills, and into an older, wilder land.

FOUR

At Garth Greggyn we camped for two days and on the third day the druids came. I half-expected the gathering to simply appear — like Otherworld sojourners in elder times — even though I knew better. The warband waited in the glen below the sacred grove, and were happy to do so since, like most people, they regarded druids in number as a menace to be avoided.

That is a curious thing. Having a bard attached to his court was high prestige for a lord, and certainly every king who could find and keep one enjoyed enormous benefit. Also, the harper's art was respected above all others, including the warrior's and smith's; sorry indeed was the celebration with no druid to sing, and winters were interminable, intolerable, without a bard to tell the old tales.

Nevertheless, let three druids gather in a grove and men began to whisper behind their hands and make the sign against evil — as if the same bard that gave wings to their joy in celebration, eased the harsh winter's passing, and gave authority to their kingmaking, somehow became a being to be feared when he joined with his brothers.

But, as I have said, men's hearts remember long after their minds have forgotten. And I do not wonder that men's hearts still quake to see the Brotherhood gathered in the grove, remembering as they do an older time when the golden scythe claimed a life in blood sacrifice to Cernunnos, Forest Lord, or the Mother Goddess. Fear remembers long, I tell you, if not always wisely.

After breaking fast on the third day Hafgan rose and stood looking at the hilltop grove, then turned to Charis saying, 'Lady, will you come with me now?'

I stared; another time Blaise might have questioned the Chief Druid's invitation, but this seemed to be a time for unprecedented events. He held his peace and the four of us began the long climb up the slope to the sacred grove.

The grove was a dense stand of ancient oak with a scattering of walnut, ash and holly. The oak and walnut were by far the oldest trees: they had been sturdy, deep-rooted youngsters before the Romans came, planted, some said, by Mathonwy, first bard in the Island of the Mighty.

Deep-shadowed and dark, with an air of imponderable mystery emanating from the thick-corded trunks and twisting limbs, and even the soil itself, the sacred druid grove seemed a world unto itself.

In the centre of the grove stood a small stone circle. The moment I set foot in the ring of stones I could feel ancient power, flowing like an invisible river around the hilltop, which was an eddy in the ever-streaming current. The feeling of being surrounded by swirling forces, of being picked up and carried off on the relentless waves of this unseen river nearly took my breath; I laboured to walk upright against it, my flesh tingling with every step.

The others did not feel it in the same way, or if they did gave no indication and said nothing about it. This, of course, was why the hill was chosen in the first place, but still I wondered that Hafgan and Blaise did not appear to notice the power flowing around and over them.

Hafgan took his place on the seat in the centre of the circle — nothing more than a slab of stone supported by two other, smaller slabs — there to wait until the others arrived. Blaise inscribed a series of marks on the ground and then stuck a stick upright over them. The sunshadow had not passed another mark on the ground before the first druids appeared. They greeted Hafgan and Blaise, and regarded my mother and me politely but coolly, while exchanging news with the two druids.

By midday all had arrived in the grove and Hafgan, cracking his rowan staff three times against the centre stone, declared the gathering assembled. The bards, thirty in all, joined him in the ring, and younger filidh and ovates began making their way round the ring with washing bowls and cups of heather water, and pouches of hazelnuts.

I was included in the circle. Charis stood looking on, a short distance away outside the ring, her face grave and intense, and

41

it came into my mind that perhaps she knew what was about to take place. Had Hafgan told her? Was that why she had been asked to accompany us?

'My brothers,' said Hafgan with staff upraised, 'I greet you in the name of the Great Light, whose coming was foretold of old within this sacred ring.' Some of the Brotherhood shifted uneasily at these words. Their movement did not go unnoticed, for Hafgan lowered his staff and asked, 'You resent my greeting — why?'

No one spoke. 'Tell me, for I would know,' said the Chief Druid. His words were a challenge; quiet, gentle, but spoken with an authority that could not be ignored. 'Hen Dallpen?'

The man singled out made a slight movement with his hands, as if to show himself blameless. 'It seemed to me a strange thing to invoke a foreign god in our most sacred place.' He looked to the others near him for support. 'Perhaps there are others among us who think the same way.'

'If so,' said Hafgan flatly, 'let them speak now.'

Several others voiced agreement with Hen Dallpen, and more nodded silently, but every man there felt the strain of Hafgan's challenge. What was he doing?

'How long have we waited for this day, Brothers? How long?' His grey eyes swept the faces of those gathered around him. 'Too long, it appears, for you have forgotten why we come here at all.'

'Why no, Brother, we have not forgotten. We know why we assemble here. But why do you castigate us so unfairly?' It was Hen Dallpen speaking out, more boldly now.

'How so unfairly? Is it not the Chief Druid's right to instruct those below him?'

'Instruct us then, Wise Brother. We would hear you.' The voice was that of a druid standing beside Blaise.

Hafgan raised his staff and turned his face heavenward, making a low moaning noise in his throat. The strange sound drifted off into the silence of the grove and Hafgan looked at those around him. 'From ancient days we have sought knowledge so that we might learn the truth of all things. Is this not so?'

'It is so,' intoned the assembled druids.

'How should we be slow to grasp the truth when it is proclaimed before us now?'

'We know many truths, Master. Which truth is proclaimed this day?' asked Hen Dallpen.

'The Final Truth, Hen Dallpen,' replied Hafgan gently. 'And it is this: the Great Light of the world has ascended his high throne and calls all men to worship in spirit and deed.'

'This Great Light you speak of, Wise Brother, do we know him?'

'We do. It is Jesu, him the Romans call Christus.' There were murmurs. Hafgan's eyes swept the assembly; many looked away uncomfortably. 'Why does his name frighten you?'

'Frighten us?' asked Hen Dallpen. 'Surely, you are mistaken, Wise Leader. We are not afraid of this foreign man-god. But, neither do we see good reason to worship him here.'

'Or worship him at all!' declared another. 'Especially since the priests of this Christus declaim against us, mocking us before our own people, belittling our craft and authority even as they seek to extinguish the Learned Brotherhood.'

'They do not understand, Drem,' offered Blaise gently. 'They are ignorant, but that does not change the truth. It is as Hafgan says, the Great Light has come and is being proclaimed among us.'

'Is that why *he* is here?' The one called Drem turned angrily to me. I saw other dark looks, and understood the reason for the coolness of our reception.

'It is his right to be here,' said Hafgan. 'He is the son of the greatest bard to draw breath.'

'Taliesin turned against us! He left the Brotherhood to follow this Jesu, and now it seems you would have the rest of us do the same. Are we to abandon old ways to chase after a foreign god simply because Taliesin did it?'

'Not because Taliesin did it, Brother,' replied Blaise, restraining his anger, 'but because it is right! He who was foremost among us knew the truth of a thing when he saw it. That alone argues for the rightness of it.'

'Well said, Blaise.' Hafgan motioned me to join him in the centre of the ring. Blaise nodded encouragement, and I stepped forward hesitantly. Hafgan placed a hand on my shoulder, and raised his staff in the air. 'Before you stands the one whose coming we have long awaited, the Champion who will lead the war host against the Darkness. I, Hafgan, Archdruid of the Cor of Garth Greggyn, declare it!'

Silence greeted this pronouncement. Even I questioned the wisdom of such a proclamation, for clearly many of the Learned Brotherhood were unhappily nursing wounds they had received at the hands of the Christian priests, and others were openly sceptical. But the words were out and could not be taken back. I stood there, quaking inside, not from anxiety only, but from the implications of the Archdruid's words: the Champion. . . leading the war host. . . Darkness. . .

'He is but a boy,' scoffed Hen Dallpen.

'Would you have him sprung full-grown into life, like Manawyddan?' demanded the druid beside Blaise. There were a few allies among the Learned Brotherhood at least.

'How do we know he is Taliesin's son? Who can attest to his birth?' wondered one of the sceptics. 'Were you there, Indeg? Were you, Blaise? And you, Wise Leader; were you there? Well?'

'I was.' The voice took everyone by surprise, for by this time they had forgotten that my mother stood looking on. 'I was there,' she said again, stepping forward. Yes, this was why she had come, not only to see her son proclaimed among the Learned Brotherhood, but to help if things went awry, which, as Hafgan had anticipated, they had.

From now on, Hafgan had said, men will begin to recognize you. That sly fox meant to give it a fair beginning.

'I bore him and watched him born.' My mother stepped into the sacred ring and came to stand beside me. So, there I was, Hafgan on one side, my mother on the other, surrounded by unhappy druids, feeling the strange power of the grove flowing around me. It is not surprising then that I should be taken out of myself to perform an act I was scarcely aware of, and remember now only in amazement.

The druids stood looking on, unconvinced. '. . . a child born without breath or life. Taliesin sang life into his still body. . . ' Charis was saying.

I felt the air shudder around me, pulsing with the power of the grove. The stones in the sacred circle appeared to change from grey to blue as around us thickened a wall of shimmering

44

glass, spun from the intense, charged air; the enmity of the druids towards me, together with my presence, had awakened the sleeping force of the *omphalos*, the centre of power on which the hill had been constructed.

I saw Otherworld beings moving among the circled stones. One of them — tall and fair, his face and clothing shining with a gleaming radiance that danced like sunbeams on water — came towards me and pointed to the Druid Seat where Hafgan had been sitting. I had never seen an Ancient One before, but part of me expected to see him and so I was not surprised. No one else noticed, of course; nor did I give any indication of the wonder taking place around us.

The being pointed to the stone slab which rested at the vortex of the hill's power. I turned to see the stone — blue now, like the rest of them, and shining faintly. I stepped up onto the stone and heard the druids gasp behind me, for only the Chief Druid may touch the stone — and never with his feet!

But I stood on the stone and it rose up. So highly charged had the vortex become that it lifted the stone, with me on it, straight into the air. From this lofty vantage I began to speak, rather the Ancient One spoke through me if that is how it was, for the words were not my own.

'Servants of the Truth, stop your whining and listen to me! Indeed you are fortunate among men, for today you witness the fulfilment many have lived and died longing to see.

'Why do you wonder that the wisest among you should greet you in the name of Jesu, who called himself the Way and the Truth? How is it that you, who seek truth in all ways, should be blind to it now?

'Do you believe because you see a floating stone?' I saw that they did not believe, though many were awed and amazed. 'Perhaps you will believe if *all* the stones dance?'

At that moment I actually believed that I could do such a thing, that I had only to clap my hands or shout, or make some sign and the stones would shake themselves from the ground to swing in whirling dance through the glistening air.

I believed, and so I clapped my hands and gave a loud

shout — it did not sound like my own voice at all, for the shout resounded over the land, echoing in the glens and valleys round about, trembling the stones of the magic ring in the earth.

Then, one after another, the standing stones began to rise.

One by one they pulled themselves from their sockets, like teeth twisting themselves from the jaw that holds them, and they rose trailing dirt to stand in the air. And then, when all were together in the air, those ancient stones began to turn.

Around and around, slowly, slowly at first, but then a little faster, each stone began turning around its own axis as it whirled in the air.

The druids looked on in horror and wonder, some cried out in fright. I thought to myself that it was a handsome sight — those heavy blue stones spinning and whirling in the shining air, as in a dream.

Perhaps it was a dream after all. If so, it was a dream we all shared together with eyes wide and staring, mouths open in disbelief.

Once, twice, and again, the stones whirled through their course. From my place on the Druid Seat, I heard my own voice ringing, high and strange, voicing a song, or laughter — I know not which — to the stones dancing in the air.

I clapped my hands again and the great stones plummeted instantly to earth. The ground shook beneath them and the dust rose in a cloud. When it cleared, we saw that some of the stones had fallen back into their socket holes; most, however, simply lay where they dropped. One or another had cracked and shattered and the ring was broken.

The stone on which I stood had settled back onto its place, and I stepped off. Blaise, his face alight with the wonder of what he had seen, rushed towards me and would have taken hold of me, but Hafgan restrained him, saying, 'Do not touch him until the *awen* has passed.'

Blaise made to step back, caught sight of the Druid Seat and thrust his finger towards it. 'For any inclined to doubt what we have witnessed this day, let this be a sign of the truth of what we have seen.'

I looked at where he was pointing and saw the prints of my feet etched deep into the stone of the Druid Seat.

So the Great Light was proclaimed among the Learned Brotherhood that day. Some believed. Others did not. And although none could deny the power of what they had seen, some chose to attribute the miracle to a different source.

'It is Lleu-sun!' some said. 'Mathonwy!' said others. 'Who else has such power?'

In the end, Hafgan lost his temper. 'You call me Wise Leader,' he said bitterly, 'but refuse to follow where I lead. Very well, from this day let each man follow who he will. I will not remain Chief of such small-minded and ignorant men!'

With that, he raised his staff in both hands and broke it over his knee, then turned his back and strode from the assembly. The Learned Brotherhood was dissolved.

We followed Hafgan from the grove — Blaise, Charis, myself, and two or three others — and returned to the glen where the warband was waiting. We broke camp at once and rode south towards Yr Widdfa. Hafgan wanted to see the great mountain again, and to show us where he was born.

He was angry for a time after leaving Garth Greggyn, but this passed very quickly and he soon appeared joyful and more content than I had ever seen him — singing, laughing, talking long and happily with my mother as we rode along — a man freed from a tiresome burden, or healed of a wearying pain. Blaise noticed the change as well, and explained it to me. 'He has been divided in his heart for a very long time. I think he wanted to force the decision back there, and now that it is over he is free to go his own way.'

'Divided?'

'Between Jesu and the old gods,' Blaise replied. 'As Chief Druid he must uphold the eminence of the ancient gods of our people, though that has become distasteful to him in the years since he discovered the Great Light.' I must have frowned or shown my lack of comprehension, for Blaise added, 'You must understand, Myrddin Bach, not every man will follow the Light. Nothing you or anyone else can do will change that.' He shook his head. 'Though dead men rise from their graves and stones dance in the air, they will still refuse. It makes no sense, but that is the way of it.'

I did not altogether believe him. I thought he was telling me the truth as he saw it, and respected his insight; but in my innermost heart I thought that if men did not believe the truth it was only because a better way of explaining had yet to be discovered. There is a way to make all men see, I thought to myself, and I will find it.

Two days later we sat on a high hill, the wind riffling the sparse grass and sighing among the bare rocks as we gazed at the cold, white-topped and solitary splendour of Yr Widdfa, Snow Lord, Winter's Fortress.

In that lonely land of brooding peaks and darksome vales it is easy to believe the things whispered before the firelight, the tales and scraps of tales men have passed to their children for a hundred generations and more: one-eyed giants in halls of stone; goddesses who transform themselves into owls to haunt the night on soft, silent wings; water maids who lure the unwary to rapturous death below the waves; enchanted hills where captured heroes sleep the centuries away; invisible islands where gods cavort in the twilight of never-ending summer. . .

Easy to believe the unbelievable there among the hollow hills.

We dismounted and ate a meal on the hilltop, then rested. I did not care to sleep, and decided to walk down to the valley and fill the water jars and skins at the stream. It was not a difficult walk, nor even very far, thus I did not pay particularly close attention to the features of the land — not that this would have helped.

I stumbled and slid down the hill, laden with skins and jars swinging from their thongs round my neck and shoulders. A quick-running stream lay in the centre of the valley, in among the tight tangles of blackthorn and elder. I found a way in to the water and set to filling the skins.

I cannot say how long I was at it, but it could not have been long. Nevertheless, when I gathered up the filled containers and stood to look around, I could no longer see the hill: a dense, grey fog had come down from Yr Widdfa and wrapped the higher hills in a clotted mass thick as wool.

I was concerned, but not frightened. After all, the hill stood directly before me. All I need do was put one foot in front of the other and retrace my steps to the top where the others waited. I wasted no time, but set off at once in the event that the others awoke and became anxious to find me missing and a fog filling the valley.

I quickly found the path I had taken down the hill and began the ascent. I walked a long time, but came no nearer the top. I stopped and peered into the swirling blankness and, try as I might, I could not make out where I was on the hillside.

I called out. . . and heard my cry muted and silenced by the thick, damp vapours.

What to do?

There was no telling how long the mist might last. I might wander the hill-track for days on end and never find my way. Worse, and far more likely, I might stumble over a rock in the path and break a leg, or step over a cliff and fall to my death. I sat down to think it through.

It seemed obvious that I had been walking in a circle — and equally obvious, as I sat there, that the fog was settling in. I had no better choice than to set off once more, as I did not relish spending a cold, wet night alone, clinging to a rock on the side of the hill. So I started walking again, but this time slowly, making certain that each step led upward. In this way, though it might take half the day, I would eventually reach our camp at the top.

And in this way I did eventually reach the hilltop — only to discover our camp abandoned and no one there. I dropped the waterskins and looked around. The mist was not as thick as in the valley, so I could, with a little difficulty, make a complete survey of the hilltop. The others were gone, leaving not a trace behind.

Strange. And frightening.

I called again and again, but heard no answering call. I went back to the place where we had eaten our meal, thinking to find some token of our presence, however small. But, try as I might, I could not locate the place. Not a crust or crumb remained to show where we had been; there was not a single hoofprint, not a blade of grass disturbed. . .

I had climbed the wrong hill! In my blind haste to escape the fog, I had lost my way, and now would have to wait until the mist cleared and I could see where and how I had made my mistake. In the meantime, I had no choice but to do what I should have done in the first place — stay put.

My cheeks burned with shame at my stupidity. I could make a stone circle dance in the air, but could not find my way to the top of a simple hill without getting lost. It was too absurd for words.

FIVE

Finding a nest among the rocks, I wrapped my cloak around me and settled myself to wait, knowing full well that I might have to spend the night there. But I did not like to think about that. Would the hollow hills claim another victim?

I did not like to think about that, either.

Later, as the deepening mist darkened towards dusk and I sat hugging my knees and trying not to be afraid, I heard a faint tinkling sound — the light jingling of a horse's tack — one of the warband coming to find me! I jumped up and called out. The sound stopped and I did not hear it again, although I stood still to listen.

'Are you there? Blaise! Who is it?'

My words fell to earth where they were spoken and there was no answer. I retrieved one of the water skins and returned to my huddle among the rocks, miserable now. I pulled my cloak more tightly around me and wondered how long it would take the wolves to find me.

I must have fallen asleep, for I dreamed, and in my dream I saw a tall, gaunt man sitting in a room painted with strange designs. His hands were stretched flat on the table before him and the eyes in his long, withered face were sunken and closed. His hair was uncut, falling around his shoulders like a net of cobwebs, and he wore a rich robe of darkest blue with a brooch and pin of silver inset with tiny moonstones.

Before him on the table was an object shaped like a large egg — a polished stone, perhaps, cradled in a holder of carven wood. Two wasted candles stood on either side of this egg-stone, guttering in the fitful wind wafting through the cracks in the walls and windows.

This man was not alone; there was another in the room as well. I could not see this other person, but knew, as one simply *knows* in a dream, that she was there with him. Oh, yes, the other was a woman. I knew this, too, before I saw her stretch her hand slowly across the table to entwine her young fingers with those of the man. He opened his eyes then, for I saw the glint of light from the candles, but his eyes were wells of darkness. . . darkness and death.

I shivered and woke.

An unusual dream, but even as I felt its lingering presence, I knew it to represent a real place, and that the man I had seen and the woman's hand I glimpsed were real.

I blinked and looked around.

Night had fallen full and darkness was complete. The wind stirred, swirling the mist and I heard again the light jingling sound. This time I did not call out, but remained silent, crouching among the rocks. The sound came nearer, but in the fog there was no telling how close it really was. I waited.

Presently, I saw a lighter patch floating in the darkness, swinging towards me through the thick, damp air. The light brightened, intensified, divided into two glowing orbs, like great cat's eyes. The jingling sound came from the lights swimming nearer.

Only when they were almost on top of me did the lights stop. I moved not a muscle, but they knew where to find me — by scent, I think, for the darkness and mist obscured all.

There were four of them, two to a torch, swarthy men in rough skin jerkins and kilts. Their bodies were well-muscled and compact, Two had huge armbands of iron and carried iron-tipped spears; all had bronze daggers in their belts. But I was not frightened of their weapons, for though they were men full grown, none were bigger than myself, a boy of but twelve summers.

Their eyes were dark, and cunning like weasel eyes. And the men stood gazing at me through the mist, shadows flickering over their faces. The torchbearers held their brands high and the other two advanced together to stand over me, jingling lightly as they moved. I looked and saw a chain with brass bells tied just below the knee of the foremost stranger. He squatted on his haunches and stared at me for a long moment, dark eyes glittering. He pressed a finger into my chest, felt the flesh and bone there and grunted. Then he saw my silver torc and raised his hand to stroke it.

After a moment he rose again and barked a word over his shoulder. The others behind him parted and I saw another figure approaching out of the mist. I stood slowly, hands loose at my sides, and waited while the newcomer came to stand before him. He was smaller than the others, but carried himself in the way of chieftains everywhere; he wore his authority like a second skin, and I had no doubt that he possessed rank among his people.

He motioned one of the torchmen closer, so that he could see me properly. In the fluttering light I saw that this chieftain was a woman.

She, too, looked long upon my torc, but did not touch it, or me. She turned to the one with the bells and uttered a short, harsh bark, whereupon he and the one beside him took me by the arms and we started off.

I was more carried than dragged, for my feet scarcely touched ground. We descended the hill and reached the valley, splashed across the stream and, from the sound of running water close by, followed the stream for a time before beginning another ascent. The slope was gradual, eventually levelling out to become a narrow track or gorge between two steep hills.

This track led a fair distance and we walked a time, one torch ahead and one behind; my companions on either side did not push me, neither did they loosen their grip, although escape was not possible — could I have seen where I was going in the mist, I would not have known where to run.

At last the track turned upward and we began a steep ascent. It was a short climb, however, and I soon found myself standing in front of a round, hide-covered opening in the hill itself. The chieftain entered and it was indicated that I was to follow. I stepped through the opening and found myself inside a large mound dwelling of timber and skin. Covered with dirt and turf on the outside, the rath, as it is called, appeared in daylight just like any of the innumerable hills around it.

There were fifteen or more people inside reclining in groups on grass pallets covered with fleeces and furs around the central fire — men, women, children and several lean dogs that looked as though they would have been more at home running the hills in a wolf pack — all of them, men and beasts alike, staring at me as I stood uncertainly in their midst.

The she-chief motioned me forward and I was brought to stand before an old woman, no larger than a girl, but white-haired and wrinkled as a dried plum. Her black eyes were sharp as the bone needle in her hand and she regarded me with frank curiosity for a moment, reaching out to touch my leg, which she pinched and patted. Satisfied with her appraisal, she nodded to the she-chief who jerked her head to the side and I was led to a pallet and pushed down upon it.

Once I was well inside the rath, the hill people seemed to lose interest in me. I was left alone to observe my captors, who, aside from an occasional glance in my direction, and a dog that came to sniff my hands and legs, appeared oblivious to my presence. I sat on the fur-covered pallet and tried to see what I might discover about these people.

There were eight men and four women aside from the she-chief and the old woman; scattered among them were five naked children whose ages were impossible to determine — the adults looked like children to me! All the adults wore woad-stained scars on their cheeks — *fhain* marks, as I was to learn. Distinctive spirals which, at the time of cutting, had the deep blue powder pressed into the wounds to colour them for ever. Individuals of the same fhain — the word means family tribe, or clan — wore the same marks.

I puzzled over who they might be. Not Picti — though they used the woad, they were too small for Painted People, who anyway would have killed me outright upon discovery. Neither were they members of any of the hill tribes I knew about. Their habit of living underground marked them for a northern people, but if so they were far south of their beloved moors.

These, I decided, could only be the *bhean sidhe*, the enchanted Hill Folk, as much feared for their obscure ways and magic, as they were envied for their gold. The *bhean sidhe* were rumoured to possess great malevolent power, and even greater treasures of gold; both of which were employed in tormenting the tallfolk, whom they delighted in sacrificing to their crude idols whenever they could catch them. And I was their captive.

The clan settled for the night and one by one fell asleep. I pretended sleep, too, but stayed awake to be ready to make my escape. When at last, judging from the sound of the snoring, everyone was sleeping soundly and peacefully, I rose, crept from my pallet to the doorway and out into the night.

The mist had cleared and the night was ablaze with stars, cold and bright, the moon already set. The surrounding hills showed as a solid black undulating mass against the deep blue of heaven. I breathed in the mountain air and looked at the stars. Here all serious thought of escape vanished. I had only to look at the jet-dark night to know that running in such darkness invited disaster. And even if I had been so determined, on the wind I heard the bark of hunting wolves.

It came to me that this was why my captors had not bothered to restrain me in any way. If I were foolish enough to tempt the wolves, so be it; I deserved my fate.

All the same, as I stood looking at the stars, I heard the rustle of the closing flap and turned to see someone emerge from the rath. As I made no move, my companion came to stand near me and I saw that it was the she-chief. She put her hand on my arm but lightly, as much to reassure herself that I was still there as to remind me that I was a captive.

We stood together for a long time so close that I could feel the heat from her body. Neither of us spoke; we had no words. But something in her touch gave me to understand that these people had some purpose for me. While not exactly an honoured guest, my presence was more than a passing curiosity.

After a while, she turned and pulled me with her back into the rath. I returned to my pallet, and she to hers, and I closed my eyes and prayed that I would soon be reunited with my people.

What the hill-dwellers wanted with me I discovered soon after sunrise when Vrisa, chieftain of the *Amsaradh* fhain — their name for themselves; it means People of the Killing Bird, or Hawk Clan — took me out to their holy place on a nearby hilltop. The hill was the highest around and took some effort to climb, but upon gaining the summit I saw a menhir, a single standing stone painted with blue spirals and the representations of various birds and animals, most notably hawks and wolves.

In her belt Vrisa wore a long, flat-bladed knife, polished and honed to mirror brightness. The man with the bells — Elac, as I would later discover — kept his hand tight on my arm all the way up the hill, and two of the others carried spears. The whole fhain made the trek up the hill, gathering round us as we came to stand beside the menhir, humming softly, with a sound like wind through dry leaves.

A braided leather rope was produced and my wrists were bound tightly. My cloak was taken from me and I was made to lie down on the sun side of the standing stone. They meant to sacrifice me; there was no doubt about that, and judging from the bones scattered around the hilltop, I was not their first offering.

But, though this might seem boastful to some, I was more fearful of being left by my people, than having my heart carved beating from my body. There was no hate, no deception or guile in these people. They did not wish me harm in the least. And indeed, did not consider the sacrifice of my life any great harm at all. In their way of thinking my soul would simply take up a new body and I would be reborn, or I would travel to the Otherworld to live with the Ancient Ones in paradise, knowing neither night nor winter. Either way, I was deemed fortunate.

That I would have to die to come into one or the other of these enviable benefits could not be helped, and consequently did not concern them over much. And since it was a journey all must make sooner or later, it was assumed that I would not greatly mind.

So, as I lay there on the ground, waiting while the sun slowly climbed its way clear of the hills round about — this would be the signal: when the first rays of the morning sun struck the menhir, Vrisa would strike with her knife — I did what any Christian would and prayed for swift deliverance.

Perhaps the knife was poorly made; perhaps it was old and should have been recast long ago. Nevertheless, as the sun struck the menhir the humming chorus loosed a mighty shout. Vrisa's knife flashed up and down swiftly as a serpent's strike.

I squeezed shut my eyes and in the same instant heard a cry.

Opening my eyes, I saw Vrisa, clasping her wrist, her face pale with pain, teeth bared as she bit back another cry. The knife's handle lay on the ground, its blade splintered into gleaming pieces like shards of yellow glass.

Elac, eyes starting from his head, gripped his spear so tightly the blood drained from his hands. Others bit the backs of their hands, some lay prostrate on the ground whimpering.

I rolled up into a sitting position. The clan's wise woman,

the *Gern-y-fhain*, pushed her way through the others to stand over me with her hands outstretched while she stared into the risen sun, chanting in their singing speech. Then she made a motion with her hands and snapped an order at the men looking on. Two of them came to me, hesitantly, the last act in the world they would have chosen, and untied the braided rope and unbound me.

Now, men will say that I broke the knife with magic. I have even heard it said that it is not surprising in the least that the knife should break since, as anyone knows, bronze cannot harm an enchanted being like myself.

Well, I was surprised and did not feel the least little bit enchanted. Also, I had not yet learned the secrets of the ancient art. I tell you only what happened. Believe what you like. But, as Vrisa's sacrifice knife flashed through the air towards my heart, there appeared a hand — a cloud hand, Elac called it. The knife struck the palm of this mysterious cloud hand and shattered.

Vrisa's wrist was already swelling. The force of her blow and the shock of the shattering knife nearly broke her wrist, poor girl. I call her girl now, for I soon learned that she was but a summer or two older than I was at the time, yet already chief of her Hill Folk tribe. Gern-y-fhain, the wise woman with the flint-sharp eyes and puckered face of a nut-brown apple, was her grandmother.

Gern-y-fhain was not slow to recognize so powerful a sign. She stepped in, raised me to my feet, and gazed long into my face. The sun was up now and my eyes filled with new morning light; she scrutinized me and turned to the others, speaking excitedly. They stared, but Vrisa advanced slowly, raised a hand to my face, pulling down my cheek with her thumb, and stared into my eyes.

The light of recognition broke across her face and she beamed, forgetting her painful wrist for the moment. She invited the others to see for themselves and I was subjected to a painless ordeal as the entire clan examined the colour of my eyes by turns.

When they had satisfied themselves that I did indeed possess the golden eyes of a hawk, Gern-y-fhain put her hands on my head and offered up a thanksgiving prayer to Lugh-Sun for sending me.

The clan had felt they needed a powerful sacrifice to offset a run of extreme ill fortune they had been having for the last three summers: poor grazing and worse lambing, two children had died of fever, and Nolo's brother had been killed by a boar. Their prospects for improved fortune were decidedly bleak when Elac, returning home from a spoiled hunt, heard me shouting on the hilltop in the fog. They thought their prayers had been answered.

Elac climbed the hill and verified I was there, then hurried to the rath, told the others what he had found and, after chewing it over among themselves, decided to fetch me along and sacrifice me in the morning. The shattered knife put a new face on it, however, and they decided that I must be a present from the gods. . . unfortunately disguised as a sub-human tallfolk youth, it is true, but a gift nonetheless.

I do not mean to make them sound like backward children, though childlike is a fair description of them in many ways. Still, they were anything but backward; on the contrary, they were wonderfully intelligent, with sharp, accurate memories and a vast store of instinctual knowledge that comes to them through their mothers' milk.

But the strength of their faith was such that they lived their lives in unquestioning acceptance of all things, trusting their 'Parents,' the Earth Goddess and her husband, Lugh-Sun, for rain and sun, for deer to hunt, for grass to graze their sheep, for the things they needed to live.

Thus, to them anything was possible at any moment. The sky might suddenly turn to stone, or rivers to silver and hills to gold; dragons might coil in sleep under the hills, or giants dream in deep mountain caverns; a man might be a man or a god, or both at once. A hand might appear in their midst and shatter a knife as it slashed towards the heart of their much-needed sacrifice. And this, too, was to be accepted.

Does this make them backward?

With faith like this it is little wonder that once they learned the Truth, they carried it a long, long way.

SIX

I thought that when we returned to the rath I would be set free. In this I was mistaken, for if I had been desirable as a potential sacrifice, as a living gift I was even more valuable. They had no intention of letting me leave. Perhaps when the purpose for which I had been sent to them was fulfilled I might depart. But until then? It could not even be contemplated.

This was communicated to me in no uncertain terms when I tried to leave the rath later that day. I was sitting beside the door to the rath and, when no one was looking, I simply got to my feet and started down the hill. I escaped but ten steps and Nolo called the dogs. Snarling, growling viciously, the dogs surrounded me until I retreated to my place at the door of the rath.

The days crawled by, and each passing moment my heart grew heavier. My people were in these hills somewhere, searching for me, worrying over me. I had not the skill to see them then, but I could feel their anxiety across the separating distance, and I knew their misery. I wept at night as I lay on my pallet: stinging tears for the sorrow I was causing my mother, and the hardship my absence meant.

Great Light, I cried, please hear me! Give them peace to know I am unharmed. Give them hope to know I will return. Give them patience to wait, and courage to endure the waiting. Give them strength so that they will not grow weary.

This prayer was to become a litany of comfort to me for a good long time. Often spoken with tears, it is true. The next day, after nearly four days of judicious contemplation, Gern-y-fhain took me by the arm and sat me down on a rock at her feet and began speaking at me. I understood nothing of what she said, but paid close attention and soon began to discern the rhythm of their speech. I nodded from time to time just to show that I was trying.

She puckered up her wrinkles and made a gesture which included the rath and everyone and everything in it. 'Fhain,' she said, repeating several times until I did the same.

'Fhain,' I said, smiling. The smiling worked wonders, for the Hill Folk are happy people and smiling indicates to them a soul in harmony with life, and they are not far wrong.

'Gern-y-fhain,' she told me next, thumping herself on the chest.

'Gern-y-fhain,' I repeated. Then I thumped myself on the chest and said, 'Myrddin.' I used the Cymry form of my name, thinking that would be closest to their speech. 'Myrddin.'

She nodded and repeated the word several times, much pleased to have such a willing and able Gift. She then pointed at each of the other clan members as they went about their various tasks, 'Vrisa, Elac, Nolo, Teirn, Beona, Rhyllha. . . ' and others. I did my best to keep up with her, and managed for a while, but when she turned to naming other things — earth, sky, hills, clouds, river, rock — I fell behind.

That ended my first lesson in the Hill Folk tongue, and began a custom that was to continue many months after that: beginning my day sitting beside Gern-y-fhain, as at Blaise's feet or Dafyd's, practising my lessons.

Vrisa took it upon herself to civilize me. For a start, my clothing was taken away and replaced with skins and fur. This concerned me until I saw that she carefully placed my things in a special basket lashed to a roofpole in the rath. I might not be leaving soon, but at least when I did it would be as I came. She then led me back outside, chattering at me all the while and glancing at me from time to time to smile, showing her fine white teeth, as much as to say, 'Be welcome, tallfolk-wealth. You are fhain now.'

It pleased her when I said her name and taught her mine. Indeed, they roared with delight when I was finally able to tell them that my name meant 'Hawk' — that confirmed them in their belief that my coming was ordained by their Parents. They watched my progress hungrily; any little thing I did pleased them all enormously. They found endless pleasure in recounting my achievements to one another around the supper fire at night. At first I considered this was because of my status as Gift; later, I learned that they treated all children that way.

Children were held in specially high regard among them. Their language proved this in that 'child' and 'wealth' were the same to them: *eurn*. This one word served both meanings.

They viewed children as others might view honoured guests — worthies deserving of consideration and respect, whose mere presence was cause for joy and a treat to be relished with pleasure and celebrated whenever possible. Thus, even though I was, in their reckoning of age, very nearly a full-grown man, I lacked the proper upbringing and so I must be considered a child until I learned enough manners to become an adult. This made an interesting period of adjustment, for in those first months I spent as much time in the company of the young as with their elders.

The summer passed quickly; time sped because I was desperate to learn their speech so that I could communicate my anxiety about my people, and learn their reason for keeping me. My opportunity came one crisp autumn night not long after Lughnasadh. We sat, as we sometimes did, before an outdoor fire on the hilltop under the stars. Elac and Nolo — first and second husbands to Vrisa — and some of the others had been out hunting that day and, after supper, began describing what had taken place.

In utter innocence Elac turned to me and said, 'We saw tallfolk in the crooked glen. Yet they are searching for their child-wealth.'

'Yet?' I asked him. 'You have known of this before?'

He smiled and nodded; Nolo nodded with him and said, 'We have all seen them many times.'

'Why did you not tell me?' I demanded, trying to keep my temper down.

'Myrddin is fhain now. Be you fhain-brother. We will leave soon; tallfolk will stop searching and go away.'

'Leave?' My anger vanished at the thought. I turned to Vrisa. 'What does Elac mean? Where are we going?'

'Snow time is coming soon. We will go to the crannog, fhain-brother.'

'When?' I felt desperation rising in me like a sickness.

Vrisa shrugged. 'Soon. Before the snow.'

It made sense and I should have known. The Hill Folk

did not live in one place very long; I knew that, but somehow failed to consider that they might leave soon for their winter home — a crannog in a hollow hill in the north.

'You have to take me to them,' I told Vrisa. 'I must see them.'

Vrisa frowned and turned to Gern-y-fhain, who shook her head slightly. 'That cannot be,' she replied. 'Tallfolk will borrow child-wealth from fhain.' They had no direct word for stealing, 'borrowing' was as close as they came and they were wonderfully resourceful borrowers.

'I was tallfolk before I am fhain-brother,' I said. 'I must say farewell.'

This puzzled them. They had no sense of parting or farewell — even death was not a strict separation since the dead one had only gone on a journey much as one might go hunting and could return at any moment, in a different body, perhaps, but essentially the same. 'What means this fayr-well?' Visa asked. 'I know it not.'

'I must tell them to stop searching,' I explained, 'to go back to their lands and leave the crooked glen.'

'No need, Myrddin-wealth,' explained Elac happily. 'Tall-folk will stop searching soon. They will go away soon.'

'No,' I said, rising to my feet. 'They are my fhain-brothers, my parents. Never will they stop searching for their child-wealth. *Never!*'

Their concept of time was equally vague. The idea of continuous, ceaseless activity could not be comprehended. Vrisa merely shook her head lightly. 'This is a thing I know not. You are fhain now. You are a gift to Hawk People, Myrddin-wealth, a gift from Parents.'

I agreed, but held my ground. 'I am a gift, yes. But I must thank fhain-brothers for letting me become a Hawk Person.'

This they understood, for who would not care to become a Hawk Person? Such a great and impressive honour would naturally engender enormous gratitude which the recipient would be duty bound to express. Yes, it made sense to them that I would wish to thank my former fhain-brothers.

What is more, they took it as a sign of my growing maturity. 'It is a good thing, Myrddin-brother. You will thank Parents tomorrow.'

'*And* fhain-brothers,' I insisted.

62

'How will you thank them?' asked Vrisa suspiciously, sensing potential trickery, her dark eyes narrowed and wary.

My answer must be innocent or she would refuse outright. 'I will give back their tallfolk clothes.'

Again this made perfect sense. To a people without skill at weaving, without looms, cloth was scarce and extremely valuable. She might be sorry to see the cloth-wealth leave the fhain, but could well understand why I wanted to give it back; and why my former tallfolk fhain, if they could not have me, would at least wish to have my clothes.

'Elac,' she said finally, 'take Myrddin-wealth to tallfolk fire ring tomorrow.'

I smiled. There was no use in pushing the matter further; it was all I was likely to get from them for the moment. 'Thank you, Vrisa-chief. Thank you, fhain-kin.'

They all smiled back and began chattering at me benignly, and I fell to working out how best to make my escape.

There were four of them in the crooked glen. I could tell even from a distance that they were my people, members of the warband that had ridden as escort. They were camped by a stream and the glimmering light of their fire reflected in the moving water. They were, from all appearances, still asleep as the sun had not yet risen above the hills to the east.

We were poised on a rock ledge on the hillside, waiting. 'I will go down to my fhain-brothers now,' I told Elac.

'We will go with you.' He indicated Nolo and Teirn.

'No, I will go alone.' I tried to sound as firm as Gern-y-fhain.

He regarded me slyly and then shook his head. 'Vrisa-chief says you will not come back.'

Indeed, that was my plan. Elac shook his head and stood up beside me, putting his hand on my shoulder. 'We will go with you, Myrddin-brother, so tallfolk do not borrow child-wealth back.'

I saw it all very clearly now, if a trifle late. If we all went down together there would be a fight. Elphin's warriors would never allow the Hill Folk to leave with me. They would try to save me, and they would likely die trying — pierced with arrows before they could draw their swords. One or more of the Hill Folk might be killed in the skirmish as well. No, I could not let that happen. My freedom was not as important as the lives of men I called my friends.

Now what was I to do?

'No,' I folded my arms across my chest and sat down. 'I will not go.'

'Why, Myrddin-wealth?' Mystified, Elac stared at me.

'You go.'

He sat down beside me. Nolo frowned and put out his hand to me. 'She-chief says husbands must go with you. Tallfolk cannot be trusted with child-wealth, Myrddin-brother.'

'Tallfolk-brothers will not understand. They will kill fhain-kin when they see you, thinking to help fhain-brother.'

That got through to Elac, who nodded glumly. He knew just how unappreciative tallfolk could be.

'Hawk Fhain fear tallfolk not at all,' boasted Nolo.

'Well, I do not wish fhain-brothers killed. That will bring great sadness to Myrddin-brother. Bring sadness to fhain.' I appealed to Elac. 'You go, Elac. Take the clothes to tall-folk-brothers.' I indicated the pile of clothing on the ledge beside me.

He considered this and agreed. I folded my cloak, trousers, and tunic as neatly as I could, frantically thinking how I might send a message that would not be misinterpreted. In the end I took off my rawhide belt and tied that around the bundle.

My people would recognize the clothing, of course, but I still needed another token to indicate my safety. I glanced around. 'Teirn,' I held out my hand, 'I need an arrow.'

I would have preferred a pen and parchment, but these were as foreign to the Hill Folk as pepper and perfume. They did not trust writing, and in this showed remarkable wisdom.

Teirn withdrew an arrow. The missiles of the Hill Folk are short, flint-tipped reeds fletched with raven feathers, unmistakable and deadly; and Hill Folk accuracy is legendary. The tallfolk tribes in the north have learned great respect for the fragile-looking arrows and the unerring hand that draws the bow.

I bent to the bundle and took the arrow, snapping it in the centre and tucking the two ends under the rawhide belt. Then, as an afterthought, I removed the silver wolfshead brooch from the cloak and handed the bundle to Elac. 'There, take this to tallfolk camp.'

He looked at the bundle and at the camp below. 'Lugh-Sun is rising,' I told him. 'Do take it now before tallfolk-brothers wake.'

He ducked his head. 'They will see me not.' With that, he scrambled over the ledge and was gone. A few moments later we saw him running towards the camp. Creeping with all the stealth and silence of a shadow, Elac entered the sleeping camp and, in an act of impulsive bravery typical of him, carefully placed the bundle beside the head of one of the sleeping warriors.

He returned to the ledge in no time and we returned to the rath a moment later. It took everything in me to keep from looking back.

I could only hope the fact that my clothes were neatly folded and deposited in their camp would somehow indicate that I was alive and knew my searcher's whereabouts but could not come to them myself. There was every chance that my message would go awry, but I trusted the Great God and hoped I had not made things worse.

Something changed inside me that day. For in giving up my clothes, it was as if I also gave up the idea of rescue. Curiously, I became more content to stay. And although I still grew heartsick and moody from time to time, perhaps I, too, began believing my presence with the Hawk People had a purpose. After that day, I no longer contemplated escape, and eventually came to accept my capture.

I did not see the searchers again, and soon after the fire of Samhain the fhain left for their winter pastures in the north. It made no sense to me why they should come south for the summer and travel north to winter, but that is what they did.

At the time, I did not know that certain regions of the north country can be as mild as any place in the south. But I soon learned that not all the land above the Wall is the bleak, rock-strewn and windblown wasteland that most people think it is. There are corners as lush and comfortable as the best land in all Britain. It was to one of these corners that we came, riding our shaggy ponies and driving our tough little sheep before us.

A crannog is not much different from a rath, save that it is actually hollowed into the heart of the hill. It is also larger; it had to be, for we shared it with our ponies and sheep on the coldest days. Ideally placed in a secluded glen, the crannog appears, to tallfolk eyes, is just another hill among many. There was good grazing for the sheep and ponies, and a stream which emptied into a nearby sea estuary.

The crannog was dark and warm and though the winter wind whined at night as it searched the rocks and crannies for places its cold fingers could reach, we lay wrapped in our furs and fleeces around the fire, listening to Gern-y-fhain tell of the Elder Days, before the Roman-men came with their swords and built their roads and fortresses, before the bloodlust came on men to make them war with one another, before ever the tallfolk came to the Island of the Mighty.

Listen, she would say, I will tell you of the time before time when the world was new-made and the Prytani ran free and food was plentiful to find and our parents smiled on all their child-wealth, when the Great Snow was shut up in the north and troubled Mother's firstborn not at all. . .

And she would begin reciting her tale, repeating in her tone and cadence and inflection the ages-old memory of her people, linking them with a past impossibly remote, but alive in her words. There was no telling how old the story was, for the Hill Folk spoke of all events the same simple, immediate way. What a Gern described might have taken place ten-thousand summers ago, or it might have happened yesterday. Indeed, it was all the same to them.

One moon waxed and waned, and another, and one day just before dusk it began to snow. Elac and Nolo and I went down to the valley with the dogs to herd the livestock back to the crannog. We had just begun when I heard Nolo shout; I turned to see him pointing off down the valley at riders approaching through the swirling snow.

Elac made a flattening motion with his hand and I saw Nolo notch an arrow to his bowstring, crouch, and. . . disappear. He simply vanished, becoming one more rock or turvey hillock beside the stream. I crouched, too, in the way they had taught me, wondering whether I might be as easily mistaken for a stone. The dogs barked and Elac whistled, silencing them instantly.

Three tallfolk riders clopped up on leggy, starved-looking mounts. Their leader said something, Elac replied and then

66

they began speaking in a much abused approximation of the Hill Folk tongue. 'We come to ask Hill Folk magic,' the rider explained in his halting, broken speech.

'Why?' asked Elac placidly.

'Our chieftain's second wife dies. She has the fever and will keep no food.' He looked at Elac doubtfully. 'Will your Wise Woman come?'

'I will ask her.' He shrugged, adding, 'But likely she will not find it worthwhile to make healing magic for a tallfolk woman.'

'Our chief says he will give four bracelets of gold if the Gern will come.'

Elac frowned disdainfully, as if to say 'Such trinkets are horse manure to us' — although I knew the Prytani valued tallfolk gold and prized it when they could get it. 'I will ask,' he repeated. 'You go now.'

'We will wait.'

'No. You go now,' insisted Elac. He did not want the tallfolk to see which hill our crannog was in.

'It is our chief!' replied the rider.

Elac shrugged again and turned away, making a pretence of going back to his sheep gathering. The riders whispered among themselves for a moment and then the leader said, 'When? When will you tell her?'

'When tallfolk go back to their huts.'

The riders wheeled their horses and rode away. Elac waited until they were gone and then motioned us forward. Nolo replaced his arrow in the quiver and we herded the sheep together and drove them back to the crannog. The others had already brought the horses in, so Elac wasted no time in speaking to Gern.

'The tallfolk chief's wife is fevered,' he told her. 'Four gold bracelets if you will heal her.'

'She must be very fevered,' replied Gern. 'But I will go to her.' And she rose and made her way out of the crannog at once. Nolo, Elac, Vrisa, and I followed.

By the time we arrived at the tallfolk settlement on the estuary, it was almost dark. The chief's house stood on timber stilts amidst a handful of lesser dwellings built at the very edge of the reeking mudflats. Vrisa, Elac, and Nolo accompanied Gern; I had come to hold the ponies, but once we arrived and

Gern looked around, she indicated that I was to join them in the chief's house.

A filthy skin hung over the door. At Elac's whistle this door-flap was drawn back and the man who had come to us in the valley emerged to motion us in. The round timber hut contained a single large room with a fire stone in the centre. Wind sifted through the poorly-thatched roof and the unfilled gaps in the wattle, making the room damp and chill. The shells of mussels and oysters, and fishbones and scales lay trampled on the floor. The chieftain sat beside the sooty dried-dung fire with two women, each clutching a dirty, squawling infant to her breast. The chief grunted and gestured across the room where a woman lay on a pallet of rushes piled high with furs.

Gern clucked when she saw the woman. She was not old, but the dubious honour of producing heirs for the chief had aged her beyond her years. And now she lay in her bed aflame with fever, eyes sunken, limbs trembling, her skin pale and yellow as the fleece under her head. She was dying. Even I — who at the time lacked any knowledge of healing — could see that she would not last the night.

'Fools!' Gern said under her breath. 'They ask magic too late.'

'Four bracelets,' Elac reminded her.

Gern sighed and squatted down beside the woman, studied her for a long moment and then dipped her fingers into the pouch at her belt and brought out a small pot of ointment which she began applying to the sick woman's forehead. The woman shivered and opened her eyes. I could see the death-look in them, although under Gern's touch she seemed to revive somewhat. Gern spoke to her softly, using the soothing words of the healer's tongue to ease the fever's grip.

Dipping back into her pouch, Gern withdrew her hand and extended it to me. Into my open palm she dropped a small mass of dried matter — bark shavings, roots, leaves, grass, seeds — nodding towards the iron cauldron hanging over the fire by a chain from the roofbeam. I understood that she wished me to put the mixture into the cauldron, which I did. I poured water into the pot and waited until it boiled. Then Gern motioned for me to bring it to her; under the foul mutterings of the chief, I dipped out a gourd.

Gern lifted the woman's head and gave her to drink. The

woman smiled weakly as she lay back. A few moments later she closed her eyes and slept. Gern then went to the chief and stood before him.

'Will the woman live?' asked the chief. He might have been speaking about one of his hounds.

'She lives,' answered Gern-y-fhain. 'See she does keep warm, and drinks the potion.'

The chieftain grunted and removed one of his bracelets. He handed the golden object to his man, who dropped it gingerly into Gern's palm lest he touch her. The slight did not go unnoticed. Elac stiffened. Nolo's hand already had an arrow in it.

But Gern looked at the bracelet and hefted it in her hand. Likely, there was much tin in the thing and little enough gold. 'You promised *four* bracelets.'

'Four? Take what you are given, and get out!' he growled in his sorry speech. 'I will not hear your lies!'

The Hill Folk drew their weapons.

Gern raised a hand in the air. Elac and Nolo froze. 'Chief thinks to cheat Gern-y-fhain?' She spoke softly, but the threat was undeniable. Her hand weaved a strange motion in the air and something fell from her fingers. The fire suddenly became a fountain gushing bright sparks.

The women screamed and threw their hands over their faces. The chieftain quickly reconsidered, glaring with red-eyed anger. He muttered and removed three more bracelets, throwing them into the flaming embers of the fire at his feet.

Quick as a flick, Gern reached into the fire and scooped up the bracelets, to the astonishment of the tallfolk. The gold disappeared into a fold in her clothing and, straight-backed, she turned and walked from the hut. We followed her, mounted our ponies, and together returned to the crannog in the winter twilight.

Two days later, Elac and Nolo took the sheep back down to the pasture and were there when the tallfolk came upon them: three riders as before and the chief with them. I was halfway down the hill and saw the riders sweep down on my fhain-brothers, scattering the sheep. I stopped and hunched myself into a motionless shape, blending instantly into the hillscape.

When the riders halted, I hurried forward.

'Give back the gold!' the chief shouted.

Elac's knife appeared in his hand. Nolo's bowstring stretched taut. The tallfolk were not unprepared. Each held a sturdy sword and a small, well-made wood-and-oxhide shield. I wondered about the weapons. Where had these men come by them? Trading with the Scotti?

'Give it back, thief!'

Elac may not have understood the word, but he knew the tone. His muscles tensed, ready to leap to the fight. The only thing that checked him was the horses. Had the Hill Folk been astride their own ponies they would have been nigh invincible to the rogues before them. But it was four against two, and the two were on foot.

The tallfolk chieftain meant to have his gold back, or the heads of those who had it on sharpened stakes outside his house. Perhaps both. As I watched, I felt the same quickening in the air around me as I had felt the day the stones danced. I knew something would happen, but did not know what it might be.

But the moment I stepped between Elac and the chieftain, I saw that the tallfolk felt it, too.

'Why have you come here?' I asked, trying to imitate Gern-y-fhain's unassailable authority.

The tallfolk started as if I had sprung full-grown from the turf at their feet. The chieftain tightened his grip on his sword and grumbled, 'The woman is dead and lies cold in the mud. I have come for my gold.'

'Go back,' I told him. 'If you think to avenge yourself on those who helped you, then you deserve what will happen to you. Turn back; there is nothing for you here.'

A fierce and ugly glee twisted his stupid face. 'I will have the gold, and your flapping tongue as well, bastard!'

'You have been warned,' I told him, then looked at the others. 'You have *all* been warned.' They were not as brave as their chief, or else they were not as stupid. They muttered and made the sign against evil with their hands.

The chief opened his mouth in a rude laugh. 'I will gut you like a herring and strangle you with your own entrails, boy!' he boasted, lowering his sword to my throat.

Elac tensed, ready to strike. I held up a hand to stay him. The chief's sword, the blade black with caked blood, came nearer. I turned my eyes to the length of jagged iron and imagined the heat that had forged it, imagined it red hot from the forge fire.

The sword-tip began to glow — duskily at first, but brightening rapidly, the fireglow spreading along the blade towards the hilt.

The chief held the weapon as long as he could, and burned his hand badly for his stubbornness. His shriek echoed in the valley. 'Kill him!' he shouted; the red welt on his palm was already blistering. 'Kill him!'

His men made no move for their own weapons had become too hot to hold, and indeed the iron in their belt buckles, knives, and arm rings was growing uncomfortably warm.

The horses jigged nervously, showing the whites of their eyes. 'Take yourselves from here and do not trouble us again,' I said levelly, although my heart was beating furiously.

One of the men turned his horse and made to ride away, but his leader was a bull-headed man. 'Stay!' Rage and frustration blackened his face. 'You!' He roared at me. 'I will kill you! I will — '

I had never seen a man carried away by such hate. And, although I have seen it once or twice since, at the time I did not know that it could kill.

The chief gagged and his words stuck — like fishbones in his throat — and he choked, making a hideous sound. Clawing at his neck, eyes bulging, he pitched from the saddle. He was dead when his body struck the ground.

The men stared at their fallen leader only for an instant, then wheeled their horses and fled back the way they had come, leaving their chief where he lay.

When they had gone, Elac turned to me and looked long into my eyes. He did not speak, but the questions were there. Who are you? *What* are you?

Nolo squatted beside the body. 'This one is dead, Myrddin-wealth,' he said softly.

'We will put him back on his horse and send him home to his own,' I told him.

With some difficulty, the three of us lifted the body and slung it across the saddle, tying the wrists and ankles together to keep it from sliding off. We turned the horse and gave the unhappy beast a slap on the rump and it trotted after the others. I breathed a prayer for the man — I did not have it in me to despise him. We watched the horses out of sight and then returned to the crannog, Elac and Nolo running on ahead in their eagerness to tell what they had seen.

Vrisa and Gern-y-fhain regarded me knowingly as they heard what had happened. Gern-y-fhain raised her hands above my head and sang the victory for me; Vrisa showed her appreciation in another way. She put her arms around me and kissed me. That night I sat beside her at supper and she fed me from her bowl.

SEVEN

The snow came to the north country. Through cold, grey days of little light and long, black nights of howling wind, I sat at Gern-y-fhain's feet beside the peat fire and she taught me her craft — the ancient arts of earth and air, fire and water that men in their ignorance call magic. I learn quickly, but Gern-y-fhain was a good teacher, as adept in her own way as Dafyd or Blaise in theirs.

It was at this time that I began to See, and it started with the peat fire, which glows so beautifully, all cherry red and gold. Not all Gerns have this ability, but Gern-y-fhain could look into the fire and see the shapes of things there. And once she awakened the ability in me, we would sit there for hours together, fire-gazing. Afterwards, she would ask me what I had seen and I would tell her.

I soon learned that my vision was more clear than her own.

As my skill improved, I could almost summon the images I chose — almost. Nevertheless, one night I saw my mother. This occurrence was as pleasant as it was unexpected. I was staring into the flames, emptying my mind for the images that would come, while at the same time reaching out for them — an act more difficult to describe than to do. Gern-y-fhain likened it to drawing water from a stream, or coaxing shy, winter-born colts down from the hills.

As I stared into the fire that cold night, I saw the form of a woman flicker before me and I drew it in, held it — much as a man might cup his hand around a candle flame — coaxed it to take shape, willed it to remain. It was Charis and she was sitting in a chamber beside a brazier glowing with charcoal. At the moment I apprehended her, she raised her head and looked around as if someone had spoken her name. Perhaps I did; I cannot say.

The image was strong and I could see from her contented

73

expression that she was at peace — which could only be, I reasoned, if my message had been received and understood in the way I had intended. At least, she was not sick with worry over me.

As I watched, the door behind her opened and she half-turned in her chair. The visitor approached and she smiled. I could not see who it was, but as the other came near she reached out. . .

With one hand in hers, he put the other on her shoulder and settled himself on the arm of the chair. She turned her head to the hand at her shoulder and brushed it with her lips. I knew then who it was: Maelwys.

This so unnerved me that I lost the image. It dissolved back into the flames and was gone. I was left with a throbbing head and a question. What did it mean?

It was not the shock of seeing my mother with Maelwys — that was logical enough; indeed, it made perfect sense that she should return to winter in Maridunum while the search for me went on. Rather, it was seeing her affection for another, affection which heretofore had been reserved for me alone. This too was logical, after all; but that did not make it easier to accept.

It is always a humbling thing to discover your own insignificance in the grand design.

I puzzled on the meaning of what I had seen for several days before giving it up. The important thing was that my mother was cared for, and that she was not overwrought for me.

I saw other things, other places. More and more often now, I recognized what I saw: Blaise wrapped in his cloak and sitting on a hill, staring up at the night sky; priest Dafyd and my grandfather Avallach hunched head-to-head over a chessboard; Elphin stropping a new sword. Other times I did not know what I saw: a narrow, rocky glen with a spring bubbling out of a cleft in a hill; a girl with raven-dark hair lighting a rushlamp with a reed; a noisome smoke-dark hall filled with glowering, drunken men and snarling dogs. . .

Always it ended the same way: the image dissolving in the flames, fading into red heat and white ash. I had no idea whether what I saw was happening, had already happened, or was yet to happen. Ah, but that would come. In time, that too would come.

Gern-y-fhain taught me other things in those dark winter days. She was pleased to have someone to tell the things she had stored up over a lifetime, and I was happy to mine that rich store. She must have known that her work was impermanent, that I would leave one day, taking all with me. Still, she gave freely. Perhaps she also knew the value I would one day place on the knowledge I was given.

When spring came again to the Island of the Mighty, the fhain travelled back to the south. They chose a rath in a different place, hoping for better grazing than they had had the previous year.

Our summer place was not far from the Wall — where the mountains enfold hidden valleys and settlements are rare. Twice that summer, when I rode hunting with Teirn, we saw troops hurrying along the ancient ridgeways. Crouching beside our ponies we watched them pass, and I sensed the upheaval in those troubled spirits; like a disturbance in the air, I felt the rolling, churning chaos as they marched by.

That was not the only indication I had of the great and terrible events proceeding along their ordained courses in the world of men. . . I also heard the *voices*.

This began soon after the second sighting of the troops. We were returning to the rath with the day's kill and had stopped to allow the ponies to drink from a stream. The sun was standing low; the sky was aglow with yellow flame. I drooped my arms across my pony's neck — we were both sweating and tired. There was not a breath of wind in the glen and the blackflies were thick and bothersome. I was simply resting, watching the sunlight dance on the rippling water, when the buzz of the flies seemed to form itself into words.

'. . . *make them understand*. . . *nearer now than ever*. . . *few years, perhaps*. . . *southeast*. . . *Lindum and Luguvallium are with us*. . . *bide, Constantius. It will not be for ever*. . . '

The words were spoken softly. A mere whisper on the breeze — but there was no breeze. The air was dead.

I looked across at Teirn to see if he heard it, too. But he remained squatting at the water's edge, cupping water to his mouth. If he heard anything he gave no sign.

'. . . *six hundred is all*. . . *orders, my friend, orders*. . . *Imperator!*. . . *more in tribute*. . . *this year than last, Mithras help us!. . . bleed us dry?. . . here is the seal, take it. . . then it is agreed. . . cannot turn aside. . . Ave Imperator!'*

The words came in gasps and snatches, many different voices, overlapping one another in a gabble of confusion. But they were voices and I had no doubt that somewhere, far or near, the words had been spoken. Although there was no sense to what I heard, I knew from the tone that a thing of momentous import was taking place.

I thought about this for a long time that night and after. What did it mean? What could it mean?

But that, I regret, I was not to discover until much later.

Not that I could have done anything about it. I was very much a part of Hawk Fhain now. I had altogether stopped thinking about running away — having come, like Gern-y-fhain, to believe that my stay with the Hill Folk was meant to be. Perhaps I was not the Gift they thought I was; indeed, they were a gift to me for I was learning much that would stand me in good stead the rest of my life.

Thus, it is no simple matter to describe my sojourn among the People of the Hawk. Even for me, the words I speak show themselves hollow, broken things beside the brimming reality that lives in my heart: the colours! — autumn fern like copper shining from the fire; and in the spring, whole mountain-sides clothed in imperial purple; greens as tender and fresh as the dawn of creation, rich as God's own idea of green; the myriad shifting blues of sea and sky and running water; the matchless white of snow newfallen; the grey of lowering thundercloud, the excellent black of night's soft wing. . .

And more: sunbright days of infinite light and pleasure; starbright nights of deep, deep slumber; seasons of goodness and right, each moment etched in elegant symmetry upon the soul; the slow Earth moving through its inexorable cycle of birth and rebirth, keeping faith with the Creator, fulfilling its ancient and honourable promise.

Great Light, I could not have loved you better than I did then.

For I saw, and I understood. I saw the order of creation; I understood the rhythm of life. The Hill Folk lived close to the order; they felt the rhythm in their blood. They had no need to understand it — they were part of it as it was part of

76

them — but through them I learned to feel it; through them I became part of it, too.

My kinsmen, my brothers! The debt that I owe you can never be repaid, but know that I have never forgotten you, and as long as men hear and remember the old stories, as long as words have meaning you will live, even as you live in my heart.

I stayed with the Hawk People another year, one more winter and spring and summer, one more Beltane and Lughnasadh, and then I knew it was time for me to return to my own. As the days began to shorten, I grew uneasy — a light flutter of the stomach when I looked to the south, a slight lift of the heart when I thought of home, the tingle of expectation that in far-off courts the future substance of my life was being shaped, that somewhere someone was waiting for me to appear.

I endured these various sensations in silence, but Gern-y-fhain knew. She could tell that my time was short and one night after supper called me outside. I took her arm and we walked in silence up the hill to stand in the stone circle. She squinted up at the twilight sky and then at me. 'Myrddin-brother, you are a man now.'

I waited for what she had to say.

'You will leave fhain.'

I nodded. 'Soon.'

She smiled a smile so sweet and sad that it pierced my soul with its tenderness. 'Go your way, wealth of my heart.'

Tears rose to my eyes and my throat tightened. 'I cannot leave without your song in my ears, Gern-y-fhain.'

That pleased her. 'Will sing you home, Myrddin-wealth. Will be a special song.' She began composing it that night.

Vrisa came to me the next day. She and Gern-y-fhain had been talking and she wanted me to know that she understood. 'You would make good a husband, Myrddin-brother. I am a good wife.'

That was true. She would have been a good wife to any man. 'I do thank you, Vrisa-sister. But —' I turned my eyes to the southern hills.

'Needs must go back to your tallfolk rath,' she sighed. Then, taking my hand, raised it to her lips, kissed it, and placed it against her breast. Beneath the warmth of her soft flesh, I could feel the beating of her heart.

'We are alive, Myrddin-brother. We are not sky-folk or Ancient Ones that have no life. Be we blood and bone and spirit — firstborn of Mother's child-wealth. . . ' she nodded solemnly, covering my hand with both of hers. 'You know this now.'

Indeed, I never doubted it. She was so beautiful, yes, and so alive, so much a part of her world that I was tempted to stay and become her husband. Quite possibly I would have, too, but the road stretched out before me and I could already see myself on it.

I kissed her and she smiled, brushing back a lock of black hair. 'I will carry you in my heart always, Vrisa-sister,' I told her.

Three nights later we celebrated Samhain, Night of the Peace Fire, thanking our Parents for the blessing of a good year. As the moon crested the hills Gern-y-fhain lit the bonfire in the stone circle and I saw other fires on other distant hilltops round about. We ate roast lamb and garlic and wild onions, and there was much talking and laughing, and I sang them a song in my own tongue, which they enjoyed even though they understood nothing of it. I wanted to leave them with something of my own.

When I finished, Gern-y-fhain rose and paced slowly around the bonfire three times in a sun-wise circle. She came to stand over me and stretched her hands over my head. 'Listen, People of the Hawk, this is the Leaving Song for Myrddin-brother.'

She raised her hands to the moon and began to sing. The tune was the old changeless melody of the hills, but the words were newly composed in my honour, recounting my life with the fhain. She sang it all: the night I had come to them, and my near sacrifice; my struggles with their language; our firelight lessons together; the incident with the tallfolk; the herding, the lambing, the hunting, the eating, the living.

When she finished, all sat in quiet respect. I rose to my feet and embraced her and then, one by one, the fhain came to say farewell — each taking my hands and kissing them in blessing. Teirn gave me a spear he had made, and Nolo presented me with a new bow and a quiver of arrows, saying, 'Do take this, Myrddin-brother. You will need it on your way.'

'I do thank you, fhain-brother Nolo. I will use it gladly.'

Elac was next. 'Myrddin-brother, as you are big as a mountain' — in truth, I had grown in my time with them and now towered over them all — 'you will be cold in winter. Do take this cloak.' He wrapped a handsome wolfskin cloak around my shoulders.

'I do thank thee, fhain-brother Elac. I will wear it with pride.'

Vrisa came last. She took my hands and kissed them. 'You are a man now, Myrddin-brother,' she said softly. 'You will need good gold for a wife.' She removed two golden bracelets from her arm and placed one on each wrist and then hugged me close.

If she had asked me to stay, I would have done so. But the matter was settled; she and the other women slipped away among the standing stones and in a little while the men went to them so that their eager love making would ensure another fruitful year. I returned to the rath with Gern-y-fhain, who offered me a blessing cup of heather beer, which I drank and then went to sleep.

Heavy-hearted, I left my Hill Folk family the next morning. They stood outside the rath and waved me away, the dogs and children running alongside my black pony as I made my way down the hill. I came to the stream in the valley where the children and dogs stopped, for they would not cross the water, and I looked back to see that the fhain had vanished. All that remained was the hilltop and the grey, sunless sky beyond.

I was in the tallfolk world once again.

EIGHT

I travelled south and east, hoping to strike the old Roman road that extended north of the Wall as far as Arderydd — or farther, for all I knew. This would lead me to Deva, City of Legions in the north, and the mountains of Gwynedd and the place where I had last seen my people. I had no better thought than to return to the hills and glens around Yr Widdfa where I had last seen the men searching for me. I never doubted whether there would be anyone there; I was certain of it, as I was certain of the sun rising in the east. They would search until they received word or sign that I was dead; without that they would search for ever.

I had only to cross their path. Time was growing short, however; one day soon the weather would break and the searchers would return home for the winter. Already the days were crisp and the sunlight thin. If I did not find them soon, I would have to ride all the way to Maridunum — a most difficult and dangerous journey for one alone.

By riding from before sunrise until well after sunset, I was able to traverse the wide, empty land with some speed. The fhain had come far north with the seasons. I did not realize how far north until I saw the great Celyddon Forest raising its black hump before me on the horizon. Apparently, we had skirted the forest to the west a year ago when travelling to winter quarters. And though the quickest route to the south lay through the forest's dark heart, I was loathe to take it.

But time was no friend to me with winter coming on. So, with my spear in my hand and my bow ready, I turned towards the forest track, hoping to pass through in three or four days.

The first day and night proved uneventful. I rode along pathways aflame with autumn colour — burning reds and golds, yellows that glowed in the falling light. Only the swish and crack of my pony's hooves in the dry leaves, and the occasional shriek of a bird or natter of a squirrel, marked our passing. Among the great stands of oak and ash, their iron-dark boles hoary and bearded with green moss, spreading elm and rowan, slender pine and massive yew, silence reigned and gave us to know with every step that we were intruders there.

The second day began with a mist that turned to a weepy, sodden rain which soon drenched me to the skin. Wet and cold, I pursued my miserable way until I came to a fern-grown clearing beside a racing stream. As I sat deciding where to cross, the rain stopped and the cloud-cover thinned so that the sun appeared a pale white disk. I slid from the pony's back, led it through the pungent fern to the water's edge and gave it to drink.

I suppose the clearing with its patch of sky above seemed a convivial place, so I started shrugging off my soaking clothing and spreading it on the rocks along the stream-bed in anticipation of the sun. And I was not disappointed.

But, as the clouds parted, I heard a crashing in the wood nearby. I dropped instinctively into my invisible posture. The noise increased, coming directly towards me, and of course I recognized the sound: a boar in full flight with a hunter right behind.

A moment later a gigantic old tusker broke through the underbrush not a dozen paces upstream. The great beast's hide was criss-crossed with scars marked in white tufts against the bristling black. And, like the battlechief that it was, the fearsome creature did not pause in its heedless, headlong flight, but plunged straight into the water, thrashed across in a frothing spray and disappeared into the wood on the other side.

Right behind came the rider. The instant the horse cleared the underbrush and leaped to the bank the sun broke through the swift-scattering cloud and a shaft of light struck like a spear heaved from on high, illuminating a most unusual sight: a mount the colour of grey morning mist — a handsome animal, long-legged and graceful, by appearances more hart than horse, white mane flying, nostrils flared to the scent of the boar. And a rider, slender and fierce, eyes wide with the excitement of the chase, hair like midnight streaming unbound behind, the sun striking the polished facets of a silver breastplate, slender arm hefting a long, silver boarspear so thin it appeared a frozen moonbeam caught in her hand.

In an instant, I knew this hunter to be the raven-haired girl I had seen while fire-gazing.

A heartbeat later, I doubted whether I had seen her at all, for the horse gathered its legs and leaped the stream as lightly as a bird taking flight. Horse and rider landed on the opposite shore and disappeared into the greengrowth on the other side, hot on the trail of the boar.

If not for the sound of the continuing chase, I might have dreamed them. But as the crackling and thumping of the hunt receded into the wood, I snatched up my clothes and threw them on again, led my pony across the stream, and rode after.

The trail was not at all difficult to follow. Still, they moved surprisingly fast, for I did not catch another glimpse of hunter or game until nearly tumbling over them in a grassy hollow in the dim forest.

The huge boar lay on its belly, legs collapsed under it, the slender shaft protruding through the massive hump of its shoulder into its chest where the leaf-shaped blade had cleft its heart; the great tusks were curved and yellow, the cunning little eyes glittered bright with bloodlust. The girl still sat her mount, and the grey horse snorted its triumph and raked the ground with a delicate forehoof.

She did not turn to me at first, although I surely made a fearful din as I burst blindly through the yew hedge; her attention was absorbed in the kill. It was a prize worthy of a champion and no mistake. Mind, I have seen boars of all sizes, and I also have seen experienced spearmen quail at the sight of a charging tusker. But I have never seen a boar so big, nor a maid so coolly composed.

Was it courage or arrogance?

The exultant glimmer in her eye, the set of her jaw, the regal posture. . . there was power in every comely line of her. I was in the presence of a woman, however young — she could not have been above fifteen summers — who chanced everything, quailed at nothing, admitted no defeat.

Only when she had drunk deep of the sight of her kill did she deign to notice me. 'You intrude, stranger.' Her speech, after the singing Hill Folk tongue, sounded odd in my ears; but I understood, for it was very like the speech of Llyonesse.

I inclined my head, accepting her appraisal. 'Forgive me, I am indeed a stranger.'

'*That*,' she pointed out, 'is not your transgression.'

She crooked a leg over her mount and slipped to the ground, then walked to the boar and stood gazing at it with pleasure. 'This one fought well.'

'I do not wonder. By the look of him, many have tried to bring him down and failed.'

This pleased her. 'I did not fail.' She loosed a wild war whoop of sheer pleasure. The cry echoed through the wood and faded, whereupon she turned to me. 'What do you here?' Her manner implied that the entire forest belonged to her.

'As you see, I am a traveller.'

'As I see, you are a dirty boy in reeking wolfskins.' She wrinkled her nose imperially. 'You do not look a traveller to me.'

'Accept that I am.'

'I believe you.' She turned suddenly and, placing a booted foot against the boar's shoulder hump, pulled sharply on the spear and drew it out. The silver shaft dripped dark red blood. She observed this for a moment and then began wiping the spear on the beast's hide.

'That skin will make a fine trophy,' I remarked, stepping closer.

She levelled the spear at me. 'So would yours, wolf boy.'

'Is everyone hereabouts as ill-mannered as you?'

She laughed, a light fillip in the air. 'I am admonished.' Her tone denied her words entirely. She returned the spear to its holder on her saddle. 'Will you stand there like a stump, or will you help me carry back my kill?'

Truly, I did not see how the monster before us could be carried back without a wagon, nor heaved into a wagon without the help of half-dozen brawny men. Certainly, neither horse could carry the weight. But the girl was not dismayed. She removed a hand axe from behind her saddle and directed me to start felling a few of the slender birches from a stand across the hollow from where we stood.

I did as I was told and together we began hacking the branches from the trees and lashing the clean poles together with rawhide strips to form a crude litter. The work went quickly and pleasantly for me, for I had the opportunity of observing her graceful body in motion.

She had removed her silver breastplate while I was cutting the trees and now worked beside me in a light blue riding tunic and checked kilt of the sort that many of the remote hill tribes wore. Her boots were soft doeskin, and at her wrists and throat were narrow silver bands set with blue stones. Long-limbed and slender, her skin smooth and delicate as milk, she nevertheless gave herself to her work with a passion I suspected she lavished on all things that happened to capture her interest.

We spoke little while we worked, enjoying the challenge of the task before us, and the rhythm of two people working as one. Once the poles of the litter had been secured, then came the difficult part: rolling the enormous carcass onto the platform. I brought my black hill pony to the boar, and we looped a length of rawhide around the boar's forelegs, and with one of the remaining poles as a lever half-dragged and half-rolled the huge carcass into position.

Grunting, sweating, heaving at the dead weight with all our strength, we nudged the carcass onto the litter, where it slipped and rolled sideways onto my leg. The girl laughed and leaped to help me; as she bent near, I drank in the warm woman-scent and the light aromatic oils she used as perfume. The touch of her hands on my skin was like a dancing flame against the flesh.

I struggled free of the boar and we continued the laborious task. Some while later we finished tying down the beast, then stood looking at one another for a moment, both flushed with pride and exhaustion at our accomplishment, and dripping sweat. 'After a hunt,' she told me, amusement glimmering in eyes the colour of cornflowers, 'I am accustomed to swim.' She paused and looked me up and down. 'You could do with a bath as well, but. . . ' she lifted a palm equivocally, 'it is getting late.'

In truth, the prospect of bathing with this beautiful young woman sent a ripple of pleasure through my loins. I did not think it so late, but she moved away without waiting for my answer, mounted her horse and rode a few paces before turning back to me. 'Well, I suppose you have earned a crust by the fire and a pallet in the stable. You had better follow me, wolf boy.'

I needed no second invitation, and likely would not have received one anyway, so took up my reins and followed. Getting the boar home was far from easy — fording the stream was the hardest part. But as the sun was touching the western hills we came within sight of a large settlement — at least twenty fair-sized timber dwellings crouching along the shores of a deep mountain lake. On a mound at one end of the lake stood a palace consisting of a great hall, stable, kitchen, granary, and temple — all of timber.

We rode down to this settlement through the trees, and the people came running to greet us. Upon seeing the boar, they shouted and gave the lady loud acclaim, which she accepted with such poise and modesty that I knew her noble born. Her father ruled here and these were his subjects and his beloved daughter. For loved she was, I could see it on the faces of those around us — she was their treasure.

As this was so, I received a rather cooler reception. Those who noticed me at all frowned, and some pointed at me rudely. They did not like seeing a filthy foundling beside her. Indeed, with very little encouragement they would have taken up the stones at their feet and pelted me away.

Did I blame them? No, I did not.

I felt decidedly unworthy riding beside her. And looking at myself through their eyes. . . Well, trotting beside their beautiful lady on a shaggy pony was an even shaggier boy dressed in leather and wolfskin, looking like something fresh out of the northern wastes, which I was; foreign and certainly not to be trusted.

But the girl did not seem to mind, and took no notice of my unease. I looked this way and that, with a growing feeling that it had been a mistake to come, that I should have fared better in the forest. We rode through the settlement, along the shingle beside the lake, and up the mound to the palace. The villagers did not come up, but remained a respectful distance away.

'What is this place?' I asked as we dismounted. Servants were hurrying towards us.

'This is my father's house,' explained the girl.

'Who might your father be?'

'You will see soon enough. Here he comes.'

I turned to where she looked and saw a giant strolling towards me with great, ground-eating strides. He was as tall as any two of the Hill Folk, taller even than Avallach, and broadly built as well, with heavy shoulders, a thick chest, and limbs like yew stumps. He had long brown hair which he wore pulled back tight and bound in a golden ring. His soft boots came to his knees and his kilt bore the red-and-green checked design of the north. Two enormous black wolf hounds bounded at his heels.

'My father,' said the girl and ran to meet him. He caught her up and lifted her off her feet in a fearsome embrace. I winced, fearing the cracking of her ribs. But he set her down lightly and came to where I stood.

The giant took one glance at the boar; his eyes grew round, and he opened his mouth and laughed, so that the timbers of his house shivered and the sound echoed from the tree-clad hills. 'Well done, lass!' He clapped hands the size of platters. 'Well done, my darling girl.'

He kissed her and turned suddenly to me. 'And who might you be, lad?'

'He helped me with the boar, father,' the girl explained. 'I told him he could have supper and a bed for his trouble.'

'It was no trouble,' I managed to squeak out.

'So that is the way of it,' the man said, neither pleased nor displeased as yet, but certainly reserving judgement. 'Do you have a name then?'

'Merlin,' I replied. The word sounded strange in my ears. 'Myrddin ap Taliesin among my own people.'

'You have people, do you?' Was he mocking me? 'Then why are you not with them?'

'I was taken by Hill Folk and was not able to escape until now,' I said, hoping that answer would save further explaining. 'My people are in the south. I am going to them now.'

'Where in the south?'

'In the Summerlands and Llyonesse.'

The man frowned. 'So you say. I do not recall hearing of such places myself — if places they are. What name do your people go by?'

'Cymry,' I told him.

'Them I have heard of at least.' He nodded, looking at my silver torc and the gold bracelets Vrisa had given me. 'They are your father's people?'

86

'Yes. My grandfather is Lord Elphin ap Gwyddno Garanhir who was king of Gwynedd.'

'Was?'

'He lost his lands in the Great Conspiracy and moved south.'

The huge man sighed sympathetically. 'A very bad time that. Aye, but still he was lucky — many a man lost more.' His voice was a rumble like wagon wheels going over a wooden bridge. 'Your father is a prince then.'

'My father died soon after I was born.'

'What of your mother? You did not mention her.'

This was odd; I had never had so much attention paid to my lineage. But then, I had never before accepted lodging from a king's daughter. 'My mother is Charis, a princess of Llyonesse. My grandfather is King Avallach of Ynys Avallach.'

He nodded approvingly, but his eyes narrowed. He seemed to be weighing me, perhaps calculating how far he could throw me into the lake, and how big the splash. At last he said, 'Royalty on both sides then. Good enough.' His eyes slid past mine to his daughter and then to the carcass of the boar which his men were gutting on the spot. 'Look at this now! Have you ever seen a finer prize? We will feast on it this time tomorrow.'

With that the remarkable man turned and strode back to the great hall, the dogs trotting after him. 'My father likes you, wolf boy. You are welcome here.'

'Am I?'

'I have said so.'

'You know all about me, and I do not even know your name — or that of your father, or where I have come, or. . . '

She smiled slyly. 'So inquisitive.'

'It is common courtesy where I come from.'

'You seem to come from everywhere and nowhere. Nevertheless,' bowing her head imperiously, she said, 'I am Ganieda. My father is Custennin, King of Goddeu in Celyddon.'

'My greetings to the both of you.'

'Our greetings to you, Myrddin ap Taliesin,' she replied nicely. 'Will you come in?'

'I will.' I inclined my head. She laughed, the sound liquid silver on the evening air. Then, drawing her arm through mine, she pulled me away. My heart nearly burst.

I slept that night on goosedown in a sleeping room next to Custennin's great hall. I shared the room with some of the king's men, who treated me politely, but accorded me no special favour. The next morning they rose and went about their various duties and I got up and went into the great hall, now empty but for the servants carrying off last night's food scraps and spreading fresh rushes over the floor.

No one took notice of me, so I drifted out into the yard and sat down on the ledge of the well and dipped out a drink from a leather cannikin. The water was ice cold and sweet and, as I drank, I thought of the journey before me that day and found the prospect a good deal less agreeable than it had been the day before.

The dipper was still at my lips when I felt cold fingers on my neck. I hunched my shoulders and squirmed round. Ganieda laughed and slipped from my reach. 'You must have been very tired,' she said, 'to stay so long abed — and you a traveller in a hurry.'

'You are right, Ganieda.' I liked the feel of her name on my tongue. She was wearing her blue tunic and kilt of the day before, but had donned a long, fleece-lined cloak against the morning chill. The silver at her throat and wrists gleamed, and her black hair had been brushed so that it shone. 'I slept well for the first time in many days, and as a consequence I have slept too long.'

'Obviously, you are exhausted,' she volunteered matter-of-factly. 'In which case, you cannot possibly leave today. Leave tomorrow when you are better rested. That makes much better sense.' She stepped shyly forward, although there was nothing at all shy about her. 'I have been thinking,' she said seriously — not too seriously, mind you, for solemnity was no great part of her nature either. 'What lovely eyes! Your eyes, Myrddin — '

'Yes?' I could feel the colour rising to my cheeks.

'They are gold — wolf's eyes, hawk's eyes. . . I have never seen eyes like this in a human being.'

'You flatter me, lady,' I replied stiffly. Was this what she had been thinking?

She settled herself on the stone ledge beside me. 'Is it far where you are going?'

'Far enough.' I nodded slowly.

'How far?'

'As far as may be.'

'Oh.' She fell silent, chin in her hand, elbow resting on her knee.

'Would it make a difference if it were not so far?'

Ganieda shrugged. 'Perhaps. . . somehow.'

I laughed. 'Ganieda, tell me what is in your mind. What have you been thinking? I tarry with you here while I should be saddling my horse and bidding Celyddon farewell.' The last word caught in my throat. Ganieda winced.

'You do not know your way through the forest. You need someone to show you.'

'I found my way thus far without a guide. I found you without a guide.'

'Blind luck,' she answered gravely. 'My father says that it is dangerous to trust in luck too much.'

'I agree.'

'Good. Then you will stay?'

'As much as I would like to, I cannot.'

Her face clouded and I swear the sunlight dimmed. 'Why not?'

'I do have a long way to go,' I explained. 'Winter is fast approaching and the weather will not hold. If I do not wish to find my death frozen on a high mountain track somewhere, I must move along quickly.'

'Is it so important — your going home?' she asked glumly.

'It is.'

And I began to tell her how it was that I came to be journey -ing through the forest.

Ganieda was fascinated. I told her much more than I intended, and would have gone on speaking just to have her remain beside me listening. But as I was explaining the way the Hill Folk moved with the seasons, a horse came pounding up the slope of the mound towards us.

Ganieda leapt to her feet and ran to meet the rider, who swung down from the saddle to kiss her. I stood slowly, disappointment scooping me hollow like a gourd, envy twisting like a knife in my gut.

The stranger had his hand loosely round her shoulder as they came towards me. Ganieda's smile was as luminous as the love between them. I was sick with jealousy.

'Myrddin, my friend,' she said as they came up — at least I was acknowledged as a friend, which seemed to indicate some slight improvement in my status — 'I want you to greet my. . .'

I regarded the weasel who had stolen Ganieda's affection. He was not much to look at — a big, overgrown youth who gazed out at the world through large, unconcerned eyes the colour of hazel wands, his long legs terminating in great flat feet. Taken altogether, he was a pleasant-enough fellow, and not more than four or five years above my age, I judged.

Still, though he had height, weight, and reach on me, I would have fought him willingly and without hesitation if Ganieda had been the prize. But the contest was over and he had won her; there was nothing I could do but smile stupidly and gnaw my heart with envy.

These thoughts went through my head as Ganieda finished, saying, '. . . my brother, Gwendolau.'

Her brother! I could have kissed him.

What a handsome, intelligent fellow. O, happy world with such men in it! Instantly, he improved enormously in my estimation and I gripped his arms in the old greeting. 'Gwendolau, I greet you as brother and friend.'

He grinned sunnily. 'I am your servant, Myrddin Wylt.' He laughed and flicked the edge of my wolfskin cloak with a finger.

Merlin the Wild. . . his joking title made my flesh crawl. I heard in it the echo of something sinister and dark. The eerie feeling passed like an arrow through a nightdark wood, as he clapped me on the back.

Ganieda explained, 'Myrddin is travelling south soon. His people are there. He has been living with the *bhean sidhe* in the north. . .'

'Really?' Gwendolau appraised me curiously. 'That explains the wolfskins at least. But how did you manage to survive?'

'My God was with me,' I offered. 'I was treated well.'

Gwendolau accepted this with a good-natured nod; then, dismissing the subject, glanced at his sister. 'Is father here?'

'He rode out early this morning, saying he would return before sunset. You are to wait for him.'

'Ahh!' He looked distracted, then shrugged. 'Well, it cannot be helped. At least I can rest until he returns. Myrddin, I give you good day. I am for my bed.' He returned his horse and led the hard-ridden animal across the yard to the stable.

'He has ridden far?' I asked.

'Yes. There is trouble on the western border of our land. Gwendolau has been warning the settlements round about.'

'What kind of trouble?'

'Indeed, is there more than one kind of trouble?'

'It is late in the year for raiding.'

'Not for the Scotti. They come across the narrows — it takes less than a day — and they row their leather boats up the Annan right into the very forest. Besides, it makes more sense to raid in autumn when all the harvests have been gathered in.'

Her words pulled me back into the world of swords and sharp conflict. I shivered at the thought of hot blood on cold iron. I looked down to the lake, mirroring blue heaven in its depths, and there I saw the image of a mighty man wearing a steel war helm and breastplate, his throat a black wound.

I recognized the man and shivered again.

'If you are cold we might go in to the fire.'

'No, Ganieda, I am not cold.' I shook my head to purge the disturbing image. 'If you will walk with me to the stable, I will leave now.'

She frowned and at that moment a raindrop splattered her cheek. She held out her hand and another drop splashed into her palm. 'It is raining,' she observed triumphantly. 'You cannot ride in the rain. Also, we will roast the boar tonight, and as you helped bring it back, you must help eat it.'

In truth, there was but a single dark cloud overhead, but the thought of the cold, wet road ahead appealed little just then. I did not want to leave, so I allowed myself to be persuaded to stay. Ganieda tugged me back into the hall to break fast on stewed meat, turnips and oatcakes. .

She did not leave my side all day, but undertook to engage me in games and music — there was a chessboard with carved pieces and she had a lyre, and had learned how to play both with skill — as if to make me forget my journey.

The day sped like a hart in flight and when I looked out through the door of the hall, the sky was alight in the west, the sun through the grey clouds edging the hill-line with amber. My horse needs a day's rest, I told myself. It is no bad thing to linger here a day.

But no longer than that, I resolved — a bit late, I admit, for it was not until I saw the sun setting that I realized that my indecision had cost me a day. A pleasant day, it is true, but a day nonetheless.

With the setting sun, King Custennin returned from his errands. He burst into the hall fresh from the saddle, his hair and cloak flying. Ganieda ran to him and he gathered her in his huge arms and spun her round.

It was clear to see that she was everything to him, and why not? As there appeared to be no other lady in that house, Custennin's daughter was his sole delight. Merely seeing her cheered him like a potent draught.

Gwendolau appeared a moment later, dressed in a silken tunic of crimson with a wide black belt. His trousers were blue-and-black checked, as was the cloak gathered over his shoulder and held with a great silver spiral brooch. His torc was silver. In all he looked the prince he was.

Ganieda returned to me as Gwendolau and her father went aside to discuss their business. They spoke for some time together — intense, arms folded, frowning — head-to-head in a corner of the hearth where the boar was roasting and sputtering over the cooking flame.

With the arrival of their lord, men began streaming into the hall. Most of them had been with Custennin, but word had gone out about the feast and there were many from the settlement invited as well. As they came in, the king and his son broke off their discussion and the lord went to greet his guests personally, embracing them heartily. Here is a man, I thought, who knows how to love his friends. What passion must he devote to his enemies?

'It is worse than I thought,' Ganieda confided.

'How do you know this?' I watched the king greeting his guests, jesting, laughing, passing horns of mead from hand to hand — the glad monarch welcoming old friends, he appeared anything but hard pressed for worry.

'I just know,' whispered Ganieda confidentially. 'He said nothing about his errand and went straight to Gwendolau without stopping for his cup. Even now he avoids drink — you see? He passes the horn but never takes a sip. Yes, the news is troubling. There will be a council tonight.'

It was as Ganieda said and, as I concentrated my attention on the scene before me, I, too, sensed the underlying current of anxiety coursing through the hall. Men talked and laughed, but too heartily and too loudly.

What have I come into? I wondered. Why am I here at all?

And I began to think of those who were waiting for me far, far to the south. It was wrong for me to linger here.

But how? I had stayed three years with Hawk Fhain and rarely felt half so much urgency as I felt now. It was different now, however. Now I stayed, I suspected, for a purely selfish reason: I stayed because I wanted to be near Ganieda. Without saying it directly, Ganieda made it clear that she wanted me to stay, too.

Ah, Ganieda, I remember it all too well.

We feasted in Lord Custennin's timber hall, aflame with light and laughter, the smoky smell of roasting meat, bright torches, eyes and jewellery gleaming, gold-rimmed horns circling among the gathered lords of Goddeu, who drank and drank, despite the example of their king, who tasted not a drop. Because of Ganieda's warning, I watched the proceedings with interest, and I was not the only one. Gwendolau watched, too — sober and intense from his seat at the high table.

When the food was finished and the chiefs called for song, Ganieda took up her lyre and sang. I thought it strange — not that she should sing, for her voice was beautiful to hear, but that a man of Custennin's wealth and influence should not have a bard or two. He might easily have kept half-a-dozen to sing his praises and the valour of his warriors.

Her song finished, Ganieda came to where I sat and tugged me by the sleeve, 'Let us go from here.'

'I want to see what is to happen.'

'No, it does not concern us. Let us leave.' She meant, of course, that it did not concern *me*.

'Please,' I said, 'just until I know what will happen. If there is trouble here in the north, men may need to know of it where I am going.'

She nodded and sat down beside me. 'It will not be pleasant.' Her tone was hard as the flagging at our feet.

Almost immediately, Custennin got to his feet and spread out his arms. 'Kinsmen and friends,' he called, 'you have come here tonight to eat and drink at my table, and this is good. It is right for a king to give sustenance to his people, to share with them in times of peace and succour them in times of trouble.' Some of those near him banged on the board with their cups and knife handles, and shouted their approval of the scheme. I noticed that Gwendolau had disappeared from the high table.

'It is also right for a king to deal harshly with his enemies. Our fathers defended their lands and people when threatened. Any man who allows his enemy to run with impudence through his land, killing his people, destroying his crops and goods — that man is not worthy of his name.'

'Hear him! Hear him!' the chiefs cried. 'It is true!'

'And any man who turns against his own is as much an enemy as the Sea Wolf who comes in his war boat.' At this the hall went silent. The fire crackled in the hearth and the rising wind moaned outside. The trap was all but sprung, but the chiefs did not see it yet.

'Loeter!' the king cried. 'Is this not true?'

I searched the hall for the one singled out, and found him — it was not difficult, for as soon as the man's name left the lips of his king those around him drew away. 'My lord, it is true,' replied the man called Loeter, a narrow-faced hulk with a belly like a sow. He glanced about him uneasily.

'And Loeter, how do we punish those who practise treachery against their own kinsmen?'

All eyes were on Loeter now, who had begun to sweat. 'We cut them off, lord.'

'We kill them, Loeter, do we not?'

'Yes, lord.'

Custennin nodded gravely and looked to his chiefs. 'You have heard the man speak his punishment out of his own mouth. So be it.'

'What madness is this?' demanded Loeter — on his feet now, his hand on the hilt of his knife. 'Are you accusing me?'

'I do not accuse you, Loeter. You accuse yourself.'

'How so? I have done nothing.'

Custennin glared. 'Nothing? Then tell me whence came the gold on your arm.'

'It is mine,' growled Loeter.

'How came you to wear it?' demanded Custennin. 'Answer me truly.'

'It was a gift to me, lord.'

'A gift it was. Oh, yes, that is true enough: a gift from the Scotti! The same who even now lie encamped within our borders, planning another raid.'

There arose an ugly murmur in the hall. Ganieda tugged at me again. 'Let us leave now.'

But it was too late. Loeter saw the thing going against him and, drunk as he was, decided to try his hand at escape, thinking to call on the aid of his friends. 'Urbgen! Gwys! Come, we will not listen to these lies.' He turned and stepped down from the table and strode to the door of the hall, but he walked alone.

'You bargained with the Scotti; they gave you gold in exchange for silence. Your greed has weakened us all, Loeter. You are no longer fit for the company of honourable men.'

'I gave them nothing!'

'You gave them safe landfall! You gave them shelter where there should be no shelter!' Custennin roared. 'Babes sleep tonight without their mothers, Loeter. Wives weep for their husbands. House timbers smoulder and ashes grow cold where once hearth fires burned. How many more of our people will die because of you?'

'It is not my doing!' screamed the wretch, still edging towards the door.

'Whose then? Loeter, answer me!'

'I am not to blame,' he whined. 'I will not have this on my head.'

'You sold our kinsmen, Loeter. People under my care lie in death's dark hall tonight.' Custennin raised his hand and pointed a long dagger at the guilty man. 'I say that you shall join them, Loeter, and join them you will, or I am no longer king of Goddeu.'

Loeter backed nearer the door. 'No! They only wanted to hunt. I swear it, they only wanted to hunt! I was going to bring the gold to you. . .'

'Enough! I will not hear you demean yourself further.' Custennin stepped up onto the table and came towards him, the dagger in his hand.

Loeter turned and bolted to the door. Gwendolau was there

with the two wolf hounds and men on either side of him.

'Do not kill me!' Loeter screamed. He turned to face Custennin, advancing towards him. 'I beg you, my lord. Do not kill me!'

'Your death will be more painless than any of those who went before you this day. I do not have the stomach to do what the Sea Wolves do to their captives.'

Loeter gave a terrible scream and fell down on his knees before his king, weeping pitifully and shamefully. All looked on in awful silence. 'I beg you, lord. Spare me. . . spare me. . . send me away.'

Custennin seemed to consider this. He gazed down at the cringing wretch and then turned back to those looking on. 'What do you say, brothers? Do we spare his sorry life?'

Even before the words were out of his mouth, Loeter was on his feet, his knife in his hand. As the knife flashed towards the king's back, there came a savage snarl and flurry of motion. Black lightning sped towards him. . .

Loeter gave one small shriek before the dogs tore out his throat.

The traitor toppled dead to the floor, but the hounds did not cease their attack until Gwendolau came and put his hands on their collars and hauled them away, blood streaming from their muzzles.

Custennin stared down at the mutilated body. 'This is what your gold has bought you, Loeter,' he intoned sadly. 'I ask you now, was it worth it?'

He made a gesture with his hand and the men before the door came and dragged the body from the hall.

I turned to Ganieda, who sat beside me, staring, her eyes fierce and hard in the light of the torches. 'He got better than he deserved,' she said softly, then, turning to me, added, 'It had to be, Myrddin. Treachery must be punished; there is no other way for a king.'

NINE

'It is a shameful business,' Custennin was saying, 'and not meet for a guest under my roof to see it. Forgive me, lad, it could not be helped.'

'I understand,' I told him, 'There is no need to ask forgiveness.'

The huge man clapped me on the shoulder with one of his paws. 'You have the grace of a king yourself. Indeed, your royal blood tells. Is it true that you lived with the Hill Folk these last years?'

'It is true.'

'Why?' he wondered, genuinely puzzled. 'A canny lad like yourself must have found many a chance to run away.'

'Oh, escape was there if I wanted it. But it was for me to stay.'

'You *wanted* to stay?'

'Not at first,' I told him, 'but I came to see that there was a purpose to it.'

'What purpose, then?'

I had to admit that I did not know, even yet. 'Perhaps it will come to me one day. All I know is that I do not regret the time I lived with them. I learned much.'

He shook his head, then. This was Custennin: a man who saw things clearly or he did not see them at all; who took direct and necessary action — as with the trouble concerning his wayward chief, Loeter; who faced matters squarely and settled accounts fairly and on time. He was a king ever mindful of the respect of his people and sought to win it daily.

'Where do you go now, Myrddin?' he asked. 'Ganieda tells me you hope to reach Dyfed before winter.'

'That is where my friends are. My own people are further south.'

'So you have said. It will be difficult.'

I nodded.

'The weather will break any day and winter will catch you up.'

'All the more reason to go quickly,' I replied.

'Yet, I would ask you to stay. Winter here with us and take up the road in the spring.' That was Ganieda's doing, surely; I sensed her hand at work in the matter. She would not ask me herself, but put her father up to it. 'It would make the time go more quickly for all of us.'

'Your offer is kind as it is generous, and I regret that it cannot be so.'

'Go then, lad. As your mind is made up, I will not ask you to change it now. Three years is a long time away from home.'

He walked with me out of the hall to the stable where he ordered my pony to be saddled; he frowned as the small horse was made ready. 'No doubt the beast is sturdy, but it is not a mount for a prince. Perhaps you would travel more quickly with one of mine.'

Custennin gestured to his horsemaster to bring one of his horses. 'It is true the breed lacks stature,' I allowed. 'Still, they are wonderfully strong and suited to long journeys. The Prytani move quickly by day or night and their ponies carry them with never a mis-step long after another horse must be rested.' I patted the neck of my shaggy little animal. 'I thank you for the offer, lord,' I said, 'but I will keep my horse.'

'So be it, then,' agreed Custennin. 'I only thought that if you took one of mine, you would have reason to come back the sooner.'

I smiled. Ganieda again? 'Your hospitality is reason enough.'

'Not to mention my daughter,' he added slyly.

'She is indeed a beautiful woman, Lord Custennin. And her manner does her father much credit.'

The lady under discussion appeared just then, took one look at the horse saddled before me. 'So you are leaving.'

'I am.'

98

'It has been three years,' said Custennin gently. 'He was a boy when they took him, Ganieda. He is near enough a man now. Let him go.'

She accepted this with good grace, though I could see she was disappointed. 'Well, he must not ride alone. Send someone with him.'

Custennin considered this. 'Who would you suggest?'

'Send Gwendolau,' she said simply, as if it were the most natural thing. They had been talking as if I was not there at all, but then Ganieda turned to me. 'You would not begrudge my brother a place at your side?'

'Indeed, I would not,' I replied. 'But it is not necessary. I can find my way.'

'And find your death in the snow,' Ganieda said, 'or worse — on the end of a Sea Wolf spear.'

I laughed. 'They would have to catch me first.'

'Are you so elusive? So invincible?' She arched an eyebrow and folded her arms across her chest. Had I Archimedes' lever, there was no moving her.

Needless to say, I had a later start than planned, but also more company. For although Gwendolau was happy to accompany me, he insisted on bringing his man, Baram, with us, saying, 'If you find your friends, I will need company on the way back.'

I could not argue with him, so would have to make the best of it. I would go with better protection, which was not to be despised, but I would go more slowly. Nevertheless, by midday we had a pack horse loaded with the provisions and fodder we would require. We left Custennin's stronghold, Ganieda standing erect, neither waving nor turning away, just watching until we were out of sight.

Two days later we reached the old Roman road above Arderydd. Aside from the blackthorn and bracken crowding thick along its lance-straight length, the stone road showed no sign of ruin or decay. The Romans built to last; they built to outlast time itself.

Once upon the road we made better time, despite the rains which settled in earnest. By day we rode beneath a heavy iron sky that leaked water over us; by night icy winds tossed the trees and set the wolves howling in the hills. Miserable we were, cold and drenched for days on end so that our evening fire did nothing to warm or cheer us.

Gwendolau proved an amiable companion and undertook to keep us all in as good humour as the dreadful weather would allow. He sang wonderfully absurd songs, and recounted long, maddeningly intricate tales of his hunting exploits — to hear him talk there was not a beast alive that did not fear his extraordinary skill. He also told me all he knew of what had passed in the world of men since I was taken by the Hill Folk. I liked him and was not sorry that he had come with me.

Baram, on the other hand, was a man to keep his own counsel, quietly expert in his ways, a sure hand with the horses, a keen eye for the trail ahead. Nothing escaped his notice, though one would have to ask him directly to find it out. Often, when I thought he was far away in his own thoughts, I would turn to him to see a smile on his broad face as he enjoyed Gwendolau's jesting.

By evening of the fifth day we reached Luguvallium, which the men in that region called Caer Ligualid; or, more often, Caer Ligal. I was for passing through quickly and camping on the road — we were so much nearer now, it was hard not to begrudge every moment's delay. But Gwendolau would not hear of it. 'Myrddin, you may be able to ride like the *bhean sidhe*, but I cannot. If I do not dry out, my bones will turn to mush inside this sodden skin of mine. I need a warming drink inside me and a roof that does not shed water on me all night long. In short, a lodging house.'

Silent Baram added his terse assent and I knew I was beaten.

'Very well, let us do as you suggest. But I have never been to Caer Ligualid. You will have to find us a place.'

'Leave it to me,' Gwendolau said, spurring his horse forward, and we galloped into the town. Our appearance drew many stares, but we were not unwelcome, and soon Gwendolau, who could coax even the most sceptical mussel to open its shell to him, had made half a dozen friends and achieved his purpose. In truth, travellers were few and becoming fewer in the north, and any news a stranger could bring was prized.

The house was large and old, a mansio of the Roman style with its large common room, smaller sleeping chambers, and stable across a clean-swept courtyard — visiting dignitaries in the old days did not often travel on horseback as we did. Both house and stable were clean and dry, and the fodder plentiful for the horses.

In all, it was an agreeable place, warm and heady with the smell of yeast from bread and beer. There was a fire in the grate and meat on the spit. Baram said not a word but went directly to the hearth and dragged up a stool, stretching his long legs before the fire.

'With the garrison empty now,' the proprietor told us, eyeing us curiously, 'we do not see so many new faces in this town.' His own face was the round, ruddy visage of a man who likes his meat and drink too well.

'The garrison empty?' wondered Gwendolau. 'I noticed there was no one on the gate. Still, it cannot be long empty.'

'Did I say it was? Och! Hang me for a Pict! Just last summer it was full to nearly bursting, and there were Magistrates thick under every bush. But now. . . '

'What happened?' I asked.

He looked at me, and at my clothing — and I think he made the sign against evil behind his back — but he answered without evasion. 'Withdrawn, they are. Isn't that what I am saying? They are gone.'

'Where?' I asked.

The innkeeper frowned and his mouth clamped shut, but before I could ask again, Gwendolau interrupted. 'I have heard the wine of Caer Ligal has special charms on a rainy night. Or, have you poured it all away since the legionaries no longer drink here?'

'Wine! Where would I get wine? Och!' He rolled his eyes. 'But I have beer to make your tongue forget it ever tasted wine.'

'Bring it on!' cried Gwendolau. The innkeeper hurried away to fetch the beer, and when he was gone Gwendolau said, 'It does not do to ask a thing too directly up here. In the north, men like to feel they know you before they say what is in their minds.'

The innkeeper reappeared with three jars of dark foaming liquid and Gwendolau raised his and drank deep. Wiping his mouth with the back of his hand, he smacked his lips and said, 'Ahh! A drink to make Gofannon himself choke with envy. It is settled, we stay here tonight if you will have us.'

The publican beamed. 'Who else would have you? And, as there is no one else beneath this roof tonight, my house is yours. The beds are not big, but they are dry. My name is Caracatus.'

Baram brought his empty jar to the table. 'Good beer,' he said, and returned to his place by the fire.

'Dry!' Gwendolau exclaimed. 'You hear, Myrddin Wylt? We will be dry tonight.'

'If a man is long on the road, he might forget the comforts of a bed,' observed the proprietor. 'Or so I am told.'

'Na, on the contrary,' replied Gwendolau. 'We have been seven days and nights on the trail and I have thought about nothing else but a hot meal in my belly and a warm place by the fire.'

Caracatus winked and confided, 'I keep no women here, but perhaps, if you were so inclined. . . ' He made an equivocal gesture and crossed his palm.

'Thank you,' replied Gwendolau, 'but tonight I am bone weary and no fit company for women, charming though they must be. We have been in the saddle since first light this morning.'

The innkeeper sympathized. 'It is late in the year for travelling. I myself would not go out unless need were very great.'

Need would have to be very great indeed, to budge him from his beer cask, I thought. Even then I doubted he would go out at all. 'It is not by choice,' I answered. 'No doubt the legionaries felt the same way about their leaving.'

This received a sly, knowing wink. 'Aye, that is the truth of it, long and short. The tears! Were there tears when the soldiers left? I tell you the streets were aflood with tears, for the women crying husbands and lovers away.'

'A sad thing to leave kith and kin behind,' observed Gwendolau. 'But, I imagine they will return soon enough. They always come back.'

'Not this time,' the innkeeper wagged his head sadly. 'Not this time. It is the Emperor's doing —'

'Gratian has much on his plate, what with —' began Gwendolau.

'Did I say Gratian? Did I say Valentinian?' scoffed Caracatus. 'The only emperor I salute is Magnus Maximus!'

'Maximus!' Gwendolau sat up in surprise.

'Himself,' smiled our host, pleased with his superior knowledge. 'Proclaimed emperor last year at this time, he was. Now we will see our interests looked to, by Caesar! And about time, too.'

So, that was what my voices had been telling me, had I but known. With the loyal support of his legionaries, Maximus had declared himself Emperor of the West and had withdrawn the troops from the north. There was only one reason for this: he must march to Gaul and defeat Gratian in order to consolidate his claim. That was the only way he could be emperor unopposed.

Deep dread crept over me. The legions gone. . .

'They will come back, you will see,' Gwendolau repeated.

The innkeeper sniffed and shrugged. 'I do not care if they return or not — as long as the Picti leave us alone. Know you, we keep these walls up for a reason.'

Baram's burring snore from the corner of the hearth brought the conversation to a close. 'I will feed you, sirs, so you can go to your beds,' said Caracatus, hurrying off to prepare the meal.

'Food and sleep,' Gwendolau yawned happily. 'Nothing better on a rainy night. Though it looks as if Baram has begun without us.'

We ate from a joint of beef, and it was good. I had not tasted beef for three years and had almost forgotten the savoury warmth of a well-roasted haunch. There were turnips as well, cheese and bread, and more of Caracatus' heavy dark beer. The meal went down well and sleep descended almost at once; we were led to our sleeping places where we curled up in our cloaks on clean pallets of straw to sleep without stirring until morning.

We were awake with the birds and found our horses already saddled. Our genial host gave us little loaves of black bread and sent us away, after receiving our promises to stay with him if ever we returned to Caer Ligal. 'Remember, Caracatus!' he called after us. 'Best *mansio* in all Britannia. Remember me!'

For once it was not raining as we started out. Baram took the lead as we rode out through the gates, and I let my horse fall in behind. There were other travellers leaving Caer Ligualid that morning — a merchant and his servants — so Gwendolau rode along beside to exchange news. Gnawing my bread, I had time to think as we rode out from the city.

Well, I thought, Maximus had declared himself emperor, or had been so declared by the legions, and now had taken his army across to Gaul — taken *our* army away to Gaul. A popular move apparently, judging by Caracatus' reaction, certain to please many who felt our taxes ill-used and our interests subverted to some greater good we never shared. Popular, to be sure. But disastrous.

Maximus — I remembered the man, yes. And I remembered the first time I saw him and knew I would not see him again. He was a brave man, and a solid and fearless general. Long years of discipline and campaigning had schooled him well. Nothing rattled him on the field; he remained cool, kept his temper and his wits. His men worshipped him. There was no doubt they would follow him all the way to Rome and beyond.

There was the hope, of course, that Imperator Maximus could do more for us in Gaul than Dux Maximus could do for us in Britanniarum, that a peace among the barbarians across the sea would provide a measure of peace for the Island of the Mighty. It was a small hope, but a hope nonetheless, and not to be despised. If anyone could do it, Maximus was the man to try.

The weather stayed dry for the while although, as the land rose to meet the mountains, the high places wore their winter mantles of white. We made good use of our time and proceeded south with all speed.

We shared a camp for several nights with our fellow travellers, the merchant and his servants. He had spent the year trading along the Wall, east to west, and, now that winter threatened, was making his late way back to his home in Londinium. As it turned out he had, as merchants will, travelled widely and traded with whoever had gold or silver in their hands, asking neither whence it came, nor how obtained. Consequently, he had dealings with Pict, Scot, Saecsen, and Briton alike.

He was a placid, talkative man named Obricus, edging into his middle years with the grace that wealth can bring. He knew his business and his tales bore the ring of truth more often than not; he was no braggart and did not speak to hear himself talk. What is more, having spent the trading year on both sides of the Wall, he was well informed about the movements of the legions.

'I saw it coming,' said Obricus, poking the night's fire with a stick. He did not appear at all happy to have seen it. 'Gaul is in trouble deep and dire. It will not last. Gratian is not strong and the only thing the Angles and Saecsens respect is strength. . . strength and the sharp point of a sword, and that none too much.'

Gwendolau chewed this over for a long moment, then asked, 'How many troops went with him?'

He shook his head. 'Enough. . . too many. All of Caer Seiont — the whole garrison — and troops from other garrisons as well — Eboracum and Caer Legionis in the south. Seven thousand or more. As I said, too many.'

'You said you could see it coming?' I asked. 'How so?'

'I have eyes, to be sure, and ears,' he shrugged, then smiled, 'and I sleep lightly. But it was no secret in any case. Most of the men I dealt with wanted to go. Could not wait, in fact — their heads full of the spoils to be won: rank for the officers, gold for the troops. So it was presents for their women, trinkets to take with them. I have seen enough of them go, and it's always the same.

'Make no mistake, the Picti knew of it, too. I do not know how they knew — I did not tell them; I tell them nothing — but they knew.'

'What will they do?' asked Gwendolau.

'Who can say?'

'Will it make them bolder?'

'They need little enough encouragement.' Obricus stabbed at the fire. 'But I tell you the truth when I say I will not come this far north again — which is why I stayed so long. No, I will not come this way again.'

Maximus had gone to Gaul, gutting the garrisons to do it, and the enemy knew. It was only the presence of the legions that kept them in check in the best of times and this was not the best of times. Gwendolau knew it, too, and he shrank into himself as the realization struck home.

'How can you trade with them?' he asked angrily, snapping a stick with his hands and throwing it into the fire. 'You know what they are like.'

Obricus had heard it before. He replied mildly, 'They are men. They have needs. I sell to whoever will buy. It is not the merchant's place to decide which man is enemy and which is friend. Half the tribes of this fly-blown island are the enemy of the other half most of the time anyway. Alliances change with the seasons; loyalties ebb and flow with the tide.'

'It will be your head on a stake, and your skin nailed to the gate. Then you will know who your friends are.'

'If they kill me, they kill their only source of salt and copper and cloth. I am more valuable alive.' He hefted the leather purse at his side. 'Silver is silver and gold is gold. I sell to whoever will buy.'

Gwendolau remained unconvinced, but said no more of it.

'I have been in the north for a while,' I said, 'and would be grateful for any news of the south.'

Obricus pursed his lips and stabbed at the fire. 'Well, the south is as ever. Healthy. Strong. There have been raids, of course, as everywhere else; there are always raids.' He paused, remembering, then said, 'Last year there was a council in Londinium — a few kings, lords, and magistrates came together to talk about their problems. The governor met with them, and also the vicarius, although he is senile and from what I hear sleeps most of the time.'

'Was anything decided?'

Obricus barked a laugh and shook his head. 'Oh, impressive decisions!'

'Such as?'

'It was decided that Rome should send more gold to pay the troops; that the Emperor should come himself to see how terrible and dangerous the situation is here; that more men and arms should be made available for our defence; that signal stations along the south-east coast should be increased; that the garrisons on the Wall should be repaired and remanned, that warships should be built and crewed. . .

'In short, that the sky should cloud up and rain *denarii* over us for a year and a day.' The merchant sighed. 'The days of Rome are over. Look not to the East, lad, our Imperial Mother loves her children no more.'

The next day we reached Mamucium, now little more than a wide place where the road divides, one part turning west to Deva, the other bending away south and east, ending eventually in Londinium. There we parted company with the merchant Obricus and continued on into Gwynedd.

The journey should have taken six days. It took many times longer. What with the rain and icy sleet in the high bleak hills it is a wonder we made it at all. But my companions were stalwart men and did not complain of the hardship. For that, I was grateful. Although it had been Ganieda's idea, I still felt responsible for them, for their comfort and safety.

At Deva, the old Caer Legionis of the north, we asked after my people. No one knew anything about a missing boy or anyone looking for one. We bought provisions and continued on into the mountains, striking south, rather than north through Diganhwy and Caer Seiont. It was further to Yr Widdfa, but the road was better and we could search the many-fingered glens and valleys along the way.

Nine days out from Deva the snow caught us. We stayed in a glen near a stream and waited until the sky cleared again. But by the time the sun shone once more the snow was up to the horses' hocks and Gwendolau reckoned that any more searching was useless.

'We cannot find them now, Myrddin, nor anyone else until spring comes. Besides, they will have gone back by now, so there is no point.'

I had to agree with him. 'You must have known it would turn out like this. Why did you come?'

I can still see his quick smile. 'The truth?'

'Always.'

'Ganieda wanted it.'

'You did this for Ganieda?'

'And for you.'

'But why? I am nothing to you — a stranger who slept one night in your father's house.'

His eyes were merry. 'You must be something more than that to Ganieda. All else aside, I would have done it anyway if my father asked. But now that I know you better, I can say that I would have it no other way.'

'Be that as it may, I free you from your errand. I will continue south alone. You may still return home before —'

Gwendolau shook his head and slapped me on the back. 'It is too late, Myrddin, my brother. We have no choice but to continue. I have heard that it does not snow so

107

much in the south, and I am determined to prove this for myself.'

Very well, as I did not greatly relish the prospect of wending my cold way alone, I let them come with me. Later that very day, we turned our horses south and did not look back. Suffice to say that the journey to Maridunum was nothing like that of three years before — half a lifetime before, it seemed to me then.

It was mean and miserable going. There were no roads, Roman or otherwise, through wild Cymry and we lost count of time on the trail — sometimes taking a whole day to traverse a single snow-bound valley, or surmount a lonely, frost-bitten ridge. The days grew shorter, and we rode more often than not in darkness — and in icy, flesh-numbing rain. Gwendolau's good humour carried us on long after Baram and I were too cold and exhausted to care whether we took another step. And though the high mountain passes were choked with snow, we somehow managed to find an alternate route when one was needed and so came at long last into Dyfed, the land of the Demetae.

I will never forget riding into Maridunum. The town glistened under a pall of new-fallen snow, and the stark trees stretched like black, skeleton hands against a pewter sky. It was late in the afternoon and we could feel the night air settling blue and hard around us. But within me a fire burned bright, for I had returned: three years late, it is true; nevertheless, I had returned.

I hoped that Maelwys was at home. I knew we would be welcome anyway, but I desperately wanted to see him to ask after my mother and the rest of my people, to learn what had happened in my long absence.

We rode through the empty streets of the town and followed the trail up to the villa. We were not surprised to find horses standing in the yard, for we had followed their tracks up the hill. As we came into the yard two servants with torches came from the hall to tend to the horses there. We hailed them as we dismounted.

'We have journeyed far to see Lord Maelwys,' I told them. 'Is he within?'

They came to meet us, holding the torches high and peering into our faces. 'Who is it that asks?'

'Tell him that Myrddin is here.'

The two looked at one another. 'Do we know you?'

'Perhaps you do not know me, but Maelwys does. Tell him the son of Taliesin waits without and would see him.'

'Myrddin ap Taliesin!' The foremost servant's eyes grew round. He shoved his companion away. 'Go! Hurry!'

There followed an awkward interval while we waited for the servant to come back. He never did. For while we waited beneath the torch, the door of the hall was heaved open and people came streaming out of the hall into the foreyard, Maelwys leading them all.

He stood for a moment, gazing at me. 'Myrddin, we have been waiting for you. . . '

Maelwys held me at arm's length and I saw the tears. I had expected a warm reception, but. . . the King of Dyfed crying for my return? That exceeded any expectations I might have had, and I knew no way to account for it. I had met the man only once.

'Merlin. . . ' The press of curious onlookers parted and Maelwys stepped away. The voice belonged to Charis, who stood in a halo of light from the doorway; tall, regal, a slim torc of gold around her throat and her hair in a hanging braid after the fashion of highborn Demetae women. Her white silk gown was long and her blue cloak richly embroidered. I had never seen her looking more a queen. She stepped towards me, then opened her arms wide and I flew into her embrace.

'Merlin. . . oh, my little Hawk, my son. . . so long. . . I have waited so long. . . ' Her tears were warm on my neck.

'Mother —' There were tears in my throat and eyes as well; I had not dared hope to find her here. 'Mother. . . I wanted to come sooner, I would have come sooner. . . '

'Shh, not now. You are here and safe. . . safe. . . I knew you would come back. I knew you would find a way. . . you are here. . . here, my Merlin.' She put a hand to my face and kissed me tenderly, then took my hand. We might have been the only people in the yard. 'Come inside. Warm yourself. Are you hungry, son?'

'We have not eaten well for two days.'

Maelwys stepped close. 'There is venison inside, and bread, and mead. Come in, everyone come inside! We will drink to the wanderer's return! Tomorrow we will celebrate with a feast!'

We were swept into the hall, aglow with torches and a roaring fire on the hearth, where the table was laid and the meal already begun. Another table was hastily prepared and platters of food produced. My mother kept my hand clasped tightly in hers, and I felt the anxiety I had lived with for the last many months begin to melt in the light and joy of reunion, even as the warmth of the hall seeped into my bones.

Gwendolau and Baram were not overlooked. I had no worry for them; they fell in naturally with Maelwys' men. Indeed, in my joy at being home once more I soon forgot all about them.

Old Pendaran, Maelwys' father, rose from his throne-like chair to greet me, saying, 'I cannot see where your wandering has hurt you at all. You look a healthy young man — lean and strong, keen-eyed as your namesake bird, lad. Come to me later and we will discuss certain matters.'

It was not likely that my mother would let me out of her sight for a moment that night, nor for many days to come. But I assured him that we would talk soon. 'There is much to say, Merlin,' said Charis. 'I have so much to tell you, but now that you are here I can remember none of it.'

'We are together. Nothing else matters now.'

A great platter of meat and bread addressed me, and a horn of mead. I sipped the warm liquid and began to eat. 'You have grown, my son. The last time I saw you —' Her voice faltered and she dropped her eyes. 'Eat. You are hungry. I have waited this long, I can wait a little longer.'

After a few bites, I forgot my hunger and turned to her. She was watching me as if she had never seen me before. 'Have I changed so much?'

'Yes and no. You are no longer the boy you were, true. But you are my son and I will always see you the same, come what may.' She squeezed my hand. 'It is so good to have you here with me once more.'

'If you knew how often I thought of this moment in the last three years — '

'And if you knew how many nights I lay awake thinking of you, wondering where you were, what you were doing.'

'I wept for the worry I caused you. I prayed for a way to reach you. That's why, when Elac saw the searchers in the valley, I sent my clothes, and the broken arrow. I meant it as a sign.'

'Oh, I took it as more than a sign, as confirmation. I knew you were alive and well —'

'How?'

'In the same way I would have known if you had been hurt or killed. A mother, I believe, can always tell. When they brought me your clothes I knew — even though the men who found them did not want to show me the bundle. They thought it meant that you were dead; the *bhean sidhe* had killed you and were taunting your friends, or some such thing. I knew otherwise. I knew you must have had good reason to do what you had done.' She paused and sighed. 'What happened, Merlin? We came back for you. We searched. We found the waterskins, found where you had huddled in the fog. . . What happened?'

And so I began to tell her about all that had taken place since that strange night. I talked and she listened to every word, and the distance between us simply shrank away to nothing, so that in the end it seemed almost as if I had never been away at all.

I must have talked long into the night, for when I finished everyone else had gone and the torches in their sconces were guttering out and the fire on the hearth was a heap of red embers.

'I have talked the night away,' I told her. 'But there is still so much to tell.'

'And I will hear it. But I have been selfish — you are tired from your journey. Come, you must rest now. We will talk again tomorrow.' She leaned forward in her chair and hugged me for a long time. When she released me she kissed my cheek and said, 'How many times have I wanted to do that?'

We stood, and she led me from the hall to the chamber that had been made ready for me. I kissed her once more. 'I love you, too, Mother. Forgive me for causing you such pain.'

She smiled. 'Sleep well, Merlin my son. I love you, and I am happy you have come home.'

I went into my room then and slept like the dead.

TEN

Maelwys was better than his word, for the next day there was indeed a feast. The servants began preparing the hall as soon as we had broken fast. Maelwys and Charis and I sat before the hearth in our chairs and talked about all that had taken place in my absence — until the doors of the hall were opened and some of the serving girls came running in from the snow outside, laughing, their arms full of holly and green ivy. They proceeded to plait the holly and ivy together and then draped it around the hall — hanging it above the doors and torch sconces.

Their happy chatter distracted us, and when I asked what they were about, Maelwys laughed and said, 'Have you forgotten what day it is?'

'Well, it is not long past midwinter's — what day is it?'

'Why, it is the day of the Christ Mass. It has become the custom of this house to observe the holy days. We celebrate tonight — your return, and the birth of the Saviour God.'

'Yes,' agreed Charis, 'and there is a surprise in it for you: Dafyd is coming to perform the mass. He will be overjoyed to see you. His prayers have not ceased since he learned of your disappearance.'

'Dafyd coming here?' I wondered. 'But that is a far distance to come. He may not make it at all.'

Maelwys answered. 'Not so far. He has begun building an abbey but a half-day's ride from this very place. He will be here.'

'Is the shrine at Ynys Avallach empty once more?' The thought did not cheer me. I loved the little round building with its high narrow, cross-shaped window. It was a most holy place; my soul always felt at peace there.

Charis shook her head lightly. 'By no means. Collen is there and two others with him. Maelwys offered Dafyd lands

112

for a chapel here and an abbey nearby if he would come and build them.'

'The work is nearly complete,' announced Maelwys proudly. 'The first of his brood will begin arriving with the spring planting.'

A thought passed between Maelwys and Charis, and the king rose from his chair. 'Excuse me, Myrddin; I must attend to the preparations for this evening's celebration.' He paused, beaming at me. 'By the Light of Heaven, it is good to see you again — it is this much like seeing your father.'

With that, he was off on his errands. 'He is a good friend to us, Merlin,' observed my mother, watching him stride across the hall.

Indeed, I never doubted it. But her words seemed offered as an excuse.

'That is true,' I allowed.

'And he loved your father. . . ' Her voice had changed, becoming softer, almost apologetic.

'True again.' I watched her face for a clue to the meaning of her words.

'I did not have the heart to hurt him. You must understand. And I admit that I was lonely. You were gone so long — missing so long. I stayed here the first winter after you were taken. . . it seemed right, and Maelwys is so happy. . . '

'Mother, what are you saying?' I had already guessed.

'Maelwys and I were married last year.' She watched me for my reaction.

Hearing her say the words, I felt the uncanny sensation that it had happened before, or that I had known it from the first. Perhaps that night when I had glimpsed her in the flames of Gern-y-fhain's fire I knew it. I nodded, feeling a tightness in my chest. 'I understand,' I told her.

'He wanted it, Merlin. I could not hurt him. Because of me, he never took a wife, hoping that one day. . . '

'Are you happy?' I asked.

She was silent some moments. 'I am content,' she said at last. 'He loves me very much.'

'I see.'

'Still, there is happiness to be found in contentment.' She looked away and her voice broke. 'I have never stopped loving Taliesin, and I never will. But I have not betrayed

113

him, Merlin; I want you to understand. In my way, I have remained true to your father. It is not for myself that I do this; it is for Maelwys.'

'You owe me no explanations or apologies.'

'It is good to be loved by someone — even if you cannot return that love completely. I am fond of Maelwys, but Taliesin has my heart always. Maelwys understands.' She nodded once to underscore that fact. 'I told you he was a good man.'

'I know that.'

'You are not angry?' She turned back, searching me with her eyes. Her hair shone in the soft winter light, and her eyes were large and, at that moment, full of uncertainty. It could not have been easy for her to do what she had done. But I felt that there was a rightness to it.

'How should I be angry? Anything that brings such happiness cannot be a bad thing. Let love increase — is that not what Dafyd says?'

She smiled sadly. 'You sound like Taliesin. That is just what he would have said.' She dropped her eyes and a tear squeezed from beneath her lashes. 'Oh, Merlin, sometimes I miss him so much. . . so very much.'

I reached for her hand. 'Tell me about the Kingdom of Summer.' She looked up. 'Please, it has been so long since I heard you tell it, Mother. I want to hear you say the words again.'

She nodded and straightened in her chair, closed her eyes and waited for a moment in silence for memory to return, then began to recite the words I had heard from the time I was a babe in arms.

'There is a land shining with goodness where each man protects his brother's dignity as his own, where war and want have ceased and all races live under the same law of love and honour.

'It is a land bright with truth, where a man's word is his pledge, and falsehood is banished, where children sleep safe in their mothers' arms and never know fear or pain. It is a land where kings extend their hands in justice rather than reach for the sword; where mercy, kindness and compassion flow like deep water over the land, and men revere virtue, revere truth, revere beauty, above comfort, pleasure, or selfish gain. A land where peace reigns in the hearts of men, where faith blazes like a beacon from every hill, and love like a fire from every hearth, where the True God is worshipped and his ways acclaimed by all. . .

'There is a golden realm of light, my son. And it is called the Kingdom of Summer.'

We put on thick woollen cloaks and joined Maelwys for a ride into Maridunum where he passed among his people, visiting their houses, giving gifts of gold coins and silver denarii to the widows and those hard pressed by life. He gave, not as some lords give who expect to buy allegiance or secure future gain with a gift, but out of concern for their need and out of his own true nobility. And there was not one among them that did not bless him in the name of their god.

'I was born Eiddon Vawr Vrylic,' he told me as we rode back. 'But your father gave me the name I wear now: Maelwys. It was the greatest gift he could have bestowed.'

'I remember it well,' said my mother. 'We had just come to Maridunum. . . '

'He sang as I have never heard man sing. If only I could describe it to you, Myrddin: to hear him was to open the heart to heaven, to free the spirit within to soar with eagles and run with the stag. Just to hear his voice in song was to satisfy all the nameless longings of the soul, to savour peace and taste joy too sweet for words.

'I wish you could have heard him as I did. Ah, but when he finished that night, I went to him to give him a gold chain or some such and in return he gave me a name: "Arise Maelwys," he said. "I recognize you." I told him that was not my name and he replied, "Eiddon the Generous it is today, but one day all men will call you Maelwys, Most Noble." And so it is.'

'Indeed, it is. He may have given you the name, but you have earned it in your own right,' I told him.

'I wish you had known him,' Maelwys said. 'Had I the power, that is the one gift I would most like to give you.'

We rode the rest of the way back to the villa in silence, not sorrowfully, but simply reflecting on the past and on the events that had led us to where we now stood. The short winter day faded quickly in a flare of grey-gold among empty black branches. As we entered the foreyard, some of Maelwys' men returned from hunting in the hills. They had been away since dawn and had a red stag slung between two of the horses. Gwendolau and Baram were with them, as I might have guessed they would be.

I realized with a twinge of shame that I had neglected to introduce my friends. 'Maelwys, Charis,' I began as they came up, 'these men before you are responsible for returning me safely. . . '

One glance at my mother's face and I stopped cold. 'Mother, what is it?'

She stared as if transfixed, her body rigid, breath coming in rapid gasps.

I touched her arm. 'Mother?'

'Who are you?' Her voice sounded strained, unnatural.

Gwendolau smiled reassuringly and began a small movement with his hand, but the gesture died in the air. 'Forgive me —'

'Tell me who you are!' Charis demanded. The blood had drained from her face.

Maelwys opened his mouth to speak, hesitated, then looked to me for help.

'We had to know for certain,' replied Gwendolau. 'Please, my lady, we meant no harm.'

What did he mean?

'Just *tell* me,' replied Charis, her tone low, almost menacing.

'I am Gwendolau, son of Custennin, son of Meirchion, King of Skatha. . . '

'Skatha,' she shook her head slowly, dazedly, 'how long since I have heard that name?'

Skatha. . . from somewhere deep in my brain the memory surfaced: one of the Nine Kingdoms of Lost Atlantis. And I remembered other things Avallach had told me in his stories. At the time of the Great War, Meirchion had sided with Belyn and Avallach. Meirchion had helped Belyn steal the ships from Seithenin — the ships that had eventually landed the remnant of Atlantis on the rock-bound shores of the Island of the Mighty.

How was it that I, who had grown up among the Fair Folk, failed to recognize them when I encountered them in Goddeu? Oh, I had sensed something — just hearing them speak had inspired a vague sensation of homecoming; I remembered the

feeling, and at the same time, wondering why I had come there.
I should have guessed.

'We did not intend to deceive you, Princess Charis,'
explained Gwendolau. 'But we had to be certain, you see.
When my father heard that Avallach was alive, and that he was
here — well, he wanted to be certain. It was important to see
how things stood.'

'Meirchion,' Charis whispered. 'I had no idea. . . we
never heard.'

'Nor did we,' Gwendolau said. 'We have been living in the
forest these many years. We tend our own, keep to ourselves.
My father was born here, as I was. I know no other life. When
Myrddin came, we thought. . . ' he left the thought unspoken.
'But we had to make sure.'

My mind staggered under the weight of understanding. If
Meirchion had survived with some of his people, who else?
How many others?

Gwendolau continued, 'Sadly, my grandfather did not
survive. He died not long after coming here. Many others died
also, before him and after in those first years.'

'It was the same with us,' offered Charis, softening.

They fell silent then, simply gazing at each other, as if
seeing in one another the ghosts of all those lost.

'You must go to Avallach,' Charis said at length, 'this
spring, as soon as the weather allows. He will want to see you.
I will take you there.'

'It would be an honour, lady,' replied Gwendolau courteously. 'And one my father would wish to repay in kind.'

Maelwys, who had held his tongue all this time, finally
spoke. 'You were welcome in my house before, but as you are
of my wife's people you are doubly welcome now. Stay with us,
friends, until we can all travel to Ynys Avallach together.'

It is a strange thing to meet someone from one's homeland
long after becoming resigned to never seeing home again. It
is a singular experience, mingling both pleasure and pain in
equal measure.

Grooms came to take the horses and we dismounted and
returned to the hall. As we walked up the long ramp to the
villa's entrance, I saw how much Gwendolau and Baram looked
like the people of Ynys Avallach and Llyonesse. They were of
the very appearance of men from Avallach's court. I wondered

how I could have been so blind, but reflected that perhaps I had not seen the similarity before because I was not *meant* to see it. Perhaps their true appearance had been hidden from me, or disguised in some subtle way. That was something I thought about for a long time.

Another surprise awaited me in the hall. We trooped in to find the hall ablaze with light, shining with torches and rushlights by the hundred, and old Pendaran standing in the centre of the hall with candles in both hands, talking to a man in a long, dark cloak, while servants bustled to and fro on brisk errands.

A gust of frosty air came in with us and the two turned to meet us.

'Dafyd!'

The priest made the sign of the cross and clasped his hands in thanksgiving and then held out his arms to me. 'Myrddin, oh, Myrddin, let Jesu be praised! You have come back. . . oh, let me look at you, lad. . . Bless me, but you have grown into a man, Myrddin. Thank the Good Lord, for your safe return.' He smiled broadly and pounded me on the back as if to reassure himself that the flesh before him was indeed solid.

'I was just telling him,' said Lord Pendaran, 'just this very moment.'

'I have returned, Dafyd, my friend.'

'Look at you, lad. Jesu have mercy, but you are easy on the eyes. Your sojourn has done you no harm.' He turned my hand and rubbed the palm. 'Hard as the slate in the hills. And here you come wrapped in wolfskin. Myrddin, where have you been? What happened to you? When I heard you were missing, I felt as if my heart had been carved out. What is this Pendaran tells me about the Hill Folk?'

'You deserve a full accounting,' I replied. 'I will tell you all.'

'But it must wait for a time yet,' said Dafyd. 'I have a mass to prepare —'

'And a feast after,' put in Pendaran, rubbing his hands with childish glee.

'We will talk soon,' I promised.

He gazed at me with shining eyes. 'It is happiness itself to see you, Myrddin. God is indeed good.'

I do not believe I ever heard a more heartfelt mass spoken than Dafyd's Christ Mass that night. The love in the man, the grace and kindness shone from him as from a hilltop beacon, and kindled in his congregation a knowledge of true worship. The hall with the holly and the ivy, and the glowing rushlights bright like stars, light glinting off every surface, warmth enfolding us, love upholding us, joy flowing from each one to every other.

Upon reading from the sacred text, Dafyd lifted his face and spread his arms to us. 'Rejoice!' he called. 'Again I say rejoice! For the King of Heaven is king over us, and his name is Love.

'Let me tell you of love: love is patient and long enduring; it is kind, never envying, never ambitious for itself, never putting on airs, or displaying itself haughtily; it boasts not.

'Never vain, never arrogant, never puffed up with pride, love behaves in a seemly manner, never rude or unbecoming. Love seeks not its own reward, nor makes demands, but gives itself withal.

'Love does not persevere to its own benefit; it is not fretful, or resentful. It takes no account of evil done to it, and pays no heed to the wrongs it suffers. Yet, it does not rejoice at injustice, but rejoices when right and truth prevail.

'Love bears all things, hopes all things, believes the best in all things. Love never fails, and its strength never fades. Every gift of the Giving God will come to an end, but love will never end.

'And so three things abide for ever: faith, hope, and love. And the greatest of these is love.'

So saying, he invited us to the Table of Christ to receive the cup and bread, which was Body and Blood to us. We sang a psalm and Dafyd offered a benediction, saying, 'My lords and ladies, it is written: Wherever two or more are gathered in his name, Jesu is there also. He is here among us tonight, friends. Do you feel his presence? Do you feel the love and joy he brings?'

We did feel it; there was not a single soul in that glowing, glittering company gathered in the hall that did not feel the Holy One's presence. And because it was so, many who heard the mass believed in the Saviour God from that night.

This, I thought to myself, is the foundation the Kingdom of Summer is built upon. This is the mortar that binds it together.

The next day Dafyd took me to see his new chapel; we talked along the way, riding out on one of those brilliant winter days when the world gleams like a thing new-made. The sky was high and clean and bright, shining pale blue like fragile bird's eggs. Eagles wheeled through cloudless sweeps of heaven, and quail strutted through elder thickets. A black-tipped fox slipped across the trail with a pheasant in its mouth, stopping to give us a wary glance before disappearing into a copse of young birches.

We talked as we rode, our breath puffing in great silver clouds in the cold air, and I told him about my life among the Prytani. Dafyd was fascinated, shaking his head slowly from time to time, trying to take it all in.

In good time we arrived at the chapel, a square timber structure set on a raised foundation of stone on top of a wooded rise. The steep roof was thatched and the eaves reached almost to the ground. Behind the chapel a springfed well spilled over to form a small pool. Two deer at the pool bounded into the brake at our approach.

'Here is my first chapel,' Dafyd declared proudly. 'The first of many. Ah, Myrddin, there is a rich harvest hereabouts; the people are eager to hear. Our Lord the Christ is claiming this land for his own, I know he is.'

'So be it,' I said. 'May Light increase.'

We dismounted and went inside. The interior had the new building smell: wood-shavings and straw, stone and mortar. It was bare of furniture, but there was a wooden altar with a slab of black slate for a top, and affixed to the wall above it, a cross carved from the wood of a walnut tree. A single beeswax candle stood upon the slate in a golden holder that surely came from Maelwys' house. Before the altar lay a thick woollen pad on which Dafyd knelt for his prayers. Light entered the room from narrow windows along the side walls, now covered with oiled skins for winter. It was similar to the shrine at Ynys Avallach, but larger, for Dafyd fully expected his small flock to increase, and had built to accommodate them.

'It is a good place, Dafyd,' I told him.

'There are far grander chapels in the East,' he said. 'Some with pillars of ivory and roofs of gold, I hear.'

'Perhaps,' I allowed. 'But do they also have priests who can fill a king's hall with words of peace and joy that win men's hearts?'

He beamed happily. 'I do not envy the gold, Myrddin, never fear.' Spreading his arms and turning slowly about the room, he said, 'This is where we begin and it is a good beginning. I see a time when there is a chapel on every hill and a church in every town and city in this land.'

'Maelwys tells me you are building a monastery as well.'

'Yes, a little distance from here — close enough to be a presence, but far enough away to be set apart. We will begin with six brothers; they are coming from Gaul in the spring. More hands will make the work lighter, true enough, but what is most important is the school. If we are to establish the Truth in this land, there must be a place of learning. There must be books and there must be teachers.'

'A glorious dream, Dafyd,' I told him.

'Not a dream, a vision. I can see it, Myrddin. It will be.'

We talked a while longer and then he led me out to walk through the unbroken snow to the pool behind the chapel. I had some presentiment of what was about to happen, for I suddenly had a hollow feeling in the pit of my stomach and a lightness in my head. I followed the priest to a little bower beside the pool with its thin skin of ice which the deer had broken to get at the water.

In the bower, formed by three small hazel trees, stood an oaken stake with a cross-piece lashed into place with rawhide. I stood for a long moment looking down at the hump of earth beneath the snow. Finally, I found my voice. 'Hafgan?'

Dafyd nodded. 'He died last winter. The foundation here had just been laid. He chose this spot himself.'

I sank to my knees in the snow and stretched myself full-length upon the grave mound. The earth was cold, cold and hard; Hafgan's body lay deep in the frozen ground. Not for him entombment in cromlech and barrow, his bones would rest in ground sacred to a different God.

The snow melted where my tears fell.

Farewell, Hafgan, my friend, may it go well with you on your journey. Great Light, shower mercy upon this noble soul and robe him in your loving kindness. He served you well with what light he had.

I got to my feet and brushed snow from my clothes. 'He never told me,' Dafyd remarked, 'but I gather something happened on your journey to Gwynedd, something unpleasant or distressing to him.'

Yes, it would have distressed him. 'He had hoped to bring the Learned Brotherhood into the Truth, but they refused. As Archdruid, I suppose he saw their refusal as a defiance of his authority, as rebellion. There was a confrontation and he disbanded the Brotherhood.'

'I thought it must have been something like that. When he returned, we had many long talks about —' Dafyd chuckled gently, ' — about the most obscure points of theology. He wanted to know all about Divine Grace.'

'Seeing that he is buried on holy ground, it would appear he found his answer.'

'He said he wanted his burial here not because he thought his bones might rest better in hallowed earth, but that he wanted it to be a sign, an expression of his allegiance to Lord Jesu. I had thought he should be buried at Caer Cam with his people, but he was adamant. "Look you, brother priest," he said, "it is not the ground, not the soil — earth is earth and rock is rock. But if anyone comes looking for me, I want them to find me *here*." So, here he is.'

It was very like Hafgan; I could hear him saying that. So, he had not died in Gwynedd as he had planned. Perhaps, after the confrontation with the druids, he had simply changed his mind. That would be like him as well. 'How did he die?'

Dafyd spread his hands in a gesture of bewilderment. 'His death is a mystery to me — as to anyone else. He was hale and well one day — I saw him at Maelwys' house; we talked and drank together. The next day but one he was dead: in his sleep, they said. He sang for Maelwys after supper, and then remarked that he was very tired and went to his room. They found him cold in his bed the next morning.'

'He went out with a song,' I murmured.

'Which reminds me!' replied Dafyd suddenly. 'He left something for you. In my joy at seeing you, I had nearly forgotten all about it. Come with me.'

We returned to the rear of the chapel where Dafyd had a little room for when he stayed there. A rush pallet piled with fleeces and skins, a small table and simple stool beside a fireplace, and utensils for eating and cooking, were all Dafyd's possessions. In the corner beside the pallet stood an object wrapped in a cloth cover. I knew what it was.

'Hafgan's harp,' Dafyd said, retrieving it and holding it out to me. 'He asked me to save it for your return.'

I took the beloved instrument and reverently uncovered it. The wood gleamed in the dim light and the strings hummed faintly. Hafgan's harp. . . a treasure. How many times had I seen him play it? How many times had I played it myself in learning? It was almost the first thing I remember about him — the long, robed frame sitting beside the fire, hunched over the harp, spinning music into a night suddenly alive with magic. Or, I see him standing upright in a king's hall, strumming boldly as he sings of the deeds and desires, faults and fame, hopes and harrowings of the heroes of our people.

'He knew I would come back?'

'Oh, he never doubted it. "Give this to Myrddin when he returns," he told me. "He will need a harp, and I always meant him to have this one."'

Thank you, Hafgan. If you could see where and when your harp has been used, you would be astonished.

We rode back to the villa then, arriving in time to eat our midday meal. My mother and Gwendolau were deep in conversation, oblivious to the activity around them. Dafyd and I ate with Maelwys and Baram, who were sitting with two of Maelwys' chiefs from the northern part of his lands. 'Sit down with us,' Maelwys invited. 'There is news from Gwynedd.'

One of the chieftains, a swarthy dark man named Tegwr, with short black hair and a heavy bronze torc around his neck, spoke up. 'I have kinsmen in the north who sent word that a king called Cunedda has been established in Diganhwy.'

Baram leaned closer, but said nothing.

'Has been established?' I asked. 'What does that mean?'

'The Emperor Maximus has put him there,' Tegwr answered bluntly. 'To hold the land, they say. Gave it to him outright, him and his tribe, if they would live there and hold the land.'

'Very generous of our emperor,' replied Maelwys.

'Generous, aye, and crack-brained.' Tegwr shook his head violently, showing what he thought of the idea.

'The land is empty and that is not good. Someone has to hold it — to keep the Irish out, if for no other reason,' I pointed out.

'Cunedda *is* Irish!' Tegwr exploded. The other chief spat and cursed under his breath. 'And he is there!'

'That cannot be,' said Baram. 'If it is, it cannot be good.'

There was something of familiarity in Baram's spare tone. 'You know him?' asked Maelwys.

'We know of him.'

'And what you know is not good?'

Baram nodded darkly, but said nothing.

'Speak man,' said Tegwr, 'this is no time to clamp jaws and bite tongue.'

'We hear he has three wives and a brood of sons.'

'Brood is right!' laughed Baram mirthlessly. 'Viper's brood, more like. Cunedda came to the north many years ago and seized land there. Since then there has been nothing but trouble. Yes, we know him and have no love for him, or his grasping sons.'

'Why would Maximus wish to establish him among us? Why not one of our own?' wondered Maelwys. 'Elphin ap Gwyddno, perhaps.' He gestured towards me. 'It was their land first.'

'My grandfather would thank you for the thought,' I replied, 'but he would not go back. There is too much pain in the place for my people; they would never be happy there again. Once, when I was quite small, Maximus asked Elphin to go back and received his answer then.'

'That is no reason to bring in a hound like Cunedda,' sneered Tegwr.

'Take the Irish to keep the other Irish out,' mused Maelwys.

'You will have to watch him,' warned Baram. 'He is an old man now — some of his sons have sons. But he is cunning as an old boar, and as mean. His sons are little better; there are eight of them, and tight-fisted to a man, whether with sword or purse. But I will say this, they look out for their own. If holding the land is what they are to do, hold it they will.'

'Small comfort that is,' muttered Tegwr.

Baram shrugged. He had, after his fashion, spoken a whole month's worth and would say no more.

In my own estimation, no matter what Tegwr and those like him might think, Cunedda's coming was no bad thing in itself. The land had to be held and worked and protected. In the time since Elphin had been driven out, no one else had claimed Gwynedd — even those who had overrun

124

it had no lasting interest in it; they cared only for the wealth it promised.

There could be, as Elphin realized, no return to the past. Better to have a known rascal like Cunedda — who could be relied upon to look out for his own interests, if nothing else — than an unknown rascal. Granting land to Cunedda could be a masterstroke of diplomacy and defence. Maximus might then more easily gut the garrison for his move to Gaul, having done what he could for the region by bringing in a strong clan to protect it. For his part, the old boar would be flattered and gratified to be so recognized by the Emperor; he might even mend his ruthless ways in an effort to win the respect of his neighbours.

Time would tell.

The others drifted into talk of other concerns, so I excused myself and took the harp to my room where I set about tuning it and trying my hand. So long had it been since I had last held a harp — in fact, the last time had been on the night I sang in Maelwys' hall.

A beautiful instrument, the harp is crafted by bardic artisans using tools and skills guarded, honed, and improved over a thousand years. The finest wood: heart of oak or walnut, carefully, gracefully cut, shaped, and smoothed by hand. Polished with a preserving lacquer and strung with brass or gut, a well-made harp sings of itself; in the wandering wind it hums. But let the hand of a bard touch those bright strings and it leaps into song.

There is a saying among bards that all songs ever to be made lie sleeping in the heart of the harp and only await the harper's touch to awaken them. I have felt this to be true, for often the songs themselves seem to teach the fingers to play.

After a time, the feel of my fingers on the strings began to come back to me. I tried playing one of the songs I liked best and managed to get through it with only a few hesitations.

For some reason, cradling the harp, Ganieda came to my mind. I had thought about her often since leaving Custennin's forest stronghold. Even though it had been in her father's mind to send Gwendolau with me, that did not lessen her concern for me. Did she, like her father, also guess I shared ancestry with the Fair Folk? Was that what attracted her to me, and I to her?

Oh, yes, I was attracted to her: smitten with that dark beauty, some might say, from the moment I saw her plunging recklessly through the wood in pursuit of that monstrous boar. First the sound of their chase and the sight of the beast thrashing through the stream, and then. . . Ganieda, suddenly appearing in the light, spear in hand, eyes bright, intense, fevered determination shaping her lovely features.

Ganieda of the Fair Folk — was it coincidence? Had chance alone brought us together? Or something beyond chance?

However it was, our lives could not go on as before. Soon or late, there would be a decision. In my heart of hearts I knew the answer already, and hoped I knew it aright.

The harp brought these things to my mind. Music, I suppose, was part of the beauty I associated, even then, with Ganieda. Already, though we scarcely knew each other, she was part of me and had a place in my thoughts and in my heart.

Did you know that, Ganieda? Did you feel it, too?

ELEVEN

Pendaran Gleddyvrudd, King of the Demetae and Silures in Dyfed, had grown weedy with the years, his muscles like rawhide cords beneath a skin of bleached vellum. His eyes were keen and bright, serving a mind that was, in its way, still alert and quick. But in his last years he had become simple. This he had in common with many whom age strips of guile and pretence.

A day or two after visiting Dafyd's chapel, I came in from walking with my mother and found him sitting in his customary place by the hearth. He had an iron poker in his hand and was jabbing at the spent logs, cracking them into embers.

'Ah! Myrddin, lad. The others have had you to themselves long enough. It is my turn now. Come here.'

Mother excused herself and I settled myself into the chair opposite him on the hearth. 'Events are galloping, eh, Myrddin? But then they always are.'

'Yes,' I agreed. 'You have seen a great many things come to pass in your lifetime.' Gleddyvrudd, the word meant Red Sword, and I wondered what kind of king he had been to win himself that name.

'More than most men, true.' He winked, and stirred the embers with the poker in his hand.

'What do you think about Maximus becoming emperor?' I asked, curious to hear what he would say.

'Bah!' He wrinkled his face with distaste. 'Upstart, you mean. What does he want to be emperor for?'

'Perhaps he thinks he can win peace for us, look out for our interests.'

Pendaran shook his bald head. 'Peace! So he takes the legions and marches off to Gaul first thing — why does he want to do that, I ask you?' He sighed. 'I will tell you, shall I? Vanity, lad. Our Emperor Maximus is a vain man, too easily

127

led by men's good opinion of him.'

'He is a great soldier.'

'Never believe it! A real soldier would stay home and protect his own and not go looking for a fight on foreign shores. Who will he fight over there? Saecsens? Ha! He will go for Gratian's throat.' He gave a derisive laugh. 'Oh, that is what we need — two strutting peacocks pecking each other's eyes out while the Sea Wolves run through us as if we were sheep in a pen.'

'If he achieves peace in Gaul, he will certainly come back with more troops for us and put a stop to it.'

'Hoo!' Pendaran hooted with glee. 'Do not believe it! He will carve up that runt Gratian and then he will fix his eyes on Rome. Mark me, Myrddin, we have seen the last of Maximus. Have you ever known a man to return from Rome? Once across the water, he is gone. A pity he took all our best fighting men with him.' He shook his head sadly, as a father might for a wayward son.

'A great pity that; a very great pity,' he continued. 'Stupid vanity! It will be his death and ours, too! Stupid man.'

Old Red Sword's grasp of the situation was surprisingly accurate. He had lived long and had learned not to be distracted by appearances and political manoeuvring. What is more, he showed me that I had placed too much hope in an ambitious man's idealism.

'But you, Myrddin, look at you. I wish Salach were here. He would want to see you.'

'Where is your youngest son?'

'Taken the orders, he has. Dafyd arranged for him to become a priest. He has gone to Gaul to receive the learning.' He sighed, 'It must take a lot of learning to be a priest; he has been gone a long time.'

I had never met Salach, although I had heard of him. He had been there when my father was killed. 'You must be very proud of him. It is a fine thing to be a priest.'

'Proud I am,' he agreed. 'A priest and a king in the same family. We are fortunate.' He turned his bright eyes on me. 'What about you; Myrddin? What will *you* become?'

I smiled and shook my head. 'Who can say, Grandfather?' My use of the word pleased him. He smiled and reached out to pat my arm.

'Ah, well, you have time yet to decide. Plenty of time.' He stood abruptly. 'I am going to sleep now.' And off he went.

I watched him go, wondering why his question left me feeling unsettled. And it came into my head that I must see Blaise very soon.

Events, as Pendaran said, were galloping. While I had dreamed away in my hollow hill, the world had continued turning and the affairs of men had continued apace: more violent incursions by Pict and Scot and Saecsen; an emperor proclaimed; armies gathered; garrisons abandoned; people moving on the land. . . Now I was in the thick of it, and felt that somehow, in some way, something was required of me, but I had no idea what it was.

Perhaps Blaise could help me find the answer. In any event, it had been nearly four years since I had last seen him and I missed him — and not Blaise only, but Elphin and Rhonwyn, Cuall and all the others at Caer Cam. This was not the only time I had thought about them since my disappearance, but there was an urgency now that I had not experienced before.

Unfortunately, I had no choice but to wait until spring opened the land to travel once more.

One moon passed and then another. With Gwendolau, and others, I rode Maelwys' hunting runs, or rambled the hills around Maridunum. The days were short, but left long nights to enjoy one another's company around the fire, playing chess or talking. Also, I began singing again as my skill and confidence with the harp returned. Needless to say, my songs and tales were welcome in the hall where my father had sung so many years before. In all it was a good time for resting and gathering strength for the year ahead. I tried to rein in my impatience and not begrudge my inactivity, but to value this quiet time for its own sake.

In this I was only partially successful. The ferment in my heart and head made it seem as if I were standing rooted in place while the world flew by me in a dizzy race.

Nevertheless, the day came at last when we bade Pendaran and Dafyd farewell and started towards Ynys Avallach and the Summerlands. For me, it was a journey back to another time: all remained precisely as I remembered it. Nothing had changed, or seemed likely to change, ever.

Maelwys travelled with us, and Gwendolau, Baram, and some of Maelwys' men as escort. Oh, we were a bold company, though, whether ranged along the road two-by-two, as we most often were, or encamped in a wooded glade in the first flush of spring. The days took wing and one day, just after midday, I saw it: the Tor, rising from the mist-clouded waters of the lake at its feet. And on the Tor the palace of Avallach the Fisher King.

Even at a fair distance I was struck by the strangeness of the palace — the place I had grown up! That the home of my childhood should appear almost alien to me struck me like a physical blow. Had I been so long in the world of mortal men that I had forgotten the grace and refinement of the Fair Folk?

It was inconceivable that such beauty, such elegance and symmetry, could fade from my mind in that time. Seeing the palace in this way was like seeing it for the first time: the tall, sloping walls with their narrow, pinnacled towers; the high-arched roofs and domes within; the massive gateposts with their flowing banners.

Indeed, the palace belonged to another world. I saw my home much the way any stranger on the road might view it when coming upon it in the mist. And I understood how easily one might believe the tales of magical beings and strange enchantments. Was the palace itself not a thing of enchantment? Half-hidden in the mists, remote on its looming Tor, and surrounded by reed-fringed waters, now shining blue, now grey slate and troubled, Ynys Avallach seemed an Otherworldly place.

But if the palace appeared strange to my eyes, the person of Avallach did not. At our approach the gates were opened and the king himself met us on the road. He shouted to see me, and I leaped from my horse and ran to his embrace.

What a reunion that was! Avallach had not changed — I eventually learned he never would — but I think I half-expected that the home of my childhood would have changed as much as I had. Everything was just the same as the day I left it.

Avallach greeted the rest of the party with equal enthusiasm — but stopped when he beheld Gwendolau and Baram. He turned to Charis and she stepped beside him. 'Yes,

Father,' she said softly, 'they are Fair Folk also; they are Meirchion's people.'

The Fisher King raised his hand to his head. 'Meirchion, my old ally. It is long since I heard that name. . . ' He stared at the strangers, then burst into a grin. 'Welcome! Welcome, friends! I am glad you are here. Come into my hall, there is much I want to hear from you!'

That night Gwendolau, Baram, Maelwys and I, held audience with Avallach in his high chamber. The Fisher King's malady came on him again, so he retreated to his chamber where he lay propped up on his red silk pallet, face white against the dark curls of his beard.

He listened to Gwendolau's recitation of the events that had brought them to Ynys Avallach, shaking his head slowly, his eyes holding the vision of a time and place now lost for ever.

'There were two ships, I have been told,' Gwendolau said. 'They were separated at sea — one reached this island. We never learned what happened to the other ship, although it was hoped we would discover one day. That is why, when my father met Myrddin — well, he thought the others had been found at last.' Gwendolau paused, then brightened. 'Still, finding you is just as good. I am only sorry Meirchion did not live to see it.'

'I, too, am sorry Meirchion is dead; there is so much we could say to one another,' he said sadly. 'Did he ever speak about the war?'

'I was not yet born when he died,' replied Gwendolau. 'Baram knew him.'

'Tell me,' said Avallach to Baram, 'for I would know.'

It was some moments before Baram replied. 'He spoke of it seldom. He was not proud of his part in it. . . ' Baram paused eloquently. 'But he allowed that without the ships we would never have survived.'

'We understand that your brother, King Belyn, was also saved,' said Gwendolau.

'Yes, with a few of his people. They settled in the south, in Llyonesse. My son Maildun rules there with him.' Avallach frowned and added, 'There was trouble between us and it has been many years since we have spoken to one another.'

'So the Lady Charis has told us,' affirmed Gwendolau. 'She also spoke of another ship, I believe.'

Avallach nodded slowly. 'There was another ship — Kian, my oldest son, and Elaine, Belyn's queen. . . ' He sighed. 'But it, like everything else, was lost.'

It had been a long time since I had thought about that lost ship. Kian and Belyn had stolen ships from the enemy fleet and had rescued the survivors of Atlantis' destruction. Kian had turned aside to save Belyn's wife, Elaine, and had never been seen again.

As a child I had heard of it, of course, but it belonged with all the other lost things of that lost world. But now, sitting in the king's chamber with Avallach and Gwendolau, I began wondering anew whether that ship was truly lost. Might it, like Meirchion's ship, have made landfall somewhere? Might there be, like Custennin's forest stronghold, another colony of survivors somewhere?

Gwendolau and Baram's presence made the possibility seem almost a certainty. If another Fair Folk settlement existed, where would it be found?

'My father has instructed me to offer you bonds of friendship by whatever token you esteem. He extends the hospitality of his hearth to you and yours now and for all time to come.'

'Thank you, Prince Gwendolau; I am honoured,' Avallach accepted graciously. 'I should like to prove that hospitality for myself, but as you see,' he lifted a hand to indicate his condition, 'travelling is not possible for me. Still, that must not interfere with the bonds of friendship — allow me to send an emissary to accept in my stead.'

'Lord, that will not be necessary,' Gwendolau assured him.

'Nevertheless, it shall be done.' Avallach turned his eyes to me. 'What about you, Merlin? Will you serve me in this?'

'Certainly, Grandfather,' I answered. Indeed, I had been wondering how I might find a way back to Goddeu and Ganieda. Suddenly, it seemed as if I were half-way there.

'But first,' continued Avallach, turning back to Gwendolau, 'I would have you speak to Belyn. I know he would be grateful for the information you bring. Would you consider going to him?'

Gwendolau glanced at Baram, who, as usual, gave no sign of what he thought or felt.

'I know you are anxious to return home, but having come this far. . .'

'Do not think of it,' replied Gwendolau. 'My father would approve, and, in any event, it is only a small delay.'

Ah, but that delay. . . another month or more before I could see Ganieda again.

'We have tarried this long,' Gwendolau said, 'a little longer will make no difference. And it furthers our purpose admirably.'

Oh, well, there was nothing to be done. It was perhaps the first time in my life that I felt the cramp of kingcraft hindering my plans. It would not be the last.

We talked long into the night. Gwendolau and Avallach were still talking when I went to my bed, and Baram, who never had much to say at any time, had given up long ago and was snoring softly in the corner as I crept from the room. I dreamed of Ganieda that night, and of a great hound with blazing eyes that kept me from her.

The next day Avallach and I went fishing as we used to do when I was a child. Sitting in the long boat with him, the sun pouring gold on the water, the reeds alive with coots and moorhens, brought that time back to me once more. The day was cool, for the sun had not gained its full strength, and a fitful spring breeze stirred the waves now and again. There was not much fishing done, but that was never the point.

Grandfather wanted to know all about what I had seen and done. For one who never moved beyond the boundaries of his own realm, he knew a surprising amount about the affairs of the larger world. Of course, in Elphin he had a constant and reliable source of news, and he always welcomed the traders that happened along the way.

When we returned to the palace, Collen was waiting for his regular audience with Avallach — a custom begun during the long winter months when Avallach, confined to his litter, had invited the priest to read to him from the holy text — a book of the Gospels which Dafyd had recently acquired from Rome. The reading had proven so beneficial to them both, they had continued it. Indeed, the brothers occasionally said mass in the great hall for the Fisher King and his people.

After recovering from his surprise, Collen greeted me warmly and we talked briefly about my 'ordeal' among the Hill Folk, before he excused himself to attend Avallach, saying, 'You must come to the Shrine when you can.'

'I will,' I promised, and did so the next afternoon.

The Shrine of the Saviour God stands to this day on a little hill above the soft, marshy ground of the lowlands in that region. In spring flood the Tor and Shrine Hill are virtual islands; occasionally, the ancient causeway leading from the Tor is under water as well. But this year the rains had not been so heavy and the causeway remained dry.

The Shrine was much as I remembered it; the mud-daubed walls were newly washed white with lime, and its high-peaked thatched roof only a little darker with age. Someone had plaited the reed thatch into the shape of a cross at the roof's crown, and a fair-sized single-room dwelling for the priests stood well down on the shoulder of the hill away from the Shrine, but these were the only changes I noticed as I approached.

I tethered my horse at the bottom of the hill and approached on foot. Collen came out of the priest's dwelling, followed by two young brothers who could not have been much older than myself. They grinned and shook my hands in the Gaulish greeting, but, besides a murmured welcome, said nothing.

'They are shy,' explained Collen. 'They have heard about you,' he added cryptically. 'From Hafgan.'

I could guess that Hafgan had told them about the dance of the stones. We walked together to the Shrine.

There is a peculiar joy of the flesh that is like no other, a joy that is as much longing as gladness. It is, I think, the yearning of bone and blood for the exultation that the spirit knows when approaching its true habitation. The body knows it is dust, and will return to dust in the end, and it grieves for itself. The spirit, however, knows itself to be eternal and glories in this knowledge. Both strain after the glory they rightfully possess, or will possess in time.

But unlike the spirit, the flesh's hope is tenuous. Therefore, in those rare times when it senses the truth — that it *will* be made incorruptible, that it *will* inherit all that the spirit owns, that the two *shall* become one — then, in those rarest of moments, it revels in a joy too sweet for words. This is the joy I felt upon entering the Shrine. Here, where good men had sanctified a heathen land with their prayers and, later, with the blood of their veins, that special joy could be found. Here in this holy place I could feel the peace breathed out upon this world from that other, higher world above.

The Shrine was clean-swept and smelling of oil, candles, and incense. The altar was a slab of stone on two stone pillars; it was very old. The silence of the Shrine was deep and serene, and as I stood in the centre of the single room, with the sunlight streaming in through the cross-shaped window onto the altar, I watched the dust motes descend slanting beams of yellow light, like tiny angels drifting earthward on errands of mercy.

Watching this, I apprehended minute and subtle shiftings in the light and shadow of the shrine. There was movement and flux, a discernable ebb and flow to these seemingly static properties. Could it be that the Powers Dafyd described, the Principalities, the Rulers of Darkness in the high places were even now encroaching on this most holy place?

As if in response to this encroachment, the single beam of light narrowed and gathered, growing finer and more intense, burning into the altar stone. The stone blazed where the light struck it, and the shadows retreated. But, even as I looked, the circle of white-gold light thickened, taking on substance and shape: the substance of silvery metal, the shape of a wine cup of the sort used in a marriage feast. The object was plain and simply made, possessing no great value of itself.

Yet, the Shrine was suddenly filled with a fragrance at once so sweet and fresh that I thought of all the golden summer days I had known, and all the meadows of wildflowers ever ridden through, and every soft moonlit night-breeze that ever drifted through my window. To look upon the cup was to sense an unutterable peace, whole and unassailable, the abiding calm of endless, enduring authority, vigilant and present — if unseen — and supreme in its strength.

It came into my mind that to hold the cup would be to possess, in part, this peace. I stepped nearer to the altar and put out my hand. The light of the cup flared, and the image faded as my hand closed around it.

There was nothing left but the sunlight streaming in through the window above the altar and my hand on the cold stone. The shadows deepened and drew closer, stealing the last of the fading radiance. And I felt my own strength flow away like water poured out onto dry ground.

Great Light, preserve your Shrine, and clothe its servants with wisdom and might; gird them for the struggle ahead!

Footsteps sounded behind me and Collen entered the cool, dark room. He peered carefully at my face — there must have been some lingering sign of my vision — but said nothing. Perhaps he knew what it was I had seen.

'Indeed, this is a holy place,' I told him. 'For that reason the Darkness will try all the harder to destroy it.'

So that my words would not alarm him, I said, 'But never fear, brother, it cannot succeed. The Lord of this place is stronger than any power on earth; the Darkness will not prevail.'

Then we prayed together. I shared the simple meal the brothers had prepared and talked of my travels, and their work at the Shrine, before heading back to the palace.

I spent the next days rediscovering Ynys Avallach. As I visited once more the places of my childhood, the thought came to me that this kingdom, this realm of the Faery could not endure. It was too fragile, too dependent on the strength and amity of the world of men. When that failed, the Fair Folk would vanish.

The thought did not cheer me.

One morning I found my mother in her room, kneeling at a wooden chest. I had seen the chest countless times before, but never open. It was, I knew, a relic of Atlantis made of gopher wood, inlaid with ivory, and carved with the figures of fanciful creatures with the heads and forequarters of bulls and the hindquarters of sea serpents.

'Come in, Merlin,' she said as I came to stand in the doorway. I went to her and sat down in the chair beside the chest. She had lifted out several small, neatly-wrapped bundles, a rather long, narrow bundle tied with strips of leather among them.

'I am looking for something,' she said, and continued to sift the contents of the chest.

One of the items on the floor beside her was a book. I lifted it gently and opened its brittle pages. The first bore a painting of a great island all in green and gold on a sea of stunning blue. 'Is this Atlantis?' I asked.

'It is,' she said, taking the book in her hands. She stroked the page with her fingertips, lightly, as if touching the face of a loved one. 'My mother's greatest possession was her library. She had many books — some you have seen. But this one stands above them all because it was her treasure; it was the last she received.' Charis turned the pages and peered at the foreign script and sighed. Looking at me, she smiled. 'I do not even know what it is about. I never learned. I saved it because of the painting.'

'It is indeed a treasure,' I told her. My eye fell on the narrow bundle beside her. I picked it up and untied the lacing. A moment later the gleaming hilt of a sword was revealed to me. Carefully, but with some haste, I stripped away the oiled leather and soon held a long, shimmering blade, light and quick as thought itself, the weapon of a dream made for the hand of a god, beautiful, cold, and deadly.

'Was this my father's?' I asked, watching the light slide like water over the exquisite thing.

She sat back on her heels, shaking her head lightly. 'No, it is Avallach's, or was meant to be. I had it made for him by the High King's armourers in Poseidonis, the finest craftsmen in the world. The Atlantean artisans, I was told, perfected a method of strengthening the steel — a secret they guarded zealously.

'I bought the sword for Avallach, it was to be a peace offering between us.'

'What happened?'

My mother lifted a hand to the sword. 'It was a difficult time. He was ill. . . his injury. . . he did not want it; he said it mocked him.' She touched her fingertips to the shining blade. 'But I kept it anyway. I suppose I thought I would find a use for it. It is very valuable, after all.'

Lofting high the wonderful weapon, stabbing the air with short thrusts, I said, 'Perhaps its time has not yet come.'

It was just something that came to my head and I said it. But Charis nodded seriously. 'No doubt that is why I saved it.'

The grip was formed by the intertwined bodies of two crested serpents whose emerald and ruby encrusted heads

137

became the pommel. Just below the red-gold hilt, I traced the script engraved there. 'What do these figures mean?'

Charis held the sword across her palms. 'It says, "Take Me Up",' she replied, turning the blade, 'and here: "Cast Me Aside".'

A curious legend for a king's weapon. By what power had she chosen those words? Did she sense in some way, however obscurely, the role that her gift would play in the dire and glorious events that birthed our nation?

'What will you do with it now?' I asked.

'What do you think I should do with it?'

'A sword like this could win a kingdom.'

'Then take it, my son, and win your kingdom with it.' Kneeling before me, she held it out to me.

I reached for the sword, but something prevented me. After a moment, I said, 'No, no, it is not for me. At least, not yet. Perhaps one day I will need such a weapon.'

Charis accepted this without question. 'It will be here for you,' she said, and began wrapping it up again.

I wanted to stop her, to strap that elegant length of cold steel to my hip, to feel its splendid weight filling my hand. But it was not yet time. I knew that, and so I let it be.

TWELVE

So it was that I found myself once more in the saddle — this time on the way to Llyonesse. Before starting out, however, I managed a short stay at Caer Cam to visit my grandfather Elphin. To say they were happy to see me would be to tell a lie through gross understatement. They were ecstatic. Rhonwyn, still as beautiful as ever I remembered her, fussed over me and fed me to bursting — when I was not lifting jars with Elphin and Cuall.

Our talk turned to matters of concern. Here, like everywhere else, men were mindful of Maximus' taking the purple, and his departure to Gaul with the troops. And they had a grim opinion of what that meant.

Cuall summed up their attitude when, after the beer jar had gone round four or five times, he remarked, 'I love the man — I will fight anyone who says different. But,' he leaned forward for emphasis, 'taking almost the whole of the British host is dangerous and foolhardy. He is grasping too high, is Maximus. Aye, but he always was a grasper.'

'Nothing good can come of it,' agreed Turl, Cuall's son, who was now one of Elphin's battlechiefs. 'There will be much blood spilled over this, and for what? So Maximus can wear a laurel crown.' He snorted loudly. 'All for a handful of leaves!'

'They came through here on the way to the docks at Londinium,' explained Elphin. 'The Emperor asked me to join him. He would have made me a governor.' Elphin smiled wistfully, and I saw how much that might have meant to him. 'I could not go —'

'You speak no Latin!' hooted Cuall. 'I can just see you in one of those ridiculous togas — how could you ever abide it?'

'No,' Elphin laughed, 'I could not abide it.'

Rhonwyn hovered near and refilled the jar from a pitcher. 'My husband is too modest. He would make a wonderful governor,' she bent and kissed his head, 'and an even better emperor.'

'At least I would not be tempted to go borrowing trouble beyond these shores. What's wrong with an emperor making his capital right here?' Lord Elphin spread his hands to the land around him. 'Think of it! A British emperor, holding the whole of the island for his capital — now, that would be a force to reckon with!'

'Aye,' agreed Cuall, 'Maximus has made a grave mistake.'

'Then he will pay with his life,' growled Turl. Bone and blood, he was his father's son.

'And we will pay with ours,' said Elphin. 'That is the shame of it. The innocent will pay — our children and grandchildren will pay.'

The talk had turned gloomy, so Rhonwyn sought to lighten it. 'What was it like with the Hill Folk, Myrddin?'

'Do they really eat their children?' asked Turl.

'Do not be daft, boy,' Cuall reprimanded, then added, 'But, I heard they can turn iron into gold.'

'Their goldcraft is remarkable,' I told him. 'But they value their children more than gold, more even than their own lives. Children are truly the only wealth they know.'

Rhonwyn, who had never born a living child, understood how this could be, and agreed readily. 'We had a little Gern that used to come to Diganhwy in the summer to trade for spun wool. She used thin sticks of gold which she broke into pieces for her goods. I have not thought of her in all these years, but I remember her as if it were yesterday. She healed our chieftain's wife of fever and cramps with a bit of bark and mud.'

'They know many secrets,' I said. 'Still, for all that they will not long remain in this world. There is no place for them. Already the tallfolk squeeze them out — taking the good grazing land, pushing them further and further north and west into the rocky wastes.'

'What will happen to them?' wondered Rhonwyn.

I paused, remembering Gern-y-fhain's words, which I spoke: 'There is a land in the west, which Mother made and put aside for her firstborn. Long ago, when men began to wander on the earth, Mother's children were enticed to stray and then forgot the way back to the Fortunate Land. But one day they will remember and they will find their way back.' I ended by saying, 'The Prytani believe that a sign will tell them when it is time to return, and one will arise from among them to lead the way. They believe that day is soon here.'

'The things you say, Myrddin,' remarked Cuall, shaking his grey head slowly. 'It puts me in mind of another young man I used to know.' He reached out a heavy hand and ruffled my hair.

Cuall was no great thinker, but his loyalty, once earned, was stronger than death itself. In older times, a great king might boast a warband numbering six hundred warriors; but give me just twelve like Cuall to ride at my side and I could rule an empire.

'How long can you stay, Myrddin?' asked Elphin.

'Not long,' I answered, and told him of my journey to Llyonesse and Goddeu for Avallach. 'We must leave in a few days' time.'

'Llyonesse,' muttered Turl. 'We have been hearing strange things from that region.' He rolled his eyes significantly.

'What strange things?' I asked.

'Signs and wonders. A great sorceress has taken residence there,' said Turl, looking to the others for confirmation. When it was not forthcoming, he shrugged. 'That is what I hear.'

'You believe too much of what you hear,' his father told him.

'You will stay the night at least,' said Rhonwyn.

'Oh, tonight, and tomorrow night as well — if you can find a place for me.'

'Why, have we no stable? No cow byre?' She wrapped her arms around my neck and hugged me. 'Of course, I will find a place for you, Myrddin Bach.'

The time passed far too quickly, and soon I was waving my farewell to Caer Cam, with only one regret — aside from not having enough time to spend there. And that was that I had missed seeing Blaise. Elphin told me that, since Hafgan's death, Blaise had been travelling a great deal and was seldom at the caer. He said the druid had told him there was strife within the Brotherhood and that Blaise had his hands full trying to avert bloodshed. Beyond that, Elphin knew no more.

The day after I returned from Caer Cam, we started for Llyonesse. Now I had never been to Belyn's realm in the southern lowlands, and knew little about it other than

141

that it *was* Belyn's realm and that Maildun, Charis' brother and my uncle, lived there with him. The Llyonesse branch of the Fisher King's family was seldom mentioned; other than Avallach's hint of a longstanding disagreement between them — and that I had only recently found out — I knew nothing at all about what sort of man his brother Belyn might be, or what sort of reception we might expect.

We travelled through country in the first blush of summer, green and promising a good harvest in time to come. It was a rough country, however, and grazing grass was short, the hills steeper, the soil rocky and thin. It did not boast the luxury of the Summerlands, or of Dyfed.

Thrust out like a finger into the sea, Llyonesse, with its crooked glens and hidden valleys, was a wholly different realm from the Summerlands or Ynys Avallach. Sea mists might rise at any time of the day or night, the sun might blaze brightly for a moment, only to be veiled and hidden the next. The sea tang on the air made the breeze sharp, and always, always there was the low, murmuring drum of the sea — a sound distant, yet near as the blood-throb in the veins.

In all, I would say the land breathed sorrow. No, that is too strong a word; melancholy, is better. This narrow hump of rock and turf was sinking beneath a dolorous weight, moody and unhappy. The strange hills were sullen, and the valleys sombre.

As we rode along our way, I tried to discern what it was that made the region appear so cheerless. Did the sun not shine as brightly here as elsewhere? Was the sky hereabouts not as blue, the hills less green?

In the end, I decided that places, too, have their own peculiar natures. Like men, a realm can be marked by the same qualities that characterize the soul: amiable, sad, optimistic, despairing. . . Perhaps over time the land takes on the traits of its masters so that it comes to reflect these traits as impressions to anyone who journeys there. I believe that certain powerful events leave behind their own lingering traces which also colour the land in subtle ways.

This was Llyn Llyonis, now known and feared by many as Llyonesse. I could understand the fear — Llyonesse was not a convivial place. And the sense of brooding sorrow increased the closer we came to Belyn's palace, which was perched on the high cliffs of the land's end, facing west. Like Ynys Avallach, it was a strong place: high-walled, gated, and towered. It was larger, for more of Atlantis' survivors had stayed with Belyn than had gone north with Avallach in those early years.

Belyn received us with restrained courtesy. He was, I think, happy to see us, but wary as well. My first impression of him was of a man given to bitterness and spite; one in whom life has grown cold. Even his embrace was chill — like hugging a snake.

Maildun, my uncle whom I had never met, was no better. In appearance he was very like Avallach and Belyn; the family resemblance was strong. He had the imperious bearing and was a handsome man, but arrogant, moody and intemperate. And, like the land he lived in, possessed of a potent melancholy that hung on him like a cloak.

Nevertheless, Gwendolau and Baram did their utmost to ensure there would be no misunderstanding of their motives. They gave the gifts Avallach had sent with them, carefully explained their reason for coming, and generally behaved as brothers long lost and lamented. They must have sensed the temper of the men with whom they had to deal, for they treated them warmly and, before our stay was over, won Belyn as a friend, if not Maildun as well.

I suppose there were important matters accomplished, but I do not remember them. My attention was otherwise engaged.

From the moment we rode into the foreyard of the palace, my spirit felt a heavy, suffocating oppression. Not fear — not yet; I had not learned to fear it — but the stifling, cloying closeness of a thing wretched and pathetic. I knew that this, and no other reason, was why I had come. And I decided to make it my affair to learn the source of this strange emanation.

I paid the required respects, and then, as unobtrusively as possible, made myself free in Belyn's palace. My first discovery was a young steward, a boy named Pelleas, I had seen lurking about. As he appeared to have no formal duties, I made him my ally and befriended him. He was eager to help me explore the palace, and I was gratified to have such a resourceful guide. Pelleas also knew quite a little about matters of court, and was not shy about revealing what he knew.

'All you see here was built later,' he told me when I asked. 'There is an older stronghold a little way up the coast — not much, mind, just a tower and an enclosure for cattle.'

For two days we had been searching the extensive grounds and buildings of the palace, and had not found what I was looking for. Time was running short; Gwendolau and Belyn were about to conclude their business.

'Take me there,' I said.

'Now?'

'Why not? Does not a steward serve a guest's every need?'

'But —'

'Well, I feel the need to go and see this tower of which you speak.'

We saddled horses and rode out at once, though the sun was already well down on its plunge towards the sea. The sea cliffs of Llyonesse possess a lonely and rugged beauty, looming over relentless waves that hurl themselves ceaselessly against black rock roots, to break and break again in frothy seafoam. On the sea side, what trees dare break soil grow as stunted, mis-shapen things: thin and with twisted branches for ever swept backward by the constant blowing of the sea wind.

The trail to the tower hugged the lea of the hills so that the wind off the sea did not buffet us so badly, but we felt the rhythmic thrumming of the waves resounding through caves deep underground.

The sun was touching the sea, pooling light like molten brass on the far horizon, when we came within sight of the tower. Despite what Pelleas had said, it was no mean thing. Many a British king would have considered himself blessed to own such a stronghold, and would have made it all his world. It was of the same peculiar white stone as Belyn's palace, which in the dying sunglow became the colour of old bone. It was square-built for strength, but tapered from its solid foundations to a series of rounded turrets so that, as we rode towards the scarp of land on which it stood, it looked like a thick neck with a face for each direction.

This, then, was where the last of Atlantis' children made their home on these foreign and forbidding shores. It was here the three crippled ships made landfall, here that Avallach and Belyn settled the remnant of their race before moving on to claim other lands.

Surrounding the fortress was a cattle enclosure of stone on

top of an earthen bank, now ruined in many places. Heather flowed about the place like a second sea, inundating the inner grounds and washing right up to the stone tower itself. We tied the horses outside the turf bank and walked in through one of the numerous gaps in the fallen wall into the inner yard.

The tower gave no signs that anyone lived within, but the deepening sense of lethargy, of hopeless woe, gave me to know that I had found the source of the oppression I sought. The tower was inhabited, but by what sort of creature I had yet to discover.

Pelleas called out a timid greeting as we came into the yard. Our shadows leaped across the derelict ground and onto the tinted stone. There was no answer to his call, but neither did we expect one. He pushed open the wooden door and we entered.

Though weak sunlight streamed through the high, narrow windows, the shadows already grew deep in the place. Opposite the entrance sat a huge, cauldron-hung hearth with two chairs nearby. But the hearth was filled with ashes, and the ashes cold.

Wooden stairs leading to the upper chambers stood at the far end of the room. As I started towards the stairs, Pelleas lay hand on my arm and shook his head. 'There is nothing here. Let us go.'

'All will be well,' I told him. My voice sounded thin and unconvincing in the place.

The upper level was honeycombed with small rooms, one leading on to the next. Twice I glimpsed the sea through an open window, and once I saw the trail we had ridden to reach the tower. But one room contained another stairway and this one was stone and led to a single topmost chamber.

I entered the chamber first. Pelleas did not care to have anything to do with this search, and only followed me because he was not willing to stay behind alone.

At first I thought the man in the chair by the window must be dead — perhaps had died this very day, this hour. But his head turned as I crossed the threshold and I saw he had been sleeping. Indeed, he had the look of one who had been asleep for many years.

His white hair hung in wisps, thin as spidersilk; his hands, crossed on his breast, were boney and long, the untrimmed fingernails thick and yellowed. His face was that of

145

one long dead: grey and spotted with blotches that faded into his moth-eaten scalp. The eyes that stared from his head were sunken pits rimmed red and weepy.

In contrast to this wraith's wasted appearance, his robe was rich velvet, embroidered with fantastic symbols and cunning designs in threadwork of gold and silver. Still, it hung on him like the rags of a corpse.

He did not seem at all surprised to see me, and I knew he was not. 'So,' he said after a moment. Just that. I felt Pelleas tug my sleeve.

'I am Merlin,' I said, using the form of my name most common among my mother's people.

He made no sign of recognition, but said, 'Why have you come?'

'To find you.'

'You have found me.' He lowered his hands to his knees, where they lay twitching feebly.

Yes, and having found him I did not know what to say to him.

'What will you now, Merlin?' he asked after a moment. He did not look at me when he spoke. 'Kill me?'

'Kill you! I have not come to harm you in any way.'

'Why not?' the wretched creature snapped. 'Death is all that is left me, and I deserve it.'

'It is not for me to take your life,' I told him.

'No, of course not. You believe in love, do you? You believe in kindness — like that ridiculous Jesu of yours, eh?' The mockery in his words was stinging sharp. As he spoke I did feel foolish for believing in such things. 'Well?'

'Yes, I believe.'

'Then kill me!' he shouted suddenly, his head snapping round. Spittle flecked his lips. 'Kill me now. It would be kindness itself!'

'Perhaps it would,' I allowed. 'But I will not take your life.'

He glared at me with those dead eyes of his. 'How not, if I told you I was responsible for your father's death.' His grisly grin sickened me. 'Yes, I murdered Taliesin. I, Annubi, killed him.'

Even as he said those hideous words, I did not believe him. He hated, yes, but it was not me he hated, nor my father. If he could have killed, I think he would have killed himself instead, but he could not. This was part of the thing that was poisoning him. Still, he knew. . . oh yes, he knew who killed Taliesin.

'You are Annubi?'

I had heard of him — not from my mother, but from Avallach, who, in his stories of Lost Atlantis, had told me about his seer. The man I had imagined bore no resemblance to the shrunken wretch before me.

'What do you want here?'

'Nothing.'

'Then why have you come?'

I lifted a hand helplessly. 'I had to come. . . to find out —'

'Go away from here, boy,' Annubi said, turning his dead eyes away from me. 'If she found you here. . . ' He sighed, then added in a whisper, '. . . but it is too late. . . too late.'

'Who?' I demanded. 'You said "*she*" — who did you mean?'

'Just go. I can do nothing for you.'

'Who did you mean?'

I saw a flicker of something cross his face — the vestige of an emotion other than hate or despair, but I did not know what it was. 'Need you ask? There is only Morgian. . . ' When I said nothing, he looked at me. 'The name means nothing to you?'

'Should it?'

'Wise Merlin. . . Intelligent Merlin. . . Hawk of Knowledge. Ha! You do not even know who your enemies are.'

'Morgian is my enemy?'

A spasm twisted his mouth. 'Morgian is every man's enemy, boy. Supreme Goddess of the Night, she has the hunger and the hate. Her touch can freeze the blood in your veins; her look can stop your heart beating. Death is her delight. . . her sole delight.'

'Where is she?' I asked, my voice a whisper in the fading light.

He only wobbled his head. 'If I knew, would I stay here?'

Pelleas, behind me, tugged on my arm. With the setting sun I felt the doom of the place increasing and wanted suddenly to be away. Yet, if there was something I could do I must do it.

'Yes, go,' rasped Annubi, as if reading my thoughts. 'Go and never come back lest you find Morgian here when you return.'

'Do you need anything?' He was so pathetic in his misery, I could not help asking.

'Belyn looks after me.'

I nodded and turned away. I had to run in order to keep up with Pelleas, who led the way back through the tower as though Morgian's breath singed the back of his neck. He reached the front door, still standing open as we had left it, and dashed outside.

I was right behind him. But before leaving that place, I knelt on the threshold and prayed a prayer against evil. Then, taking up a handful of white pebbles from the path, I marked out the sign of the cross before the door. Let it be a warning, I thought. Let her know who it was she had chosen to fight.

Our party left Llyonesse the next day, but the sense of lingering doom stayed with me a very long time. Riding back through that cheerless land was no great help, serving only to reinforce my already doleful mood. Gwendolau and Baram felt it, too, but less keenly. For a time, Gwendolau tried to keep up his usual travel banter, but it became too much and eventually he lapsed into moody silence like the rest of us.

I did not feel myself until the Tor came into view across the marshland. By then, just seeing the Glass Isle was enough to make our hearts leap in wild relief. In any event, my mother was waiting for me at the gate — which I wondered about, until I realized that she had guessed about Morgian and Annubi.

'They left here on the night your father was killed,' she told me, her voice soft and low. We were sitting in a corner of the hearth and it was very late at night. Nearly everyone else had gone to their beds. Charis had waited until we were alone to tell me. 'I never found out where they had gone.'

'But you guessed.'

'Llyonesse? Of course it was a possibility.' She made a small, empty gesture. 'I should have told you.'

I remained silent.

'I know I should have told it all long before now. . . but I could not bring myself to it — and then you were gone. So —' She made that curious gesture again, a small warding off movement of her hand against an unseen adversary. But then she settled herself, straightened her back, and squared her shoulders. 'Well, you must know the truth.

148

'After my mother was killed in that ghastly ambush —' she broke off, but continued in a moment. 'Forgive me, Merlin, I did not know how hard these words would be.'

'Your mother was killed?'

'That is what started the war between Avallach and Seithenin. Well, in the ninth year Avallach was wounded in a battle — I knew nothing about it; at the time I was bull dancing in the High Temple. When I returned home, my father had taken another wife, Lile. She was a young woman who had a knack for healing and she nursed my father. He was grateful to her and married her.'

'Lile? I do not remember her. What became of her?'

'No, you would not remember. She disappeared when you were very young.'

'Disappeared?' That was an odd way to put it. 'What happened to her?'

Charis shook her head slowly, but more from puzzlement than sorrow. 'No one knows. It was only a few months after Taliesin was killed; I had come back here to live. And although Lile and I were not the best of friends, we had learned to respect one another; there was no trouble between us.' Charis smiled, remembering. 'She liked you, Merlin. "How is my little Hawk today?" she always asked when she saw you. She liked holding you, rocking you. . . ' she shook her head once more. 'I never understood her, Merlin. I never did.'

'What happened?'

'The last time anyone remembers seeing her was in the orchard; Lile loved her apple trees. Many of them she had brought with her from Atlantis — can you believe it? Apple trees. . . all that way, through so much turmoil. And they live, they thrive here. . . such a long way from home we all are. . . ' Charis paused and swallowed, then continued.

'It was dusk. The sun had set. One of the grooms saw her riding out earlier; she told him she was going to the orchard. She spent so much time among her trees. But when she did not come back, Avallach sent men to the orchard. They found her horse tethered to a tree. The animal was half crazed with fear. Its haunches were streaked with blood and there were deep scratches across its shoulders as from a wild beast, although no one had ever seen anything like them before.'

'And Lile?'

'Of Lile there was no sign. She was not found, nor ever seen again from that night.'

'And you never spoke of her after that,' I said.

'No,' my mother admitted, 'we did not. If you ask me why, I cannot tell you. It did not seem appropriate somehow.'

'Perhaps she was carried off by a wolf, or bear,' I suggested, knowing full well that was not the answer.

'Perhaps,' answered Charis, as if considering it for the first time. 'Perhaps by someone or something else.'

'You have not mentioned Morgian,' I reminded her.

'Morgian is Lile and Avallach's daughter. When I returned home to meet Lile, Morgian was already three years old. She was a beautiful little girl. I liked her then. I did not see much of her, however, because preparations for leaving Atlantis took absolutely every moment. And yet, I remember her playing in the gardens. . . and, even then, with Annubi. She was always with Annubi.'

'She is not with him now.'

Charis considered this. 'No, I suppose not. Anyway, after the cataclysm we came here and she grew up like any other child. I did not pay much attention to her; she had her interests, I had mine. But she came to dislike me for some reason, and I always felt awkward and ill-at-ease with her. Things were not well between us, and I never understood why.

'Once, after Taliesin's people had come, she tried to steal Taliesin's affection for herself. It was done very clumsily and did not succeed, of course. But it set her against me.' Charis paused, choosing her next words carefully. 'And this is why I believe she caused Taliesin's death. I do not know how it was done, or whether she meant me to die instead, but I have always known she was behind it.'

I nodded. 'You are right, Mother. Annubi told me *he* was responsible, but he was lying.'

'Annubi?' There was pain and pity in the word.

'I think he hoped to anger me so that I would kill him. He wanted release, but I could not do it.'

'Poor, poor Annubi. Even now I do not have it in me to despise or hate him.'

'Annubi is Morgian's creature now. His misery is complete.'

'He was once my friend, you know. But our world changed

and he could not. It is sad.' She raised her eyes from the dying embers on the hearth and smiled weakly. 'Now you know it all, my son.'

She stood and kissed my cheek, resting her hand lightly on my shoulder. 'I am going to my bed. Do not sit up too long.' She turned to go.

'Mother?' I called after her. 'Thank you for telling me.'

She nodded and moved off, saying, 'It was never meant to be a secret, Hawk.'

THIRTEEN

I will say nothing of the journey north to Goddeu, except that it was opposite in most respects from the journey south the winter before. Such is the difference in travelling from one season to another. Avallach sent men with us, as did Maelwys. Both men were anxious to secure the friendship with a powerful ally in the north.

This is not to say that men in the north were not anxious for the same thing. The mood in the land had changed with the seasons: fear was growing; slowly it was creeping across the wide, empty hills to touch men's hearts and minds. I saw this in the faces of those who watched us pass; I heard it in their voices when they spoke; I tasted it on the wind, which seemed to cry:

The Eagles are gone! All hope is lost! We are doomed!

That such a change could take place in so short a time amazed me. The legions were greatly diminished, true, but they were not *all* gone. We were not abandoned. And our hope had never rested entirely with Rome in any case.

Always, from the very first, a man trusted the blade in his hand, and the courage of his kinsman. *Pax Romana*, well and good, but the people looked to their king for protection first, and only after to Rome. The tangible, present king protected his people, not the vague rumour of an emperor who sat on a golden throne in some far-off land no one knew.

Had we grown so weak and soft that the shift of a few thousand troops made us faint with fear? If we were doomed, fear is what doomed us, not invasion or threat of invasion by screaming Saecsen hordes and their woad-washed Picti minions. After all, there had been invasions and threats of invasions for many years now and the presence of the Eagles had not prevented either.

So now the Eagles had flown. What of that? Was Britain no

longer a foe to be feared? Could we not look after ourselves?

I was convinced that we could. If Elphin and Maelwys could raise again their warbands, others could do the same. And *that*, not the presence or absence of Roman legionaries, was where our future lay. I knew this with a certainty that increased with every Roman mile north.

Custennin received us in good spirits. He was delighted to see that his investment had borne such a rich return. Gifts were exchanged again and again. Even I received a gold-handled dagger from him for my negligible part in bringing everyone together. The expansive mood was such that he declared a feast for the third night of our stay in order properly to celebrate the new pledges between all our peoples.

As feasts go, it was an elaborate affair, taking fully two days to prepare. And yet there was something austere about it. It was the same austerity I had noticed on my first visit — as in the small matter of the lack of a bard. I had remarked on it then, but did not know its cause. Now, of course, I did: Custennin, despite his British name, was of Atlantean descent. This meant that the wilder, more passionate expressions of emotion were not to be indulged. It was the same with Avallach.

Nevertheless, the inclusion of so many Britons in Custennin's court meant that austerity and revel achieved an amiable balance. There was food enough, and the smoky-tasting heather beer of the Hill Folk by the barrel — how he had come by that, I cannot say, unless someone had learned from one of the fhains how to brew it — so that the festivities were indeed vivid.

I seem to remember singing a great deal, loudly, and not always with my harp. Although it is doubtful anyone noticed any lapse on my part.

Except Ganieda.

Everywhere I turned. . . Ganieda. Watching me, her dark eyes shining, waiting and watching, silent, keeping her own counsel. In truth, since our frosty reunion, she had not spoken three words to me in as many days.

I had expected a warm welcome from her when I returned. Not a shower of kisses, certainly — but a smile, a welcome cup, something. Instead, as I stood awkwardly just inside the doorway of her father's hall, fresh from the trail, she merely looked at me, neither smiling nor frowning, but as one judging the value of a pelt offered for trade.

The feeling was so strong in me, I made a joke of it, holding my arms out and turning round slowly. 'What will you give for this handsome hide, lady?'

Apparently, she did not appreciate the jest. 'Handsome indeed! Why on earth would any noble-born lady be interested in a hide as dirty and smelly as the one I see before me?' she replied coolly.

I must admit that my time in the saddle had exacted a price. I was not the freshest flower to bloom in the forest. A bath in the lake would put matters right, I thought, but the exchange began our reunion uncomfortably. And I thought that perhaps I had been mistaken about how it was between us; or that Ganieda had second thoughts about me. She had, after all, had plenty of time to change her mind.

To make matters worse, it was late on the fourth day before I finally found another chance to speak to her alone — had she been avoiding me? — and that left only two days before we were due to depart once more. I felt the time fleeing away, so cornered her in the kitchen behind the great hall.

'If I have said something to offend you,' I told her directly, 'I am sorry. Only tell me and I will make it right.'

She appeared pensive, her mouth pulled into a pretty pout, her brows wrinkled. However, her voice was cold and clear as ice. 'Surely, you flatter yourself, wolf boy. How could you possibly offend me?'

'That is for you to say. I can think of nothing I have done.'

'What you *do* makes no difference to me.' She turned and started away.

'Ganieda!' She froze at her name. 'Why are you doing this?'

Her back was towards me and she did not turn round to answer. 'You seem to imagine that there was something between us.'

'It was not all my imagining, surely.'

'Was it not?' She turned to look at me over her shoulder.

'It was not.' At the moment, I was less certain than I sounded by far.

'Then that is your mistake.' Still, she turned towards me once more.

'Perhaps you are right,' I conceded. 'Are you not the dauntless maid who hunted Twrch Trwyth, Lord Boar of Celyddon, and killed him with a single thrust? Are you not the lady of this great house? Is not your name a delight on the tongue, and your voice a joy to the ear? If not, then I am indeed mistaken.'

This made her smile. 'Your tongue wags well, wolf boy.'

'That is no answer.'

'Very well, the answer is yes. I am the one of whom you speak.'

'Then I have made no mistake.' I stepped towards her. 'What is wrong, Ganieda? Why this coldness at our meeting?'

She crossed her arms and turned away again. 'Your people are in the south, and my place is here. It is as simple as that and nothing can change it.'

'Your logic is unassailable, lady,' I replied.

That spun her round. Her eyes snapped angrily. 'Do not think to make me out a fool!'

'Then why are you behaving so foolishly?'

Her face contorted in a frown. 'You have said it, and you are right. It is foolish to want something that you cannot have and know you cannot have, and yet go on wanting.'

I could not imagine her lacking anything she wanted — not for long, anyway. 'What do you want that you cannot have, Ganieda?'

'Are you blind as well as stupid?' she asked. The words were harsh, but her voice was soft.

'What is it? Only tell me and I will get it for you if I can,' I promised.

'*You*, Myrddin.'

I could only blink in confusion.

She lowered her eyes and clasped her hands nervously. 'You asked and now I have told. . . It is you that I want, Myrddin. More than anything I have ever wanted.'

Silence grew to the point of breaking. I reached out to her, but could not touch her and my hand fell away.

'Ganieda,' my voice sounded painfully coarse in my ears, 'Ganieda, do you not know that you have me already? From the moment I saw you astride the grey stallion, plunging through the stream in a spray of diamonds and the sun dancing in your hair — from that very moment I was yours.'

155

I thought this would make her happy and, indeed, she smiled. But the smile faded and the sorrowful frown returned. 'Your words are kind. . . '

'More, they are true.'

She shook her head; the light glinted on the slim silver torc at her throat. 'No,' she sighed.

I stepped closer and took her hand. 'What is wrong, Ganieda?'

'I have already said: your place is in the south, and mine is here with my people. There is nothing to be done about that.'

Already she was thinking further ahead than I. 'Perhaps nothing need be done about it — for now. And later, who knows?'

She came into my arms. 'Why do I love you?' she whispered. 'I never wanted to.'

'It is possible to search for love and find it. More often, I think, love finds us when we are not even searching,' I told her, wincing a little at the presumption of my words. What did I know of such things? 'Love has found us, Ganieda, we cannot turn it away.'

With Ganieda nestled in my arms, the clean-washed scent of her hair filling my nostrils, the living warmth of her against me, the softness of her skin under my hand — these things made me want to believe what I said, and I did. With all my heart I believed it.

We kissed then and with the touching of our lips I knew that she believed it, too.

'Well,' Ganieda sighed, 'this has solved nothing.'

'No. Nothing,' I agreed.

But what did that matter?

Needless to say, when the time came for us to return to Dyfed, I hesitated, hoping to hold off the time of leaving indefinitely. This I actually managed to do for a few days, and they were happy days. Ganieda and I rode in the forest and walked along the lake, we played chess before the fire, I sang to her and played my harp, we talked late into the night so that dawn found us groggy and yawning, but unwilling to part. In short, we did all the things lovers do and it did not greatly matter whether we did anything at all as long as we were together.

I see her now: her dark hair braided with silver thread entwined; her blue eyes glinting beneath long, dark lashes; the soft, bird's egg blue of her tunic; the swell of her breasts beneath the thin summer fabric; her long, strong legs; the golden bracelets on her sun-browned arms. . .

She is the essence of female to me: bright mystery, clothed in beauty.

Sadly, I could not hold off the day of leaving for ever. I had at last to return to Dyfed. Still, I put the best face on this that I could devise.

So, while the others readied the horses, Ganieda and I walked hand in hand along the pebbled shingle of the lake. The clear water lapped at the stones under our feet while out on the lake swallows darted and dived, skimming the surface with the tips of their wings.

'When I return, it will be for you, my soul; it will be to take you from your father's hearth to my own. We will be married.'

If I thought this would cheer her, I was mistaken. 'Let us be married at once. Then you would not have to leave at all. We could stay together always.'

'Ganieda, you know I have no hearth of my own. Before we can be married, I have to make a place for you, and to do that I must first make a place for myself.'

She understood this, for she was noble through and through. She smiled unexpectedly. 'Go then, wolf boy. Make yourself a king, then come and claim your queen. I will be here waiting.'

She leaned close and kissed me. 'That is so that you will remember who it is that waits for you.' She kissed me again. 'That is to spur you to your task.' Then, putting her hands on either side of my head, she pressed her lips to mine in a long, passionate kiss. 'And that is to hasten your return.'

'Lady,' I replied when I could breathe once more, 'if you kiss me again I will not be able to leave.'

'Away with you then, my love. Go this very instant, for I would have you return all the sooner.'

'It may take time, Ganieda,' I warned her. Hoping to make our parting easier, I pulled the gold band from my arm. I held it up. 'This was given me by Vrisa, my Hill Folk sister, so that if ever I found a wife, I could claim her. With this, I claim you, Ganieda.' I slipped the ring of gold onto her wrist. 'And when I return I will make good my claim.'

She smiled, encircling my neck with her arms, drawing me close. 'I live for that day, my love.'

I hugged her tightly to me. 'Take me with you,' she whispered.

'Oh, yes. At once,' I answered. 'We can live in a wooded bower on walnuts and gooseberries.'

Her laughter was full and free. 'I detest gooseberries!'

Taking my arm she spun me around and pushed me towards the path leading back up the hill. 'I will not live on nuts and berries in a mud hut with you, Myrddin Wylt. So, you get on that sorry horse of yours and ride away at once. And do not come back until you have won me a kingdom!'

Ah, Ganieda, I would have won the world for you if you had asked!

It was high summer when we rode into Maridunum. Beltane had come and gone while we were on the road. We had seen the hilltop fires bright under the stars, and had heard the mysterious cries of the Hill Folk drifting on the midnight wind. But there was no midsummer fire for us, nor did we think it wise to join in the celebration at one of the nearby settlements. More and more, Christian folk kept away from the old customs as the paths of the new ways and the old diverged.

Of course, many of Maelwys' people had become followers of the Christ — especially since Dafyd's coming. But there were some with us who observed the old ways, so to make up for the missed revel, I played the harp and sang.

And it came to me while I was singing — watching the ring of faces around the night's fire, their eyes glinting like dark sparks, gazing raptly as the song kindled and took light in their souls — it came to me that the way to men's souls was through their hearts, not simply through their minds. As much as a man might be convinced in his mind, as long as his heart remained unchanged all persuasion would fail. The surest way to the heart is through song and story: a single tale of high and noble deeds spoke to men more forcefully than all of blessed Dafyd's homilies.

I do not know why this should be, but I believe it to be true. I have seen the humble folk crowd into the chapel in the wood to receive the mass. In all sincerity they kneel before the holy altar, mute, reverent, as they should be, but also uncomprehending.

Yet I have seen the eyes of their souls awaken when Dafyd reads out, 'Listen, in a far country there lived a king who had two sons. . . '

Perhaps it is how we are made; perhaps words of truth reach us best through the heart, and stories and songs are the language of the heart.

However it is, I sang that night and the men listening heard a song they had never heard before: a song of that same far-off country Dafyd told about. I had begun making songs, although I did not often sing them before others. This night I did and it was welcomed.

When we finally reached Maridunum, it was market day and the old stone-paved streets were awash with bleating, clucking, squealing livestock and their shouting handlers. We were wearily pushing our way through the confusion when I heard a voice ring out, saying: 'Behold, you Briton men and women! Behold your king!'

I craned my neck, but with the market swirling round the horse's flanks I could see nothing. I rode on.

Again the voice proclaimed. 'Sons of Bran and Brut! Listen to your bard. I tell you your king passes by, hail him in all respect.'

I reined the horse to a halt and turned in the saddle. A way parted through the crowd and a bearded druid stepped into view. He was tall and gaunt, with his blue robe hanging over his shoulder. His mantle was bound at his waist with rawhide and a leather pouch dangled from this crude belt. He held his staff raised as he came forward, and I saw that it was of rowan.

He approached. The others riding with me also stopped to watch.

'Who are you, bard?' I asked. 'Why do you call after me the way you do?'

'For the giving of a name, a name is required.'

'Here among these people, I am called Myrddin,' I told him.

'Well spoken, friend,' he said. 'Myrddin you are, but Wledig you will be.'

The flesh of my scalp prickled at his words. 'I have given my name,' I told him, 'I will hear yours, unless something prevents you.'

His brown face wrinkled in a smile. 'Nothing prevents me, but I am not in the habit of giving my name where it is already known.'

He stepped slowly closer. The men behind me made the sign against evil with their hands, but the druid ignored them; his eyes never left my face. 'Tell me now that you do not know me.'

'Blaise!'

I was out of the saddle and into his arms before another word could be spoken. I gripped his shoulders hard, feeling the solid muscle and bone beneath my hands. It really was Blaise in front of me, though I had to touch him to believe it. He was much changed. Older, thinner, tough as a pine knot, his eyes blazing like pitch torches.

'Blaise, Blaise,' I shook him and pounded him on the back, 'I did not recognize you, forgive me.'

'Not recognize the teacher of your youth? Tch, Myrddin, are you going soft in the head?'

'Let us say that a satirizing voice from the market throng was the last thing I expected.'

Blaise shook his head gravely. 'I was not satirizing you, my lord Myrddin.'

'And I am no lord, Blaise, as you well know.' His talk made me uncomfortable.

'No?' He threw back his head and laughed. 'Oh, Myrddin, your innocence is beyond price. Look around you, lad. Who is it that men's eyes follow when he rides by? Who do they speak of behind their hands? What tales are winging through the land?'

I shrugged in bewilderment. 'If you are talking about me, I am sure you are mistaken. No one takes notice of me.' I said this into virtual silence, for the market had grown very quiet as the crowd watched, catching every word.

'No one!' Blaise raised a hand to the throng around us. 'In the day of trouble, these people will follow you to the grave and beyond — and you call them no one.'

'And you talk too much — and too loudly. Come with us, you disagreeable druid, and let me stop your yammering with bread and meat. A full belly will make you sensible.'

'It is true I have not eaten for many days,' Blaise allowed. 'But what of that? I am used to it by now. Yet, I would welcome a drink to wash the dust from my throat, and a long talk with my good friend.'

'That you shall have, and all else besides.' I climbed into the saddle, put down a hand to him and pulled him up behind me. And we rode on to Maelwys' villa together, chattering all the way.

There was the usual ceremony at our arrival, the usual greetings and welcomings — which I would have found gratifying, but for the fact that they kept me from my friend. There was so much we had to say to one another, and yet now that we were together all the urgency and longing I might have felt in his absence, but did not, suddenly sprang into being. I had to talk to him *now*!

Be that as it may, it was still some time before we could speak together alone — indeed, I began to think it had been more private in the market-place!

'Tell me, Blaise, where have you been? What have you been doing since last I saw you? Have you travelled? I heard there was trouble within the Brotherhood, what news of that?'

He sipped his watered wine and winked over the rim of his cup. 'If I had remembered that you were this inquisitive, I would not have acknowledged you in the square.'

'Do you blame me? How long has it been? Five years? Six?'

'If a day.'

'Why did you call out to me in front of everyone like that?'

'I wanted your attention.'

'And that of every man, woman, child, and beast in Maridunum as well apparently.'

He shrugged good-naturedly. 'I only spoke the truth. I care not who hears it.' Blaise laid aside the cup and leaned towards me. 'You have grown well, Hawk. All the promises of childhood are being fulfilled, I can see it. Yes, you will do.'

'I seem to be growing into my saddle. I tell you, Blaise, I have seen more of this Island of the Mighty than Bran the Blessed himself in these last years.'

'And what have you seen with those golden eyes of yours, Hawk?'

'I have seen the mood of the people change — and not for the better; I have seen fear spreading through the land like a plague.'

'That I have seen as well, and I can think of fairer sights to look upon.' He raised his cup and tossed down the last of the wine and wiped his moustache with his sleeve. 'There is trouble in this land of ours, Hawk. Men are turning their backs on the truth; they toil at sowing lies.'

'The Learned Brotherhood?'

'Hafgan, God keep his soul, was right to dissolve the Brotherhood. A few came over to us at first, but now most of them have gone back. They have chosen a new Archdruid to lead them — a man named Hen Dallpen, you may remember him.'

'I remember.'

'So the Learned continue the councils and observances, and Hen Dallpen leads them.' His voice became low with dread. 'But, Hawk, they are falling away; they are sliding back into the old ways — the very thing I have been trying to prevent.'

'What do you mean, Blaise? What old ways?'

'Truth in the heart,' he said, repeating the age-old triad, 'strength in the arm, and honesty in the tongue. This the druid kind have taught for a hundred lifetimes. But it was not always so.

'There was a time when we, like all the unenlightened, believed that only living blood would satisfy the gods —' He paused, forcing the next words out with an obvious effort. 'Just a few days ago, in the hills not far from here, the Chief Druid of Llewchr Nor kindled the midsummer fire with a Wicker Man.'

'No!' I had heard of human sacrifice, of course — I had nearly been one myself! But this was different, darker, perverse and wilfully unholy.

'Believe it,' Blaise answered gravely. 'There were four victims burned to death in that hideous wicker cage. It sickens me, Hawk, but they have persuaded themselves that our present troubles have come upon us because we have abandoned the old gods to follow the Christ, and the only way to fight powerful magic is with even more powerful magic. So they have revived the murderous customs.'

162

'What is to be done?'

'Wait, that is not all, Myrddin Bach. There is more. They have turned against *you*.'

'*Me*? Why? What did I —' Then it came to me. 'Because of the dancing stones?'

'Partly. They believe Hafgan was deluded by Taliesin and induced to follow Jesu. Therefore, they have turned against Taliesin, but he is dead and beyond their schemes, so now they seek to destroy you, his heir. It is suggested that his soul lives on in you.' He spread his hands by way of explanation. 'You possess a power none of them ever imagined existed.'

I could only shake my head. First Morgian, now the Learned Brotherhood — I, who had never lifted a hand against another in my short life, was now the object of hatred by powerful enemies I did not even know.

Blaise felt my distress. 'Worry not,' he said, gripping my arm, 'neither fear. Greater is he that is in you, than he that is in them, eh?'

'Why should they want to harm me?'

'Because they fear you.' He gripped my arm with a hand of iron. 'I tell you the truth, Myrddin, it is because of who you are.'

'Who am I, Blaise?'

He did not answer at once, but neither did he look away. His intense eyes peered into mine as if he would search me out inside. 'Do you not know, then?' he asked at last.

'Hafgan talked about a Champion. He called me Emrys.'

'There, you see?'

'I do not see at all.'

'Well, perhaps it is time.' He released my arm and leaned down to retrieve his staff. Taking it up, he held the smooth length of rowan wood over me and began declaiming: 'Myrddin ap Taliesin, you are the Long-Awaited One, whose coming was foretold with wonders in the sky. You are the Bright Light of the Britons, shining against the gathering gloom. You are the Emrys, Immortal Bard-Priest, the Keeper of the Spirit of our People.'

Then he knelt down, and laying the staff aside, took up the hem of my tunic and kissed it. 'Look not with disfavour upon your servant, Lord Emrys.'

'Have you lost your reason, Blaise? It is only me, Myrddin.' My heart beat in my throat. 'I am not — not what you said.'

'You are and will be, Hawk,' he replied. 'But why look so downhearted? Our enemies are not beating down the door.' He laughed and the intensity of the moment passed. We were, once more, just two friends talking beside the fire.

A steward came to refill our cups. I lifted mine and said, 'Health to you, Blaise, and to our enemies' enemies!'

We drank together and the old bond between us grew stronger. Two friends. . . there are stronger forces on earth, perhaps, but few as tenacious and enduring as the bond between true friends.

FOURTEEN

That autumn, when the weather finally broke towards winter, Blaise and I returned to my long-abandoned lessons. I studied with greater intensity now because I had the hunger, and because I so wanted to make up for lost time — committing the stories and songs of our people to memory; sharpening my powers of observation; increasing my store of knowledge about the earth and her ways, and those of all her creatures; practising the harp; delving deep into mysteries and secrets of earth and air, fire and water.

But it soon became apparent that in the realm of things men call magic, my knowledge outstripped his. Gern-y-fhain had taught me well; what is more, the Hill Folk possessed many secrets even the Learned Brotherhood did not know. These I possessed as well.

The winter proceeded, one cold leaden day following another, until at last the sun began to linger longer in the sky and the land to warm beneath its rays. It was then that I reached the end of Blaise's tutelage. 'There is nothing more I can give you, Hawk,' he told me. 'On my life, I cannot think of another thing to teach me. Yet, there are many you might teach me.'

I stared at him for a moment. 'But there is so much — I know so little.'

'True,' he said, his lean face lighting in a grin. 'Is that not the beginning of true wisdom?'

'I am in earnest, Blaise. There must be more.'

'And I am in earnest, too, Myrddin Bach. There is nothing more that I can teach you. Oh, a few of the minor stories of our race, perhaps; but nothing of import.'

'I cannot have learned it all,' I protested.

'True again. There is much more to be learned, but I am not the one to teach you. Whatever else there is, you must learn it on your own.' He shook his head lightly. 'Do not look so downcast, Hawk. It is no disgrace for pupil to leave master behind. It happens.'

'But will you not go with me?'

'Where you go, Myrddin Emrys, I cannot follow.'

'Blaise —'

He raised a cautionary finger. 'Nevertheless, see that you do not confuse knowledge with wisdom, as so many do.'

Well, we did continue on together, but not as before. In fact, more and more, I found myself the master instructing Blaise, who professed to marvel at my acuity, and said so many flattering things that I became embarrassed to open my mouth in front of him. But in all it was a good and profitable winter for me.

When spring opened the roads to travel once more, I rode out with Maelwys and seven of his men — all of us armed — to make the first circuit of his lands that year. We spoke with his chiefs and received their accounting of how the people of each district and settlement had fared the winter. On occasion, Maelwys settled disputes and administrated justice in cases that exceeded the chief's authority, or acted in place of the chief to spare hard feelings.

He also told each chief that he wanted young men for his warband, and that from now on the year's increase would go to its support. No one objected to the plan and, in fact, most had foreseen it and were only too glad to do their part.

Maelwys showed himself an astute ruler: by turns sympathetic, indulgent, stern, unyielding — but always fair and just in his dealings and judgements.

'Men resent unfairness,' he told me as we rode between Clewdd and Caer Nead, two points along the ring of hillforts that served to protect his lands. 'But they despise injustice. It is slow poison, and always deadly.'

'Then you have no fear, lord, for your judgements are the heart of justice.'

He cocked his head to one side as he regarded me. The others rode behind us, talking idly among themselves, so he spoke what was on his mind. 'Charis tells me that you have given your heart to Lord Custennin's daughter.' That lightning came out of a clear blue sky. I did not know my mother surmised so much, or so accurately.

The colour rose to my cheeks, but I answered him straight out. 'Her name is Ganieda and, yes, I love her.'

Maelwys considered this, and for a moment all I heard was the soft plod of the horses' hooves over the new green turf. Then the king said, 'Have you given a thought to your future, Myrddin?'

'I have, lord,' I said, 'and it is on my heart to make my way as soon as may be so that I may go and take Ganieda from her father's hearth to my own.'

'So that is how it is between you.'

'That is how it is.'

'Then perhaps on our return to Maridunum we should do some talking.'

That was all he said and, indeed, it was all he needed to say. We arrived shortly at the next, and last, settlement: Caer Nead, a cluster of wattle huts and briar-fenced cattle yards within sight of a small hillfort.

Maelwys was anxious to get back to Maridunum before nightfall and so we did not tarry in Caer Nead, but conducted our business quickly. By midday we were ready and left as soon as decorum allowed. There was no great hurry; the distance was not far. Yet I noticed that, the closer to home, the more anxious Maelwys became. I did not say anything, and I do not think anyone else would have noticed in any case. But I watched his jaw set firm and his mouth turn down in a hard, straight line. The words he spoke grew more terse and the silence between them longer.

So I tried to discover what it might be that was troubling him, and could come to no conclusion. . . until I saw the smoke.

We saw it together. I gave a shout just as Maelwys reined up. 'Fire!'

He took one look at the hill-line before us. 'Maridunum!' he cried, and put leather to his mount.

We all followed him in his breakneck flight. The smoke, at first a thin, shadowy wisp in the air, blackened and thickened into a huge dark column. Closer, we could smell the stench of burning and hear the screams of the townsfolk.

The raiders had held off until they could be certain of their reception. I imagine they thanked their heathen gods with every breath in their bodies upon learning that the king was away and the town virtually unprotected.

But they were overcautious. Or perhaps they had lingered too long with their boats before coming inland. However it was, we caught them in midst of their destruction, our horses hurtling down on them without warning. We took them on the points of our swords as we charged through their scattering ranks in the old market square.

Though they fought with some courage when cornered, they were no match for mounted warriors seeking blood vengeance. In a matter of a few moments the corpses of a score of Irish raiders lay sprawled in the stone-flagged square.

We dismounted and began pulling down the burning straw of the roofs so that the fire did not spread, then turned to the bodies of the dead raiders to retrieve what they had stolen. The town was quiet, and except for the crackle of flames and the grating cry of the carrion birds already gathering for their feast, the air was dead still.

That should have been a warning, I suppose. But the fight was over and we were already starting to cool down. No one expected an ambush.

We did not even realize what was happening until the first spears were already whistling through the air. Someone screamed and two of our party fell with spears in their stomachs. The Irish were on us instantly.

We learned later that there were three big warboats in the Towy — each carrying thirty warriors. All of these, save the twenty whose blood stained the stones at our feet, came on us at once with a tremendous roar. Seventy against seven.

The next moments were a terror of confusion as we ran to the horses and leaped to our saddles. But the raiders were streaming into the square from all directions and we were too close bound to make a charge. In any event, the square was soon so crowded we could hardly swing our swords. I saw one of our men hauled from the saddle and his brains dashed out beneath his own horse's hooves.

I saw Maelwys struggling to rally us to his side, his arm rising and falling again and again as he struck out at those surrounding him. Spears splintered before his blade and more than one man went down screaming.

I took up the call and drove towards him.

Into my path leaped two spearmen. The horse shied and dodged, nearly pitching me from his back. The animal's hooves slipped against the smooth stone and it fell, rolling onto its side, pinning my leg.

One spear thrust past my ear, another jabbed towards my chest. I swung with my sword and knocked it aside, kicking myself free of my mount as it thrashed to its feet.

I rolled up to face two more raiders, making four together, all with iron-tipped spears levelled on me. One of them gave a shout and they rushed me.

I saw the enemy move towards me, saw their faces dark and grim, saw their eyes gleaming hard like sharp iron. Their hands were tight on the shafts of their spears, their knuckles white. Sweat misted on their faces and the cords tightened on their necks. . .

I saw it all and more — all with dreadful, heart-stopping clarity as the speeding flow of time dwindled to a bare trickle. Every action slowed — as if all around me was suddenly overcome with an impossible lethargy.

I saw the spearheads edging towards me, swinging lazily through the air. My own blade came up sharp and smart, biting through the wooden shafts, slicing the spearpoints from the hafts as easily as striking the heads of thistles from their stems. I let the force of the blow spin me away so that, as my attackers fell forward behind their blunted spears, I was gone.

I scanned the melee. The square churned and writhed with the fight. The sound was a booming, featureless roar — like that of blood racing through the ears. Our warriors, horribly outmanned, strove valiantly, fighting for their lives.

Maelwys held his own across the square, leaning low in the saddle, hewing mightily. His arm flailed with a fierce and violent rhythm. His blade streamed scarlet ribbons.

He had been identified, however, and more and more of the enemy lumbered towards him in that strange, languid motion brought on by my heightened awareness.

I put out my hand and caught up the reins of my mount, swinging up into the saddle. I turned the horse's head and urged it forth towards Maelwys.

Moving with the easy roll of the horse beneath me, I swung the sword in my hand first on the left and then on the right, slashing, slashing, striking again and again, my blade a shining circle of light around me. Men toppled like cordwood in my wake as I forced my way to the king's side.

My sword sang, ringing clear and true as it struck, relentless as the sea swell driven before the storm. We fought together, Maelwys and I, and soon the stone under our horses' hooves was slick with blood.

But still the enemy swarmed around us in fighting frenzy, slashing with the knives in their hands and jabbing with their spears. None dared come within the arc of my blade, however, for that was certain death. Instead, they tried for my horse, stabbing at its legs and belly.

One howling fool leaped at my bridle strap, hoping to drag the horse's head down; I gave him something to howl about as his ear left his face. Another lost a hand when he made a clumsy thrust at the animal's flanks. Yet another collapsed in a quivering heap when the flat of my blade came down hard on the crown of his leather war helm, as he made to leap for me.

These things happened leisurely, almost laughably so, each action deliberate and slow. Thus, I had time not only to react, but to plan my next move and my next, before the first had been completed. Once I fell into the uncanny rhythm of this strange way of fighting, I found that I could move with impunity among the absurdly lethargic enemy.

So, striking again and again, striking and whirling away, while my hapless opponents floundered and lurched around me, flailing uselessly, with sluggish, inept movements, I joined a bizarre and terrible dance.

The bards speak with reverence of Oran Mor, the Great Music — elusive source of all melody and song. Very few have the gift to hear it. Taliesin had the gift — or something more than that. But I heard it then: my limbs throbbed with it, my swinging arm told out its unearthly rhythm, my sword sang with its brilliant melody. I was part of Oran Mor, and it was part of me.

There came a rallying cry and Maelwys' houseguard came clattering into the square. They had ridden from the villa, where the townspeople had fled, and were hurrying to our aid now that it was clear the awaited attack would not come there.

But a few heartbeats later, I knew the battle was broken. A rising wave of exultation rose within me and I heard a high, keening call, a war chant, a victory cry, and recognized my own voice soaring up from my throat.

The reaction of the enemy was immediate. They turned to meet the source of this unnerving sound and I saw, in that extraordinary clarity, black despair fall across their features. They were undone. And they knew it.

My cry rose into a song of triumph, and I leaped to the aid of my sword brothers who were hard pressed, sweet exhilaration sweeping through me and out of my mouth in the song. No one could stand before me, and the Irish fled lest they be trampled beneath my horse's hooves or carved by my swift blade.

Now I was in one place, freeing a man being dragged to his death, now in another, snatching a weapon from a foe and flinging it to an ally. Once I saw a man falling and reached out, caught him, and hauled him back into the saddle. All the while, my voice rose in joyous celebration. I was invincible.

I saw Maelwys clear the path and ride to meet me, three of his own behind him. I raised my sword in salute as he came up, and I saw, under the sweat and blood, his face white and his eyes staring. His sword arm was gashed, but he paid it no heed.

He put a trembling hand out to touch me and I saw his mouth move, but the words were slow in coming.

'You can stop now, Myrddin. It is over.'

I grinned and loosed a wild laugh.

'Look!' he said, shaking me. 'Look around you. We have beat them back. We have won.'

I peered through the mist that had risen before my eyes. The bodies of the dead lay deep upon the square. The stench of death clawed at my throat.

I shuddered as with a sudden chill, and began to shake from head to foot. The last thing I saw was the sun bright in my eyes and the clouds swirling above me, swirling like the wings of circling birds.

I remember arriving at the villa, and the drone of hushed voices around me. I remember drinking something very bitter, and then vomiting. I remember waking cold in fire-shot darkness to the sound of steel on steel. I remember floating lost in an immense sea as booming water roared around me.

Lastly, I remember climbing up a sharp slope to stand on a wind-bitten rock ledge in a blood-red dawn. . .

When I awoke all was well with me once more. The battle frenzy that had come on me was gone and I was myself. My mother regarded me closely, and pressed her hand to my forehead, but allowed that whatever ailment had possessed me had vanished. 'We were worried, Merlin,' she told me. 'We thought you had been wounded, but there is not so much as a bruise on you, son. How do you feel?'

'I am well, Mother.' That was all I said. There was no explaining what had happened when I did not know myself.

After breaking fast, I heard a commotion outside and walked out into the forecourt where I found Maelwys surrounded by his houseguard — some of whom had fought with us the day before. Rarely were all of them at the villa, however, as he kept them circulating his lands, riding the borders, keeping watch.

News of the attack had summoned those who had not been present the day before, both warriors and chiefs. There were many townspeople there as well, swelling the ranks of those gathered in the forecourt.

Maelwys had been speaking to them but, when I came out, silence descended over the throng. Thinking only to join them, I came to stand beside the king. A man pushed his way to me, and I saw that it was Blaise.

He raised his staff and lifted his voice in song:

'Three thirties of bold warriors have gone down before
    the thirsty blade;
The blood of the vanquished is silent,
    black is their mourning;
The eyes of the enemy feed the birds of death;
    let each mouth make entreaty.
From the heart of the hero a champion springs —

great of skill, a giant in battle;
He has hewn the savage with sharp steel;
    terrible were their war cries.
Hail him men of valour; exalt him in your midst;
    let his name rise on wings of welcome!
Make homage to the Lord of your Deliverance,
    who with walls of iron has defended you.
Brave men! Princes of noble birth! Make of Myrddin
    a name of praise and honour.

When he had finished, Blaise lowered his hands and, stooping before me, laid his staff at my feet. Then he backed slowly away. For a moment the people stared in silence. No one moved.

Then a young warrior — the one I had saved from a fall in the battle, I think — stepped forward. He drew his sword from its sheath at his side and, without a word, laid it beside the druid's staff. Then he knelt down and stretched out his hand to touch my foot.

One by one, each of the warriors there followed their sword brother's example. They drew out their blades, knelt, and put out their hands to cover my feet. Several of Maelwys' chiefs, caught in the spell, added their swords to the pile and knelt to touch my feet as well.

It was something warriors did when vowing allegiance to a new battlechief.

But Maelwys had not been badly injured, let alone killed; he was still a skilled and able leader. I turned to the king to find he had stepped from beside me. I was standing alone before the people. What could this mean?

'Please, lord,' I whispered, 'this honour is yours.'

'No,' he declared. 'It is yours alone, Myrddin. The warriors have chosen who they will follow.'

'But —'

Maelwys shook his head. 'Let be,' he replied gently. Then, stepping behind me, he raised his hands over my head. 'Hear me, my people. Look upon the one you honour. You have made him your battlechief. . . ' he paused and lowered his hands to my shoulders, 'This day I make him my son, and heir of all I possess.'

What?

Blaise was there and ready. 'This is an auspicious day, lord,' he said, 'allow me to confirm you in your good intent.' So saying, he unwound the rawhide belt from around his waist and bound our hands together at the wrist.

To Maelwys he said, 'Lord and King, as your hand is bound, is it your wish to bind your life to the son of your wife?'

'That is my wish.'

'Will you honour him with sonship, bestowing him with lands and possessions?'

'That I will do gladly.'

Turning solemnly to me Blaise said, 'Myrddin ap Taliesin, will you accept this man to be your guardian and your guide?'

It was happening so fast. 'Blaise, I —'

'Answer now.'

'As he has accepted me, so will I accept him.' I gripped Maelwys' hand and he gripped mine.

Blaise drew his knife and nicked our wrists, so that our blood mingled. 'So be it,' he said, untied the thong and released us. Then, indicating the pile of swords at my feet, he said, 'Will you also accept the fealty of these men who have sworn loyalty to you with their lives?'

'Likewise, I accept the honour and fealty of these brave men. I give my life as pledge to them.'

A shout went up from the people and the warriors leaped forward and grabbed up their swords and began beating them against their shields, making a terrible din. 'Myrddin! Myrddin! Myrddin!' they cried, my name a chant on their lips.

Then I was lifted up and carried into Maelwys' hall on the shoulders of my men. As I crossed the threshold, I saw my mother standing just inside the door. Charis had seen all that had taken place and her face glowed with love for me. She stepped towards me and raised her hands, and I saw she held a sword across her palms: the Fisher King's sword.

I took up the sword and lifted it high. The men around me redoubled their acclaim, shouting and cheering and calling my name. And I sang with joy, until the timbers rang with the sound.

For this was the day I won my kingdom.

BOOK TWO

FOREST LORD

ONE

Black is the hand of heaven, blue and black,
    and filled with frozen stars.
And stars and stars and stars. . . and stars.
Who are you, lord?
What is your name? Why do you look at me so?
Have you never seen a man disembowelled?
Have you never seen a living corpse?
Black is the day. Black is the night.
And black the hand that covers me.
Deep in Celyddon's black heart I hide.
In a forest pool I glimpse the face
    beneath the antlered helm,
        and I stare.
I stare until the stars stream overhead.
The red moon screams.
The birds and wild creatures take flight at my coming.
The trees taunt me.
The flowers of the high meadows turn their
    faces from me.
The crooked glens echo sharp accusation.
The racing waters mock me. . .
Rain and wind, blast and blow, snow and sun.
Bright fire of the sun.
Silver moon glow.
Silver water from the soul of the mountain.
Sing fair stars of heaven!
Lift your voices, Children of the Living God!
Sharp as spearpoints are your shining songs.
Life and death are they to me.

Ave! Ave, Imperator!
Listen to the bleak wind howl through your
    empty halls.
Listen, High One! Hear the bones of the brave
    rattle in nameless graves.
King Eagle, attend your offspring;
    lift your hand and sustain them
    with the crumbs of your
    banquet hall.
They hunger for justice; they weep.
Only the King of Eagles can ease their craving.
Rivers flow and waters rise.
See fast ships fly over the sea.
Away, away. . . always away.
Take flight, my soul, away.
What is it that remains when life is gone?
How much of a man endures?
Like a beast among beasts I go.
Naked,
    feeding only on the roots of the field,
    drinking only rain,
    I am a man no more.
Broken rocks bruise my flesh, cold winds wrack
    my sorry bones.
I am undone!
I am as one cast out from the hearth of my kinsmen.
I am as one living in the shadowlands.
I am as the dead.
Shall I sing the seasons?
Shall I sing the ages of our Earth,
the days of men past and yet to come?
Shall I sing fair Broceliande?
Shall I sing drowned Llyonesse?
Pwyll, bring the Hero's Cup!
Mathonwy, bring my harp!
Taliesin, wrap your bright cloak around my shoulders!
Lleu, gather your people into your bright hall!
For I shall sing the Kingdom of Summer!

Mad Merlin . . . mad . . . you are mad Merlin . . . mad . . .

TWO

Oh, Wolf, happy Wolf, monarch of the green-clad hills, you are my only friend. Speak to me now. Give me the benefit of your wise counsel. Be my advocate and my protector.

Nothing to say, wise friend? What is that? A story?

If it pleases you, Hill Lord. I take up my harp. Hear, O People of Dust. Hearken well to the tale I shall tell:

In elder days, when the dew of creation was still fresh on the earth, Great Manawyddan ap Llyr was lord and king over seven cantrefs of Dyfed and this is the way of it.

Now Manawyddan was brother to Bran the Blessed, who himself was king of the Island of the Mighty, holding all kings and kinglets beneath him, even as he held all lands as his own. But Bran had journeyed to the Otherworld and tarried long, so Manawyddan took the kingship in his brother's place, as was his right to do. And there was not a better king in all the world than Manawyddan, and no better place for a kingdom than the wild hills of Dyfed, for these were the fairest lands in all the world.

It came about that Pryderi, prince of Gwynedd, came before Manawyddan seeking friendship for their two houses. Manawyddan received him gladly and offered a feast. So, the two friends feasted and took their ease, engaging in pleasant conversation and delighting in the songs of Manawyddan's skilful bard, Anuin Llaw, and the company of Manawyddan's beautiful queen, Rhiannon, of whom many wondrous tales are told.

After the first evening's sitting, Pryderi turned to Manawyddan. 'I have heard,' said Pryderi to his host, 'that the hunting runs of Dyfed are unmatched by any in the world.'

'Then you must heartily thank the one who told you, for truer words were never spoken.'

'Perhaps we might hunt together, you and I,' suggested Pryderi.

'Why, Cousin, we could go hunting tomorrow — that is, if nothing prevents you,' replied Manawyddan.

'Indeed, I thought I should grow old in waiting for you to ask,' said Pryderi happily. 'As it happens, nothing prevents me. Let us go tomorrow.'

On that very morrow, the two friends set out with a company of bold companions. They hunted all the day and at last stopped to rest and water their weary horses. While they waited, they climbed a nearby mound and lay down to sleep. As they slept, there came the sound of thunder; very loud thunder it was, so they awoke. And with the thunder came a thick, dark mist — so thick and so dark that no man could see his companion next to him.

When the mist finally lifted, it was bright everywhere, so that they blinked their eyes and put up their hands. When they lowered their hands once more, however, they looked out and saw that everything had changed. No more were there trees or rivers or flocks or dwellings. No animal, no smoke, no fire, no man, nothing save the hills, and those were empty, too.

'Alas, lord!' cried Manawyddan, 'What has become of our company and the rest of my kingdom? Let us go and find them if we can.'

They returned to Manawyddan's palace and found only briars and thorns in the place where his sparkling hall had been. In vain they searched the valleys and glens, trying to spot a dwelling or settlement, but only a few sickly birds did they see. And they both began to feel mournful for their loss — Manawyddan for his wife Rhiannon, who was waiting for him in their chamber, and all his brave company as well; and Pryderi for his companions and the fine gifts Manawyddan had given him.

There was nothing to be done, so they kindled a fire with the briar thickets and slept that night hungry on the cold, hard ground. In the morning they heard the sound of dogs barking, as dogs will when the scent of game inflames them.

'What can that mean?' wondered Pryderi.

'Why stand here wondering when we can find out?' said Manawyddan and leaped up at once to saddle his horse.

180

They rode in the direction of the sound and came to a birch copse in a hidden glen. At their approach a score of fine hunting hounds came racing from the copse, shaking violently with fear, their tails low between their haunches. 'Unless I miss my guess,' remarked Pryderi upon seeing the dogs, 'some enchantment lies upon this little wood.'

No sooner had he spoken these same words, when out of the copse burst a shining white boar. The dogs cowered to see it, but after much urging, took up the trail and ran after it. The men followed until they drew near to where the boar stood at bay against the hounds.

Upon seeing the men, the white boar broke free and ran off once more. Again the men gave chase and again found the boar at bay against the hounds, and again the boar broke free when they came near.

Well, they pursued the boar until they came to a great fortress which neither of them had ever seen before, and they marvelled to see it. The hounds and the boar ran inside the stronghold and though the two men listened for the dog's barking, as long as they stayed they heard not a sound more.

'Lord,' said Pryderi, 'If you will, I shall enter this fortress and seek what has become of the dogs.'

'Lleu knows that is not a good idea,' replied Manawyddan. 'Neither you nor I have ever seen this fortress before, and if you ask my counsel, it is this: stay far from this strange place. It may be that whoever has placed the enchantment on the land has caused this fortress to appear.'

'It may be as you say, but I am loath to give up those fine hounds.' So, Manawyddan's good advice notwithstanding, Pryderi urged his reluctant horse forward and entered the gate of the fortress which was before them.

Once inside, however, he could see neither man nor beast nor boar nor dogs nor hall nor chamber. What he did discover was a great stand of marble stone. And hanging above the stand by four golden chains, whose ends extended upward so that he could not see any end to them, was a huge bowl of the finest gold he had ever seen, and Pryderi was no stranger to fine gold.

He approached the marble stand and saw Rhiannon, Manawyddan's wife, standing still as the stone itself, her hand touching the bowl.

'Lady,' said Pryderi, 'what do you here?'

As she made no answer, and as the bowl was of dazzling beauty, Pryderi thought no ill and came to where she stood and put his hands on the bowl. In the selfsame instant that he touched the bowl his hands stuck to the bowl and his feet stuck to the stand, and there he stood as one made of stone.

Awhile and awhile Manawyddan waited, but Pryderi did not return, and neither did the dogs. 'Well,' he said to himself, 'there is nothing to be done but go in after him.' And in he went.

There he saw, as Pryderi had seen, the magnificent golden bowl hanging by its golden chains. He saw his wife Rhiannon with her hand to the bowl, and Pryderi likewise. 'Lady wife,' he said, 'friend Pryderi, what do you here?'

Neither made to answer him, but his words provoked a response nonetheless, for no sooner had he spoken than the sound of a very great thunder echoed through the mysterious fortress and the mist rose up thick and dark. When it cleared, Rhiannon, Pryderi, the golden bowl and indeed the fortress itself were gone and not to be seen any more.

'Woe to me,' cried Manawyddan when he saw what had happened. 'I am all alone now with neither companions nor even dogs for company. Lleu knows I do not deserve such a fate as this. What shall I do?'

There was nothing to be done but go on with his life as best he could. He fished the streams and caught wild game, and began to till the soil, using a few grains of wheat he had in his pocket. The wheat flourished and in time he had enough to sow an entire field, and then another, and another. Great the wonder of it, for the wheat was the finest the world had ever seen!

Manawyddan bided his time and waited out the seasons until at last the wheat was so ripe he could almost taste the bread he would make. So, looking at his wonderful crop, he said to himself, 'I am a fool if I do not reap this tomorrow.'

He returned to his bothy to sharpen his wheat knife. The next morning when he came in the grey dawn to harvest his long-awaited crop, he found only naked stalks standing in the field. Each stalk had been snapped off where the ear joins to the stem and the grain carried off, leaving only stubble behind.

Much distressed, Manawyddan ran to the next field and saw

that all was as it should be. He examined the grain, which had ripened nicely. 'I am a fool if I do not reap this field tomorrow,' he said to himself.

He slept lightly that night and awoke with the break of day to reap his grain. Upon coming to the field, he saw that, as before, only naked stalks remained. The grain had been carried off. 'Alas!' he cried. 'What enemy is doing this to me? Lleu knows he is completing my downfall. If this keeps on I will be destroyed and all the land with me!'

With that Manawyddan hastened to his last remaining field. And behold, it was ripe and ready to be harvested. 'I am a fool if I do not reap this field tomorrow,' he said to himself, 'more, I will be a dead fool, for this is my last hope.'

And he sat down right where he was, intending to watch through the night and so catch the enemy that was destroying him. Manawyddan watched, and towards midnight what must have been the greatest uproar in the world reached his ears. He looked and saw the greatest host of mice ever assembled, so large a host he could scarce believe his eyes.

Before he could move the mice had fallen upon the field, each one scaling a stalk and nipping off the ear and carrying off the grain in its mouth, leaving only a naked stalk behind. Manawyddan rushed to the rescue of his field, but the mice might have been midges for all he could catch them.

One mouse, however, was heavier than all the others and could not move so quickly. Manawyddan pounced upon it and put it in his glove. He tied the opening with string and took the mouse prisoner back to his bothy. 'Well, as I would hang the thief that has ruined me,' he said to the mouse, 'Lleu help me, I will hang you.'

The next morning Manawyddan went out to the mound where this whole misadventure had begun, taking the mouse in the glove. And there he set two forked sticks upright in the ground at the highest part of the mound.

All at once a man appeared, riding by the foot of the mound on a thin-shanked horse. The man's clothes were worse than rags and he appeared a beggar. 'Lord, good day to you,' the beggarman called out.

Manawyddan turned to observe him. 'Lleu be good to you,' he replied. 'These past seven years I have seen not one man in all my kingdom, save yourself this very moment.'

'Well, I am only passing through these desolate lands,' the beggar told him. 'If it please you, lord, what work are you about?'

'I am executing a thief.'

'What sort of thief? The creature I see in your hand looks very like a mouse to me. It is scarcely fitting for a man of your exalted position to touch an animal like that. Surely, you will let it go.'

'Between you and me and Lleu, I will not!' said Manawyddan hotly. 'This mouse, and his brothers, have brought about my destruction. I mean to execute punishment upon it before I starve to death, and the judgement is hanging.'

The beggar went on his way and Manawyddan set about fixing a stick for the crossbeam between two forks. He had done this when a voice hailed him from below the mound. 'Good day to you, lord!'

'Lleu smite me if this is not becoming a busy place,' muttered Manawyddan to himself. He looked around and saw a fine noblewoman sitting on a grey palfrey at the foot of the mound.

'Good day to you, lady,' he called back to her. 'What brings you here?'

'I was only riding by when I saw you toiling up here. What work are you about?' she asked full politely.

'I am hanging a thief,' explained Manawyddan, 'if that is anything to you.'

'Indeed, it is nothing to me,' said the lady, 'but the thief appears to be a mouse. Still, I should say punish it by all means were it not so demeaning to a man of your obvious rank and dignity to hold commerce with such a low creature.'

'What would you have me do?' asked Manawyddan suspiciously.

'Rather than see you disgrace yourself further, I will give you a coin of gold to let it go.' She smiled winsomely as she said this and Manawyddan was almost persuaded.

'You speak well for this sorry mouse, but I am determined to end the life of the creature that has ended mine.'

'Very well, lord,' replied the lady haughtily, 'do as you wish.'

Manawyddan returned to his grim task, and taking the string from the glove, he tied one end around the mouse's neck. And as he drew the creature up to the crossbeam, there came a shout from the foot of the mound. 'Not a freckle on a face have I seen in seven years to this day, and now I am accosted at every turn,' he grumbled.

So saying, he turned around to meet an Archdruid with a score of ovates as retinue ranged behind him. 'Lleu give you good day,' said the Archdruid. 'What sort of work is my lord about?'

'If you must know, I am hanging a thief which has brought about my destruction,' replied Manawyddan.

'Forgive me, but you must be a fragile man indeed. For that appears to be a mouse in your hand.'

'It is a thief and destroyer, nonetheless,' snapped Manawyddan. 'Not that I should have to explain myself to you.'

'I require no explanation,' the Archdruid told him. 'But it grieves me full well to see a man of your obvious renown exacting punishment on a helpless creature.'

'Helpless is it? Where were you when this mouse and its myriad companions were devastating my fields and bringing about my demise?'

'As you are a reasonable man,' said the Archdruid, 'allow me to redeem the worthless creature. I will give you seven gold pieces to let it go.'

Manawyddan shook his head firmly. 'That will not do. I will not sell the mouse for any amount of gold.'

'Still, it is not seemly for a man of your rank to kill mice in this way,' countered the Archdruid. 'Therefore, let me give you *seventy* pieces of gold.'

'Shame on me if I sell it for twice that amount of gold!'

The Archdruid would not be put off. 'Nevertheless, good lord, I will not see you defile yourself by harming that animal. I will give you a hundred horses and a hundred men and a hundred fortresses.'

'I was lord of thousands,' replied Manawyddan. 'How should I take less than what I had?'

'As you will not accept that,' the Archdruid said, 'please name your price that I may meet it.'

'Well, there is a thing which might persuade me.'

'Name it and it is yours.'

'I wish the release of Rhiannon and Pryderi.'

'You shall have that,' promised the Archdruid.

'Between me and Lleu, that is not all.'

'What else then?'

'I wish the removal of the spell of enchantment from the realm of Dyfed and all my holdings.'

'You shall have that as well, only release the mouse unharmed.'

Manawyddan nodded slowly and looked into his hand. 'That I will do, only first I will know what this mouse is to you.'

The Archdruid sighed. 'Very well, you have the better of me. She is my wife — otherwise I would not ransom her.'

'Your wife!' cried Manawyddan. 'Am I to believe such a thing?'

'Believe it, lord, for it is true. I am the one who laid the enchantment upon your lands.'

'Who are you that you should seek my destruction?'

'I am Hen Dallpen, Chief of Druids in the Island of the Mighty,' replied the Archdruid. 'I acted against you out of revenge.'

'How so? What have I ever done to you?' For indeed, Manawyddan could think of nothing he had ever done to anger any man, be he priest or druid.

'You took the kingship of Bran the Blessed, and in this you did not obtain the blessing of the Learned Brotherhood. Therefore, I took it upon myself to enchant your kingdom, which I did.'

'I will say you did,' grumbled Manawyddan unhappily. 'What of my fields?'

'When some of those who follow me learned of the wheat, they begged me to turn them into mice in order that they might destroy your fields. The third night my own wife went with them, and she was heavy with child — although if she had not been so, you would not have caught her. But since she was and you did, I will give you Rhiannon and Pryderi and lift the spell from Dyfed and all your lands.' The Archdruid finished by saying, 'Now I have told you all, please release my wife.'

Manawyddan glared at the Chief Druid, 'I am a fool if I let her go now.'

'What else do you wish?' sighed the Archdruid. 'Tell me and let there be an end to this matter between us.'

'I wish that once the enchantment has been removed from the land there will never be another spell cast.'

'You have my most solemn promise. Now will you let the mouse go?'

'Not yet,' stated Manawyddan firmly.

The Archdruid sighed. 'Are we to be at this all day? What else do you require?'

'One thing else,' replied Manawyddan. 'I require that no revenge be taken because of what has happened here — neither on Rhiannon, or Pryderi, or my lands, or people, or possessions, or the creatures under my care.' He looked squarely in the Archdruid's eyes. '*Or* upon myself.'

'A cunning thought, Lleu knows. For indeed, had you not struck on that at last, you would have suffered far worse than anything you have suffered until now and all harm would be on your own head.'

Manawyddan shrugged. 'A man must protect himself however he can.'

'Now release my wife.'

'That I will not do until I see Rhiannon and Pryderi coming towards me with glad greetings.'

'Then look if you will,' said the Archdruid wearily. 'They are coming even now.'

Pryderi and Rhiannon appeared; Manawyddan hurried to meet them and they greeted him gladly and began to speak of what had happened to them all.

'I have done all you asked, and more than I would have done had you not asked,' implored the Archdruid. 'Do the one thing I have asked and release my wife.'

'Gladly,' replied Manawyddan. And he opened his hand and the mouse ran free.

The Archdruid scooped it up and whispered some words in the ancient secret tongue into the mouse's ear, and instantly the mouse began to change back into a comely woman whose belly swelled with the child she was carrying.

Manawyddan looked around the land and saw that every house and holding was back where it should be, complete with herds and flocks. And all the people were back where they should be, so that the land was inhabited as once before. Indeed, it was as if nothing had changed at all.

Only Manawyddan knew differently.

Here ends the Mabinogi of Manawyddan, my friend Wolf. Yes, it is a sad story in many of its parts. But I think you will agree that its end redeems.

What is that you say? Yes, there is more to it than first appears. How astute you are, O Wise Wolf. Of course, there is always more than meets the eye, or ear. This tale conceals a secret at its heart.

He that has ears to hear, let him hear!

THREE

The ravens croak at me from the treetops. They speak rudely; no respecters of persons, they say, 'Why do you not die, Son of Dust? Why do you cheat us of our meat?'

I am a king! How dare you affront me! How dare you slander me with insinuations!

Listen, Wolf friend, there is something I must tell you. . . Oh, but I cannot . . . I cannot! Forgive me. Please, you must forgive me, I cannot tell it.

Well, I am in misery. The scant trickle of my little spring as it drips from the rock is as my very life, my blood. Hear the bitter wind weeping among the cruel rock crags. Hear how it moans. Sometimes soft and low, sometimes as if to tear at the roots of the world. Sometimes a sigh or a thin, crooning song from the throat of a toothless hag.

I wander without sense or purpose: as if the aimless movement of my limbs is atonement for sins too loathsome to utter, as if in the slow, purposeless shuffling of one foot after the other I will find some release. Ha! There is no release!

Death, you have claimed all the others, why do you not claim me?

I shout. I rave. I cry into the depths of darkness and my voice falls into a pit of silence. There is no answer. It is the unknowing silence of the grave.

It is the unyielding silence of despair, black and eternal.

I was a king. I *am* a king. This rock I squat upon is all that is left to me; it is all my realm. Once better lands were mine. Away in the wealthy southland I raised my throne and Dyfed flourished. Maelwys and I were kings together, after the custom of the proud Cymry of old.

All the world turns back, turns back, turns again to the old ways, the forgotten yet familiar ways. In the old ways there is certainty and solace, there is the empty form of comfort. But there is no peace.

Hear then if you will, friend Wolf, the story of a man.

There was a feast following that first victory. How my sword did shine! Oh, it was a beautiful thing. Perhaps, I valued it too much. Perhaps, I tried too hard, attempted too much. But tell me, my Lord Jesu, whoever has attempted more?

We burned the Irish warboats, throwing in the corpses of the raiders before firing them and setting them adrift on the outrunning tide. The red flames danced and the black smoke rose to heaven and our hearts beat for joy. Maridunum was saved that day, suffering little more than a few dwellings lost and a few roofs fired. Ten of our people were killed — six of those were warriors.

Still, we had survived, and before the summer was out the first of Maelwys' new warband began arriving. We raised eighty that year. And sixty the next — Demetae and Silures; the dual clans of Dyfed produced fierce warriors.

Great Light, I see them: astride their tough ponies, ox-hide shields slung over their shoulders, spearpoints burnished sharp, the bold checked cloaks fluttering from their shoulders, torcs and armbands gleaming, their hair braided and bound like their horses' tails, or free-flying under their war caps, their eyes dark and hard as Cymry slate under smooth brows, and firm the set of their jaws. It was joy itself to lead such men.

We rode the circuit together, the ring of hillforts guarding our lands. And we erected timber platforms on the coastal hills for beacon fires. These were manned from the first summer on, until winter made an end of the warring season. And yes, we were attacked again and yet again — the barbarians knew that Maximus had gone, and the cream of the British troops with him — but we were never taken by surprise.

This was a good time for Maridunum. The weather was a boon companion to the land: days full of clear skies and sunlight, and an evening's rain to quench the thirsting root. All things flourished and bore fruit. Despite constant harrassment of raiders, our herds and flocks increased; our people thrived and were content.

That first autumn of my kingship — when I was certain my place was established — I spoke openly of my love for Ganieda to my mother and Maelwys. It was decided that a messenger should be sent to take word to Custennin of my intentions. We chose six of our company and sent them north to Goddeu with gifts and letters, both for the lord, and for my bride. I would have gone myself, but it is not done that way; and besides, I was needed in Maridunum.

The day the messengers rode out was a crisp, golden day in autumn, just after Samhain. The warmth of summer had lapsed, and nights could be cold, but still the days were fair, with the fire-tint brightening summer's greens. I stood in the road and watched them out of sight, thinking that only the winter, a few grey, wet months, a little space of darkness and cold, separated me from my light, my Ganieda.

Only one winter. Then I, too, would ride out to fetch my bride from her father's hearth and bring her home.

And it was much like I imagined it to be.

I spent a restless winter, riding with the hunting bands when I could, watching clouded skies shift over the land as they brought rain and a little snow now and then. I fussed with Maelwys' hounds; bathed in the heated bath; played chess with Charis, losing more often than winning; strummed my harp and sang in the hall of an evening; and generally haunted the villa like the restless shade I was — all the time waiting for the days to shorten and trees to bud.

'Be at ease, Merlin, you are as tense as a cat about to pounce,' Charis told me one night. It was after mid-winter, just after the Christ Mass, and we were at the nightly game of chess. She always played, with either Maelwys or me as her partner. 'You cannot make the days fly faster than they will.'

'That I know only too well,' I replied. 'If it had been for hoping, spring would have been with us long since.'

'You are so eager, my soul.' She looked at me over the chessboard, and I caught a hint of sadness in her voice and in her glance.

'What is it, Mother?'

Charis smiled and moved a gamepiece on the board. 'I was only thinking.'

'Yes?'

'These years have themselves flown, it seems to me. Was it so long ago that Taliesin came with his harp to my father's house?' She lifted a hand to my cheek. 'You are very like him,

Merlin. Your father would be proud to see he has sired such a noble son.' She lowered her hand and pushed a gamepiece with a fingertip, then sighed. 'My work is nearly finished.'

'Your work?' I moved one of the pieces, not caring which one, or where.

Charis countered the move. 'You will be Ganieda's responsibility from now on, my Hawk.'

'You make it sound as if I were going away across the sea. I am only moving into the chambers across the courtyard.'

'To me it will be as if you have travelled to the end of the earth,' she said solemnly. 'From the day you are married, you and Ganieda are one. You will give all of yourself to her, and she to you. You will be a world together and that is as it should be. I will have no place in it.'

I knew what she was saying, but I made light of it. I did not like to think that something that would bring me such happiness would cause someone I loved such pain. I wanted everyone to share my joy, and so Charis did, but her joy was bittersweet and could be no other way.

A little later, when we bade each other good night, she hugged me more tightly, and held me more closely. It was the first of many small farewells for us that helped ease the greater.

The day did finally come when I rode out for Goddeu myself, taking a score of warriors for company. We did not fear attack on the road, but the enemy was becoming more bold with each passing season. Also, we had heard of a hard winter north of the Wall; this would send the hungry Picti and Scotti out on the war trail all the sooner.

Riding with twenty of my best was only prudent, and it would serve to set an edge to winter-dulled skills. But aside from the usual spring-swollen rivers and mountain passes that had not yet thawed, the journey proved unremarkable. Indeed, it seemed to me as if I had travelled the Goddeu road so often that I remembered every rock and bush and ford along the way.

Nor did we lack for travelling companions. For, despite the rumours of raiders of one sort or another, there were many others on the road as well. More than normal for early spring. It was as if men knew that the days of free-ranging trade over longer distances were drawing to a close and were anxious to do what they could before the end came.

Yet, there was an air of exuberance, of carefree comradeship — although that might have been my own mood colouring things for me. Oh, but it was a fine journey.

And the day I rode into King Custennin's lakeside stronghold, my heart swelled to bursting. It was a glorious day, all sun bright and adazzle with lights off the lake. Cleanswept the sky, deep and azure blue; the woodland flowers full and sweet on the gentle air; the trees absolutely piping with birdsong — it was a grand day. Every man should have such a wedding day.

Although the actual ceremony was yet some time away, the day I rode into Goddeu and saw Ganieda standing before the door of the king's great hall — dressed in a cream-white mantle fringed with golden tassels and worked in emerald green thread, with white wildflowers plaited in her black hair — that day, that instant, my soul was married to Ganieda's.

We were so happy!

I do not remember catching her up to sit before me in the saddle, although they say I did — coming at her on the run and leaning low to sweep her away with me in a wild and joyous ride. I only remember her arms around my neck and her lips on mine as we galloped along the sparkling lakeshore, the horse's hooves striking up showers of diamonds for us.

'How did you know I would come today?' I asked, when we dismounted at last outside Custennin's palace.

'I did not know, my lord,' Ganieda answered with mock solemnity.

'Yet you were ready and waiting.'

'As I have been ready and waiting each day since the first flowers bloomed.' She laughed that I should marvel at that. 'I would not have my love find me otherwise.'

'I love you, Ganieda,' I said. 'With all the heart and soul in me, I love you. And I have missed you.'

'Let us never part again,' she said.

Just then I was hailed from the doorway, and Gwendolau appeared. 'Myrddin Wylt! Is that you? But for the wolfskin on your back I would not know you, man. Unhand my sister and let me look at you.'

'Gwendolau, my brother!' We gripped arms in the old greeting and he beat me happily about the shoulders with his hands.

'You have changed, Myrddin. Look at how you have filled out. And what is this?' He raised a hand to my torc. 'Gold? I thought gold was the sole right of kings.'

'It is and well you know it,' said Ganieda. I smiled to hear the possessive note in her voice. 'Does he not look every inch a king?'

'A thousand pardons, lady,' he laughed. 'I need not ask how it has gone with you, for I see you have weathered well.'

'And you, Gwendolau.' The year had wrought its change in him as well. He appeared more like Custennin than ever, a veritable giant among men. 'It is good to see you.'

'Allow me to see to your men and their horses,' he said. 'You and Ganieda have much to discuss, I should guess. We will talk later.' And, with a happy slap of my back, he walked off at once.

'Come,' Ganieda tugged on my hand, 'let us walk awhile.'

'Yes, but first I must pay my respects to the lord of this place.'

'That you can do later. He is hunting today and will not return until dusk.'

So we walked, and our path led us into the woods where we found a leafy bower and sat down on the sunwarmed grass. I held Ganieda in my arms and we kissed, and if I could have stopped the world from turning, I know I would have. Just feeling the sweet, yielding weight of her in my arms was earth and sky to me.

Great Light, I cannot bear it!

FOUR

No. . . no, listen Wolf, my mind is calm. I will continue:

Custennin was well disposed to the match. Gwendolau must have given his father a good report of my kinsmen and lineage. Indeed, he could have done nothing else. The joining of our houses would be to affirm honourable and long-established ties, something both Avallach and Maelwys were anxious to do as well.

The south needed the north, and needed it strong. The attacks that year-by-year drove deeper into the heartland invariably originated in the north; Picti, Scotti, Attacoti, Cruithne: these were all northern tribes. And the Saecsen and Irish, who were becoming bolder and more belligerent with each passing season, when they came, they came across the sea and into Ynys Prydein from the unguarded north.

But the incessant raiding was driving the few stable and trustworthy Britons north of the Wall back into the south — those that, like Elphin and his people, had not already left long ago. So it was becoming more and more difficult to hold the middle ground between the war-lusting north and the civilized south.

Without strong northern allies the south became more vulnerable than ever. Rome had realized this from the beginning, of course. The Eagles built the Wall — more a symbolic demarcation than an actual defence, although it was that, as long as the garrisons were manned. But the true defence of the south had been, had always been, the strength of the northern kings.

This strength was faltering. It is no wonder that the southern Britons had begun to look fearfully to the north as both the cause of their troubles and their salvation. It was to the benefit of both to form strong alliances, and there is no stronger tie than blood.

Kinship would do what the administrative might of Rome could not. Or we would all go down together.

As king, this was to be my work. I saw, perhaps more clearly than others, the desperate need for accord between kingdoms. The few and feeble attempts at friendship between the north and south, good though they were, were not enough.

If we were to survive we would have to find and welcome ways of encouraging the northern kingdoms, and supporting them. This would mean putting away the petty concerns of rank and wealth, the small rivalries of small men, for the greater good of all. On this the future depended. On this we would stand or fall.

I began thinking of one great kingdom made up of all the smaller kingdoms, united, yet each independent of the others, and all contributing to the general welfare and security. Not an empire, nor a state: a nation of tribes and peoples, ruled by a Council of Kings, each lord with an equal say. This was important, for, if we were to survive the barbarian onslaught, it would have to be as a single united entity presenting one, unassailable front, not the fractious scattering of divided kingdoms — which is what we were.

I began dreaming of this great kingdom made up of smaller kingdoms. This great kingdom would be ruled by a single great king, a paramount king, or chief king — one elected from among the Council of Kings to rule over all. A High King whom the lower kings, princes, lords and noblemen would serve.

You might say, as others have said, that this was foolishness, or at best the idle whimsy of a self-important young ass. Better, they said, to stand tall and demand our rights as citizens of the greatest empire the world has ever known.

'Petition Rome!' they cried. 'We are citizens. Protection is our right, is it not? Send to the Emperor with petitions. Bring the legions back, tell him. Now that Maximus wears the purple, he will listen. He will not let us be burned and bled by savages.'

But Maximus did not long wear his imperial robe and laurel circlet. When he marched on Rome, as I knew he would — rather, as old Pendaran Gleddyvrudd had predicted — Theodosius, son of Theodosius the Conqueror, captured him and marched him into the Senate in chains. A few days later,

Magnus Maximus was beheaded in the Colosseum. And it was not only the man that died that day: the dream of empire was extinguished in the blood-soaked sand before those jaded, jeering crowds.

Bring the Eagles back!

Yes, bring the Eagles back. Bring them all back, for all the good it will do. Is everyone blind? Can no one see?

Never did we shelter beneath the Eagle's wings. *We* were the Eagle. When the first Romans had laid their roads and forts across the countryside and then turned aside to other, more pressing matters elsewhere, who took up the standard? Who buckled on the breastplates? Who took up the gladius and pike? Whose sons filled the garrison rosters all those years? Who took Roman names and paid tax in Roman coins? Who raised the cities and built the great villa farms?

Was it Rome?

Oh, by all means bring the Eagles back. I would have them see how well the Briton wields the tools he has been given. For that is what we have always done. Rome left long, long ago, but we did not know it. Instead, we flattered ourselves, and were likewise flattered to be sure, that we were favoured children of Mother Rome.

Foster children, maybe. I will not say bastard children, for once Rome did look kindly on us, and from time to time sent her agents to help us look after our affairs — for a price, always for a price. Our wonderful Mother was always more interested in the corn and beef and wool and tin and lead and silver that we produced and paid to her in tax and tribute, than she was interested in our welfare.

Yet that was in the best of times, my friends. What do you suppose she thinks of us now — if she thinks of us at all?

The truth is a bitter draught, but drain the cup and we will find our strength in it. We are not weak; we are not bereft of hope. Our hope is where it always was: in our own hearts, and in the strong steel in our hands.

Yes, I began seeing the vision of a free people ruling themselves without let or hindrance from distant emperors whose hearts had grown cold; a nation of Britons ruling Britons for the good of all who sheltered in this fair land, high and low alike. . .

It was Taliesin's vision: the Kingdom of Summer.

FIVE

The heavenly star-host wheels through the sky, the seasons spin away in the slow dance of years. I squat on my rock and the rags of my clothes flap around me. Summer sun bakes and blisters, winter wind slices flesh from bone, spring rain soaks to the soul, autumn mists chill the heart.

Yet, Merlin endures. Destiny waits while Merlin squats on his rock above dark Celyddon. Forest Lord. . . Cernunnos' Son. . . Wild Man of the Wood. . . Myrddin Wylt. . . Merlin. . . he of the Strong Enchantment, who walked with kings, the very same, who now grubs among rotting apples for his food — and the future must wait.

How is that, Wolf? The kingmaking? Have I not? Then I will tell you.

Dafyd came to Maridunum the day of the victory feast, and he performed a rite of consecration for me as part of my kingmaking. With Maelwys and Charis, and several of the chiefs who had been summoned by news of the raid, Dafyd and I rode to the chapel, where, crowded together in the sweet silence round the altar, we all knelt and prayed for God's blessing on my reign.

Dafyd then anointed me with holy oil, touching my forehead in the sign of the cross; and he anointed my sword as well, saying, 'Behind this wall of steel shall Our Lord's church flourish.'

We all said 'Amen' to that. He blessed me from the holy text, then kissed me with a holy kiss, and I him, whereupon each of the others in the room knelt and stretched forth their hands to cover my feet as sign of their submission to me. All except Maelwys, of course, but he embraced me like a father.

In this way was I made King of Dyfed.

I began my reign in the usual way, I suppose: I shared wine with the men who would follow me. I distributed gifts among them and accepted their pledges of fealty. There was singing — Blaise came with four of the Learned Brotherhood, who gave us such song as is reserved for, well, for a king's ears alone — and the feasting continued for three more days.

Between the time Blaise had handed me my kingship — I still think of it as his doing; but what of that?; the druids of old were kingmakers and it was their right — and the time of my crowning, he had vanished. Only to reappear again with a golden torc. Pendaran had said he would give me his torc and also the throne he had occupied for nearly fifty years. But as he was still somewhat active in the affairs of the realm, that hardly seemed right. Since there had never been a time when three kings ruled in Dyfed at once, Maelwys ordered a new torc to be made instead.

Blaise must have guessed that this would be the case, and he swept into the hall bearing the torc in his hands, as if it were the kingship itself that he held. At his appearance the hall fell silent. Men stared at the object he held. Had they never seen that ring of gold before?

I admit, his entrances and exits could be arresting, but I saw nothing unusual about his bearing a torc to me. Perhaps it was because I saw it in the hand of a friend, while others saw it in the hand of the bard, and the more significant for that. However it was, he caused quite a stir.

He bade me kneel before him while he stood over me with the torc, as if with a talisman of power. In the eyes of the Cymry, I suppose it was a charmed thing. The church had power, most would allow, but so did the images and rites of old, which had the additional benefit of being hallowed by long tradition. It was all well and good to be anointed by the priest in the chapel in the wood. Better still to receive the torc of kingship from the hand of a druid.

Well, I had both.

'Is this necessary?' I hissed under my breath. The hall had fallen silent; every eye was on me. 'I've already been consecrated.'

'Is it killing you?' he whispered as he bent the soft yellow metal in his hands, spreading the ends to fit around my neck. 'Just be quiet and let me do this.'

He held the torc before me, and I saw that it had two bears' heads carved at the ends; their eyes were tiny sapphires, and each wore a collar of equally small rubies. I stared in astonishment. Where on earth did he get it?

'Did you steal it?' I whispered to him as he placed the torc around my neck.

'Yes,' he said. 'Now be quiet.'

He gently pushed the two ends of the torc together and, lifting his hands to my head, made the kingship speech in the old tongue. It is doubtful anyone in the hall, or even in all of Dyfed, knew the old Briton language any more — the Dark Tongue, men called it, from before Rome came. Nevertheless, they appreciated the significance of it just then.

Blaise, Jesu bless him, was trying his best to help me with all he had. He was showing the people gathered there that in the new king all past and future were brought together. He was reminding them of the old ways, in the same way Dafyd had shown the way of the future.

But the old ways are evil ways — I have heard that said by more ignorant clerics than bears thinking about. Convenient, perhaps, to a priesthood neither knowledgeable nor tolerant of things belonging to another priesthood and another time. Much in elder days was evil, I admit; I am not like one of those pig-headed fools who stare into the embers of a dying fire and think to see the kindling of tomorrow's flame. But neither do I deny the good where I find it.

And there was some good, I assure you. In every age, there is some good. God is ever present, ever eager to be found if men will look. I know I searched.

Blaise understood this, too. He wanted me to enjoy the dual blessings of past and future, thinking that the people would follow me more readily. He too believed in the Kingdom of Summer.

Unlike me, however, he thought the people would need to be coaxed towards it. I believed I had only to throw the doors open wide and all would rush in gladly. But then, I was very young.

Blaise, of course, knew better — which is why he went round telling all those stories about me. 'What men believe, Hawk,' he told me once, 'that is what they follow. Their hearts are willing — all men *want* to believe. Very few can follow a dream, even a true and beautiful dream. But they will follow a *man* with a dream. So,' he smiled deviously, 'I am giving them a man.'

When he put the bear's head torc on my neck, I tell you I felt a king. It was without doubt a king's torc and, wherever he had found it, I knew a king had worn it. Perhaps many kings. Indeed, it was a thing of power.

The torc, Wolf, I wear it still. See? Ganieda liked it, too. Yes, she did.

After that Maelwys and I began making plans for repairing the hillforts — not that they were in poor repair. But none of them were supplied any more, nor stocked with grain and water; a few lacked strong gates, and most had gaps in the walls, and mud-choked wells. The people were using thorn bushes or briar hedges to close them — which worked well enough to keep cattle from wandering, but would be no defence at all against Saecsen or Irish spears. No one actually lived in the hillforts any more, had not for a long, long time. But Maelwys foresaw the day when fully stocked and gated forts would be required.

We also began planning the series of coastal beacons; the first, as I have said, were built that summer when the warriors began arriving. From the beginning, there was much activity around the villa, and in Maridunum. The mood was high. In all it was a good summer.

I did not often have time to stop and reflect upon my good fortune, but in those days I prayed as I had never prayed before: for my people, for strength, for wisdom to lead. Mostly for wisdom. It is a lonely thing to be a king. Even sharing the burden with Maelwys it was not easy for me.

For one thing, many of the younger warriors had apparently chosen me for their sovereign. They more or less attached themselves to me, looking to me to lead them. Maelwys helped me as he could, and Charis too, but when men hold you as their lord, there is not much anyone else can do. It is up to you and you alone how best to lead them.

We spent many long nights, Maelwys and I, talking, talking, talking. Rather, Maelwys talked and I listened, carefully, to every word. He taught me much about the handling of men, and in the teaching taught me much about life.

I also saw a good deal of Blaise, and of Dafyd. And in the autumn, just before Samhain and the end of harvest, I travelled to Ynys Avallách with Charis, and then went on to

Caer Cam to see Grandfather Elphin and the others. I stayed with them — such good people, such noble hearts — until the last leaves clung to the trees and the winds turned cold off the sea and then went back to the Tor where Charis was waiting to return to Dyfed.

The Isle of Apples, which is what some called it, had not altered in so much as a stone out of place. Time was frozen there, it seemed; no one aged, nothing changed. And nothing dared intrude on the holy serenity of the place. It remained, remains still, an almost spiritual place, a place where natural forces — like time and seasons and tides and life — obey other, perhaps older, laws.

Avallach now spent most of his time perusing the holy text with Collen, or one of his brother priests from Shrine Hill, as it had become known. I think he had it in his mind to become something of a priest himself. The Fisher King would have made a very strange, albeit compelling, cleric.

That autumn, I remember, he began showing the first interest in the Chalice, the cup Jesu had used at his last supper, and which the Arimathean tin merchant Joseph had brought with him in the days of the first shrine on Shrine Hill.

For some reason, I did not mention to him that I had seen an image, or vision, of the cup. I do not know why. He would have been keenly interested to hear of it, but something held me back — as if it was unseemly to say anything about it just yet. I remember thinking, 'Later I will tell him. We must get back to Maridunum.' Although we were in no particular hurry at the time, it seemed best to let it go.

That autumn, also, I sent my messengers to Ganieda. Whereupon, I settled down to a drear winter of the most restless waiting I have known. But that I have already told. . .

SIX

How long, Wolf? How long, old friend, have I sat here upon my rock and watched the seasons fly? Up they swirl, winging back to the Great Hand which gave them. . . they fly like the wild geese, but never more return.

What of Merlin? What of the Wild Man of the Wood, eh? Will he never more return?

There was a time when. . . never mind, Wolf, it does not matter. Orion's Belt, Cygnus, the Great Bear — these things matter; these things are important. Let all else fade and fall. Only the eternal stars will remain when all else is unthinking dust.

I watch the winter stars glitter hard in the frozen sky. Were I not so forlorn I would conjure a fire to warm myself. Instead, I watch the high cold heaven perform its inscrutable work. I gaze at the hoar frost on the rocks and see the patterns of a life there. I stare at the black water in my bowl and I see the shapes of possibility and inevitability.

I will tell you about inevitability, shall I? Yes, Wolf, I will tell you and then you will know what I know.

We were living in Dyfed. I was ruling my people, little by little helping them to see the vision of the Summer Realm. It was in my mind that if I could only show my people the shape and substance of the kingdom I meant to create, they would follow me willingly.

I had no hint, then, of the forces arrayed against me. Oh, we struggle against a cunning adversary. Never doubt it. We move about on our crust of earth and we imagine we see the world as it is. What we see is the world we imagine.

No man sees the world as it is.

Unless, perhaps, granted sight by the Enemy. But I will not talk of him. Ask Dafyd, he will tell you. He will find it easier, for he has never had to stand against him face to face. Words alone are useless to describe the repugnance, the repulsion, the utter loathsome abhorrence. . . Ah, but let it go. Let it go, Merlin. Linger not upon it.

I remember when he came to me. I remember his young face, full of hope and apprehension. He little appreciated what he was doing, the young fool, but he knew how badly he wanted it, how much it mattered to him. Of course, I was flattered a little and I saw some benefit in it for both of us, or I would not have allowed it. As it was —

What? Have I not? Pelleas, Wolf; I am speaking of Pelleas, my young steward. Who else?

Along with Gwendolau and some of Avallach's people, I had ridden to Llyonesse to hold council with Belyn. We were hoping to make a treaty among us to uphold one another through the barbarian incursions that had become more than annoying of late. We needed the help of those south of Mor Hafren and along the far southern coasts where the Irish had begun making their landfalls in the hidden little bays and inlets. Once ashore, they could strike north or east as they would.

Maelwys and Avallach believed that by linking the coastland with a system of watchtowers and beacon fires, we could discourage these landings, perhaps even end them. For if the Irish knew they would be met in force at each landing, and that their losses would outweigh their gains at every turn, they might abandon the war trail for more peaceful pursuits.

So we took the plan to Belyn. He was not easy to convince; he did not like the Irish any more than we did, but working with us would force him out of his cherished isolation. He much preferred his solitary way. But in the end, Maildun argued for us and won Belyn's support.

The night before we were to leave Llyonesse, Pelleas came to me. 'Lord Merlin,' he said, 'forgive me for disturbing your rest.' I had retired early to my chamber — haggling always taxes me, and after three days of it I was weary.

'Come in, Pelleas, come in. I was enjoying a small cup of wine before going to sleep. Will you share one with me?'

He accepted the cup I offered him, but he did not drink. I could see by the look on his face that it had cost him a great deal already to come here, and that he had a matter of some importance on his mind. Tired as I was, I did not rush him, but let him come at the thing in his own time.

I sat down on the edge of my bed and offered him the chair. He sat, holding the cup in his hands, staring into it. 'What is it like in the north?' he asked.

'Oh, it is a wilder country, to be sure. Much of it is woodland and there are mountains and moors where nothing grows but the peat moss. It can be a lonely place, but it is not so bleak and terrible as men make out. Why do you ask?'

He shrugged. 'I have never been to the north.'

Something in his voice made me ask, 'Is that where you think I live?'

'Do you not?'

I laughed. 'No, lad. Dyfed is only across Mor Hafren, not far from Ynys Avallach. It is no great distance.' He was embarrassed by this, so I went on to explain. 'The northland I was talking about is far, far north indeed. It is many and many days ride — above the Wall itself.'

He nodded. 'I see.'

'I lived in that region for a time, you know.' His head came up at these words. 'Yes, I did. I lived with Hawk Fhain — a clan of Hill Folk who follow their herds from grazing to grazing all over the region up there. But the land goes even further north than that.'

'It does?'

'Oh, indeed, it does. There is Pictish land further north. Now that *is* a forbidding place, where they make their homes.'

'Do the Picti really paint themselves blue?'

'For a fact they do. In various ways. Some of them even stain their skins permanently in the most intricate patterns — the fiercer warriors do this.'

'It must be something to see,' he said cautiously.

'You should see it sometime,' I replied, sensing this was what he wanted from me.

Pelleas shook his head slowly and sighed — I think he had rehearsed it. 'No, that is not for me.'

Again I made the required response. 'Why not?'

'I never can go *anywhere*.' His voice had risen, and the words were a lament. 'I have never even been to Ynys Avallach!'

Here we had come to the thing he wanted to say. 'What is it, Pelleas?' I asked gently.

He started up from his chair so quickly, some of the wine splashed over the rim of the cup. 'Take me with you. I know you are leaving tomorrow — I want to go with you. I will be your steward. You are a king; you will need someone to serve you.' He paused and added desperately, 'Please, Merlin, I must get away from here or I will die.'

The way he put it, I was not entirely certain that he would not fall down dead immediately upon our departure. I thought about this. I had no real need of a steward, but there might be a place for him in Maelwys' house. 'Well, I will ask Belyn,' I offered.

He threw himself back into the chair in a slump. 'He will never let me go. He hates me.'

'That I heartily doubt. No doubt the king has other things on his mind and —'

'Things more important than the welfare of his own son?'

'His son — ' I looked at him closely. 'What are you saying?'

He took a hasty sip from the cup. His secret was out and now he was steeling himself for the fight he sensed would come. 'I *am* Belyn's son.'

'I must apologize,' I told him, remembering our first meeting and how I treated him as a servant. 'I seem to have mistaken a prince for a steward.'

'Oh, that I am. At least, I am no prince,' he sneered.

'Make it plain, please, I am tired.'

He nodded, his eyes downcast. 'My mother is a servant in this house.'

I understood perfectly. Pelleas was Belyn's bastard and the king would not acknowledge him. He felt his only chance to make a life for himself lay as far from Llyonesse as he could get. For the same reason Belyn would not acknowledge him, the king was not likely to let the lad go either. I told him this.

'Would it hurt to try?' He was so desperate. 'Please?'

'No, it will not hurt to try.'

'Then you will ask him?'

'I will ask him.' I rose and took the cup from his hand. 'Now you are leaving and I am going to sleep.'

He rose but made no move towards the door. 'What if he says no?'

'Let me sleep on it tonight. I will think of something.'

'I will come for you in the morning, shall I? We can ask him together.'

I sighed. 'Pelleas, leave it to me. I have said I will help you if I can. That is all I can do at this moment. Let us leave it there for tonight.'

He agreed, apprehensively, but I think he was not displeased. Nevertheless, at cock's crow the next morning, Pelleas was standing at my door, ready and eager to see which way his fate would swing. As there would be no getting rid of him until the thing was done, I agreed to see Belyn as soon as may be.

In fact, it was not until we were making ready to depart, that I was able to speak to Belyn alone. Thinking my chances were greater without anyone else looking on, I had to wait — and endure Pelleas' pleading stares — to find my chance.

'A word, Lord Belyn,' I said, seizing my opportunity as we walked from the hall. Gwendolau and Baram, and the others, had left moments before and we trailed after.

'Yes?' he said stiffly.

'I am interested in one of your servants.'

He stopped and turned towards me. If he guessed what I had in mind, he did not show it. 'What is your interest, my Lord Merlin?'

'As a new-made king, I am without servants of my own.'

'You want one of mine, is that it?' He smiled frostily and rubbed his chin. 'Well, name him, whoever you fancy, and if I can spare the man he is yours.'

'You are most generous, lord,' I said.

'Which one?' he asked absently, turning to the door once more.

'Pelleas.'

Belyn swung back to face me. His eyes searched mine to determine what I knew.

'I understand he has no formal duties,' I volunteered, hoping to make it easier for him.

'No — no formal duties.' He was working furiously on this, weighing implications and possibilities. 'Pelleas. . . ah, you have spoken to him about this?'

'Yes, briefly. I did not wish to say too much until I could consult you.'

'That was wise.' He turned away again and I thought he would leave the matter there. Instead, he said, 'What says Pelleas? Would he go, do you think?'

'I believe I could persuade him.'

'Then take him.' Belyn took a step towards the door and hesitated, as if to change his mind.

'Thank you,' I said. 'He will be well treated, on that you have my word.'

He only nodded and then walked away. I think I sensed relief in his mood as he moved off. Perhaps in this arrangement he saw an answer to an awkward dilemma.

Pelleas, of course, was overjoyed. 'You had better collect your things and saddle your horse,' I told him. 'There is not much time.'

'I am ready now. My horse was saddled before I came to you this morning.'

'Very certain of yourself, were you not?'

'I had faith in you, my lord,' he replied happily and ran off to bring his things.

If I thought that was the end of it, I was mistaken. No sooner had Pelleas disappeared than I became aware of a presence watching me. I turned back to the empty hall to see that it was not empty now. A figure, swathed head to foot in black, stood in the centre of the great room.

My first instinct was to flee but, as if in answer to my thoughts, the stranger said, 'No, stay!'

I waited as the figure approached. The full black cloak was ornately worked in tiny, fantastic designs all in black and gold thread, the tall boots likewise; black gloves covered the hands nearly to the elbow, and the head was covered in a hood-like cap that had a gauzy black material attached to it, so that the face was veiled from view.

This strange apparition came to stand before me and I felt a dizzying sensation, as if the stone beneath my feet had lost its solidity, stones become fluid mud. I put out my hand to the doorpost beside me.

The black-robed figure studied me intently for a moment. I could see eyes glittering behind the veil. 'Have we met?' asked the stranger in a voice deceptively cordial — coming, as it was, from so forbidding an aspect. And it was female.

'We have not, lady, for I feel certain I would recall it.'

'Oh, but we know one another, I think.'

She was right in this, for I knew full well who it was that addressed me. My own dread had told me, if nothing else.

'Morgian,' I said, my tongue finding movement of its own. How quickly her name leapt to my tongue.

'Well met, Merlin,' she replied politely.

At the speaking of my name I felt a delicious thrill, sensual and seductive — like that a man might feel in succumbing to some forbidden pleasure. Oh, she had many kinds of power and knew their various uses well. I actually wanted her, at that moment.

'How is my dear sister?' she asked, taking a half step and lifting the gauze from her face. At last we stood face to face.

Morgian was beautiful, very much like Charis; the family resemblance was strong. But at the moment my mother was the furthest person from my mind. I stared into a face of seeming exquisite and compelling beauty.

I say 'seeming', because I am not at all certain now that it was not enchantment. She was of the Fair Folk, of course, and had the natural elegance of her race. But Morgian far exceeded this. Hers was the dreamlike beauty of a vision: heart-rending, flawless, perfect in all its parts.

Her hair gleamed like spun gold, pale and shimmering; her eyes were large and luminous, flecked with the green fire of matched emeralds beneath golden lashes and smooth, gently-arched brows; her skin was white as milk, contrasting with the deep blood red of her lips. Her teeth were even and fine as pearls.

Yet. . . and yet, around her, or behind her, like spreading black wings, or a living, invisible shadow, I saw an aura, brooding dark and ugly, as if made up of all the nameless horrors of nightmare. This thing seemed alive with churning, writhing torment, and it clung to her — although whether it was part of her, or she part of it, I cannot say. But it was a real presence, as much as fear or hate or cruelty are real.

'You are long in answering, Merlin,' she said, lifting a hand to my face. Even through the fine leather of her glove, I could feel the cold fire of her touch. 'Is something wrong?'

'Charis is well,' I said, and felt I had betrayed my mother merely by uttering her name.

'Oh, I am glad to hear it.' She smiled and I was shocked

to feel genuine warmth in her smile. Immediately, I thought I must be mistaken in my estimation of her. Perhaps she did care after all, perhaps the evil I sensed in her was of my own imagining. But then she added casually, as one might upon suddenly thinking of it: 'And what of Taliesin?'

The words were malice itself — a poison dagger in the hand of a skilful, hateful enemy.

'Taliesin is dead these many years,' I intoned flatly. 'As you well know.'

She appeared taken aback by this news. 'No,' she gasped, shaking her head in mock disbelief, 'he was so alive when last I saw him.'

It was a wicked thing to say. I did not think it needed a reply.

'Well,' Morgian went on, 'perhaps it could not be helped. I imagine Charis was devastated by his death.' The word was precise as a knife prick.

I reached for a weapon as well. 'Indeed, but her grief was not without some consolation at least.'

This drew her interest. 'What consolation could there be?'

'Hope,' I replied. 'As my father was a believer in the True God, he had won eternal life through the grace of Lord Jesu, the Christ. One day they will be reunited in Paradise. That is the hope and promise that sustains her.' It was a clean thrust and I felt the blade go in.

She smiled again and I felt the power leap up in her, as it reached out to me like a hand poised to slap. 'We need not dwell upon such unhappiness,' Morgian said. 'We have other things to discuss.'

'Do we, lady?'

'Not here; not now. But come and visit me again,' she invited. 'You know the way, I think. Or Pelleas will show you. We might become friends, you and I. Oh, I should like that, Merlin, to be your friend.' Those striking green eyes narrowed seductively. 'You would like that, too. I know you would. There is much I could teach you.'

Such was the power of the woman that even though words like 'friend' were so unnatural, so alien to her, I still believed she meant it. Her charm could beguile and it could confuse and convince; it could make the most impossible, repulsive suggestions seem logical and attractive.

I said nothing, so she continued, 'Oh, but you are soon leaving, are you not? Well, another time. Yes, we will meet again, Merlin. Trust on it.'

The prospect chilled me to the marrow. Great Light, spread your protecting wings around me!

She pulled the veil across her face once more and stepped back abruptly. 'I must not keep you,' she said, and turning away made a small flicking motion with her hands.

I could move once more, and lingered there no longer, hurrying from the hall and through the corridor beyond, anxious to put as much distance between Morgian and myself as possible. Outside, the horses were ready and I vaulted to the saddle without a backward glance.

Gwendolau was waiting with the others and regarded me closely as I swung into the saddle, perhaps sensing something amiss. 'One other will be coming,' I told him. 'Pelleas is riding with us.'

'Is everything well with you, Merlin? You look as if someone has just danced across your grave.'

I forced a laugh. 'There is nothing wrong with me that a good day's ride will not cure.'

He climbed into his saddle beside me. 'Are you certain?'

'Yes, brother, I am certain.' I gripped his arm; I needed the reassurance of flesh just then. 'But I thank you for your concern.'

The big man shrugged amiably. 'I am only thinking of myself. My sister would flay me alive if I let any ill befall her husband.'

'For the sake of your oversized hide, I will try never to let that happen,' I told him with a laugh, and felt Morgian's influence receding.

Pelleas came alongside a moment later. He had a small bag slung on the back of his horse and a great grin on his face. 'I am ready,' he announced happily.

'Then let us ride, my friends,' called Gwendolau. 'The day is speeding before us!'

We rode out from the forecourt and through the tower-bound gates of Belyn's palace, and no one came to see us away.

SEVEN

They say Merlin slew a thousand thousand, that the blood of the enemy ran red upon the land, that rivers stank with floating corpses from Arderydd to Caer Ligualid, that the sky darkened with the wings of feasting birds flocking to the battlefield, that the smoke of the cremation fires rolled to the very dome of heaven. . .

They say Merlin mounted to the sky, taking the shape of an avenging hawk to fly away to the mountains.

Yet, when the voices of the searchers rang in the wood, where did Merlin hide? In what pit did Merlin cower while they cried out to him?

O, Wise Wolf, tell me why was the light of the sun taken from me? Why was the living heart carved from my breast? Why do I haunt the desolate wastes, hearing only the sound of my own voice in the mournful sigh and moan of the wind on bare rock?

Tell me also, fair sister, how long has it been? How many years have passed me here in Celyddon's womb?

What is that you say? What of Morgian?

Ah, yes, I have often wondered. . . what of Morgian?

That first time, of course, was just the brandishing of weapons between foes. She wanted to see who it was she would destroy. She wanted to savour the exquisite hunger before the kill. She was the cat taunting the mouse, trying her claws.

But I do not think she was entirely certain of me then. The meeting was necessary, because she was not a fool and she would not presume to begin her battle without first assessing the strength of her adversary.

Strange to say, but I believe Morgian's offer of friendship was genuine — that is, as genuine as anything about her could be. She meant it, although she could not have had the slightest idea of true friendship because she was not capable of it. But she was so hollow, so empty of all natural feeling that she could adopt any posture as it occurred to her; she used emotion as one might use a cloak, changing when it suited her. Still, she believed what she felt — amity, sincerity, even love of a perverse sort — until she abandoned it in favour of another, more practical weapon.

Thus, Morgian could make the incredible offer of friendship to me, and make it seem genuine, because she herself believed it — if only for as long as it took her to say it. In that sense, it was not a trap. She no doubt thought it might be advantageous to her in some way to have me as an ally and so spoke sincerely. This was part of her treachery: she could change as quickly as the wind, and put the full force of her being behind the moment's intent.

For Morgian there was no higher ideal, no greater call to be heard above the deafening shriek of her own all-consuming will. There was no core of human pity or compassion to appeal to.

There was only Morgian, rarest beauty, frozen and fatal, mistress of the sweet poison, the warm kiss of death.

Though she ultimately meant me harm — make no mistake about that, I did not — Morgian had not come to join battle with me that day. Only, as I have said, to try her weapons and see what mine might be. I have no clear idea of what she discovered about me in that regard, although she revealed much about herself.

But she was *vain*! Such vanity is rare in a human soul. But then, Morgian is no ordinary human, and possesses no ordinary soul.

EIGHT

Ganieda! What do you here, my soul?

Ohhhh, your flesh is so white. . .

Go back, go back! I cannot bear it. . . Please, go back.

Drink a little water, Hawk. You thirst; you rave. Your chalybeate spring will revive you.

Gods of stream and air, gods of hills and high places, gods of wells and water springs, gods of the crossroads, forge, and hearth . . . All gods bear witness! Observe this mortal before you. What is his failing that he should suffer so? What was his sin that his torment should be unending?

Is it that he strived too hard, reached too far, attempted too much? Tell me! I defy you!

The gods are silent. They are mute idols with mouths of stone; there is no life in them.

Look out upon Hart Fell. . . is it day or night? Sun and stars in the sky together. . . it is so bright!

What does this mean, Wolf? Look you, and speak forthrightly. Tell me now, what do you observe?

Red Mars rising in a coal-black sky, yes. What does this signify? Does its fresh ruby colour mean that one king is dead, and there shall be another? Of course, but there are always kings and kings. Why should their decline or ascent be noticed by the heavens? Very great kings these, then. Oh, aye, very great!

And you, fair Venus, accompanying Sol on his fiery course, what about this double ray of yours, cleaving the air like a war axe? Division, surely. The realm cloven as with the stroke of Saecsen steel.

A king dead, a new king reigning: division. Ruin shall proceed from this, surely. Who among us is mighty enough to prevent this destruction? Who is wise enough to advise us?

O, Taliesin, speak to your son! My father, I would hear

your voice.

What is this? The music of a harp? But no harper do I see, nor bard is there to play. Yet, I hear it — the wonderful music of the harp.

Look Wolf, he comes! Taliesin comes!

See him climbing the mountain path; his blue cloak is flung over his shoulder; his staff is strong rowan; his tunic is white satin, his trousers tanned leather. He shines! I cannot look upon his face. He gleams with the glory of the Otherworld. His countenance is bright to rival the light of heaven.

Father! Speak to your wretched offspring. Give me wise counsel.

Behold, Myrddin, I answer your summons. I will speak to you, my son, and I will give you benefit of my wisdom. Hear then, if you will, and gain all that I have learned since my journey in this worlds-realm began:

Praise the Great Creator, the Lord of Infinite Compassion! Honour him and perform heartfelt worship, all creatures! My own eyes have beheld him; we have walked together in Paradise. And often we have observed you, Myrddin, my son; we have heard your cries and discussed your sore predicament between us, the Lord and I.

Fear not what will happen to you, Hawk. The King of Heaven has covered you with his hand. Even now his angels surround you; they stand ready to do your bidding. Listen to the one who knows the things of which he speaks: your life was given to you for a purpose, dearest flesh of my flesh. How should that purpose not obtain?

So, take heart and put away your sorrow. After a little time, there will come a hermit to this shrine of yours. Do not send him away, my son. Rather welcome him; do as he bids, and he will give you a great blessing.

When you have received this blessing, go out into the world again. Go you back to your lands and your people, take up your staff once more. There is much work to be done, brave Myrddin. I tell you the truth, while you have lain here sunk beneath your heavy grief, Darkness has not been idle.

Therefore, it is time to rise up, strap steel to your hip and helm your head with iron. It is time, Myrddin, now, before the pathways to the Kingdom are overgrown and lost. Once lost, Bright Star, they will no longer be found; even with much searching they will not be found.

Remember well the Kingdom of Summer and let its light become your prow star. . . let its song be a victory song on your lips. . . let its glory cover you, my beautiful son. . .

No! Do not go, my father! Do not leave me alone and forlorn! Please, stay but a little. . . *Taliesin!*

He is gone, Wolf. But did you see how his face shone when he spoke to me? It was not the vision of a fevered brain. Never that. Taliesin came to me; my father spoke to me. He spoke to me and I heard the sound of his voice.

Yes, and I heard his stern warning.

NINE

If I am crazed, if I am mad, if I am mad. . . mad I am and
there is no help for Myrddin.

But wretched as I am before all the world, I was not
always the scrag of hair and bone you see shivering on filthy
haunches with flies biting his nether parts. Was Myrddin ever
king in Dyfed, Wolf?

Aye, that he was. . . he was. . . He was, and nevermore
will be. Wild Man of the Wood I am. Yet, while I live, the
creatures of the forest hearken to me, for I am their lord.

Let the Forest Lord speak forth his prophecy!

No scribes attend me, no servants have I to give account of
what I shall say. Pelleas, where are you, boy? Have you, even
you, deserted me, Pelleas?

Intelligent words are uttered to the winds. Wise words
from the Soul of Wisdom go unheeded. Let it go, let it go.
The bard's *awen* will not be chained; it moves as it will and no
mortal hand may make bold to bid or restrain. Let it go, fool!

Stir up the flames, read the glowing embers and tell us
something of happiness. Great Light, in this bleak place, you
know we need some kindly cheer. What is it that shines up at
me from the bed of ashes?

Behold! Ganieda dressed in fine linen, clothed with the
purity of new-fallen snow. Bearer of my soul, keeper of my
heart, she walks on a carpet of rose petals, a peerless maid,
chaste before her lord. Her smile is as the golden sunshower;
her laughter like a silver rain.

Pray to the God who made us, Dafyd! Praise him most
eloquently for the gift he has given this day. Amen, so be it!

My marriage day was all a day of wedding should be. I
have heard my grandmother speak of her marriage to Elphin,
and the celebration that it was. For unlike Taliesin and Charis,
who had no celebration — and likely needed none — Elphin

and Rhonwyn had been wed in fine old Celtic style and they wanted to see me wed in like manner.

Consequently, the Cymry of Caer Cam bestowed on that gladsome day all the fire and verve of their happiness. Not that Maelwys was to be outdone — he would have hosted the celebration, but Ganieda was Custennin's daughter and Custennin's the feast, as was his right. Maelwys had to content himself with housing the celebrants.

In truth, I remember little of the day. All is shadow next to the daylight of Ganieda, bright and shining star. She was never more beautiful, more graceful and serene. She was love embodied for me, I swear it; and I hope I was for her.

On that fine day, we two stood before Dafyd in the chapel and we gave each other the gift of rings after the Christian custom, and spoke out the eternal promises that would bind our souls, as our hearts had already been bound by love — and as our bodies would be joined later that night.

Ganieda's black hair was brushed and shining, it hung in long braids entwined with silver thread; she wore a circlet of spring flowers, pink as a maid's blush — they filled the wooden chapel with their fragrance. Her mantle was white, and white embroidered; on each tassel hung a tiny gold bell. Over one shoulder was draped the marriage cloak she had woven that winter: a fine expanse of imperial purple and bright sky blue in the cunning checked pattern of the north country; it was held by a great, gold brooch. There were golden bracelets on her wrists and bands of gold on her arms. She wore sandals of white leather on her feet.

The most beautiful of the Fair Folk, she was a vision.

I scarcely recall what I wore — no one took notice of me beside her; I know I took no notice of myself. In my hands I carried the slim golden torc that was my wedding gift to her. She would, after all, be a queen and should have a torc like the great queens of old.

Dafyd, his dark robes brushed clean, his face glowing like the bride's beside me, held up the holy text for all to see, and he pronounced the marriage rite. When he finished, we laid our joined hands on the pages of the sacred book and repeated vows to one another as Dafyd instructed, whereupon he made a prayer for us.

In his great benevolence, Dafyd allowed Blaise to come

forward and sing the joining of our souls after the manner of the bards, which he did with simple and elegant dignity. The harp was deeply appreciated by all gathered in the chapel — there is something about a harp, and a true bard's voice lifted in song, that bestows great blessing on all who hear it.

And I think it was something Taliesin would have done himself, if he had lived to see his son's wedding day.

As the last notes of the harp faded, we left the chapel, emerging to find that the whole of Maridunum had come to see us wed, thronging the chapel yard. As soon as they saw us, they gave forth a mighty shout — led by the warriors of my warband, who acted as if *they* were the ones taking a queen. They were so pleased.

But then, Ganieda could have conquered any army with charm alone; the young men of my warband were firmly under her spell, and they loved her.

We rode back to the villa surrounded by a noisy sea of well-wishers. Between the shouted blessings of the townsmen and the singing of the warband, the far hills rang and rejoiced with the happy sound.

Custennin had brought his cooks and stewards with him, and all the supplies they would need for the feast — including six head of fine, fat cattle on the hoof, a dozen casks of heavy mead, and some of his good heather beer. The rest — pigs, lambs, fish, mountains of turnips and tender spring vegetables — he bought in the market at Maridunum. Maelwys kept trying to get him to accept the use of his own stores but, other than a few spices the cooks had forgotten to bring, Custennin would not hear of it.

Ah, we feasted well. It brings the water to my mouth to recall it. Although, at the time, my only appetite was for Ganieda. It may well have been the longest day of my life: would the sun *never* go down? Would the twilight never come, when I would bear Ganieda away to the sleeping-place that had been prepared for us to share our first night together? I kept looking at the sky and finding it still light.

So, we sang, and the jars and cups went round, and the meat was served up and the loaves of hot bread, and the steaming vegetables, and the sweetmeats. We sang some more — Blaise and his druids provided endless music on their

219

harps — and I do not think even Taliesin could have filled that hall with a better sound.

Oh, but Taliesin *was* there; he was there, Wolf, he was *there*. You only had to look at my mother's face to know it: Taliesin's spirit infused the day; his presence was a sweet fragrance everywhere. Charis had rarely appeared more fair, more radiant. Likely, she was living her own wedding day in mine.

'Mother, are you enjoying yourself?' I asked; a needless question, for a blind man could have seen it.

'Oh, Merlin, my Hawk, you have made me very happy.' She drew me to her and kissed me. 'Ganieda is a wonderful young woman.'

'Then you approve?'

'How sweet of you to pretend that it mattered. But since you ask — yes, I approve. She is what every mother would have for a daughter, and as a wife for her son. No woman could ask for more.' Charis put a hand to my cheek. 'You have my blessing, Merlin — a thousand times if once.'

It was important for Charis to say this to me, since her own father's refusal to bless her marriage is what had driven her and Taliesin away. Even though Avallach had become reconciled in the end, it had caused them both considerable pain.

Subtle are the workings of God's ways: if Elphin and his people had not been driven from Caer Dyvi, if the Cymry had not come to Ynys Avallach, if Charis and Taliesin had not been driven from the Isle of Apples, and if they had not come to Maridunum, and if. . . and if. . . well, then I would never have been born, and I would not have been taken by the Hill Folk, and I would never have met Ganieda, and I would not be a king of Dyfed now, and this would not be my marriage day. . .

Great Light, Mover of all that is moving and at rest, be my Journey and my far Destination, be my Want and my Fulfilling, be my Sowing and my Reaping, be my glad Song and my stark Silence. Be my Sword and my strong Shield, be my Lantern and my dark Night, be my everlasting Strength and my piteous Weakness. Be my Greeting and my parting Prayer, be my bright Vision and my Blindness, be my Joy and my sharp Grief, be my sad Death and my sure Resurrection!

Yes, Charis loved Ganieda, a circumstance from which I derived unexpected pleasure. It was joy itself to see them together, fussing over the preparations before the wedding, knowing that I was the object of devotion in their warm womanly hearts, and the living link between them. May such love increase!

They were, both of them, Faery Queens, tall of stature and elegant in every detail, perfection in movement, harmony made flesh, beauty embodied. To see them together was to catch breath and pray thanks to the Gifting God.

Men speak foolishly of the beauty that slays, though I believe such a thing may exist. But there is also a beauty that heals, that restores and revives all who behold it. This is the beauty Charis and Ganieda possessed. And it greatly cheered Custennin and Maelwys to see it; those two kings glowed like men aflame with their good fortune.

I tell you the truth, there was never a more joyous company gathered beneath one roof than gathered beneath the roof of Maelwys' hall that wedding day.

O Wolf, it was a fine and happy day.

And it was a fine and enchanting night. My body was made for hers, and hers for mine. The delight of our lovemaking could have cheered whole nations, I believe. Even now the smell of clean rushes and new fleece, of beeswax candles and baking barley cakes makes my blood run bold in my veins.

We slipped unnoticed from the feast — or perhaps by common consent the celebrants chose *not* to attend to our leaving — and flew to the courtyard, where Pelleas had my horse saddled and ready. I took the reins from him and swung myself into the saddle, and reached down for Ganieda, and settled her before me in the saddle, and, with my arms around her, I caught up the bundle Pelleas offered and clattered from the courtyard.

No one gave chase, as is the usual custom: pretending that the woman has been carried off by a rival clansman and so must be saved and avenged. It is a harmless game, but such pretence had no place in our wedding. There was about our marriage such an air of rightness and honour that merely to suggest otherwise would have made vulgar a sacred thing.

The moon shone fair among a scattering of silver-gilt clouds. We rode to a nearby shepherd's bothy which had been prepared the day before. It was a single-roomed hut of thick wattle-and-mud walls and a roof of deep thatch — little more than a hearth and bed place. Maelwys' serving women had done a good job of turning the rude room into a warm and inviting chamber for a young couple's first night. It had been swept, and swept again, the hearthstone scoured, the walls washed with lime. Fresh rushes had been cut, and fragrant heather for the bed, which was piled high with new fleeces and a coverlet of soft otter fur. Candles had been set, the hearth prepared, and bouquets of spring flowers bunched and placed around the room.

As it was a warm night, we lit a small fire in the hearth — only enough to cook the barley bannocks which Ganieda would serve to me for our ritual first meal together. In the glimmering firelight, the shepherd's bothy could have been a palace, and the clay bowl in which Ganieda mixed the water and barley meal a chalice of gold. Ganieda might have been the enchantress of the wood, and I the wandering hero entrapped by my love for her.

I sat cross-legged on the bed and watched her deft movements. When the hearthstone was hot enough, she shaped the little cakes and placed them on the stone. We did not speak all the while, it was as if we were no longer ourselves alone; no, we were all the young people who had ever loved and married, joining life to life, the latest in a living chain stretching back countless eons to that first hearth, that first coupling. There were no words for this moment.

The barley cakes cooked quickly, and Ganieda placed them gingerly in the gathered hem of her mantle and brought them to me. I took one, broke it, and fed her with half even as I ate half myself. She chewed solemnly and then turned to lift the cup she had poured out while the bannocks were baking.

I held the cup to her lips while she drank, then drained the warm, sweet wine in a single gulp. Then the cup clattered to the floor and her arms were around my neck and her lips were on mine and I was tumbling backwards onto the bed, Ganieda's body full upon me, the scent of her silky skin filling my head.

And then there was only the night and our passion and, after, the sweet deep darkness of sleep in one another's arms.

I woke once before morning and heard a light whistle on the breeze. I crept from the bed and looked out of the door to see, outlined in the light of the sinking moon, Gwendolau, astride his horse. He rode at a respectful distance, keeping watch over us through the night.

I slipped back beneath the coverlet and into Ganieda's embrace, and fell asleep once more to the rhythm of my wife's soft breathing in slumber.

TEN

Deep in the black heart of Celyddon, with wolves and stags and grunting boars for company, does Myrddin abide. Is he alive or is he dead? God alone knows.

O happy Wolf, look into the fire and tell us what you see.

Ah, the steel men. Yes, I see them, too. All in steel from helm to heel. Big men, fearless men. Bristling with spears like an ash forest. See the knotted muscles of their arms; see the quick, deadly movements of their strong hands; see the fearless thrust of their jaws. They know that this day's light might be their last, but they are not afraid.

That one! See him? Look at the span of his shoulders, Wolf. See how he sits his saddle — as if he was part of the beast he rides. A magnificent man. Cai, yes, that is his name: a name that kindles fear in the heart of the foeman.

Here is another! See him, Wolf? A champion among champions he is. His cloak is blood red and his shield bears the cross of the Christ. His is a name the harpers will sing for a thousand years: Bedwyr, Bright Avenger.

And those two there! Oh, look — have you ever seen such dread purpose, such grim grace? Sons of Thunder. That one is called Gwalchmai, Hawk of May. The other is Gwalchaved, Hawk of Summer. They are twins, one in heart, one in mind, one in action — as alike as two may be and still be two. There is no matching the swiftness of their blades.

Each of these men is worthy of the rank of king; each is a lord in his own land. Who is there to lead such men? Who can be their Battle Lord? Where is the man to be king over kings?

I do not see him, Wolf. I do not see him for a long time yet.

No, these men do not live now, and not for many long years. Their time is not come. We have time yet to find a chieftain for them, Wolf. And we will. . . we must.

The day after Taliesin's visit — a day, a year, does it matter? — I saw the hermit as he promised. Squatting before my miserable cave, high up in the mountain, I saw him coming a long way off. He was climbing, following the trickle of my spring as it wends down into the valley to join one of Celyddon's myriad streams.

He came on foot, and slowly, so that I had time to observe him. His cloak was dun, his feet were shod in high boots, and he wore a wide-brimmed hat on his head to keep off the sun. A strange hermit, I thought, to travel in such array.

As he approached, I saw that his steps were purposeful, deliberate. His was not the aimless gait of a wandering wayfarer; he knew his destination — it was this very cave, and him who lived within. He had come to Hart Fell to find Mad Merlin.

Find him, he did.

'I give you good greeting, friend,' he called when he saw me watching him.

I waited until he came closer — there was no use in shouting at him. 'Will you sit? There is water if you thirst.'

He stood a moment, looking round. At last his eyes came to rest on me. They were sky blue, and just as cold and empty as the heaven above him. 'I would not shun a cup of water.'

'The spring is there,' I told him, indicating where the water ran from the rock. 'I said nothing about a cup.'

He smiled and went to the spring, bent and sucked in a few mouthfuls of water — enough for appearance' sake, I thought, not enough to satisfy real thirst. And yet he had no water-skin with him.

When he sat down again, he removed his hat and I saw hair as yellow as flax — like that of a Saecsen prince. But his speech was good Briton. 'Tell me, friend, what do you up here?'

'I might ask the same of you,' I grunted by way of answer.

'It is no secret,' he said, laughing. 'I have come to find a man.'

'And have you found him?'

'Yes.'

'How fortunate for you.'

He smiled broadly. 'You are the one they call Merlin Ambrosius — Myrddin, the Emrys. Are you not?'

'Who would call me that?'

'Perhaps you are not aware of the things men are saying about you.'

'Perhaps it does not interest me what men say.'

He laughed again, as if the sound should win me. But the laughter, like the smile, did not touch his eyes. 'Come now, you must be somewhat curious. They are saying you are a king of the Fair Folk, that you are divine. They say you are a mighty warrior, invincible.'

'Do they say also that I am mad?'

'Are you mad?'

'Yes.'

'No madman would speak so rationally,' he assured me. 'Perhaps you only feign madness.'

'Why would any man feign that which is most hateful to him?'

'To make himself seem mad, I suppose,' the wanderer answered thoughtfully.

'Which would be madness itself, would it not?'

The stranger laughed again and instantly I hated the sound.

'Speak plainly now,' I said, challenging him, 'what do you want of me?'

He met my challenge with his empty smile. 'Just to speak with you a little.'

'You have come a long way for nothing, then. I do not wish to speak to anyone.'

'Perhaps you would not mind listening,' he replied, picking up a stick. He scratched in the dirt for a few moments, then looked up at me suddenly and, finding my eyes on him, said, 'I am not without influence in this world. I could do things for you.'

'Do this for me then, if your influence extends so far: go away.'

'I could do great things for you, Myrddin Emrys. Tell me what you want — anything you desire, Myrddin, I will do it, or see that it is done.'

'I have told you what I desire.'

He moved closer. 'Do you know who I am?'

'Should I?'

'Perhaps not, but I know who you are. I know you, Myrddin. You see, I am an Emrys, too.'

At his words, a slow, inexorable dread crept over me. I felt very old and very weak. He reached out to me and his touch was cold as stone. 'I can help you, Myrddin,' he went on. 'Let me help you.'

'I need no one's help. This place is a palace,' I told him, lifting my hand to my barren surroundings. 'I have all I need.'

'I can give you all you desire.'

'I desire peace,' I snapped. 'Can you give me that?'

'I can give you forgetting — it amounts to the same thing in the end.'

Forgetting. . . that would be a blessing. The hateful images pursue me, they haunt my waking, they steal my sleep. To forget — ah, but at what price?

'It seems to me that I might forget the good along with the bad,' I told him.

The stranger grinned happily and shrugged. 'Good, bad — what of that? It is all the same in the end.' He leaned still closer. 'I can do more for you. I can give you power, Myrddin. Authority such as you have never dreamed existed. It can be yours.'

'I am content with such power as I have, why should Merlin the Wild need more?'

His answer was quick, and I wondered how many others he had tempted with his vapid promises. Oh, yes, I knew who he was now. My time with Dafyd was never in vain. And, though I was no longer certain of the Guiding Hand, I could see no sense in going over to the enemy.

'Myrddin,' he said, making my name a mockery on his lips, 'it is such a little thing for me to do. I would do it in an instant. Look,' he raised his stick and pointed out across Celyddon's dark folds to the east. 'There is where the sun rises, Myrddin. There is where the heart of the Empire beats.' And I seemed to see, glimmering on the far horizon, the imperial city with its strong walls and palaces. 'As emperor, you would rule the world. You could destroy the hated Saecsens once and for all. Think of all the suffering you could save. One wave of your hand, Myrddin, that is all it would take.' He held out his hand to me.

'Come with me, Myrddin, together we could make you the greatest emperor this world has ever seen. You would be rich beyond all riches; your name would last for ever.'

'But Myrddin would not,' I told him. 'You would see to that as well. Be gone, I am tired.'

'Are you such an honourable man?' he spat contemptuously. 'Are you so righteous?'

'Words, words. I claim nothing.'

'Myrddin. . . look at me. Why will you not look at me? We are friends, you and I. Your lord has left you, Myrddin. It is time to find one more trustworthy. Come with me.' His fingers were nearly touching mine now. 'Come, but we must go at once.'

'Why is it that when you speak I hear only the vacant howl of the tomb?'

That made him angry. His face changed and he was formidable. 'You think you are better than I am? I will destroy you, Myrddin.'

'As you destroyed Morgian?'

His eyes gleamed maliciously. 'She is beautiful, is she not?'

'Death wears many faces,' I said, 'but its stench is always the same.'

The heat of his anger leapt up instantly. 'I give you one last chance — in fact, I give you Morgian, my finest creation.' He assumed a soothing aspect as he thought of this new tactic. 'She is yours, Merlin. Do what you like with her. Yes, you will be her master. Take her. You can even kill her if you wish. Destroy her as she destroyed your father.'

Black anger swarmed before my eyes like wasps. My body began to shake. I tasted bile on my tongue. I jumped to my feet. '*You* destroyed my father!' I cried, hearing my voice echo in the long valley below. I stood and put two fingers in my mouth and whistled high and long. 'Leave while you can.'

'You cannot send me away,' the creature said. 'I go when and where I will.'

At that moment, the she-wolf came running up the trail, snarling, ears flat to her head, fangs bared.

He laughed. 'Do not think to frighten me away. Nothing on earth can harm me.'

'No? In the name of Jesu the Christ be gone!'

The wolf closed on him. He turned and dodged aside as she leapt, jaws slashing for his throat. Still, he had moved, and was already fleeing back down the mountainside as Wolf gathered herself for a second leap. She would have given chase, but I called her to my side, where, still snarling, I patted her head until the hackles melted into her back and she was calm once more.

So, my first visitor left me without a farewell. I was still trembling when Wolf growled once more, low in her throat, a warning growl. I looked down the defile, thinking to see the stranger returning. And there was someone approaching, but even from a fair distance I could tell it was another.

He was a gaunt stick of a creature, rough featured and hairy, wearing pelts of at least six different beasts. He stumped up the mountainside with the long, regular strides of one used to long journeys afoot, looking neither right nor left, but coming on apace.

And well he might, for a storm had sprung up out of nothing, as it can do in the mountains. Rags of black clouds were flying down the mountainside and I could taste rain on the cooling wind. Mist rolled over the rocks, taking the visitor from my sight.

I waited, comforting the she-wolf at my side. 'Be still, Wolf, we will hear what this one has come to say. Perhaps this guest will be more to our liking.' Although that did not appear likely, because of Taliesin's promise, I was of a mind to see it through.

He came in sight again, stepping from the mist when he drew near, and hailed us in a bold voice. 'Hail, Wild Man of the Wood! I bring you greetings from the world of men.'

'Sit down, friend, there is water if you thirst.'

'Water will serve where wine is scarce,' he replied. I watched him as he scooped water into his hand and slurped it up noisily. He did not appear a man over-used to holding the guest cup, but what of that? Did I look a king of Dyfed?

'It is thirsty work, climbing this slate mountain of yours, Myrddin.'

'How do you know my name — if it is my name?'

'Oh, I have known you for a very long time. Should a servant not know his master?'

I stared at him. His face was long and horsy; his brows black, his cheeks red from the sun and wind. His hair hung to his shoulders, loose like a woman's. I know I had never seen him before.

'You speak of masters and servants. What makes you think I have anything to do with either?' I asked, and then framed a more pertinent question. 'How did you know where to find me?'

'The one who sent me told me where to find you.' That was all he said, but his words made my heart leap within me.

'Who sent you?'

'A friend.'

'Does this friend have a name?'

'Everyone has a name — as you well know.' He scooped up more water and then wiped his hands on his skin jerkin. 'My name, for instance, is Annwas Adeniawc.'

A most unusual name — it meant Ancient Winged Servant. 'I see no wings, and you are not as ancient as your name implies. And there are indeed many masters in this world, and even more servants.'

'All mortals serve, Myrddin. Immortals also. But I have not come to talk about me — I have come to talk about you.'

'Then you have come for no purpose.' The words were out before I could stop them. *Do not send him away*, Taliesin had said. I need not have worried, for my visitor took no notice of my rudeness.

'Once loosened, the tongue wags on, does it not?' This was said with great good humour. Annwas apparently enjoyed himself. He glanced around my scree-covered abode, and then turned his eyes to the west, over the vast, rumpled bearskin of Celyddon. 'Men say the light dies in the west,' he remarked casually. 'But if I told you it rises there, would you believe it?'

'Would it matter very much what I believed?'

'Myrddin. . . ' he shook his head lightly. 'I should have thought that all these years of solitary meditation would have taught you something about the power of belief.'

'Has it been many years then?'

'More than a few.'

'Why come to me now?'

The narrow bones of his shoulders hunched in a shrug. 'My lord wills it.'

'Am I to know your lord?'

'But you *do* know him, Myrddin. At least, you once did.' Annwas turned to look at me directly. I felt sympathy flowing out from him. He bent his long frame and settled cross-legged on the bare ground. 'Tell me now,' he said softly. 'Tell me about the battle.'

It was then that the rain began.

ELEVEN

The first drops splattered over us, but neither one moved. The storm grew, staining the sky violet and black like a wound — from which the rain gushed like blood.

'The battle, Myrddin; I have come to hear you tell it.' Annwas held my gaze in his and made no move, despite the rain.

It was a moment before I could speak. 'What battle would that be?' I asked, dreading the answer. Darkness swirled around me, around the mountain itself in the form of a midnight mist that boiled out of nowhere. A rising wind began wailing among the crags, driving the rain.

'I think you know,' said Annwas gently.

'And it seems to me you know a great many things no man can possibly know of another!' I glared at him, feeling the wrath seethe in my soul once again. The wind screamed my defiance.

'Tell me,' he insisted gently, but his insistence was firm as rock. 'It will come easier once you begin.'

'Leave me!' I hated him for making me exhume those long-dead bones. The she-wolf leapt to her feet, snarling. Annwas lifted his hand to her and she subsided with a whimper.

'Myrddin,' the voice was soft as a mother's crooning to her babe, 'you will be healed. But first we must cut out the disease that poisons your soul.'

'I am happy as I am,' I gasped. Breath came hard to me. The wind howled now, and cold rain fell in stinging sheets upon us.

Annwas Adeniawc reached out his boney hand and touched my arm. 'No one is happy in hell, Myrddin. You have carried your burden long enough. It is time to lay it down.'

'Burden it may be, but it is all I have left!' I screamed, tears of rage and pain mingling with the rain on my face.

232

The hermit rose and went into my cave. I sat where I was until he called me. When I looked, there was a fire burning brightly just inside the entrance. 'Come in from the rain,' Annwas said. 'I will cook us something to eat while we talk.'

How long has it been since I had warm food in my belly? I wondered, and found myself going in to join him. I do not know where he found the small pot to hold the meaty stew, nor where he got the meat, nor the grain to make the bread. But as I watched him prepare the meal, and smelled it cooking, the fight went out of me and I began, haltingly, to tell him. . . and, God help me, I told him everything.

Ganieda went north that spring, to her father's house in Celyddon. It seems a woman needs to be near her own when a babe is born. I was against it, but my wife could be a most persuasive woman, and in the end Ganieda had her way.

I arranged the journey, taking every precaution, seeing to every detail personally, for I knew I would not be able to travel with her. She sought to reassure me. 'It will be lovely in Goddeu in the summer. You come when you can, my soul. Elma will be so surprised.' She kissed me. 'You are right to have a care for the journey, but nothing will happen to me.'

'It is not an afternoon's ride in the woods, Ganieda.'

'No, no it is not. And you are right to remind me. But I am not so far along with child that sitting a horse will be a hardship.' She stood up straight and smoothed her mantle over her still-flat stomach. 'See? I have not even begun to show. Besides, I am a most fearsome hand with a spear, am I not, love? I will be safe.'

Jesu, I should have gone with her!

'Anyway, I could not for one moment imagine having a baby without Elma to help me,' she continued. Elma was midwife to her mother, and the nearest thing to a mother Ganieda remembered. And, as I said, a woman needs to be with her own when the birth pangs begin. 'You worry for nothing, Myrddin. Gwendolau rides to meet us. And, if I do not leave soon, he will be here even before I start out.'

'Better still,' I remarked.

'Come with me, then.'

'Ah, Ganieda, you know I cannot. The towers, the horses, the warband must be trained —'

She stepped close and put her hands on my shoulders as she settled lightly in my lap, where I sat in my chair. 'Come with me, husband.'

I sighed. We had had this discussion before. 'I will follow as soon as I can,' I told her. It was only a few months. Ganieda had to set out now, while she could still make the journey safely and in some comfort. I was to follow when my summer's work was finished, joining her in the autumn. The babe would not be born until deep winter, so there was plenty of time for us to be together once I arrived in Goddeu.

The crops were well in when she finally set out. I sent her with thirty of my warband, and she took four of her women for company. Half as many would have sufficed, but I was of a mind to be cautious and Maelwys agreed, insisting that it was better safe than sorry. 'I would do the same if I stood in your place,' he told me.

It was still early in what was coming to be known as the warring season, so the actual risk of the travellers running into trouble on the road was not great. Also, I had devised a route that kept them well away from the coasts. The only likely danger would be when they reached the Wall, and by then Gwendolau would have met them and they would be a force of fifty or more. There was no danger.

So, Ganieda left Maridunum one bright morning with her escort and I watched her go, feeling the warmth of her lips on my mouth as she turned her mount and joined the others, leaving the yard and striking off along the old road.

Oh, it was a jolly band. And why not? Ganieda was going home to have our baby and the world was a wondrous place. She waved farewell to me until she was out of sight; and I waved, too, until the flank of the hill took her from view. Then I said a prayer for her safety — not the first, nor the last, mind you — and went about my duties.

A balmy summer followed close on the heels of spring. The thirty returned in due time with the report that all had been well on the road and after. They had seen Ganieda to her father's house and stayed there to rest the horses for a few days before turning back. Custennin was delighted to have his daughter home and sent his regards and the message that all was well with him and his realm. It was a quiet sum... them; there had been no raids.

I was relieved, at last, and turned my attention to finish... g my tasks, so that I might ride after her as soon as may be.

Maelwys and I worked hard, dawn to dusk every day, and retired to our beds exhausted. More than once, Pelleas had to wake me from my chair at the table so that I could stumble to my chamber. Charis had charge of the king's household and servants so that we could collapse each night with food in our bellies without having to think about that, too, or I fear we might have starved.

The watchtowers along the coast were mostly finished and the relay towers inland well begun; the new men had received their first summer's training; our horse herd had been increased by twenty-eight sturdy colts, and a few hides of land cleared for future grazing.

You see, already I was thinking of horses, breeding for size, strength, courage and endurance. It was to be a fight won on horseback by a force of mounted fighting men like the old Roman *ala*.

Well, we had an early autumn and at last I could leave. I chose thirty to go with me. Rather, I took thirty from the three hundred who clamoured to be allowed to ride at my side. I have no idea why I took that many. It had been in my mind to take only a third of that number but, when the time came, the choice was not so easily made and I had not the heart to turn them away.

It took but a day to gather supplies and provisions, and we set out for Celyddon.

The days were indeed golden. It had been a good summer and bountiful crops were coming under the scythe everywhere; the herds appeared healthy and well grown; every holding and settlement boasted new dwellings, and occasionally even a hall. The fear that had grown in the land with the last few years had receded a good deal, given even a brief respite from the worrying raids. Everywhere men were encouraged and hopeful.

After many days on the trail we came to Yr Widdfa, a bleak and forsaken land when compared to the rich south. But even here summer had worked its manifold miracles and the flocks had swelled their numbers, and men were content. We camped one star-filled night in a high mountain pass and awakened to frost on the mountain heather. We saddled our snorting mounts and started down that morning into the stepped lowlands falling away towards the Wall.

The day was dazzling clear and I could see Celyddon's dark mass spreading on the far horizon. A few more days and we would reach its outermost fringe. A few days after that and I would sleep once more in Ganieda's arms.

When we reached the forest I sent scouts on ahead to announce our arrival. Custennin would welcome the news, I knew, and so would Ganieda.

Oh, my soul was restlessness itself. Our long separation had been harder on me than I knew, for the thought of holding her again filled me with an exquisite ache. My saddle became a prison and time could not pass quickly enough. I slept little; thoughts of Ganieda and our child made me fretful in my desire to be with her. I had so much to tell her about all that had happened in her absence. I believe I would have ridden through the night, if that were possible in tangled Celyddon.

My torment was sweet, but it was torment all the same.

At last, however, at last the day of arrival dawned and I was awake before anyone else, knowing that if we rode hard we could reach Custennin's palace by midday. The scouts would have reached them the night before, I reckoned, and Ganieda would be waiting. I meant to make her wait as short as possible.

The wood awakened around us as we rode through the night-quiet forest along the narrow track. We stopped a little after sunrise and broke fast — I allowed the men to dismount, but only while they ate and then it was back in the saddle and hurrying on.

At midday we reached the crest of the last hill where the track widened somewhat as it wound down through the forest towards Goddeu. We could not see Custennin's stronghold of course, but we were close.

The first warning came a little while later.

We had stopped at a stream to rest and water the horses before continuing on the last stretch of the journey. A few of my men had crossed the stream to give more room to those behind; and they had spread out along the bank.

I heard a shout as I knelt, scooping water to my mouth.

'Lord Myrddin!' My name echoed in the close wood. 'Lord Myrddin!'

'Here I am,' I answered. 'What is it?'

One of my fourth-year warriors came running to me. 'Lord Myrddin, I have found something you should see.'

'What is it, Balach?' I read nothing, save concern, from the look on his face.

'Mantracks in the mud, lord.' He raised his arm to point downstream from us. 'Just there.'

'How many?'

'I would not like to say. My lord should see for himself.'

'Show me where they are.'

He led me downstream to the place he had indicated. I splashed my way through the water to the other side of the stream and there on the muddy bank I saw the footprints of a score or more men. There were no footprints on the opposite bank — the group had not crossed the stream, they had come out of it. . .

Saecsens!

It was something Saecsens did when travelling in heavily forested country: follow the natural pathway of the stream. This is how they traversed difficult country unknown to them. . .

And now they had come to Celyddon.

What is more, they were ahead of us — how far ahead I could only guess. The tracks were still fairly fresh, not more than a few hours old. Unfamiliar with the land, they would go slowly. We might overtake them on horseback. Great Light, help us catch them!

I gave the order to mount up at once, and told my warriors to ready their arms and to remain alert to an ambush. Then we rode.

Our precautions seemed unnecessary. We saw no more tracks and, if I had not seen them myself, I would have thought Balach had imagined them. Although we stopped from time to time simply to listen, we heard nothing but the light chatter of squirrels and the scolding of crows.

We rode on towards Goddeu, and despite the apparent peace of the wood, deep foreboding drew over me — a dread to make my heart leaden in my chest. Fear came at me from out of the sunfilled forest — whispers of disquiet, of hushed alarm.

I raced ahead.

Then the horses grew nervous. I believe they can smell blood at a fair distance.

Well in front of the warband now, I crested a knoll and came into view of Goddeu, quiet beside the mirror-smooth lake. The sun shone full on the trail ahead and I saw the bodies there.

I spurred my horse forward to the place and flung myself from my saddle. It was a party of women. . .

Oh, Good God, no!

Ganieda!

I knelt and turned over the first one. A maid with dark braids. Her throat had been severed.

The next had been pierced through the heart and the front of her white mantle was stained deepest crimson. The body was still warm.

Ganieda, my soul, where are you?

I stumbled unseeing to a knot of tumbled corpses. What the brutal Saecsen axes had done to those once-beautiful bodies made me weep and gnash my teeth. Some had been ravaged before being murdered, and their clothing had been torn from their limbs. For the love of God — the ugly wounds between their legs! All had died horribly.

May heaven shut me out for ever, I wish that I had died that day!

There were seven young women in that group. But Ganieda was not among them. Oh, please, Loving Father! My heart grasped that tiny hope as I lurched on. Behind me the first of the warband were thundering up.

I do not know what made me turn from the track. Perhaps the soft shimmer of pale blue among the shadows. . .

I walked towards the fallen tree, an old stump long dead. There, on the far side were two more women slumped across the body of a third. I lifted them aside, gently, gently. . .

Ganieda's women had died protecting their lady with their own bodies.

But the barbarians had seen Ganieda was pregnant. Oh, they had made great sport of killing her.

Great Light, I cannot bear it!

Oh, Annwas, I see her body before me. . . I feel its fleeting warmth in my hands. . . I taste again her blood on my lips as

I kiss her cold cheek. . . I cannot bear it . . . Please, do not make me tell it!

But you want to hear. You want to hear me say the thing most hateful to me of all I know. . . Very well, I will tell it all, so that all may know my anguish and my shame.

Ganieda had taken many wounds. Her mantle was sodden with thickening blood, and rent in several places as they had tried to strip her naked. One lovely breast had been carved from her body, and her proud, swelling stomach had been run through with the point of a sword. . . Loving God, please, no! Stabbed — not once but again, and again, and yet again.

My legs would not hold me. I fell across the body of my beloved, a great cry of grief tearing from my throat. I raised myself and held Ganieda's beautiful face in my hands. It was not beautiful any more, but twisted in horrific agony, bespattered with blood, her clear eyes cloudy and unseeing.

Beasts! Barbarians!

And then I saw it: protruding from one of the stomach wounds. . . Dearest God! . . . reaching for life it would never know was a tiny, unborn hand. Blue and still, minutely veined, its tiny wrist extending from the wall of the dead womb. . . the hand of my babe, my darling child. . .

TWELVE

Thunder boomed in my head. Voices like angry hornets buzzed loud in my ears. *BEASTS! BARBARIANS!* The ground rolled away on every side like the swelling sea. I stumbled, fell, picked myself up and ran. Merciful Father, I ran, vomiting bile, gagging, choking, running on.

Behind me came a shout, and the ringing scrape of men drawing steel. The horn sounded. The Saecsens had been sighted.

Farewell, Ganieda my soul, I loved you better than my life.

It was a different Merlin who turned to meet the foe that day. My sword was in my hand, whirling, flashing — the regal blade of Avallach — and my horse was careering headlong into a company of Saecsen warriors, but I have no memory of drawing sword or reining horse to the fight.

Merlin was no longer present; I stood off and watched from a very great distance as an unthinking, unfeeling body performed the practised actions of war.

The body was mine, but Merlin had fled.

I saw faces rise before me. . . grim faces mouthing strange curses to unknown gods. . . hate-filled faces vanishing beneath flailing hooves. . . hideous faces writhing on severed heads as my sword carried them off . . .

The battle frenzy was on me; I burned with it. And the enemy felt the white heat of my killing rage. None could stand against me and, as the enemy force was a small one, it was easily overcome.

As the rest of my warband gathered to me, some of them wiping blood from their weapons, I sat in the saddle, staring blankly into the sun, my sword resting on my thigh.

I felt a hand on my arm. 'Lord Merlin,' began Pelleas, 'what is it?' His voice was as tender as a mother's with a fevered

240

child. 'What did you see?'

The smoke from Custennin's stronghold ascended before us, and on the wind came the sound of shouting in the distance. I lifted the reins in my hands and urged my mount forward. 'Lord Merlin?' Pelleas asked, but I did not answer. I could not speak; besides; what answer could I make?

The barbarians we had engaged on the road had been returning to watch the ford — perhaps to ambush anyone on the trail and prevent them from coming to Custennin's aid. Their main party had gone ahead to attack Goddeu.

Even as my warband took this in, I was away, my horse pounding down the slope towards the lake that lay between us and Custennin's timber halls. As before, my body moved of its own accord. I knew nothing of what I did — only that which one man might observe of a stranger.

I was first to the fight, throwing myself into the thick of it. If there was a conscious thought at all, I believe it was that one of the Saecsens' hated axes would swiftly find my heart.

They had fired the first buildings they came to. Smoke roiled through the air, black and thick. Fair Folk dead lay on the ground, mostly women overtaken while hastening to the safety of the hall. I dropped six enemy before they knew I was among them, and five more Saecsens died before they could lift blade against me.

It was a band of forty all told; and with my thirty and those of Custennin's men who were not away on a day's hunting with Gwendolau, we easily outnumbered the enemy and made short work of them.

In truth, it was over almost before it began. My men had dismounted and were cleaning their weapons and looking among the dead for the wounded, beginning to assess the damage and take account of the losses, when we heard horses thundering into the settlement.

Gwendolau and his hunting party had seen the smoke, and they had ridden off their horses' hooves returning to the defence of their home. They came flying in, all alather, Gwendolau at their head with Baram at his side. He took in the situation before him, even as he drew his horse to a halt. He looked to his father first — who was standing with a hand on the collar of one of his dogs, trying to keep the animal from further worrying the throatless corpse before him — and then he saw me.

'Myrddin! You —' he began. The quick smile of relief faded, as the implication of what he saw hit him. Not even Custennin had guessed as yet. 'No!' he cried, startling those around him anew. 'Ganieda!'

He ran to me, seizing the bridle strap. 'Myrddin, she was going out to greet you! She was so happy, she —' He turned horror-filled eyes to the way we had come, thinking, I suppose, to see her returning safely behind us and knowing he would not.

He looked to me for an answer, but I sat mute before him, the brother of my beloved, who was no less brother to me.

Custennin came forward. Whether he also knew what had happened to his daughter, I will never know. For, in the same instant, we heard a sound to make the blood run cold:

A low, booming horn, like a hunting horn, but lower, meaner, a brutal, hateful rasping sound, created to inspire terror and despair in those who must face it. It was the first time I had heard it — though not the last, dear God in heaven, not the last — yet, though I had never heard it, I knew well enough what it was. . .

The great battlehorn of the Saecsen warhost.

We fifty turned as one man to see our doom sweeping down the hill to meet us: a massed Saecsen battlehost five hundred strong!

They ran to join battle, screaming as they came. I swear the ground trembled beneath their pounding feet! Some of the younger warriors had not encountered Saecsens in full battle array before — it was still rare enough then — and they saw the half-naked, fearless barbarians flying towards us, war axes glinting cruelly in the hard light, their powerful legs racing, racing like death to embrace us, their long wheat-coloured braids flying as they came.

I heard more than one man curse the day of his birth and prepare to die, when he beheld that awful sight.

We were outmanned ten to one — it took no scholar to reckon that! But we were a mounted warband. And a battle-trained horse is an incalculable asset in a fight, especially against Saecsens and their like who fight only on foot.

The fear all had felt at seeing the enemy was thrust aside as men remounted and readied themselves for the attack. Gwendolau called my name, but I did not respond, for I was already spurring my horse forward. I intended to meet the whole Saecsen host alone.

There were shouts for me to rein up, to halt and wait — and then Gwendolau took command and organized the charge, dividing our small force into two groups to try to split the onrushing wave. Our only hope lay in penetrating their battle line — smashing through once and again, again and again, wearing at them, taking as many as we could out of the fight each time, but never allowing them to close on us or surround us. We were too few, and they were too many — we could not survive a pitched battle.

As for me, I had no hope at all. I had no plan, no volition but to ride and fight and kill, to slay as many of my beloved's murderers as possible before being slain myself. I tell you I did not care to live, I did not care to continue breathing the air of this world if my Ganieda was not also alive to breathe it.

Lord Death! You have taken my heart and soul, you must also take me!

The wind of my passing whistled along the upraised blade in my hand. My mount's iron-shod hooves dug into the soft ground and flung the turf skyward. My cloak flew out behind me like a great wing and I screamed. . .

Yes, I screamed at the devil's spawn before me, my voice awesome and terrible, rending heaven with its cry:

Earth and Sky bear witness!
I am a man, see how I die!
See how my sword breaks forth, flashing lightning!
See how my shield dazzles like the noontide sun!
See how my arm strikes fierce judgement!

Make ready your graves, Earth!
Open wide your insatiable maw
    to swallow the food I give you.
Gather your mists and clouds, Sky!
Weave your sombre vapours
    to make a funeral shroud for the dead I bring you.

Hear and obey! I, Myrddin Emrys, command you!

I screamed and my scream was terrible to hear. I laughed, and my laughter was more terrible still.

Alone, I flew to meet the Saecsen host. Alone, I hurtled towards them, bereft of sense and feeling. . .

Insane.

The tall horsetail standard which the Saecsen carried into battle loomed before me: a cross on a pole bearing a wolf's skull on either end of the crosspiece, with a human skull in the middle, and the three fringed with horsetails of red and black. I drove straight towards the thing with the point of my sword.

I do not know what I thought, or what I intended to do. But the force of my charge was such that upon reaching the battle-line the first enemy I encountered were simply swept beneath my steed's pummelling hooves and I was carried well into their midst as I made for the standard. The standard-bearer, a tall, muscled chieftain, dodged to the side. My blade came level and, with the momentum of my charge behind it, neatly sliced the solid pole in half, as if it had been a dry reed.

The Saecsen battlechief — an enormous brute with pale yellow hair hanging in long braids from his temples — stood beneath the standard with his House Carles around him, staring in amazement as the emblem sank like a stone. The cry of outrage reached my ears as a mild and distant sound, for I had once again entered that uncanny state where the actions of others were as languorous and slow as those of men half-asleep.

The flying, careering warhost became a massive, lumbering thing, heavy-footed and dull, without speed or quickness, overcome by a languid torpor. Once again, as in the battle at Maridunum, I became invincible, dealing death with every well-calculated blow, hewing down mighty warriors with effortless strokes, my movements perfect in their deadly grace.

The clash of battle reached my ears like the sound of water washing a far-off shore. I moved with elegant precision, striking boldly and with vengeance, my sword a living thing — a streaming crimson dragon spitting doom.

The enemy fell before me. I carved a swathe through their close ranks as if I was the scythe and they the corn standing for harvest. I struck and struck, and death fell with every stroke like judgement.

The battle surged around me. Gwendolau's charge had succeeded in driving through the enemy the first time, but the second charge had bogged down. There were simply too many Saecsens against us, and we were too few horsemen. Even when a man killed with every stroke, as my men did, two more barbarians leapt up to drag him from the saddle before his blade was clear of the dead weight.

I did what I could for those closest to me, but my charge had carried me into the centre of the Saecsen warhost, out of reach of most of my warband. All around me I saw good men dragged down and hacked to death by those wicked axes. There was nothing I could do about it.

The battlelord, a fair-haired giant, rose up before me with an enormous hammer in his hand. Slavering with rage, he bellowed his challenge to me and planted his feet, swinging that hammer, thick-sinewed shoulders and arms bulging with the effort. He stood like an oak tree as I urged my horse towards him. Sunlight glinted in his yellow hair, his blue eyes clear and unafraid, taunting me, the hammer in his hands dripping blood and brains from the skulls he had smashed.

I spun towards him and waited until he swung the hammer up for the killing blow. My first stroke ripped low across his unprotected stomach.

A lesser man would have fallen, but the golden giant stood his ground and swung the hammer down with such force that his wound burst. Blood and entrails gushed forth, and I laughed to see it.

The hammer swung wide; and as his hands came down to grab his belly, I plunged the point of my sword through his throat. Dark blood spewed out over my hand.

He stood a moment, his eyes rolling up in their sockets, then collapsed. I jerked the blade free, laughing, laughing, roaring with the absurdity of it.

I had slain the Saecsen battlechief! He had murdered my wife and unborn child, and I had felled that great brute with a child's trick. It was simply too absurd for words. I wept with laughter until I tasted the tears in my mouth.

When their war chief went down, the barbarians fell into confusion. They had lost their leader, but not their heart. And none of the cold-blooded ruthlessness, either. They still fought with crazy courage. If anything, losing their leader inspired them to higher, more reckless valour. Now they fought for the honour of accompanying their battlelord into Valhalla, the great Hall of Warriors in their wretched Otherworld.

So be it. I helped as many as possible earn that privilege.

But my sword brothers were not so fortunate. Too many of them were driven down that day. I remember turning as the tide of battle receded from me momentarily, turning and looking out over the field to see only a small handful of my valiant warband still holding their own against the barbarians. So few. . . and they were all that was left.

I made to ride towards them, but the gap closed again and they were lost. That was the last I ever saw of them alive.

A dreadful earnestness stole over me — a murderous fury. I slashed and struck with all my strength, as if my heart would burst. I killed and killed again. I began to fear that there would not be enough enemy to slake my thirst for blood. I gazed about me and there were more dead now than living, and I despaired.

'Here I am! Here is Merlin, take me!'

Mine was the only voice on the field. The barbarians stared at me with cow-stupid eyes, mute before my righteous rage, the strength going out of their hands.

'Come to me!' I cried. 'You who exult in death, come to me! I will cover you in glory! I will give you the delight of your hearts! Such a splendid death I will give you! Come! Receive the doom you deserve!'

They looked at one another with wide and staring eyes. There must have been seventy or more of them left to face me. Oh, the fighting had been cruel.

But I blazed, Annwas; I blazed with a fierce and righteous fire and the enemy quailed to see it. Their courage flowed away like water.

They stood staring and I raised my blade and called upon heaven to witness their destruction. Then I put spurs to my mount, and that spirited animal responded, though its head drooped and its nostrils streamed blood, it lifted its hooves and bolted straight towards the barbarians.

The sun itself was dim compared to the brightness of my blade as I hacked and hewed through them. Seventy men, and none could lift an axe against me. They fell like toppled oaks, going down into death's dark cavern clutching their wounds and crying.

Blood soaked the soil beneath their feet, staining the turf the colour of wine. They could not stand up for the blood. I chopped with my sword, cleaving their unprotected heads from crown to chin. They dropped dead to the blood-wet earth.

The slaughter was appalling.

In the end, the few who still lived threw down their weapons, turned and fled. But even these did not escape my vengeance. I rode them down from behind, galloping over their stumbling bodies, turning upon them again and again, until not one remained in the world of the living.

Then it was over. I sat in my saddle and gazed out over a hideous carnage. Saecsens lay thick on the ground and I screamed at them:

'Get up! Get up, you dead! Take up your arms! Arise and fight!' I taunted them. I challenged them. I screamed at them and cursed them even in death.

But there was no longer anyone to hear my taunts.

Five hundred Saecsens lay dead upon the ground and it was not enough. My grief, my hate, my rage still burned within me! Ganieda was dead and our child with her, and Gwendolau, Custennin, Baram, Pelleas, Balach, and all the brave men of my warband — all the quick and bright, their hearts beating and breath in their lungs, alive to love and light, now were stiffening corpses. My friends, my wife, my brothers were dead, and the blood price I claimed that day, mighty though it was, could not pay the debt.

Oh, Annwas, Winged Messenger, I myself slaughtered hundreds. Hundreds, do you hear?. . . *hundreds*. . .

And it was not enough!

I looked out on the battlefield shimmering in the heat haze of a midday sun. So still. . . so still. . . and silent — save for the croak of the circling birds; for already the carrion crows were flocking, picking at the eyes of the dead. In this I knew the stark reality of war: all men, friend and foe alike, are food for the scavenging beasts.

I saw Lord Death moving among the tumbled corpses, rubbing his fleshless hands and grinning his lipless smile as he gazed upon my wonderful work. He greeted me.

247

Well done, Myrddin. Such a handsome harvest; I am pleased, my son.

My horror could not be contained. Dark mist rose up before my eyes; the voices of the dead filled my ears with cries of sharp accusation. The bloody earth mocked me; sky and sun jeered. The wind laughed. I fled the field, seeking refuge in Celyddon's deep, black heart. I fled to the nameless hills, to the rock-bound mountains, to this barren outcrop with its cave and spring.

And here, Annwas, here is all Myrddin Wylt's kingdom. Here is where I have dwelt, and ever shall dwell.

Death! You have taken all the others, why have you not taken me?

THIRTEEN

I raised my head and looked out across the night-filled valleys. The storm had passed, and the stars shone brightly. The air was scented with pine and heather, and from the forest below came the bark of a hunting wolf — a single short cry in the darkness.

At my feet Wolf pricked her ears; her golden eyes flicked to mine, but she did not move. The small fire Annwas had made still burned; the pot bubbled and the cakes were baked. He sat watching me, his face sorrowful and serene.

'Do you hate me now, Annwas?' I asked in the silence of the snapping fire. 'Now that you know what I have done — do you despise me for it?'

He did not answer, but picked up a bowl and ladled stew into it and offered it out to me. 'I can hate no man,' he replied gently, offering me the bowl. 'And this is not a time for judgement.' He broke one of the little loaves he had made and handed it to me. 'We will eat now, and you will feel better.'

We ate together in silence. The food was good, and I did feel better. The fire warmed me, and the stew — how long had it been since I had meat in my stomach? — soon made me drowsy. I sopped the last of my broth with the bread and stuffed that into my mouth, then laid the bowl aside and drew my cloak around me.

'Sleep now, Myrddin,' Annwas told me. 'Sleep well.'

It seemed only an instant, but when I opened my eyes again the new-risen sun flamed the high peaks, and larksong fell golden from the sky. Annwas had the fire burning brightly and had brought water in the pot for me to drink.

'So, you are still here,' I observed, pouring water into my bowl and lifting the bowl to my mouth.

'I am,' he nodded.

'I am not going back with you,' I told him bluntly.

'That will be your decision, Myrddin.'

'Then you are wasting your time. I will not leave this place.'

'As you have said. But I tell you I have not come to take you away from here.'

What did he want from me? 'Then why have you come?'

'To save you, Myrddin.'

'Do I look in need of saving?'

'Your work is not finished,' he replied. 'In the world of men, affairs continue apace, and darkness covers nigh all. It has even reached these shores. Yes, the Great Darkness men have feared is here; it has gained a foothold on the Island of the Mighty.'

I glared at him, for his words disturbed me more than I liked. 'What do you expect me to do about it?'

'I tell you merely what is.' Annwas handed me half of the second loaf he had made the night before. 'What you do about it is for you to decide.'

'Who are you, Annwas Adeniawc? Why have you come to me like this?'

He smiled gently. 'I have told you, Myrddin. I am your friend.'

Then he rose and stepped to the cave entrance. 'Come with me now.'

'Where?' I demanded suspiciously.

'There is a stream in the glen below —'

'Yes?'

'We must go there.'

That was all he said. He turned and started down the trail. I watched him go for a moment, and decided that I would not go. But he stopped, turned, and beckoned me. I rose and followed.

The stream was not large, but it was running with the rain from the night before and there were deep pools round the boulders, and it was into one of these pools that Annwas led me. 'Set aside your cloak, Myrddin,' he instructed, stepping into the water, 'and your clothing.'

My clothing, as he generously called it, was little more than a filth-crusted loincloth. It fell from me as I shrugged it off. 'I have already been baptized,' I said.

'I know,' replied Annwas, holding out his hand to me. 'I just want to wash you.'

'I can wash myself.' I drew back.

'Na, na, I know, I know. But come, let me do it for you this once.'

I stepped into the cold water; my flesh prickled and I began shivering. Annwas took my hand and brought me to stand facing him. He dipped water with the bowl in his hand and poured it over me. Then he produced a chunk of soap — the hard, yellow kind such as the old Celts used to make in huge blocks for the whole clan, from which each household carved off what it needed — and he began to wash me.

He washed my arms and chest, then turned me to scrub my back. 'Sit,' he commanded, and I sat down on a nearby rock while he washed my legs and my nasty, matted hair and beard.

All this he did quickly and cheerfully, as if it were his life's chief fulfilment. I allowed him to do it, thinking it strange to be washed like this — me a grown man, being washed by another grown man.

But it did not *feel* strange. It felt comforting; more, it felt appropriate. This, I imagined, was how the emperors of the east came to their thrones.

Oh, it was good to be clean. Clean! How long had it been? How long?

He washed my hair and then, to my surprise — although nothing about Annwas should have surprised me by now — he brought out scissors and a razor of the Greek variety, and, kneeling before me in the water, he set about shaving me, first clipping the tangled curls short, then scraping the skin smooth with the honed edge.

When he finished he laved water over me with the bowl and then said, 'Arise, Myrddin, and go forth to meet the day.'

I stood, water streaming from me, feeling the sickness of all the sick years, the years of waste and grief and death flow away. I stood, and that sick skin sloughed from me and I was clean once more, clean and in my right mind.

I stepped from the rock pool and picked up my cloak, though loth was I to put on that filthy thing again.

Annwas had foreseen my predicament. 'Leave the cloak where it is. You will not need it.'

Well, perhaps he was right. The sun was bright and warm — still, it would not always be so. The mountains were cold at night; I would need it then. I stooped to pick it up again. 'Leave it,' he said.

And he turned to point down the trail. 'See,' he said, 'one comes who will dress you in clothes appropriate to your rank.'

I looked where he was pointing and, heaven bless me, I did see a lone figure toiling up the track, leading two saddled horses.

'Who is it?' I turned to Annwas, who had come to stand beside me.

'Someone whose love has carried you further than you will ever know.' His words seared into my heart, but his glance did not condemn me. 'He comes, and I must go.'

'Stay, friend.' I put out my hand to him.

'I have done what I came to do.'

'Will we meet again?'

He held his head to one side for a moment, as if appraising me. 'No, I think that will not be necessary.'

'Stay,' I insisted. 'Please, stay.'

'Myrddin,' he said, gently, gripping my hand tightly in his own, 'I have ever been with you.'

One of the horses on the trail below whinnied. I turned to see that the man labouring up the trail had approached more closely, and his form seemed familiar. Who could it be? I took a step closer.

'Farewell, Myrddin,' Annwas called, and when I turned towards him he was gone.

'Farewell, Annwas Adeniawc, until we meet again,' I called, and then sat down on the rock to wait until my visitor should present himself to me.

FOURTEEN

I did not have long to wait, for the man followed the trail up through the scree directly to the stream where I sat upon my rock. He did not see me — his eyes were raised to the cave still some way above, where he meant to find me.

I should have recognized him, but did not. He laboured up the trail and when he made to stop at the stream, I stood — thereby giving him considerable fright: meeting a naked man on a mountainside at sunrise was not what he expected.

'Greetings, friend,' I said as I stood. 'Forgive me for startling you, that was not my intention.'

'Oh!' He gave a little shout as he jumped back, as one might from a viper. But instantly his face changed. I knew him then, but the truth could not be accepted at once. And he recognized me. 'My lord Merlin!'

He dropped the reins and sank to his knees, tears starting into his eyes. His hands shook as he reached out to me, and he grinned like one demented with delight. 'Oh, my lord Merlin, I dared not hope —'

I stepped towards him hesitantly. 'Pelleas?'

'My lord. . . ' Happy tears streamed down his face. He clutched at my hand and clasped it to him, his body quivering with excitement.

'Pelleas?' I still could not believe it. 'Pelleas are you really here?'

'I am here, my master. Pelleas is here. I have found you at last!'

I shivered with a chill and he came to himself somewhat, although still ecstatic. He jumped up and ran to the horses, which had wandered a few paces, and, delving into the bag behind the saddle of the second horse, brought out a brightly coloured bundle. 'You are cold,' he said, 'but these will warm

253

you.' He unwrapped the bundle and began spreading clothing out on a boulder.

I drew on the finely-woven yellow tunic and blue-and-black checked trousers, then sat down and pulled on the soft brown leather boots and tied them at the knee. When I stood up again, Pelleas held out for me a deep blue cloak edged all around with wolf fur. It was a cloak made for a king; indeed, it was my own cloak remade — my old Hill Folk wolfskin new-sewn.

I gathered it over my shoulders and he stepped before me with a brooch in his hands — I recognized the ornament: two stags facing, their antlers entwined, ruby eyes gleaming fiercely at one another. The brooch had belonged to Taliesin; it was one of the treasures Charis kept in her wooden chest at Ynys Avallach.

Pelleas saw my wondering look as he fastened the fold of my cloak. 'Your mother sends this with her greetings.'

Suddenly, there were so many things I wanted to know, so many questions I needed to ask. I asked the first that occurred to me. 'But, Pelleas, how did you know where to find me?'

'I did not know, my lord,' he said simply; he fastened and stepped away. 'There, you are a king once more.'

'You mean —' I stared at him. 'You mean you have been searching for me all this time. . . these many years? It has been years, has it not? Of course it has, look at you, Pelleas — you are a grown man now. I — Pelleas, tell me, how long has it been? How long have I been away?'

'You have been away a fair time, lord. Many years.'

'A good many?'

'Yes, lord, a good many.'

'How many?'

He shrugged. 'Not so many that the name of Myrddin Emrys is not still remembered and revered in the land. In fact, your fame has increased most wonderfully. There is not a corner of the Island of the Mighty that does not know and fear you.' He fell to his knees once more. 'Oh, Merlin, my master, I am so happy to have found you at last. . . '

'How you must have searched — have you never stopped searching?'

'Until this moment, never. And if I had not found you just now, I would have gone on searching.'

254

I was awed by his devotion to me, and shamed by it. I turned away from him. 'I am not worthy of your sacrifice, Pelleas. God alone is worthy of such devotion.'

'As one cares for another, does he not also care for God?'

I heard a certain priest in his words. 'You have been listening to Brother Dafyd.'

'Bishop Dafyd,' he said, smiling.

'Bishop, is he now? Tell me, how is he?'

'Well,' Pelleas replied. 'Well and happy. He is run off his legs by his monastery, but men half his age cannot keep up with him. His heart is young still, and he is well. Indeed, he is the marvel of the realm.'

'And Maelwys? Does he fare as well?'

'My lord, Maelwys has joined his fathers.'

I do not know what answer I expected. But I felt Maelwys' loss sharply then and it came to me what my absence from the world of men had meant. 'And Elphin? What of Elphin?'

'Likewise, lord. Many years ago. And the Lady Rhonwyn as well.'

Fool! What did you think, lurking up here in your hovel, haunting the rock wastes like a wraith? What did you think? Did you not know that men mark their years differently, that their spans are less? While you squatted up here in your squalid misery, nursing your unholy grief, your friends and kinsmen grew old and died.

'I see,' I replied at length, much saddened. Maelwys, Elphin, Rhonwyn — gone, all of them. And how many others with them? Great Light, I did not know!

Pelleas had gone to the horses and now returned with food. 'Are you hungry? I have bread and cheese and a little mead. It will cheer you.'

'Let us eat together,' I said. 'I would welcome nothing more than to break my long fast with a friend.'

While we ate, he told me something of his search, which carried him to every corner of Celyddon. 'I thought you dead,' I told him when he finished. 'I saw them all dead — Custennin, Gwendolau, my warband. . . Ganieda — all dead, and you with them. I could not face it. Merciful Father, forgive me, I fled.'

'So many dead that day,' he replied gravely, 'but not all. I lived — and Custennin, too. I saw you ride away, did you know? I even called after you, but you did not hear me. Even then,' his face brightened, 'even then I knew that I would find you one day.'

'You must have been very certain. Certain enough to bring two horses.'

'Celyddon is great, my lord, but I never gave up hoping.'

'Your faith has been rewarded. I would reward you, too, but I have nothing. Even had I a hundred kingdoms, the gift would still be as nothing compared to the gift of your devotion, Pelleas. Has a man ever had such a friend?'

He shook his head slowly. 'I have my reward,' he said in a hushed voice. 'I seek no other than to serve you once more.'

We finished eating in silence and then I rose, brushing crumbs from my clothing. I breathed the mountain air deep into my lungs and it was the air of a world much-changed. While I had hidden in my cave, the darkness had grown strong. What I had now to do was to discover where the light still burned, and how brightly.

Pelleas bundled up the remaining food and joined me. 'Where do you propose to go, Lord Myrddin?'

'I hardly know.' I turned to the spring and cave above us on the mountainside. It now appeared a cold and forlorn and alien place. 'Does Custennin still abide in Celyddon?'

'Yes, lord. I was with him earlier in the spring.'

'And my mother — does she stay in Dyfed?'

'She has returned to Ynys Avallach.'

'I see. And what of Avallach?'

'He is well enough. But, as ever, he is troubled from time to time by his injury.'

I turned and asked sharply. 'If Charis is in Ynys Avallach, who rules in Dyfed?'

'Lord Tewdrig — a nephew of Maelwys.'

'And in the Summerlands?'

'A lord named Elyvar,' replied Pelleas, and added hesitantly, as if breaking bad news, 'but there is another over him — called Vortigern. Indeed, this. . . this *man* — he has set himself as king over all the lords of Britain.'

'A High King.' Oh, Vortigern, yes. I have seen your face in the fire; I have seen the shadow of your coming. Yes, and I have heard the thunder of your fall.

'What is it, my lord?'

'It is nothing, Pelleas. Vortigern rules in the Summerlands, you were saying?'

'In Gwynedd, Rheged, and Lloegres as well. He is a most ambitious man, lord, and most ruthless. He stops at nothing to win his way.'

'I know about him, Pelleas. But do not worry, his days are not long in the land.'

'Lord?'

'It is something I have seen, Pelleas.' I turned my eyes to look down into the valley where the dark folds of the trees gathered around the feet of the mountain. Four riders were making their way towards us along the banks of the stream.

I should have been surprised — especially after all these years alone — but part of me expected them, I think, for upon seeing them I knew who they were and why they had come. I knew also who had led them to me.

'The enemy has wasted no time,' I said, remembering my first visitor and his subtle guile. Well, I had not been tricked — sick in heart and mind as I was, by the Good God's grace I was not tricked. And now I was insane no longer. I was healed and whole again.

Ancient Enemy, do your worst! I, Myrddin Emrys, defy you!

Pelleas watched the riders approach for a moment. 'Perhaps we should leave now, master.'

'No,' I told him. 'You ask where we will go. I think these men have come to escort us on our way.'

'Where?'

'To see a wonder in the land — the man who has made himself a king higher than any other since kingship began in this island.'

'Vortigern's men! I was not followed, Lord Myrddin, I swear it!'

'No, you were not followed. They were sent by another.'

'We still have time — let us flee.'

'Why, Pelleas, we have nothing to fear from these men. Besides, I would like to meet this Vortigern face to face. I have never seen a High King before.'

Pelleas made a face. 'He is not much to look at, I am told. And those who value their lives and land stay as far away from him as possible.'

'Nevertheless, I will go and pay my respects to the man who has held the island in my stead.'

We waited while the riders toiled slowly up the steep slope, and it gave me time to observe them closely. They were three stout fighting men with bronze armbands and oxhide shields, and another, darker man who, judging by the oak staff behind his saddle, was a druid. Though it was early morning, all appeared worn and travel weary, their horses drooping with exhaustion. Their errand was an important one, I gathered; they had not lingered on the way, but had driven themselves hard to find me.

When they were close enough, I greeted them and called them to me. 'Hail, travellers, the Forest Lord welcomes you!'

They reined up at this and then sat looking at one another for a moment, muttering under their breath. 'Who are you?' the foremost rider, the druid, asked curtly.

'That you already know, for I have told you. I might well ask who you are, but I am not in the habit of asking questions when the answer is known to me.'

'You know who we are?' asked one of the others, coming a few cautious steps closer.

'I do,' I assured him.

'Then maybe you also know why we have come.' He cast a disapproving glance at Pelleas beside me, as if Pelleas had spoiled their secret.

'You have come to take me to meet your lord, one called Vortigern, who makes himself a king.' They did not like this answer, but it was true and they did not challenge my meaning for I spoke civilly enough.

'We have come,' replied the druid, 'to find one called Merlin Embries.'

'And you have found him,' I said. 'It is he that addresses you.'

The druid did not appear convinced. 'The man we seek was already old when I was a child. You cannot be Merlin.'

'Then indeed you do not know who it is you are searching for.'

He puzzled on that for a moment. 'They say Merlin is of the Fair Folk,' pointed out the rider beside him. 'That would explain it.'

'Your horses are tired, and you are nearly falling out of

258

your saddles. Dismount; rest yourselves and your animals. Eat something and regain your strength for our journey back.'

This shocked them more than anything I had said so far. They had thought to take me by force; the notion that I might go willingly had never occurred to them.

'We mean to take you with us,' the second rider stubbornly warned me.

'Have I not already said that I will go? I desire to speak with your lord.'

The druid nodded and signalled the others to dismount. He swung himself down from the saddle and came to stand before me. 'Do not try to escape. I am a druid; I have power. Your tricks will not work on me.'

I laughed. 'I would speak lightly of power, friend, for I know whence your power comes. I tell you the truth, I have faced your lord and was not overcome. I will not be overcome by you. Darkness has no power over light, and no power on earth can move me if I do not wish to be moved. It is by my free choice alone that I go with you.'

He frowned and turned to the others, barking orders to unsaddle and water the beasts. 'We will rest here a while,' he said.

'Help them with the horses, Pelleas. I must say my farewells.' I turned and began walking back up the hill to my cave to find Wolf.

Well, Wolf was not to be left behind so easily. At first, I feared for the horses, but I need not have worried, for at the sight of her with me the animals took her for a dog and accepted her as they would any hunting hound. The men were not so easily persuaded.

'Get that killer away!' cried one of the riders, leaping to his feet, his dagger drawn and held out before him — although what protection that would have offered, I cannot imagine.

'Sit down,' I told him. 'Be silent. She will not harm you if you do not provoke her. And put that knife away; if she wanted your life, nothing would save you, least of all your sorry blade.'

The man stared at the golden eyes of the wolf, then at mine. He made the sign against evil with his left hand and muttered under his breath. I heard what he said, and told him, 'You have nothing to fear, Iddec.'

His fright did not leave him and he clutched the knife even tighter. 'How do you know me?' he rasped.

'I know a great many things,' I replied.

One of the other riders heard what I said and came closer, giving the wolf a wide respect. 'Then you know what we mean to do —' he began.

'Yes, Daned, I know.'

'Shut up!' shouted the druid. 'It is a trick! Tell him nothing!'

'He *knows*!' shouted Daned. 'We cannot keep it from him.'

'He knows nothing unless *you* tell him!'

'He called me by name,' insisted Iddec. 'Both of us — he knew us both.'

The druid, Duach, flew at the warriors. 'He heard you talking among yourselves. You've probably named yourselves to him a hundred times since we first saw him.'

The two glanced at one another, unconvinced. Grumbling, they went back to unsaddling their horses. Duach turned on me. 'Leave them alone,' he said. 'They may be foolish enough to believe your lies; nevertheless, they will slit your throat right smart if I tell them to.'

Wolf beside me growled deep in her throat, and the druid stepped back. 'Get rid of that animal if you would save its life.'

'Do not raise your voice or hand against me again, Duach, if you would save yours.'

Pelleas had watched all this silently and now came close. 'I do not care for their manner, lord. Perhaps it is a mistake to go with them.'

I put my hand on his shoulder. 'Worry not, Pelleas. Nothing will happen to me that is not ordained. And as I said, we go with them not because they want me to, but because I choose it.'

He remained sceptical, so I added, 'Besides, it is the quickest way I know to announce to the world that Myrddin Emrys has returned to the land of the living.'

FIFTEEN

Vortigern, he of the thin red beard and narrow, wary eyes, had been an able battlelord once upon a time. Now he sat on his handsome throne, a jaded, sated old glutton; world weary, wretched, and sick with dread. His once-strong shoulders drooped and his paunch spread beneath his richly-woven mantle, the firm muscle of a warrior running to flesh and fat.

His pouched eyes still maintained the guile and cunning that had brought him to this place, however; and, for all his troubles, he still managed the air of a king, sitting in his great hall surrounded by his minions and mercenaries.

My first glimpse of the man who had brought so much ruin upon the Island of the Mighty did little to alter my opinion of him: in truth he was a bane and a curse upon the land. But as I watched him struggle with his dignity — a battle-scarred old badger backed to the wall — I understood him better, and I determined not to hold against him the things he had done. Justice would find him soon enough, of that I was certain sure, and it was not for my hand to hold the balance.

Looking back on it now, I see he was a shrewd and calculating man who had survived desperate times. If he had acted too much for love of himself first and his people last — and he had, oh yes, he had — some of his designs at least stemmed the on-rushing Saecsen tide. Because that, too, had been in his selfish interest.

True, he was reaping the harvest of his folly now, but not all of his decisions had been bad. He had done what he could with the sorry mess he had found, always making the best of a bad bargain. Indeed he had little enough help from the mewling, squabbling lords and chieftains around him. And if I in my madness had not forsaken my people and my land, who knows? — perhaps Vortigern would not have found the foothold he needed to ascend to the high throne.

Things might have been very different, indeed, if I had not deserted Britain.

None of that could be helped. What had happened, had happened, and there was no undoing it. Nevertheless, the day of reckoning was dawning for Vortigern and he knew it. But at least I would not raise my hand against him, and I would show him what mercy I could. God knows, he was a man in need of a friend.

The four who had sought me — the druid and three of Vortigern's bodyguard — brought me with all haste to where he waited in Yr Widdfa. We had travelled quickly and uneventfully, leaving the forest for the open hills two days after starting out. I was glad to see the wide, empty hillscape once more; after the closeness of the forest, the open spaces seemed like freedom itself.

It was not all gladness to me, however, for in the end I bade farewell to Wolf. A creature of the forest, she stopped at Celyddon's furthest edge and would go no further.

Farewell, faithful friend, your long vigil is over. You are free to go your way.

Upon reaching the king's camp, I was ushered before him without demonstration. The High King sat in the sunshine outside his tent, surrounded by mounds of stone and building material, and scores of labourers. Vortigern rubbed his grizzled chin and stared at me, a curious gleam lighting his hooded eyes. In his demise he had gathered to himself a body of druids, looking once more to the old ways for his hope, no doubt. Vortigern's druids regarded me with icy contempt; they knew me and hated me with the lively enmity of lost men confronting their doom.

'You are the one they call the Emrys?' Vortigern asked, finally. He was not, I suppose, much impressed by what he saw before him, expecting, as men do, someone of greater stature, or more marked appearance.

'I am known by many names,' I replied. 'Emrys is one of them, Merlin is another. Among my people I am called Myrddin.'

'Do you know why I have sought you?' He turned the heavy amber ring on his finger, and waited for me to answer.

'Work on your stronghold is going badly. Your druids blame an evil spirit for the failure of your masons to raise a decent wall.' I shrugged and added, 'In short, you require the blood of a virgin-born man to secure your foundations.'

This threw the druids into an indignant fluster. I think they really believed they could deceive me in the matter. But Vortigern only smiled at their consternation. 'What did you expect?' he told them. 'Is there any doubt this is the man we require?'

'He is an evil spirit himself,' said Vortigern's chief druid, a malevolent creature named Joram. 'Do not listen to him, my king, or he will confuse you with his lies.'

Old Vortigern waved the druid silent and said, 'And are you indeed a fatherless child?'

'My father was Taliesin ap Elphin ap Gwyddno Garanhir,' I told him. 'Names that used to be lauded in this land.'

'I know these names,' Vortigern said respectfully. 'They were men of great renown in Cymry.'

'Ah, but this Taliesin was not mortal!' declared Joram. 'It is well known to the Learned Brotherhood that he was an Otherworld being.'

'That will be news to my mother,' I replied coolly, 'and to anyone who knew him.' Some of those attending Vortigern laughed aloud.

'And where are they who knew him?' The chief druid stepped menacingly towards me with his rowan staff before him. It was so sad to see that fool mimicking the Learned Masters of old. Hafgan would quake with wrath to see it; he would have broken the man's staff over his insufferable head. 'Where are they who knew Taliesin?' demanded Joram triumphantly, as if proving me guilty beyond doubt. Guilty of what, I cannot say.

'Dead and in their graves,' I admitted. 'It has been a long time. Men grow old and they die.'

'But not you, eh, Myrddin Emrys?'

'I am as you see me.'

'I see a *young* man before me,' replied Vortigern, seeking, I think, to divert Joram and save my life, 'one who has not long used a razor — surely he cannot be the son of this Taliesin who died long before I myself was born.'

'Lord and King,' replied Joram quickly, 'do not let his appearance dissuade you from your plan. He is of the Fair Folk who live long and do not age as other men.'

'Hmmm,' uttered Vortigern. I could see he was in a spot. He bore me no ill will, and was even sorry, now that he had seen me, to have carried the scheme this far. 'Well, perhaps, if he *is* the son of Taliesin, he knows a thing or two — how about it, Myrddin? Do you know a way out of our difficulty?'

I addressed Joram with my answer. 'Let Joram say before us all why the stones fall each night and lay waste the day's work.'

Joram puffed out his cheeks, but remained silent.

'Come now,' I insisted. 'If you cannot tell us why the work fails, how is it you can declare with full certainty that my sacrificed blood will save it?'

He glared at me, and turned to his lord in protest, but Vortigern silenced him. 'Well, we are waiting, Joram.'

'It is well known already,' the false druid said. 'Each night while the workmen sleep, the evil spirit of this place troubles the foundation and overturns the stones. No matter how high the wall is built during the day, by morning it is rubble.' He took a deep breath and continued condescendingly. 'Therefore, the remedy is sure — the blood of a man virgin-born will bind the stones fast and the evil spirit will trouble it no more.'

'The evil is in your mind, Joram,' I told him. 'There is no evil spirit at work here, and no man virgin-born, save one only.'

Vortigern smiled craftily. 'Tell us, Wise Myrddin, what is the cause?'

'The ground hereabouts appears solid, but beneath it lies a pool filled with water. For this reason the ground gives way beneath the weight of the stone and the walls cannot hold.'

'Liar!' shouted Joram. 'It is a trick to save his life!'

'The truth of what I say can be easily proven,' I replied calmly. 'Vortigern, send your men to dig a ditch and you will see I speak the truth.'

Pelleas, who had stood by me all this time, managed to look both relieved and worried by this turn of events. 'Are you certain, master?' he whispered, as Vortigern called for workmen to carry out my orders.

'I know what I am doing, Pelleas,' I told him. 'But watch, there is more to come.'

I pointed out to the workmen where to dig and they set about it at once. It took some time for the hole to reach the proper depth, and with each shovelblade full the druid's satisfaction increased. For it appeared there would be no water.

But when the hole reached man height, one of the workers with an iron pick swung down and struck a piece of rock. The rock broke and he pulled out his pick to swing again and all at once water began bubbling up into the hole. In the end, the men had to scramble out to keep from being drowned.

Vortigern's court looked on in wonder as the gushing water filled the hole to the very top.

'Well done, Myrddin!' cried Vortigern. He turned sharply to Joram and demanded, 'What do you have to say to that, traitor?'

Joram had nothing to say. He held his tongue and fumed darkly at me. His fellows, clustered around him, muttered oaths and incantations against me, but they had no power and their spells fell like spent arrows at their feet. I understood then how very low the art of the bard had fallen, and it saddened me.

Taliesin, forgive your weaker brothers if you can. Ignorance spreads to every quarter on the wind, and truth is spurned and reviled.

Vortigern asked me then to name my reward, and I answered, 'I will not take silver or gold from you, Vortigern.'

'Take land then, friend,' he offered.

'Nor land,' I said. I wanted nothing from his hand. Indeed, how could I take from him a thing that was not his to give?

'Very well, let it be as you say. But I will have you share meat with me tonight. And,' his eyes gleamed wickedly, 'there will be an entertainment.'

I was given a tent in which to rest and refresh myself before supper. Pelleas and I retired and I slept, waking when a servant brought a basin for me to wash. Then we were led back to the hall and given seats at the high table next to Lord Vortigern. The druids were still there, still furious, their faces dark with rage and menace, but they were huddled next to the hearth and did not share Vortigern's table tonight.

'Welcome, friend Myrddin!' cried Vortigern when he saw me. The guest cup was pressed into my hand. 'Was Hael! Drink, friend! And fill your cup again!'

I drank and returned the cup. It was filled again, but I left it on the board and took my place beside the king. The meal was remarkable only for the quantity of food prepared. Vortigern and his retinue appeared to have endless appetites, but easily pleased palates. The fare was common — black bread, roasted meat — all cooked well enough, but ungarnished and unspiced.

Vortigern gave himself to his meal; I see him now, hunched over his plate, tearing meat from his knife with his teeth. Poor Vortigern, there was not a noble sinew in his body. How far he had overreached himself.

He did not speak during the meal, but when at last he wiped the grease from his lips with his sleeve, he turned to me. 'Now for a drink and some diversion, eh, Myrddin?'

Pelleas, who had served me through the meal so that he could remain by my side, did not like the sound of that. He gave me a warning look, but Vortigern had no mischief in mind for me.

The High King called for his chief bard and Joram shuffled forth warily. 'Do not think I have forgotten your treachery to me, druid,' said Vortigern, as the bard came to stand before him.

'If you would find treachery,' answered Joram sullenly, 'you have but to look no further than the one sitting at your right hand.'

'Enough of your slander!' the king snapped. 'I will hear no more from you.' He beckoned the captain of his bodyguard to him and declared before all the court, 'These men, who I entrusted with my life, have shown themselves false before me. They are worse than traitors. Draw your sword and kill them at once.' This was Vortigern all over — efficient, if ruthless, and eager to secure the friendship of powerful men who could help him. The soldier's steel came ringing from its sheath.

He hoped by this display to win me, for he turned to me and said, 'As these blind magicians were so eager for your blood, surely they will not mind my asking for theirs.'

There was nothing I could do for them; Vortigern was determined. But I wanted them to know, at last, who it was they had sought to destroy. 'If you please, Lord Vortigern, the reward you offered — I would claim it now.'

'By whatever god you worship, Myrddin, you shall have it. What do you propose?'

'A story,' I replied. 'Before they die, I would have them contemplate the power of a true bard.'

Vortigern had hoped for something more exotic, but he smiled graciously and ordered a harp to be brought to me. I took my place before the table and tuned the harp, as Vortigern's company gathered around me. I do not think that even then I knew precisely what I would say but, as I fingered the strings of the harp, searching for a melody, the words began forming on my tongue of their own accord and I knew that I had been led to this place and the words would be given in turn.

The harp nestled against my shoulder, I turned to Joram and said, 'As you show so little respect for the high bardic arts of old, I will tell you a true tale.' Lifting my voice to the hall, I said, 'Listen well, all of you.'

I gathered my cloak around me, closed my eyes and began to speak as one would speak to children. And this is the tale I told:

There was an eagle, and the father of eagles, who lived long, protecting his realm with beak and claw. One day a shrew came to Eagle and squatted beneath the oak where Eagle maintained his eyrie. And there he stayed until Eagle should speak to him.

'What do you want?' demanded Eagle. 'Tell me quickly, for I shall not suffer the like of you beneath my noble abode.'

'It is but a little thing,' replied Shrew. 'Only come down closer so that I may speak my matter plainly. For I grow dizzy shouting up at you like this.'

Eagle, being impatient to have an end to the matter, did as he was bade and flew down to meet Shrew. 'Well, here I am,' said Eagle. 'What do you want?'

'My voice is raw,' said Shrew, 'from all this shouting. Please come nearer.'

Eagle put his head near and, all at once, Shrew leapt upon his neck and bit it with his sharp teeth, so that Eagle was wounded grievously and died as his blood rushed out. Thereupon Shrew ran away so that no one ever saw him again.

When the other beasts and birds learned that Eagle had been wickedly killed, they were aggrieved and angry, for the exalted bird had been their king. They buried their lord and looked among themselves for a new king. 'Who can take Eagle's place?' they lamented. 'For none there is the like of our lord.'

But the fox was crafty and cunning. Seeing his chance, up he jumped and said, 'Does not our lord leave heirs behind? Let his oldest son be our lord.'

'For a fox, you are a foolish one,' replied the otter. 'The young eagles are only nestlings. They cannot even fly.'

'But they will soon grow up. Meanwhile, let us elect someone to stand guard over them, until the eldest of the three has come of an age to take up the lordship of the forest.'

'Well said,' declared the ox. 'Who will do this thing which you suggest?'

To speak plainly, none of the other creatures were willing to take on the care of nestlings, for the oak was high and eaglets are touchy birds and always hungry. 'Shame on you all,' cried Fox. 'Since none of you will undertake the care of the eaglets, I will do it — even though I am not the most worthy creature among you.'

So Fox set about raising the nestlings and, when the eldest of the three had come of age, the animals of field and forest came together beneath the noble oak and held council to make Eagle their king.

No sooner had they placed the crown on his head than did Fox take him aside and whisper to him, 'Do not be deceived, the other animals of the forest love you not at all. Why, when you and your brothers were nestlings they would have let you starve. You were not esteemed then, and I think the matter has not improved.'

'These are worrisome tidings,' replied young Eagle. 'Were it not for you, I would not be alive today.'

'True, but let us keep our wits about us. If you will take my counsel, I will guide you. Together we shall prevail against all comers.'

So young Eagle took Fox as his chief advisor to do swiftly whatever he deemed best to do for the good of the forest and them in it. Needless to say, Fox grew fat on his portion, and his red pelt grew sleek and rich.

By and by there came grumblings from beyond the forest that a great herd of pigs, having despoiled their own realm, were eager for new lands to seize. Fox came to young Eagle and said, 'Lord, I like not the things that I am hearing about these pigs.'

'Nor do I,' replied Eagle. 'You are the canniest of creatures, what is to be done?'

'Well, now that you say it, I believe a plan has come to me.'

'Speak it out, friend. For all we know the pigs may be on their way here now.'

'In the marshlands on the edge of the forest dwell a fair number of rats —'.

'Rats! I will have nothing to do with those vile creatures!'

'Oh, they are vile indeed. But it seems to me that if we were to take but a few of them into our service they would give us tidings regarding these pigs and we should be well informed of their intentions and so protect ourselves against them.'

'That is a bold plan,' answered Eagle, 'and as I have none better, so be it.'

So it was. A company of rats came into the forest that very day.

Fox saw to it that the rats lived well, receiving the best portion from his hand. Oh, he treated them like kings every one. In this way he won their confidence, so that when one day he came to them with tears in his eyes, they all looked about them for the cause of their provider's sorrow. 'What ails you, friend Fox?' they asked.

'Why, do you not know? The king has ordered me to send you all away — you who have been nothing but faithful to him from the first day to this.' And Fox sobbed so that his fur became soggy. 'Alas, I fear I must do as my king bids, for I have no goods or lands of my own and cannot keep you of myself.'

Hearing this the rats grew wrathful. They murmured against Eagle. 'Let us kill this mad king and raise Fox in his place. Then we will not lose our living; in fact, we might increase it.'

So saying, up they rose and by stealth killed young Eagle while he slept. When Fox saw that the rats had done what he knew they would, he raised the alarm. 'Woe! Woe! Our king is murdered! Help!'

The forest creatures rushed to his aid and all saw how Fox savagely killed the rats, and many were impressed. With his proud coat all bespattered with blood, Fox turned to the others and addressed them: 'I knew no good could come of having rats, and now worse has come to worst. I have killed the traitors, but once again we are without a king. Still,' he said sincerely, 'I am prepared to serve you well and wisely, if you will have me.'

'Who else has done so much for us?' shouted the badgers.

'Who else has done so much for himself?' muttered Ox and Otter.

Nevertheless, Fox was made King of the Forest and began his ignoble reign. That very night the two remaining eaglets took counsel with one another. 'Surely, with Fox reigning over us we are not long for this world. Let us fly to the mountains, for we will neither of us wear the crown now.'

'No, but at least we will stay alive,' answered the youngest. And they flew from the forest at once. The eaglets lived in the mountains, biding their time.

Fox made himself free with the ruling of the forest and increased his wealth as much as he liked, for no one could gainsay him. One day, however, the pigs he had lied about to young Eagle suddenly appeared. Fox was greatly distressed to see them, but sent word that they should come to him, which they did.

The pigs' leader was a great, meaty boar with the scars of many battles on his hide. Fox took one look at him and knew he had met his match. But he plucked up what little courage he possessed and said, 'My, you are a handsome pig, and so strong. Tell me of your errand here, and perhaps I can help you.'

The pigs looked long at one another and greatly marvelled, for no one had given them such a grand welcome. 'Well, lord,' replied Boar, 'as you see we are a fruitful breed, more quickly abounding than any other of forest or field. And, try as we might, the land cannot long sustain us and we must go out and find new feeding grounds.'

'Your story moves me,' replied Fox cannily. 'As it happens I have need of a strong companion, for although I am king, I am not well liked by those I must rule. In fact, though it grieves me full well to say it, they daily seek to destroy me.'

'Say no more,' answered Boar, 'I am the friend you seek. Only give us land to call our own and as long as I live I will protect you and serve you as loyal battlechief.'

'Land you shall have,' said Fox happily, 'and I would give you more besides, but the forest cannot maintain so great a host of pigs. I understand that even now pigs other than yourselves are on their way here to thieve and despoil.'

'Never let that worry you, lord,' answered Boar, 'we are fully able to hold our own and keep all others out.'

'Only do that and you shall not find me a miserly master,' Fox told him. 'For the less I must give to other pigs, the more I can give to you. Ask who you may and they will tell you, I always reward those who serve me.'

So the bargain was struck then and there, in just that way. Boar and his pigs settled themselves on the edge of the forest where they could guard the trails and keep any other creatures out. This they managed to do exceedingly well, for there are not many creatures willing to risk the wrath of a bold, battle-wise tusker.

Fox lavished gifts upon his army of swine, listening to their squeals of pleasure as if to a chorus of bards singing his praises. Both master and servants flourished far beyond their worth, much to the dismay of their fellow creatures of the forest.

But, by and by, the day came when the pigs became greedy, as pigs will do. They looked around and grunted to one another their misgivings. 'We do all the work and it is Fox who grows fat.'

Boar agreed with his chieftains and declared, 'I have heard you, brothers, and I agree. Now I will do something about this, as you shall see.'

It so happened that the young eagles had grown up and had become restless in the mountains. Said one to the other, 'I am not lying when I say I am sick of living like this while pigs overrun our forest with impunity.'

'You speak my thoughts exactly, brother. Let us go down to the forest and seek redress. It may be that we will win our own back. If not, we will at least be dead and no longer take notice of what vile creatures are ruling in our place.'

At once they flew off, streaking like comets through the clouds towards the forest.

Fox awoke from a happy nap to see a very disturbing sight:

an army of pigs arrayed against him, lead by Boar, his thick pelt bristling. 'What news, friends?' Fox asked.

'It seems to us that you have dealt falsely with us,' declared Boar. 'Frankly, this state of affairs cannot continue.'

'Am I to believe what I hear?' wondered Fox. 'How can you say this to me? I have given you all I have, keeping but little for myself to live on — the rest is yours.'

'Indeed, you give us the rest — which is little enough for earning the hate of all the other creatures,' grunted Boar. 'Now we want the best!'

Though they were only swine, they were not ignorant. They knew that Fox had been blaming all the problems of his reign on them. Thinking quickly, Fox said, 'There may be something in what you say. I must think me how best to right this wrong I have done you.'

Boar turned a suspicious bead of an eye on Fox, but said, 'What will you do?'

'I will give you a further half of all I possess, which will make you equal with me. We will rule the forest together, you and I — which, it seems to me, is a far better bargain than your like will find in many long years of looking.'

Boar liked what he heard, for Fox was ever clever at saving his fine red pelt and knew right well the soothing words to say. Still, Boar would not be made the fool; so he said, 'Saying is one thing, doing is another. Give me a token of your troth and I will believe you.'

Fox made tears come to his eyes. 'This, and after all I have done for you. Well, if there is no other way —'

'There is none,' declared Boar confidently.

'Then I will do as you require.' With that he turned and started off through the forest.

'Wait!' cried Boar, and all the pigs with him shouted, too. 'Where do you think to go?'

'Why, you are not so stupid as to think I keep my treasures hereabouts, where anyone can stumble over them?' Fox replied. 'I must go to my den to fetch the token you require.'

'Go then,' sniffed Boar. 'We will await you here.'

And Fox turned tail and ran away.

The pigs waited through the day and then through the evening and then through the night, but Fox did not return. And, when dawn came rose-fingered in the east, Boar roused himself and said, 'I am thinking that Fox is not returning. Nevertheless, we will wait until midday, and if our lord has not shown hide or hair, we shall surely go after him, and he will rue the day he deceived us.'

Needless to say, Fox did not return. For, by midday, he was far, far away, going to ground in his own lands in the west. And in their rage the pigs began uprooting trees and bushes and flinging them into the air with their tusks. Meanwhile, the two eagles, flying over the forest, looked down and saw the commotion the pigs were making over Fox's disappearance.

'Well, brother,' said the older eagle, 'if we are to have our revenge and save our lands, it appears that we must be the first to find Fox, or there will be nothing left of him worth finding.'

So, on they flew to harry Fox in his den. And that is where they are flying even now.

I stood in silence with my cloak wrapped round me. 'My tale is finished. He who has ears to hear, let him hear!'

The warriors filling Vortigern's hall stared at me nervously; the chief druid gripped his staff with both hands in a paroxysm of impotent rage. He had heard my children's tale and understood its hidden truth, and it angered him that I saw so much so clearly. He knew, at last he knew in his very soul, he was no match for me.

'There, Joram,' I said softly. 'Now you know the power of a true bard.'

Yes, and soon the rest of the world would remember as well.

You kings asleep in your mead halls, wake! Gather your warbands, arm your warriors, fill their hands with strong steel!

You warriors sunk in your cups at your lord's table, arise! Burnish your weapons, sharpen your blades, scour your warcaps, and paint bright your shields.

You people of the Island of the Mighty, stand! Stop your trembling; take heart, and make ready rich welcome. For the Soul of Britain is stirring again. Merlin is coming home.

BOOK
THREE
PROPHET

ONE

Vortigern had gone to ground in the west, in his native lands, choosing high Yr Widdfa's bleak hills for his last battleground. There he hoped to erect a fortress strong enough to keep the young eagles from stripping the flesh from his brittle bones, strong enough to keep the battling boar from uprooting him.

For it was as I had said in my story, fox Vortigern had played his last trick and now cowered in the hills, awaiting the judgement of those he had wronged, and those whose greed he had inflamed. The young eagles, Aurelius and Uther — younger brothers of Constans, murdered son of the slain Constantine, first High King of Britain — gathered warriors in the south. Hengist, the boar, awaited the arrival of reinforcements for his Saecsen warhost from his homeland. It would be a race to see which enemy would reach miserable, driven, fox Vortigern first.

Vortigern knew all this, of course, and early the next morning, as I was preparing to leave, the High King called me to him.

'I would not detain you unduly, Myrddin, for I esteem you highly. But if you would tarry with me but a little, I would speak with you, and I would deem it a service worth high reward.'

I was eager to be away, anxious now to seek out my mother in Ynys Avallach and let her know I was still alive. It rankled me to delay even a moment more; although I held no ill will towards the High King, there was nothing more to say to Vortigern. I had done what I had come to do, and even now word was winging across the land that I had returned.

I could hear the voices:

Myrddin Wylt is come! . . . Merlin the Enchanter has appeared! . . . The Great Emrys is alive again, awakened from his long sleep. . . Did you see? He defeated the druid bards of

277

the High King and had them all beheaded. . . He is here, I have seen him, Merlinus Ambrosius, King of Dyfed, has returned for his kingdom! . . . Did you hear? He has foretold Vortigern's doom! . . . Merlin lives again!

Yes, the Emrys had returned with the doom of the usurper in his hand. Vortigern, for all his sins and vices, was no mouse. What he had done he had always done boldly, with impunity. If his doom was to catch him up, he was game to hold it off as long as he could, by whatever means possible. But he wanted to know what shape it would take, so to prepare himself to fight or to flee — which is why he sent for me now.

'I have nothing more to tell you, Lord Vortigern,' I said. 'There is nothing else to say.'

'Perhaps not, but I would speak nonetheless,' the High King replied. He lowered himself heavily into his chair, a handsome thing carved with Imperial eagles on the armrests. His bloated face was haggard in the early morning light. 'I did not sleep last night,' he paused and I waited, 'for fear, Myrddin, for fear of a dream. . . '

He looked at me cannily. 'They tell me you are one who knows portents and dreams. I would have you tell me the meaning of mine, for I fear it greatly and believe it betokens much.'

'Very well, Vortigern, tell me your dream and, if I find a meaning in it, I will tell you.'

The grizzled red head nodded absently and he was silent for a moment, then began abruptly. 'I saw the pit the workmen dug at your bidding and at the bottom they struck a great stone and it broke and the water gushed forth — as it did, you know — and then you ordered the water to be drawn off by means of a ditch. This was done and, when the pool was carried away, a great cavern was discovered, and in it two great stones like eggs.'

He paused to swill some wine from a cup, and then continued, never looking at me with his eyes, but staring at the dead embers on his hearth. 'Inside the stone eggs were two dragons that came forth to battle one another. The first was white as milk, and the other — the other was red as blood. And they fought one another, shaking the very ground with their furious fight.

'Oh, it was terrible to behold! Their jaws foamed, their

tails thrashed, and with their claws they slashed one another. Flames flew out from their mouths! First the white would be above, and then beneath, and the same with the red dragon. Sorely they wounded one another, I tell you, and when neither could fight any more, they dragged themselves back to their eggs and slept, only to fight once again when they had rested.

'That is all, though it filled me with such terror that I awoke at once.' Vortigern dashed down the last of the wine and sat back, fixing his narrow eyes on me at last. 'Well, what say you, Myrddin? What of these dragons in the pit and their fierce fight?'

I answered him forthrightly, for I had seen the meaning in my mind as he spoke. 'Yours was a true dream, Vortigern. And here is its meaning: the dragons are kings yet to come, who will contend with one another for the Island of the Mighty — white for the Saecsen horde, blood red for the true Sons of Britain.'

'Which is fated to win, Myrddin?'

'Neither will triumph over the other until the land is united. In truth, the man has not been born who can bind the tribes of Britain together.'

He nodded again, slowly. 'What of me, Myrddin? What will happen to Vortigern?'

'Do you really want to know?'

'I must know.'

'Even now, Aurelius and Uther are sailing from Armorica —'

'So you have said,' he snorted, 'in that tale of yours.'

'They will arrive with fourteen galleys and put ashore tomorrow in the south. Meanwhile, Hengist has gathered his war brood and they march to meet you now. Your enemies are arrayed on every side. As you have done much evil, much evil will be done to you. Yet, if you would save your life, you must flee, Vortigern.'

'Is there nothing else I can do?'

I shook my head. 'Flee, Vortigern, or stay and face the wrath of those you have wronged. Make no mistake, Aurelius and Uther seek the blood price for their brother; they mean to pluck back their realm, and the kings of Britain march with them.'

'Is there no hope for me?' This was spoken softly, but

without self-pity. Vortigern knew what he had done and, likely, had long ago weighed out the losses against the gains.

'Here is your hope, Lord Vortigern, and the hope of our people: from the events which you have set in motion will arise a king who will hold all Britain in his hand, a High King who will be the wonder of the world — a Chief Dragon to utterly devour the white dragon of the pit.'

He smiled grimly and stood. 'Well, if I am to flee, I must be about it. Will you accompany me, Myrddin? I would have you with me for your presence is a balm to me.'

'No,' I told him. 'My road lies another way. Farewell, Lord Vortigern. We will not meet again.'

Pelleas and I departed the camp as Vortigern called his chieftains to order the march east, where he hoped to elude the vengeance of the brothers swooping down on him. It would go ill with fox Vortigern, yet there was nothing for it but to face the justice he had so long denied.

We were well away from the stronghold, riding down between the crease of the hills and out of sight. Pelleas, glancing a last time over his shoulder at the heads of the druids adorning a row of pikes along the ridgeway, sighed with relief. 'That is over.'

'For Vortigern, yes,' I replied, 'but not for us.'

'We ride to Ynys Avallach, do we not?'

'We do, but our stay there will not be long.'

'How long?' he asked, dreading my answer.

'A few days,' I told him, 'that is all. I wish it were more, believe me.'

'But —' He was remembering his master's temperament and how quickly moods and plans could change. 'But it is not to be.'

I shook my head gently. 'No, it is not to be.'

We rode on a pace or so, and then I reined up. 'Pelleas, listen carefully to me now. You have found me and brought me back to the world of men, and I thank you for that. But it is in my mind that you will soon curse the day you begged my service. You will wish, perhaps, that you had never wasted a day in searching for me.'

'Forgive me, my lord, but your own heart will prove traitor before I do,' he swore. And I knew he meant it with all that was in him.

'What I have to do will earn no man's thanks,' I warned him. 'It could be that before I am through I will be despised from one end of this island to the other, with every hand raised against me and those who stand with me.'

'Let others make their choice; I have made mine, my Lord Merlin.'

He was in earnest, and now that I knew he understood how hard it would be, I knew I could trust him with both our lives. 'So be it,' I said. 'May God reward your faith, my friend.'

We rode on then, considerably lighter of heart than before, for we had spoken the bond between us and our old places had been reclaimed. Pelleas was content, and so was I.

Aurelius and Uther, sons of Constantine by separate mothers and as different as dawn and dusk, would end Vortigern's reign with swift justice. Aurelius, the elder of the two, would be the next High King and would prove an inspired leader. His mother was Aurelia, the last flower of a noble Roman family — a claim which Constantine himself could make somewhat less certainly — whose forebears included a governor, a vicarius, a long line of distinguished magistrates, and scores of well-married and highly-revered women.

But Aurelia took fever and died suddenly when Aurelius was three years old. And Constantine, fresh from his victories over the harrying Pict, Scot, and Saecsen, had become smitten with the daughter of one of the defeated Saecsen leaders. In a fit of generosity towards the vanquished, he married the fair-haired beauty, a girl named Onbrawst. Little Uther was born a year later.

Both boys, near enough in age, were raised together in the old Roman manner, under the tutelage of a household servant. Their older brother, Constans, pledged to God from birth, was schooled apart, living with the priests at the little monastery at Venta Bulgarum. When Constantine was murdered by one of his slaves — vengeful Pict whose clan had been defeated years before — old Gosselyn, Archbishop of Londinium, became afraid for the younger boys' lives. He took Aurelius and Uther under his wing.

When, as a result of Vortigern's manipulations, Constans met his sorry end, Gosselyn wisely removed the boys from harm, sending them to an obscure priory in King Hoel's lands in Armorica — near enough to keep an eye on, far enough away not to be a threat to Vortigern's ambition. There they had grown to manhood, biding their time until they could return and claim their rightful place in the world.

This they would do, but they would soon need help if they were to advance the High Kingship beyond the mark made by Vortigern. Hengist would see to it that they had no rest, no opportunity to consolidate their gains, and the other kings, once Hengist was beaten back, would grant them no peace either. In short, they would need my help.

Pelleas and I moved swiftly. He led and I followed, agog at the changes wrought in the land since I had last been in it — especially in the settlements where fear accomplished its bleak work. Walls were everywhere, made of stone, and high. Most of the older, more expansive towns were abandoned — murderously difficult to defend — in favour of smaller, half-hidden stone-built settlements that were less conspicuous, and less inviting to the barbarian eye.

It seemed as if all dwelling places of men had shrunk in upon themselves. Streets, where there *were* streets, were narrower, the houses smaller and tighter. Everything appeared crowded and huddled together, cowering before the darkness that grew and grew.

This both saddened and outraged me.

By God's Holy Name, we are the Children of the Living Light! We do not cower in our dens like frightened livestock. This is the Island of the Mighty, and it is ours by right! The foeman challenges that right to his everlasting peril, but by the Great Good Light we will not be moved!

Yet, wherever I turned my eyes we *were* being moved — in body and in spirit. Back and back, retreating before the armies of the night we fled. We were no longer certain of our right or our ability to defend ourselves and our homeland. And, unless something was done soon, this retreat would become a rout.

I took heart that the land itself was solid as ever — not that anyone could change it very much. Trees grew tall for timber; fields, when they could be planted in peace and left to harvest, flourished; cattle and sheep gave good meat, leather, and wool; the old Roman mines were still worked and provided tin and lead and, more importantly, iron for weapons.

There was strength and consolation in this, to be sure. Still, it would take more than healthy agriculture to embolden the hearts of men. It would take a swift, certain demonstration of leadership: success in battle, turning back the onrushing barbarian tide. For this reason, I was anxious to meet Aurelius.

In this young eagle called Aurelius I saw great potential. Perhaps he could become the High King I had seen, the one men needed to restore their faith.

Oh, I had seen Aurelius from afar — in the firemists, in the black oak water of the seeing bowl — and I knew him, after a fashion. But I needed to meet him, to sit down and talk with him and observe what kind of man he was. Only then could I be certain if Britain had a worthy High King.

Purposefully, I stayed well away from my old lands in Dyfed. I was not yet ready to witness what changes had been wrought there and much preferred my memory of the place. My sudden appearance would be awkward, to say the least, for those ruling there now. News of my return would hasten to Maridunum — now called Caer Myrddin, Pelleas informed me blithely — and that would cause confusion enough. Besides, I was not at all certain what I should do, and there would be time to decide that later, after I had met with Aurelius.

Before that, however, I had but one desire: to return to the only home I knew, to see my mother. In truth, I never stopped to think what commotion my sudden appearance at Ynys Avallach would provoke. In my mind the place was always so serene, so remote from the frantic strivings of the larger world, I imagined — if I had any thought at all — that, simply setting foot onto the Isle of Apples, I would instantly fall under its peaceful enchantment, occupying the same place I had always occupied. *'Oh there you are Merlin, I wondered where you had gone.'* As if I had merely departed no further than the next room and had now returned but a moment, a small space of heartbeats, later.

For me, at least, it was something like that. For Charis and Avallach, it was something else entirely.

After the first flurry of sensation at the announcement of my arrival — there was now a gatehouse at the end of the causeway leading to the Fisher King's palace — the glad cries of welcome, and the tears — my own and my mother's — it still took some time for the place to recover its normal, staid dignity.

283

I had been missed, and sorely, my death contemplated and wondered at ten thousand thousand times since my disappearance. I had, selfishly I suppose, vastly underestimated my own value in my mother's life.

'I knew you were still alive,' Charis told me later, when the excitement had diminished. 'At least I think I would have known if you had been dead. I would have felt it.'

She sat holding my hand in her lap, clutching it as if afraid to let it go lest she lose me again so soon. She beamed her pleasure, the light bright and shining in her eyes, and glowing from her face. I do not believe I had ever seen her so happy. Except for this, and the fact that she had once again adopted the fashion of the Fair Folk, she was unchanged.

'I am sorry,' I said. How many times had I said that already? 'Forgive me, I could not help myself. I never meant to hurt you, I —'

'Hush.' She bent her head and kissed my hand. 'It has all been said and forgiven. It is past and done.'

At these words, and the truth behind them, the tears started to my eyes once more. Could one ever be worthy of such love?

That night I slept in my old room and the next day went fishing with Avallach, sitting on the centre bench while he poled the flat-bottomed boat along the bank to his favourite place. The sun danced on the lake surface and the reeds nodded in the warm breeze; a heron stalked the green shallows, looking for frogs, and nervous moorhens jerked and clucked on the mossy shore, and I felt like a child of three once more.

'What was it like, Merlin?' Avallach asked me. He stood poised with the spear.

'To be insane?'

'To be alone with God,' he answered. 'I have often wondered what it would be like to be in his presence — to see and hear him, to worship at his feet.'

'Is that who you think I was alone with?' It shamed me to realize I had not acknowledged it before. But through years of contemplation Avallach had grown sensitive to the life of the spirit.

'Who else? The Great Lord himself,' he said happily, 'or one of his angels. Either way, a very great honour.' At that moment a fish flashed beneath the stern of the boat and Avallach's spear flashed in the same instant and he drew it back out of the water with a fine pike wriggling on the barbed tines.

As he carefully removed the fish, I sought a reply. Of course, I had been sustained in the wild. At the time I had never questioned it, considering that my years of living with the Hill Folk had stood me good stead in surviving in the wilderness. But even that, surely, had been the Good God's hand at work, preparing me.

And at last he had appeared to me — I knew that, and had not dared admit it to myself aloud. But Avallach had seen it, and accepted it with the greatest enthusiasm and just a little pious envy. I marvelled at his faith.

'You are fortunate among men, Merlin. Most fortunate.' He bent and took up the pole once more and pushed the boat further along the reed-grown bank. 'I, who would dearly love to spend but a moment in my Lord's presence, must content myself with visions of his sacred cup.'

He said this matter-of-factly, but he was as serious as he was sincere. 'You have seen it, too?' I asked, forgetting that I had never told him *I* had seen it myself.

'Ah, I thought so.' Grandfather winked at me. 'Then you know.'

'That it exists? Yes, I believe that it does.'

'Have you touched it?' he asked softly, reverently.

I shook my head. 'No. Like yours, mine was a vision.'

'Ah. . . ' He sat down in the boat and held the dripping pole across his knees. The quiet lapping of the water against the boat's hull and the chirking of a frog filled the silence. When he spoke again, it was as a man sharing a confidence with a brother; never before had he spoken to me like this.

'You know,' he said, 'I have believed until this moment that the Lord's Cup was denied me for the great sin of my life. . . '

'Surely, grandfather, your sins are no greater than any other man's. Far less, I should think, than many I could name. And you have Jesu's forgiveness. . . '

My attempt to ease his mind was a thin one, and it is doubtful he even heard me, for he continued, 'I gave life to Morgian.'

At the sound of the name my heart turned leaden in my chest. Morgian. . . what had *she* been up to while I was lost to the world of men? Something told me her hands had not been idle. I saw her as a black spider spinning webs of alluring death around her.

'Where is Morgian?' I asked, dreading the answer. I had to know.

Avallach sighed wearily. 'She is in the Orcades — a group of small islands in the northern sea. A good place for her, I think; at least she is far from here.'

I had heard of this island realm, called Ynysoedd Erch, in the British tongue: the Islands of Fear. And now I knew why. 'What does she there?'

The Fisher King sighed wearily. No one who has not so mourned can know the pain of a parent whose child has gone wrong. But he bore his torment like the king he was, neither pitying himself nor excusing himself. 'What Morgian does only Morgian knows. But we hear lately that she has married a man, a king named Loth, and has borne him children.

'I know nothing of the man nor his unfortunate spawn, but there are tales of great wickedness in the north, and terrors that defy description. It is Morgian's handiwork, of course, but what she intends I cannot guess.'

I could guess well enough what she intended. 'Is anything known of these children?'

'Only that they live. But no, there is no word. . . no certain word about any of this. Just traveller's tales and dark rumours.'

Morgian had learned patience, I will give her that. She was biding her time well, no doubt steeping herself in her craft and the forbidden lore of the ancients, gaining strength and black wisdom. She could wait, knowing perhaps that her best time to strike had not yet come. There would be chaos in the land soon, and she would have her chance. When she struck there would be no mistaking it.

It was clear to me from that moment that the problems of Britain could not be considered wholly apart from Morgian. The very fact that she had taken a Briton king as husband — the people of the Orcades are Briton rather than Pict or Irish — could only mean that her ambitions had blossomed since I had last seen her. Then she might have been content with a soul or two to torture, now she wanted an entire realm.

Great Light, be the strong shield before your warriors, be the very steel in their hands!

It occurred to me to use the seeing bowl to determine what Morgian was about. Although I shrank inwardly from an encounter with her, I could have done it. But it seemed best to me not to interfere or draw attention to myself in any way. I did not know what powers she possessed. Very likely, she already knew I was back among the living — if not, she soon would. Better to let her wait and wonder. It never serves to let an enemy know your strength and position.

'Listen to me, Avallach,' I told him. 'You have no reason to feel guilt for Morgian. You are not responsible for her evil.'

'Am I not?' He frowned as if something foul lay on his tongue. 'I gave her life, Merlin. Oh, what would I give if . . . if —'

'If and if and if! Do you hear yourself?' I said hotly. 'If cannot change *is*!'

He looked at me with mild reproach for my temper. 'No, nothing is changed, Merlin,' he said sadly. 'We all must bear our failures to the grave.'

We spoke no more about this and went on to talk of happier things. Still, I wondered why his words stirred such a response in me.

'But he does blame himself,' said Charis later when I told her about it. 'He believes himself responsible.'

'One man cannot make himself responsible for the actions of another,' I insisted.

Mother smiled. 'One did, once. Or have you forgotten? Is there anything to prevent it happening again?'

I had not forgotten, but I remembered it now anew, and in a slightly different light. Was Charis suggesting that Avallach might be contemplating an atoning act on behalf of Morgian? Here was something new to think about. 'You cannot let him do it,' I said earnestly. 'You must not.'

'Merlin,' she said soothingly, 'what is the matter? You are troubled, son. Tell me.'

I sighed and shook my head. 'It is nothing; it will pass.' For some reason I thought of Maelwys, and I asked about him. 'Tell me, how did Maelwys die?'

'There was an attack on Maridunum,' Charis explained. 'We fought off the invaders, having met them on the coast. The battle was over and he was returning to the villa with some of his men. There was an ambush and the villa was fired. . . '

As she spoke, my mind filled with images of such horror and pain that I trembled to see them. My mother broke off her recitation. 'Merlin, what is wrong?'

It was some moments before I could speak. 'There is great hardship coming,' I replied at last. 'Many will fall in the darkness and many more will be lost to it.' I regarded her grimly, hating what I had seen. 'Surely, no one alive now has ever endured such calamity.'

'I have, Merlin,' she said gently, answering the note of hopelessness in my voice. 'I have endured, and so has Avallach, and all the rest who came with us.'

'Mother, look around, there are few left now — fewer every year.'

It was a cruel thing to say. I do not know why I said it, and the instant the words were out of my mouth I would have given my eyes to have them back.

Charis nodded sadly. 'It is true, my Hawk. There are fewer of us every year. Maildun, my brother, died in the winter.' She lowered her eyes. 'We will not last. I used to hope that we might find a way to survive here; I thought that with your father — through Taliesin and I — we might survive in that way. But it was not to be. Yes, our days upon the land are nearly over and soon we will follow the rest of Earth's first children into the dust.'

'I am sorry, Mother. I should not have spoken so. Forgive me.'

'It is the truth, Merlin. You need never apologize for the truth.' She raised her head and looked me square in the eye, and I saw I was mistaken if I thought her words meant *she* had given up. 'But there is a greater Truth that must not be silenced ever: the Kingdom of Summer. As long as I am alive, it too is alive. And it lives in you, Merlin, and in all who believe and follow.'

The Kingdom of Summer. . . was it only a dream of paradise? Or could it be made real, here and now? Could men of flesh and blood inhabit such a place?

Once Taliesin had conceived it, had sung its shape in the heart, there could be no turning away from it. To deny the Summer Realm now would be to acquiesce to defeat, and ultimately to evil itself. For whenever the vision of a greater good has been proclaimed in the world of men, it must be striven for even unto death. Anything less is denial, and denial mocks the Great Light that inhabits the vision and gives it life. Turning away from good once it is known is wilfully turning towards evil.

Taliesin had set an enormous burden upon my shoulders, for it fell to me to bring the Summer Kingdom into being. Would that I had his voice, his gifts! I might have sung it into existence.

Look! I can see him with the harp in his hands, the shimmering notes spinning from his fingers, his face glowing with the reflected glory of his song. . . and oh! such a song, words streaming from his throat as through a living doorway from the Otherworld, his fair hair shining in the torchlight, the whole world still and breathless to hear the heartbreaking beauty of his song. . . I see him and I weep. Father! I never knew you!

I stayed at Ynys Avallach until the new moon and let the timeless serenity of the place reclaim my soul. I would have need of serenity in the turbulent days ahead.

Then, on a cool, bright morning, Pelleas and I rode out once more to begin the long, impossible task of saving the Island of the Mighty.

TWO

I found Aurelius and Uther on the road returning from the battle with Vortigern. The old Fox had come to a messy end: locked in a burning tower, deserted by his closest allies. Even his son, Pascent, had fled to the coast, leaving his father to face justice alone. Thus the fight had been short and sharp, and decisive. The two brothers were still flushed with exultation when I met them a little north of Glevum, near where they had finally run Vortigern to ground.

Aurelius had been instantly proclaimed High King by those who supported him. I saw him and shuddered: he was so young!

'You were scarcely his age when you took the torc,' Pelleas whispered to me as we waited to be ushered before him.

True, I suppose, but I had hoped for a little more maturity to work with — I groaned for the work ahead. Young Aurelius was High King in name only; his biggest battle lay before him, for he had yet to win the support of the majority of smaller kings, most of whom thought themselves eminently qualified to rule the roost now that Vortigern was gone.

Winning fealty would be a rough campaign in itself; it did not need Hengist to make it more bloody than it already promised. I knew that many of the lesser lords would not be convinced by anything other than brute force. That was bad enough, but Hengist had yet to be dealt with. In short, I saw nothing for it but to advise Aurelius to make quick work of any who would not uphold him.

If he would listen to me. I had no right to expect that he would. Pelleas was more optimistic. 'Everyone has heard of Myrddin Emrys,' he told me. 'Of course he will see you. He will welcome you like a brother!'

Like a disreputable uncle, as it turned out. But he did agree to meet with me, which was something. I sat across the board from Aurelius in his skin tent, and we drank mead together while he watched me and tried to make up his mind about me. Uther had already made up his mind, and fussed and fidgeted in the background, trying to be noticed by his older brother so that he could say what he thought — which would in no way be complimentary, I was sure.

Aurelius had a brooding look, accentuated by a head of curly dark hair cut close to his skull in the Imperial manner, and dark, dark eyes, set deep under even dark brows. He had a high, noble forehead and a well-formed, unlined face, now sun-browned from his days on the road.

He also had Maximus' sword. Though I had not seen it since meeting the Duke of Britain that day in Elphin's stronghold when I was a small boy, I recognized it at once: the fine-honed steel, the bronze hilt wrapped with braided silver, the great eagle-carved amethyst winking purple in the pommel — there is not another like it in all the world.

How he had come by it, I could guess. How he had managed to keep it was the real marvel. If Vortigern, or anyone else, had known about it, he would not have lived to see this day. Old Gosselyn saved the boys, and he saved the sword; in so doing, he preserved more than he knew.

Aurelius looked me over carefully as I came to stand before him. The expression of vague disdain tugging at his features gave me to know that he thought little of the intrusion of an unexpected madman into his plans.

But, like it or not, we were stuck with each other. For neither of us was there anyone else. It all came down to us. I could accept that, but I did not know if Aurelius could.

'I am glad to meet the famous Merlin at last,' Aurelius said, trying out his best diplomacy. 'Your fame precedes you.'

'As does yours, Sire.' I used the newly-adopted epithet to show my support of his claim to the High Kingship. This pleased him immensely and the light came in his eyes.

'Does it indeed?' He wanted to hear it from my lips.

'How should it not? You have vanquished the usurper Vortigern and have collected the blood debt owed you these many years — and this in most impressive fashion. All the world is singing your praises.'

Whether or no he was true High King material, this little speech of mine would tell.

He smiled, but shook his head slowly. 'Not all the world, surely. I can think of a fair few who are singing their own praises even now — and some were men who marched with me but a few days ago.'

So he did not rise to the bait. Well done, Aurelius! My next probe sought different territory. 'Well, what of them? What does it matter what a few self-important grumblers think?'

'I only wish that *I* could dismiss them so easily. In truth, Merlin, I need those grumblers every one. They are all that stand between me and Hengist —' he flashed a sudden smile, ' — between my rump upon the throne and that blood-lusting Saecsen's. I like to think the Britons would prefer mine.'

'Yours is an admirable rump, my king,' I agreed with mock solemnity. 'Much to be preferred to any Saecsen rump.' And we both laughed. Pelleas and Uther stared at us as if we were drunk in our cups.

'My lord brother,' protested Uther, unable to hold himself back any longer, 'you have only just met this man and already you bespeak confidences to him.'

'Only just met? Oh, I think not, Uther. I have known the man for a very long time, it seems to me. And we have been testing one another since he walked into this tent.' Aurelius turned back to me. 'I will trust you, Merlin Ambrosius. You will be my counsellor —' Here Uther snorted loudly and shook his red locks in sharp disapproval. 'He will be my counsellor, Uther! I need an adviser, and we are not exactly neck deep in volunteers.'

Uther subsided, but Aurelius had warmed to the matter on his heart. 'Yes, another score left this morning — left the picket before dawn. My lords and chieftains are deserting me, Merlin. I have delivered them from Vortigern, and now they turn against me.'

'How many warriors are left?'

'There are two hundred here, and five hundred follow a day behind.'

'Seven hundred is not a man too many to take on Hengist,' growled Uther.

'Yes,' admitted Aurelius ruefully, 'and half of those are Hoel's men and they must return to Armorica soon.'

'It is worse than I thought,' I told him.

Aurelius dashed down the last of his mead and sat looking

glum. Uther paced dejectedly. How quickly the moods of the young can shift!

'Though not as bad as it might be,' I began. 'I have friends in the west, and in the north. I believe we can count them among your supporters.'

'The north!' Aurelius slapped the board with his palms. 'On my life, Merlin, if I had the north behind me, the south and midlands would fall in line.'

'The west is where the true power lies, Aurelius. It always has. The Romans never understood that, and so never really conquered this island at all.'

'The west?' sneered Uther, as if it were a disease. 'Cattle thieves and corn merchants.'

'So the Romans thought,' I replied. 'And where is Rome now?'

He glared lethally at me as I continued: 'But go to Dyfed and Gwynedd, and see for yourself — the Cymry are still there. Still ruling their clans with dynasties that stretch back five hundred years, a thousand! And they are as strong as ever, stronger perhaps now that Rome can no longer bleed them of men and tribute. Cattle thieves and corn merchants! Arms alone do not make a king strong, it takes cattle and corn as well. Any king who finally understands that *will* be High King indeed.'

'Well said, Merlin! Well said.' Aurelius slapped the board again. 'What do you propose? Shall we ride to the west first? Or to the north?'

'To the west —'

'We will go at once. Today!' Aurelius stood up, as if he would dash out and leap upon his horse.

Standing more slowly, I shook my head. 'I will go alone.'

'But —'

'I do think it best if I go alone. It has been a long time since I lived there. It would be well for me to see how matters sit first, before arriving with an army. Let me win them for you before you have to deal with them.'

'What do we do while you play at kingmaking?' demanded Uther. The last word was a slap in my face.

'Kingmaking is exactly what I *am* playing at, Uther, my lad,' I growled. 'Make no mistake. You won a great victory, yes — over an old man already exhausted and sore beset.'

He bristled at this, glowering murderously at me, but I was ruthless. 'Neither you nor your brother will last the summer without me and my *kingmaking*, and that is the way of it.'

'Have we no choice in the matter?' he whined.

'Of course, you have a choice. You can listen to me and do as I say, or you can find yourselves a shallow grave beside the road somewhere and scoop the dirt over your faces, or high-tail it back to Armorica to languish in Hoel's court the rest of your miserable lives.'

I let them have it between the eyes, but they took it like men and did not cringe. They did not like it, but neither did they yelp like spoiled children. If they had, I would have ridden from the camp and never returned.

So, it was a start. Aurelius' clear thinking prevailed over Uther's hot-blooded impulsiveness and I was firmly installed as the High King's counsellor — future High King, I should say, for we had much work to do before his rump could sit that throne.

That very afternoon Pelleas and I rode for Dyfed, taking with us only a few golden armbands Aurelius sent along for presents, to be given as I saw fit. These would be welcome, of course, a polite gesture; although the canny Cymry would not be won by gifts of gold. They would want to know who this upstart High King was, and what he was made of; eventually, they would want to meet him in the flesh. That would come, in time, but I wanted to prepare the way.

My first glimpse of my one-time homeland caused my throat to tighten and my eyes to mist. We had stopped a little way off the old Deva road on a hilltop overlooking the broad humps of the western hillscape. Those high, handsome hills, with the wind fingering the long grass and ruffling the new heather, spoke to me of a happier time — a time when a new-made king rode the hills with his proud warband, working tirelessly to make safe his realm.

We looked to the sea in those days. Now the invaders were firmly planted on our own soil. Vortigern had *given* Hengist and his brother Horsa their own lands along the south-eastern coast, in exchange for protection. While it was true that the Fox had no better alternative — so contrary were the kings beneath him, *they* would have sided with Hengist if Vortigern had not done it first! — the bargain proved disastrous in the

294

end. Hengist not only nipped the hand that fed him, he meant to take it off clean to the shoulder!

After a little time, Pelleas urged the horses forward and we started down into the long, crooked valley that wound between the hills leading in due course to Dyfed. We camped that night in a grove beside a quick-running burn, and arrived in Maridunum — Caer Myrddin, now — at sunset the following day.

In the dying light — like fiery embers of a fading fire — all crimson and gold and white, the town appeared unchanged, its walls solid, its streets paved, its houses square and upright. But it was an illusion; as we rode slowly through the streets I saw that the walls were breeched in places too numerous to count, the streets broken, the houses tumbled. Dogs ran in the ruins, and somewhere a baby bawled, but we saw no one about.

Pelleas would turn his head neither right nor left, but rode straight on without a sideways glance. I should have done the same, but could not help myself. What had happened to the town?

Maridunum had never been anything more than a scruffy, scuffling market town. Even so, it had life. Apparently that life was over and it had become the habitation of homeless dogs and phantom children. Having passed through Maridunum, as bad as it was, I was in no wise ready for the shock of seeing my old home and birthplace — the villa on the hill. It was as if I had ridden through the town and back in time a few hundred years. For the villa was gone and in its place stood a hillfort with a timber hall and palisade, and ringed with steep ditches — something common enough in the northern wilderness, but unseen in the civilized southland for ten generations or more.

For all the world, it appeared a Celtic settlement from before the Eagles set foot on the Island of the Mighty.

Pelleas led us up the path and waited below the gates, which were already shut against the night, although the sky was still light in the west. But the timber gates were opened readily enough following Pelleas' call, and we ambled into a compound crowded with clusters of small log-and-thatch huts surrounding a great hall of dressed timber, impressive in its proportions. Of the villa that had once stood on this very ground, there was no sign.

In Taliesin's time this seat of Demetae and Siluri power

had been ruled by Pendaran Gleddyvrudd, who in later years shared the throne with his son Maelwys and, briefly, even with me. Red Sword was long dead, of course and, alas, so was Maelwys.

Times and needs change. No doubt the hillfort was immensely more practical for its occupants. But I missed the villa, and found myself wondering whether the little chapel in the woods still stood, or whether it, like the villa, had been replaced by an older temple to an older god.

Pelleas nudged me. 'They are coming, master.'

I turned to see men issuing from the great hall, a few with torches in their hands. Their leader was a mature man of goodly stature with greased hair tied at the nape of his neck, and a huge golden torc on his neck. He looked enough like Maelwys that I knew Pendaran's bloodline to be healthy.

'Greetings, friend,' he said with casual friendliness, nevertheless eyeing me with keen interest. 'What brings you here?'

'I have come,' I answered, 'to seek a home I once knew.'

'It will be dark soon — too dark for searching out a settlement. Stay with us tonight,' his eyes had strayed to my harp behind the saddle, 'and we will help you find the place you seek in the morning.'

It was Tewdrig himself who addressed me; he had inherited Maelwys' generous nature. But I replied, 'In truth, *this* is the place I am looking for.'

He stepped closer and, putting his hand on the bridle of my horse, peered up at me. 'Do I know you? Tell me if I do, for I cannot remember ever seeing you within these walls.'

'No, there is no reason you should know me. It is many years since I have been here — when this hillfort was a villa still, and Maelwys was its king.'

He stared in disbelief. 'Myrddin?'

A murmur of excitement passed among those gathered round. One young man ran back into the hall and, a moment later, more men, and women, were streaming out into the yard.

'I am Myrddin,' I said quietly. 'And I have returned, Tewdrig.'

'You are welcome here, my lord. Will you come in and sit at my table?'

'That,' I said, climbing down from the saddle, 'we will be most happy to do.'

Pelleas and I were conducted into the great hall by the entire throng. News of my coming flitted like sparks on the wind among them and the hubbub grew around us. Although the hall was spacious, soon it was filled with a crush of people, all buzzing with excitement, so that Tewdrig had to shout in order to be heard.

'Lord, your arrival here is unexpected. If only you had sent your man ahead to warn us of your coming, I could have prepared a feast for you. As it is. . . ' he gestured vaguely round the hall. Although not bedecked with festive finery, it was no shabby place. I gathered from a glance that the Demetae and Silures still possessed much wealth and, hence, much power.

'As it stands,' I told him frankly, 'is how I wanted to see it.' I had not overlooked his use of the word *warn*, for despite his welcome, which was genuine, it bespoke the worry in his heart. I could calm his fears with a word, but I decided to let it wait for a moment, the better to see how he was made.

Tewdrig ordered food to be brought, and beer in the guest cup — a huge silver bowl with double handles — offered me by a comely girl with long dark braids. 'This is Govan, my wife,' Tewdrig offered, by way of introduction.

'Welcome, friend,' Govan replied demurely. 'Health to you, and success to your journey.'

With that I took the cup from Govan, lifted it by the handles and drank. The liquid was pale, frothy and cool, reviving my appetite admirably. 'It appears the brewer's art has reached new heights since last I held such a cup as this,' I commented. 'This is a draught worthy of any king.'

'You shall have a butt of it to take with you when you have concluded your business here,' Lord Tewdrig replied.

He was trying his best to get me to speak of my errand, without asking outright, which would have been ungracious. I could imagine the thoughts spinning in his head. If Myrddin, the former lord and king of this realm, had returned, it could be for one reason only: to reassert his claim to the throne and take back his lands. Where, he wondered, did that leave him exactly? The fact that I had not arrived with a warband at my command was not lost on him, and it made him wonder.

'I thank you most heartily,' I told him, replacing the cup. At that moment food was brought from the kitchens and the platters laid on the board. We took our places — I sat on his left, Govan with his infant son Meurig on his right — and we began to eat.

While we ate, I remarked on the changes I'd noticed in the town, and in the caer. Tewdrig lamented the passing of the town, and the necessity that had occasioned the construction of the hillfort. 'The villa could not be saved,' he said, 'although we have kept what treasures we could.' He pointed to the floor near the hearth, where I saw the old mosaic floor of red, white and black tiles that had adorned Gleddyvrudd's hall.

So sad, to lose something so fine. And we were losing so much that would never be replaced. 'Was it very bad?' I asked, wondering.

He nodded his head slowly. 'Bad enough. The same raid that took Maelwys, took the town and villa also. My father, Teithfallt, saved what he could, but there was not much.'

When supper was finished, a few of the younger boys who had seen the harp behind my saddle pushed one of the braver of their number forward to beg their lord's indulgence; they had a request of me.

Tewdrig was on the point of sending the audacious lad away with a stern rebuke for his affrontery, but I interceded. 'I would be most happy to sing them a song, Lord Tewdrig.'

The boy's eyes grew round, for he assumed I had known his request even before he spoke it. In truth, I had seen the same look on too many young boys' faces in the presence of a bard not to know what it meant.

'Bring me my harp, Gelli,' I told him. He stared, wondering how I knew his name. Like so many things since my madness, I did not know myself, until I had said it. But once spoken, I knew the thing I said to be true.

'Well,' said Tewdrig, 'do not stand there gaping like a fish on the beach. Fetch the harp, lad, look you quick!'

I sang from the tale of the Daughters of Llyr and pleased the whole of Caer Myrddin. They clamoured for more when I finished, but I was tired and so laid my harp aside, promising I would sing again another time, and people began shuffling off to their sleeping-places. Queen Govan bade us good night and carried the yawning Meurig away. Tewdrig ordered more beer and we withdrew, accompanied by Pelleas and two of the king's advisers, to his private chamber behind a woven wicker partition at the end of the hall.

It was clear that the lord of Caer Myrddin meant to have a full explanation of my presence, if it took all night. I had seen enough that evening to know that Tewdrig was an honourable man; and, no matter how things fell between us, he would do what honour required.

Therefore I decided to put a quick end to his anxiety.

We settled in chairs facing one another; a rushlight hung from the beam above, casting a ruddy circle of light, like a glimmering mantle thrown over us. One of his men filled silver-rimmed horns with beer and passed them to us. Pelleas stood behind my chair, silent, expressionless, his tall, handsome form like that of a protecting angel — which, in a way, he was.

Tewdrig drew a big draught and wiped the foam from his drooping moustache with a thumb and forefinger, eyeing me all the while. I noticed that neither of his men drank with him. 'It has been,' he said slowly, amiably, 'an interesting night. Too long have the songs of the bard been absent from my hearth. Thank you for filling my hall with joy tonight. I would reward you for your song. . . ' he paused and looked at me squarely, 'but something tells me you would accept nothing but what you came here to receive.'

'Lord and king,' I said quickly, 'have no fear for your throne on my account. I have not come to claim it — although I could make good that claim if that were my intent.'

'But it is not?' He rubbed his chin absently.

'No, it is not. I have not come to take back my lands, Tewdrig.'

His eyes went to his men and a secret signal passed between them, for instantly the tension in the room — subtle, but quite present — melted away. More beer was poured and they all drank. A crisis had been averted.

'I tell you the truth, Myrddin,' said Tewdrig. 'I did not know what I would do with you. This is your realm, and rightly; I avow it before you. I would not challenge your right. . . but I have been king here these many years, and my father before me. . . '

'There is no need to explain, Tewdrig. I well understand. For this reason I deem it best to let my claim lapse. Too much has happened, too many years have passed for me to take back my throne. Myrddin will not be king again.'

Tewdrig nodded sympathetically, but offered no response.

'No,' I continued, 'I will not be king again, but in remembrance of a time past when I was a king of Dyfed, I have come to ask your support for another who desperately needs your help.'

'If he is a friend of yours, Myrddin,' Tewdrig said expansively — it was relief talking, to be sure — 'we will offer whatever aid you deem best. You have but to name it.'

I leaned forward. 'Wiser not to promise before the boon is asked. Nevertheless, the need is such that I would hold you to it regardless. But no, no, it cannot be like that, for it is no small thing I ask.'

'Ask it, friend.'

'High King Vortigern is dead —'

'Vortigern dead!'

'How?' asked one of Tewdrig's men. 'When?' asked the other.

'Only a few days ago. He was killed by Aurelius, son of Constantine, the true High King. Aurelius has taken his father's place for now, but there are many who consider themselves more worthy to sit the High King's throne. Even now, those who fought at his side turn against him. I expect Aurelius will not last the summer —'

'Without support.'

'Without friends,' I said.

'I had little love for Constantine, and less for Vortigern; they were both arrogant, foolish men. It is because of Vortigern that we suffer the Saecsen wrath now.' Tewdrig paused and took a long drink, then placed the horn aside. 'If Aurelius had come here himself to ask for aid, I would have sent him away right quick. But you, you, Myrddin, you intercede for him. Why?'

'Because, my lord Tewdrig, he is all that stands between us and the Saecsen horde.'

Tewdrig chewed on that for a while. 'Is this so?'

'If it were not so, I would not have come to you like this. In truth, Aurelius is all we have.'

'But we have arms,' insisted one of Tewdrig's advisers. 'And we have men and horses to use them. We are more than a match for any Saecsen warband.'

'Are you indeed?' I asked scornfully. 'When was the last time you stood with a naked blade in your hand under the blast of Saecsen battlehorns, while a host of Saecsen Berserkers flew towards you over the battleground?' The man made no reply. 'I tell you that Hengist has assembled the greatest war host yet seen in the Island of the Mighty. And, before the summer is through, he means to have the throne — he *will* have it, too, for we are too busy squabbling among ourselves to take arms against him.'

'There is something in what you say,' allowed Tewdrig.

'There is truth in what I say.'

'What would you have us do?' the king asked.

'Two things,' I said. 'First, put aside any notions you might have that you will become High King — that cannot happen. Then, gather the warbands of the Demetae and Silures and ride with me to pledge them to Aurelius.'

'For how long?' asked one of the men.

'For as long as he needs them. For ever.'

Tewdrig pulled on his chin and looked from one to the other of his counsellors. 'This is something that cannot be decided tonight,' he said at length. 'It is late. I will sleep on the matter and give you my decision in the morning.'

'It will wait until morning,' I agreed, rising, then added a warning, 'but no longer. Rest well, Tewdrig.'

THREE

I arose early the next morning for Tewdrig's decision. But the king could not be found. His chamber was empty and no one would say where he went, nor when. I could but wait for him to return — and think the worst while I waited.

Midmorning, at Pelleas' insistence, I broke fast on a few little barley cakes and some watered wine. Then I went outside and walked around the caer, trying to see the old place beneath the new one. It was what I imagined grandfather Elphin's Caer Dyvi in Gwynedd must have been like: all industry and bustle clustered behind a stout earthen rampart topped by a timber wall.

And the people! Were these the same folk I had led in my brief time as king? They dressed not as the Britons I remember, but as the Celts of an older time: the women in long, colourful mantles; the men in bright-checked breeches and tunics; and all with the distinctive plaid cloaks of the Cymry. Their hair was worn long and bound back to hang in tight braids or loose ponytails. Wherever I looked, gold, silver, bronze or copper glinted from every throat and wrist and arm and shoulder — all worked in the cunning designs of the Celtic artisan.

Low-built houses, most of notched logs topped with a neat reed-thatched roof, sheltered one another with but narrow lanes between them, filling what had been the square courtyard of the villa. Tewdrig had a smith whose forge and hut occupied the mound where the old pagan temple had been. The forge was of stone, no doubt the selfsame stone of the temple.

Very well, in the day of strife when men worship steel for their salvation, let the temples become ironworks!

But this morning, so bright with summer's rich promise, the storm clouds seemed far away. Very far, indeed, from this realm of peace. On such a day I feared that Tewdrig's decision would go against me.

Surely, his advisers would say, *there is no need to further the claims of an upstart king. What is it to us if he boasts Imperial blood? If Aurelius would be High King, let him win the throne by the might of his sword. Whatever happens it is his business and none of ours; we have our own affairs to worry about.*

I could hear them coaxing Tewdrig to do what he was already inclined to do anyway, and I feared my efforts had been wasted. More, if I had misjudged the temper of the Demetae and Silures I had once ruled, how could I expect to fare any better with the kings of the north? Perhaps if I *had* pressed my claim to the kingship. . . perhaps, then. . . but no; the seed was sown. I would have to wait for the harvest.

And wait I did — like a hound waiting before the badger's hole. When *would* Tewdrig return?

At last — anxious, exasperated, tired of waiting — I dozed off for a light sleep before supper and was roused a short time later by Pelleas' nudge on my shoulder. 'Wake up, master. Lord Tewdrig has returned.'

I sat up instantly alert. 'When?'

'Just now. I heard the shout when the horses entered the yard.'

I stood and splashed water on my face from the laving bowl on the table, dried myself on the linen provided and then, straightening the folds of my cloak over my shoulder, went out to meet the king.

If I was taxed by my ordeal of waiting, Tewdrig appeared exhausted by his. Eyes red-rimmed, face grey with dust and fatigue, he obviously had not slept and had ridden very much further than planned. But a thin smile pulled at the corners of his mouth and, seeing that, I took hope.

'Bring me my cup!' he shouted as he strode into the hall. 'Bring cups for us all!'

I waited for him to come to me, and to speak the first word.

He in turn waited for the cups to be brought and his road-thirst slaked before he would speak. He drank deep and long, drawing out the moment full length. 'Well, Myrddin Emrys,' he said at last, lowering the cup and wiping his moustache with the back of his hand, 'you are looking at King Aurelius' most formidable ally.'

I wanted to let out a wild whoop of joy, but contained myself and simply replied, 'Indeed, I am glad to hear it. But why formidable?'

Tewdrig shook his head wearily, 'That I *must* be to have won against my lords and chieftains — all of whom put up a great resistance to your scheme, using iron-cast arguments which I was hard-pressed to beat down.'

'But you did beat them down.'

'Aye, that I did.' He eyed his counsellors while they stood grimly, their mouths pressed into firm scowls. 'And with no help from anyone here!' He looked at me once more and raised a hand to knead the back of his neck. 'Bless me, Jesu, I wheedled and bargained as if my life depended on it —'

'As well it might!' I told him.

'Be that as it may,' Tewdrig continued, 'I have done well by you this day, Myrddin Emrys. I have bent my honour no little way for you, and do not mind bending it further to tell you that I consider you as deep in my debt as ever any man was.'

'So be it. It is a debt I will repay gladly; for I count it gain to be indebted to so worthy a lord.'

'You should have seen me, Myrddin. Lleu's own tongue flapped in my head this day, and Lleu's logic was on me. Why, Lleu himself could not have argued better!'

Flushed anew with his victory, he bolted down some more beer and continued recklessly, 'When I left here I thought only to give my chieftains a chance to confirm my own thoughts in the matter. Yes, it's true: I was against it. But the more they talked, the more they argued — the more I hardened my heart to their cries.

'Make no mistake, I meant to find reason to refuse you, Myrddin. But I heard in their counsel the sounds of self-satisfied, small-minded men and I did not like that noise. In truth, it frightened me. Have we become so safe, our realm so secure that we no longer need the help of our brother kings? Are we now invincible? Or, have the Saecsens taken wings and fled home over the sea?'

'That,' Tewdrig growled triumphantly, 'is what I asked them, and they had no answer. There it is, Myrddin: I strove against my own chieftains, and I prevailed.' He lifted his cup and I took one up and lifted it to his. 'I drink to the new High King, may his spear fly true!'

We drank and, giving my cup to Pelleas, I raised my hands in the bardic declamation, saying, 'Your loyalty will be rewarded, Tewdrig. And because of the faith you have shown this day, you will win a name that will endure for ever in the land.'

This pleased him enormously, for he broke into a wide-toothed grin. 'My warriors will uphold that loyalty a hundred-fold! Let no one ever say that Dyfed did not back its king.'

I remained at Caer Myrddin another day and then set out with Pelleas and one of Tewdrig's advisers — Llawr Eilerw, one of the two who were always with him — and a small force of ten warriors as escort. We rode at once to the north, for I wanted to present Aurelius with as much support as I could gather before returning to him. Partly out of vanity, I suppose; ashamed as I am to say it, I wished to demonstrate my power to him, to gain his confidence. It was in my mind that I would need his complete trust, and very soon.

With Dyfed in hand, I could go to the northern kingdoms without feeling the beggar. Tewdrig ap Teithfallt was well respected in the north and, as I have said, the ties between the two regions were ancient and honourable. I anticipated no trouble and, indeed, received none.

Along the way, Llawr told me all that had happened since I had lived and ruled in Dyfed — most of which had come down to him from his elders, since he was in no wise old enough to have remembered it of himself.

It seems that word of the Goddeu massacre eventually reached Maridunum. Maelwys was heartbroken, but since my body had not been found there was some hope that I still lived.

'King Maelwys held firm to his dying day the notion that you were alive,' Llawr told me as we journeyed through the cool mountain passes of Yr Widdfa one afternoon. 'All those years, and he would never hear a word but that you would return one day.'

'I wish it could have been sooner,' I replied sadly. 'He died in the raid that took the villa, I believe?'

'That he did — and more than many with him.' Llawr's tone betrayed no emotion. Why should it? The events he spoke of had happened before he had been born, and the world he described was different from the one he knew. 'The barbarians came at us from the east, so the beacons were no use. They were on us almost before the alarm could be given. We beat them back, of course, but we lost Maelwys and the villa to them that day — Maelwys to an axeblade, the villa to the torch.'

I was silent for a time, out of respect for Maelwys, and all that he had given me of himself. Great Light, grant him a place of honour at your feast.

'Teithfallt succeeded him?' I asked a little while later.

'Yes, a nephew — Salach's youngest son.'

'Ah, Salach, I had forgotten about him. He went to Gaul to become a priest, did he not?'

'So he did, I am told. He had returned some years earlier to help Bishop Dafyd with his church — the bishop was getting old and required a younger hand take over certain duties. Salach had married and fathered two sons: the eldest one, Gwythelyn, already dedicated to the church, and the other, Teithfallt, he dedicated to Dyfed and its people.'

'In time Teithfallt distinguished himself in the eyes of Maelwys' lords as a canny battlechief, so when the king was killed it was natural they should choose him. Teithfallt ruled well and wisely and died in his bed. Tewdrig already shared the throne with his father as war leader, and he became king upon Teithfallt's death.'

'So that is the way of it,' I mused. The realm was in good, strong hands, and that was how it should be. I could never be a king again, even if I wanted to be; Aurelius needed me, the Island of the Mighty needed me, far more than Dyfed ever did, or would. It was clear to me that my Lord Jesu had placed my feet on a different path; my destiny lay another way.

If I had any qualms about returning to the north — to the scene of my beloved Ganieda's hideous death — they were swallowed up in the desire to see, at long last, her grave. Since my healing, I no longer felt the insane morbidity that had consumed and nearly destroyed me. I did feel the fleeting emptiness of a grief that would remain with me for ever. But it was not unbearable to me, and not without the upward-looking hope that we would one day be reunited on the other side of death's many-shadowed door.

So, before coming into Custennin's old stronghold in Celyddon, I had Pelleas conduct me to my wife's grave. He waited outside the little grove with the horses while I went in alone, as into a secluded chapel to pray.

I will not say that the sight of that small mound lying in the wooded glade, now much overgrown with woodbine and vetch, did not move me: I wept to see it, and my tears were sweet grief to me.

A single grey stone stood over the mound where her body lay in its hollowed-oak coffin. The stone, a single slab of slate, had been worked, its surface smoothed and trimmed, and an elaborate cross of Christ incised on its face. And, beneath the cross, the simple legend in Latin:

HIC TVMVLO IACET
GANIEDA FILIA CONSTENTIVS
IN PAX CHRISTVS

I traced the neatly-carved words with my fingertips and murmured, 'Here in this tomb lies Ganieda, daughter of Custennin, in the peace of Christ.'

There was no mention of the child, nor of my heart, as there might have been, for in truth both were buried with her.

All in all, it was a tranquil place, near where she had died; and if the gravesite was not much visited any more, at least it was hidden from the casual desecrations of unthinking wayfarers.

I knelt down and prayed a long prayer, and when I rose I felt peace reclaim its place in my soul. I left the grove content in heart and mind.

Then Pelleas and I returned to where our escort waited and we continued to Goddeu.

I should have known what to expect. I should have been prepared. But I was not. Too much had happened in too short a time, it seemed, and the sight of Custennin and Goddeu, unchanged, shocked me as much as the change in Maridunum had shocked me. But there he stood, bold and big as the day I first had seen him: proud monarch of Celyddon, Fair Folk king, great battlechief and ruler of a haughty people.

Like Avallach and others of their race, the years had not touched Custennin, nor would they. He even maintained the same appearance as when I knew him before — in everything, including the two black wolf-hounds crouching at his heels.

I swung down from the saddle as he approached and went to him. Without a word he gathered me in his powerful arms and crushed me to him, as I had seen him do with Ganieda countless times. 'Myrddin, my son,' he murmured in his deep voice. 'You have come back from the dead.'

'I have indeed,' I replied.

He pushed me away and held me at arm's length, looking at me. There were unshed tears in his eyes. 'I never thought to see you again. . . ' his eyes slid past me to Pelleas, whom he acknowledged with a nod, 'but Pelleas insisted you were still alive and he never stopped searching for you. Would that I had had his faith. . . '

'I only wish I could have come sooner.'

'Have you seen Ganieda's grave?'

'I have just come from there. It is a good stone.'

'Yes, I had the priests at Caer Ligal make it.'

I noticed he said nothing about his son, so I asked: 'What of Gwendolau?'

'He is buried on the field where he died. I will take you there if you like — but you will remember the place.'

'I have never forgotten it.' Nor would I ever.

'We have spoken our respect for the dead, and that is good and proper,' Custennin said. 'Now let us talk of the living. I have another son, for I have taken a wife in recent years and she has just given birth to a babe.'

This was good news and I told him so. Custennin was well pleased, for the birth of this child meant a great deal to him. 'What is his name?'

'Cunomor,' he told me, 'an old name, but a good one.'

'May he grow into the stature of his illustrious ancestors,' I said lightly.

'Come inside and rest from your journey. We will eat and drink together,' Custennin said, pulling me along with him. He held me by the arm as if he were afraid that I might disappear again if he relaxed his hold for even an instant. 'And then you will meet my new son.'

We did eat and drink together. And I greeted his son — who looked precisely like all newborn babes everywhere. I sang in Custennin's hall and fell asleep that night thinking about the first night I had sheltered under his roof: an awkward boy dressed in wolfskins, half-wild and alone, and hopelessly infatuated with the most beautiful girl I had ever seen.

The next morning I walked out to the place where Gwendolau was buried and I prayed for the Good God's mercy on his soul. It was evening when the reason for my visit arose. 'Well, Myrddin Wylt,' said Custennin, slapping a dog leash against his leg, 'what news of the wider world beyond this forest?'

We were walking together at the near fringe of the forest; a new dog which Custennin was training ran on ahead of us. 'There is news at last,' I replied; this was the king's way of saying that he was ready now to talk. 'Vortigern is dead.'

'Good!' He stared at the trail ahead. 'Health to his enemies!'

'Yes, and there were not a few of them.'

'Who is to be High King in his place?'

'Need anyone?' I asked, probing his mind on the subject.

He glanced quickly at me to see if I was serious. 'Oh, yes, I think so. Despite what Vortigern became, it is a good thing. Each year the Saecsen grow bolder; they take more. For each king to defend his own little patch — that is becoming too difficult. We must help one another if any of us are to survive. If a High King can make this happen, I support him.' He broke off abruptly.

'But?'

Custennin stopped walking and turned to me. 'But what we need is not another Vortigern, sitting in his mead hall, drunk on ambition and power, bloated with gold-lust, feasting the Saecsen and giving them land because he is too much a coward to confront them on the field of battle. . . ' He spat his venom and then paused. When he spoke again he was cooler. 'What we need is a war leader — a battlechief over all others, leading all the armies as his own.'

'A *Dux Britanniarum*,' I said, musing, 'Duke of Britain — supreme commander of all armies in the land.'

'Yes, *that* is what we need — not another Vortigern.' He started walking again.

'We would still need a High King,' I ventured, 'to keep the other kings in their place.'

'Oh, aye,' agreed Custennin, 'and to keep the war host supplied from the coffers of the kings beneath him. But on the battleground the supreme commander must wield a power above even the High King. In battle there is enough to worry about, without having to wonder whether you will offend this lord or that in some obscure way, or run out of supplies because someone did not send the aid he promised. The way we fight,' he lamented, 'it is a wonder we are still here at all.'

A plan was taking shape in my mind. 'What if I told you your thoughts could become reality?'

Custennin laughed. 'I would say you were an enchanter indeed — the Chief Enchanter of the Island of the Mighty!'

'But would you support the man?'

'How could I not? I have already said I would.' He looked at me slyly. 'Does such a man exist?'

'Not yet, but he will. Soon.'

'Who?'

'The man who killed Vortigern. . . men, rather. There were two of them — brothers.'

'Brothers.'

'What is more, they have already won the support of the kings of Dyfed for their claim to the High Kingship.'

Custennin mulled this over in his mind for a moment. 'Who are these remarkable men?'

'Aurelius and Uther, sons of Constantine. I believe that with the Cymry kings and the kings of the north on his side, Aurelius will be High King.'

'And the other — this Uther?'

'He could well be the battlelord you speak of.'

Custennin began to see what I was seeing. He nodded, then asked, 'The lords of the west will follow him?'

'They will,' I assured him. 'I have spoken to them as I am speaking to you now. On their behalf, Tewdrig sends his adviser — the one who rides with me — so that you will know that what I say is true: the lords of the west support Aurelius.'

Custennin slapped the leash sharply across his palm. 'Then the lords of the north will support him as well.' He smiled grimly. 'And by the god you serve, Myrddin, I pray that you are right.'

'Right or wrong,' I said, 'this new king and his brother are the only hope we have.'

The next day Custennin sent messengers out to his lords and chieftains to gather in Goddeu to voice their approval of his plans to support Aurelius as High King, and Uther as his supreme war leader. I could guess what Custennin's lords would think of the idea, but I did not know what Uther would say.

That, I would soon discover.

FOUR

I cannot say Uther was overjoyed to hear what the lords of the north had decided: that they would support Aurelius, *if* Uther would lead the war host. Uther, fancying himself High King material, rebelled at the thought, considering it somehow beneath him.

I delivered the ultimatum only moments after our arrival from Goddeu. Custennin, like Tewdrig, had sent advisers with me, and Aurelius had seen them as we entered camp — cold and wet, for it had been misting rain all day. The king summoned me before I could even change into dry clothing. Both Aurelius and Uther had listened to my summary, and Uther spoke first:

'So, the yapping dog is to be thrown a bone to keep him quiet — is that it?' I did not reply, so he continued, thrusting his fist in my face. 'You put them up to this! *You*, Merlin the Meddler.'

Aurelius looked on placidly. 'Uther, do not take on so —'

'How should I not, brother dear? I am to be made a simple spear-bearer and you sit by and say nothing,' Uther sulked. 'I should be a king at least.'

'It was Custennin's idea,' I told him. 'And it was his lords who added the condition of your leading the war host, not me. Still, I think it is no bad thing.'

'Consider it, Uther,' said Aurelius, seeking to smooth his brother's ruffled feathers, 'of the two of us, you *are* the better warrior.'

'True,' sniffed Uther.

'And as I am the older, the kingship falls to me.' Aurelius fixed him a stern glance.

'Also true,' Uther admitted.

'Then what is to prevent you from becoming this Supreme Commander?'

'It is an insult,' sneered Uther.

I bit back the words that were stinging my tongue like wasps.

Aurelius put a hand on his brother's shoulder. 'Since when is it an insult to lead the greatest army in the world?'

Uther softened. Aurelius pressed home his point. 'Is it an insult to be the Supreme Commander of all the Britons? Think of it, Uther! Hundreds of thousands of men at your command — a thousand thousand! — all looking to you, trusting you for their lives. You will win great renown, and your name will be remembered for ever.'

Shamelessly, Aurelius preened his brother's vanity. And not without the desired effect.

'The greatest army in the Empire,' Uther murmured.

'In an older time,' I put in, 'the war leader was called *Dux Britanniarum*. It means Duke of Britain. Magnus Maximus held the title before he became emperor.'

'You see? Not since Emperor Maximus have we had a *Dux Britanniarum*. A noble title, Uther, and it is yours — yours alone.' Here Aurelius broke off. He stepped backward a pace and raised his arm in the old Roman salute. 'Hail, Uther, Duke of Britain!'

Uther could not help himself any longer; he burst into a grin, answering, 'Hail, Aurelianus, High King of the Britons!'

They fell laughing into one another's arms like the overgrown boys they were. I let them have their fun, and then announced, 'Now then, Tewdrig and Custennin await an answer from you both. Their advisers are gathered in my tent and wish to speak with you before riding back to report to their lords. I suggest you do not keep them waiting even a moment longer.'

I do not know where Aurelius had come by his tact, but it was a well-honed tool with him and he used it like a craftsman. And that was not all; he also possessed a high and noble dignity which he could wield when it suited him, and this, on more than one occasion, won the day for him when words alone were not enough. To say that he coaxed and flattered the advisers who had come to see him would cheapen his art, for he was far more subtle than that.

He never coaxed, but he persuaded; he never flattered, but he encouraged those around him to think the best of themselves. Uther, of course, he had a different way with. Still, he was never devious or dishonest. The Imperial blood ran true in his veins and it was not in him to disgrace it.

As I came to know Aurelius, I came to honour him and to love him. He was what our people needed. He would be a true High King to unite all kingdoms with his power, just as Uther would be the battlechief to lead them on the field of battle. Together they made a most formidable force. Although, there was never any doubt in my mind which one of the two was the wiser and stronger.

Uther simply did not have his brother's character. He was not to blame, perhaps, for this lack. Men of Aurelius' stamp are rare. It was merely Uther's poor luck to have Aurelius for a brother and to be forced to live his whole life in his brother's shadow. In consequence, I undertook never to compare one of them against the other, nor ever to praise Aurelius in Uther's hearing — nor out of it — without also praising Uther.

A small thing, you may think, but empires have foundered on less.

With the kingdoms of the west and the north behind Aurelius, the stiff-necked lords of Lloegres in the south were suddenly faced with an almost insurmountable obstacle to winning the High Kingship for themselves or one of their own. Most, seeing the prudence of capitulation — if not the wisdom of unity — fell in with the powerful west and north in their support of Aurelius.

For others, in whom the white-hot fires of ambition burned, and blinded, it was a challenge that could not be ignored. They would fight Aurelius for the throne and quench the fire once and for all in blood. Woefully, many a good man lost his life to an ally who, on another day, might have been fighting Jutes and Saecsens instead.

It was a painful purging, but necessary. Aurelius would be king of all, or king of none. There was no other way.

I rode with him, always by his side, upholding him in battle as Taliesin had done for Elphin in another day. I will say that they had need of my help through that long, difficult summer. Aurelius, so sure and forthright ordinarily, would at times misdoubt himself and grow discouraged. 'Nothing can be worth *this*, Merlin,' he would moan, and I would embolden him with heartening words.

Uther had no stomach for fighting allies, but he was a warrior, and had a warrior's soul; he could dare, and do, many things other men would shrink from. And this earned him a fearsome reputation in the land: Uther, it was soon whispered abroad, was Aurelius' wolfhound — a cold-hearted killer who would tear throat and heart out of any man at his master's slightest command.

He was not so much cold-hearted as he was loyal, and his loyalty — to his brother, to the High Kingship itself — knew no bounds. In this, Uther earned my respect; his steadfastness was sprung from love — a love both genuine and pure. There are not many men who love so selflessly as Uther loved Aurelius.

This flame-haired firebrand lavished no love on me, however. He distrusted me with the same unreasoning suspicion many so-called enlightened men adopt in the presence of someone or something they cannot comprehend. He tolerated me, yes. And in time he came to accept me and even to value my counsel. For he saw that I meant him no harm, and that I shared his love of Aurelius.

Well, we three were a sight to behold: riding here and there with our troops, most of whom were unmounted — there simply were not enough horses to go round; hungry all the time; tired and dirty and sore; wounded and sick. But we were tenacious. We had fastened on the High Kingship, like hounds on the scent of the stag, and we would not be put off.

One by one, the warbands of Lloegres fell to us. One by one, we added the fealty of southern lords to Aurelius' rule: Dunaut, lord of the belligerent Brigantes; Coledac, lord of the ancient Iceni and Catuvellauni; Morcant, lord of the industrious and independent Belgae; Gorlas, lord of the contentious Cornovii. Proud, arrogant men, each and every one of them. But they all bowed the knee to Aurelius before it was through.

Then, in the last shining days of false summer, just before the autumn rain spread its dripping cloak over the land, we turned to face Hengist at last.

It was not the best of circumstances. We might have waited through the winter, nursing our strength, healing our wounds, biding our time until the next spring. We might even have paused to crown Aurelius properly. But the thought of suffering the Saecsen horde even one more season on British soil rankled with Aurelius. 'Let them crown me later,' Aurelius said, 'if there is anything left to crown.'

Besides, as Uther pointed out, it would only give Hengist time to amass more men for, certainly, more ships would come across the Narrow Sea with the spring floods. Also, there was no telling how long the lords of Lloegres would remain loyal; they might forget their promises in the long winter months ahead. Best to strike now and settle the matter once and for all.

That would have been my counsel in any case. Hengist had already grown stronger through the long summer. He had been joined by his brother Horsa, with six more shipfuls of warriors. They had encamped themselves along the eastern shores — called the Saecsen Shore even by the Romans, who had built fortresses to keep the warships from raiding the coast. Now the Saecsens owned these fortresses and the land around them — lands they had been given by Vortigern, and other lands and strongholds they had not been given.

We marched to the east, to the Saecsen Shore, to the very doors of the fortresses themselves if need be, for we were determined to carry the fight to Hengist come what may. We need not have worried whether the barbarian would meet us. They were eager for blood; indeed, it had been a thirsty summer for them.

Aurelius raised his standard, the Imperial Eagle, and pitched his tent beneath it on a hill overlooking a ford on the River Nene. Somewhere across the river, well hidden, Hengist's war host was waiting.

'This will suit our purpose,' declared Aurelius. 'The Eagle will not fly from this hill until all the Saecsens are driven into the sea!' With that he plunged his sword into the turf in front of his tent and he went in to rest.

For men who had existed on a steady diet of war all summer, there was a surprising air of excitement in the camp. Men talked earnestly to one another, they laughed readily and loudly, they went briskly and happily about their tasks in a mood of high anticipation.

The reason for this, I came to understand, was partly that they trusted Uther to lead them wisely. He had shown himself an inspired leader, a natural battlechief: quick, decisive, yet cool in the heat of the clash, a consummate horseman and skilled with spear and sword — in short, more than a match for any who drew blade against him.

But part of the reason for the high spirits was that at last we were meeting the real enemy. Tomorrow we would fight Saecsens — *not* subdue an ally. There would be a true foe arrayed on the field against us, not a would-be friend. And this thought lifted the spirits of the warriors.

As I was going to my tent, Uther stopped me on his way to meet with his battlechiefs. 'Lord Emrys,' he said, the light taunt always in his voice, 'a word.'

'Yes?'

'It would be well to have a song tonight. I am thinking the war host would fight the better tomorrow for a song to set the fire in their hearts.'

The men appeared in excellent fettle to me, and in any event there were two or three other harpers in the camp, for some of the other kings travelled with their bards, and these often sang for the men. All the same, I replied, 'It is a good idea. I will ask one of the harpers for you. Which would you like?'

'*You*, Myrddin.' He used the Cymric form of my name, something he rarely did. 'Please.'

'Why, Uther?' I had caught something in his tone I had never heard from him before.

'The men would feel better,' he said, his eyes sliding from mine.

'The men.' I said and was silent.

He could endure only so much silence, so at last he burst out, as if the words had been trapped inside him, 'Oh, very well, it is not for the men only.'

'No?'

'*I* would feel better for it.' He smacked his fist angrily against his thigh, as if the words had cost him dearly. But he looked at me with something like pain in his eyes. Or fear. 'Please, Merlin?'

'I will do it, Uther. But you must tell me why.'

317

He stepped close, and spoke low. 'Well, there is no reason you should not know. . . ' he began, and halted, searching for words, 'My scouts have returned from across the river. . . '

'And?'

'If their count is accurate — and I trust with my life that it is — we will face an enemy war host larger than any other since fighting began in this island.'

'That is not saying very much. How large?'

'Were we five times our own number we still would not match them man for man.' He spat the words. 'Now you know.'

So, Hengist had been busy all summer and his efforts had born fruit. 'But the men are not to know — is that it?'

'They will learn it soon enough.'

'Tell them, Uther. You cannot let them discover it on the field tomorrow.'

'Would it serve a purpose, do you think, to have them worry with it through the night?'

He walked off without another word, and I went on to my tent and bade Pelleas string and tune my harp, so that I could sing as Uther requested. I rested, and then, after supper, when the war host had gathered round the huge fire-ring Uther had ordered to be made, readied myself.

It was in my mind that there were many people — very many, if not most now alive — who had never heard a true bard sing. Certainly, the young warriors of our war host had never heard. It saddened me to think that more than a few would go to their graves tomorrow never having known, nor felt the power of the perfected word in song. Therefore, I was determined to show them.

I stripped and washed myself, and then dressed in my finest clothes. I owned a belt made of spiral discs of silver which had been given to me by one of Aurelius' lords; this Pelleas polished until it shone and I tied it around my waist. I scraped my hair back and bound it with leather. I donned my fine cloak of midnight blue, and Pelleas arranged the folds precisely and fastened them at my shoulder with Taliesin's great stag's-head brooch which Charis had given me. I took up the harp and stepped out into the night to sing for the massed war bands of the Island of the Mighty.

The stars shone like bright spearpoints to the low-rising moon's silver shield, and I sang. Straight and tall before them, I sang: I was a dancing flame against a wall of fire; I was a wild tempest in their midst; I was a voice falling like bright lightning from an uncertain sky; I was a shout of triumph at the Gates of Death.

I sang courage in the heart and strength in the arm; I sang bravery, valour, and gallantry. I sang honour.

I sang the power of Holy Jesu to save their living souls from eternal night, and my song became a high and holy prayer.

Awe descended over the warriors as the song came shining from my lips. I saw their faces bright and lifted up; I saw them changed from mortal men to warrior gods who would gladly die to defend their brothers and their homes. I saw a great and terrible spirit descend over the camp: deadly Clota, spirit of justice in battle, the dark flame of destiny cupped in her hand.

Here it begins, I thought; here is where the winning of Britain begins. . . Now, this night.

FIVE

Uther awakened the camp early. We broke fast and pulled on our battledress in the dark, and then moved into position. Now we sat on horseback on the crest of the hill above the ford, awaiting the sunrise. Across the sleepy Nene the Saecsen war host assembled: ten thousand strong, moving inexorably down the opposite slopes like the shadow of a mighty cloud on a sunny day. But it was no shadow darkening the land. Great Light, there were too many of them!

Hengist had indeed grown strong; he must have been building his forces throughout the long summer, swelling his war host with Saecsens from home. And not Saecsens only. There were Angles, Jutes, Frisians, Picti, of course, and Irish Scotti as well. All had answered Hengist's summons to the husting.

In contrast, our own troops appeared to have dwindled away since the night before when they had seemed as numerous as the starry host itself. Uther's scouts had told the truth: they were five to our one.

'Lleu and Zeus!' swore Uther when he saw them. 'Where can they have come from?'

'Never mind,' I told him. 'It is where they are *going* that matters.'

'Well said, Merlin,' answered Aurelius. 'Today we send them to meet their ill-famed Woden — and let them explain to him why they were bested by so few Britons!'

Aurelius and Uther then fell to discussing the battle plan for a moment but, as everything was in readiness and all had been said before, there was little more to do. Uther saluted his brother and moved off to take his place at the head of his troops. 'Pray to your Lord Jesu, Merlin; I am certain he will hear you and grant us the victory today,' Uther called after him.

This was the first interest in Jesu that Uther had ever

exhibited, if interest it was. I answered him, 'My lord hears your voice, Uther, and stands ready to aid all who call upon him — even now!'

'So be it!' came the reply. Uther snapped the reins and the horse trotted off.

The Britons were to advance slowly to the river and wait for the enemy to come across. We did not care to fight with our backs to the water, although taking the enemy midway in the stream might offer a slight advantage — *if* we could keep the battle line stretched out. The danger in this was that, once through the line, the barbarian could swarm around our flanks and gain the high ground behind us.

To keep that from happening, Uther determined to hold a third of the war host back, to reinforce the flanks if the Saecsens began to overwhelm them. Aurelius would lead this rear guard, and I, as was my custom, would ride beside him. Pelleas rode beside me, stalwart and grim. Together we had determined to protect the High King come what may.

Aurelius commanded the remnant of Hoel's men who had not returned to their lord. With us was Gorlas, who, next to Tewdrig, possessed the largest mounted warband.

At Uther's command, the foremost line started forward, horses and men together. At the last moment, when the two armies closed on one another, the horsemen would whip their mounts to speed, meeting the first wave of foemen with the lightning of steel and the thunder of pounding hooves.

Our warriors started down the long slope. As expected, the enemy started forward as well — some even reached the river-bank and leapt into the water. But Hengist had foreseen the folly of this type of attack and corrected it before committing himself to an indefensible position. The Saecsen line halted on their own side of the river and waited, raising a great cry of challenge to us.

I could hear their taunts from where I sat. Aurelius jerked the reins back and forth, causing his horse to toss its head and snort. 'Where did they learn that?' he wondered aloud, then looked at me. 'What will Uther do now?'

We did not have to wait long for the answer, for speeding towards us came a messenger, who reined up with a sharp salute. 'Lord Uther asks that you join him on the field at once.' The excitement in his voice made it quiver.

'Very well,' replied Aurelius. 'Anything else?'

'Hold the centre,' said the messenger, repeating his commander's words.

'Hold the centre? That is all?'

The messenger nodded once, wheeled his horse and sped back to join his commander.

Aurelius signalled Gorlas to follow and we started down the hill to the river. At first we did not see what our battlechief intended — perhaps Hengist would not guess either! — but, as we came up behind Uther, the whole front rank, all horsemen, swung out and rode quickly upstream leaving the footmen behind. We moved in to fill the gap Uther left, and to wait.

Hengist greeted this change in the battle array with long blasts on the great Saecsen war horns — those blood-chilling harbingers of doom. The din along the riverbank was deafening.

The Picti danced their defiance, and struck out at easy targets with their evil arrows; Jutes and Frisians banged their spears against their hide-covered shields; Scotti, naked, hair limed and pulled into spiked crowns, their bodies stained with woad, wailed their air-splitting battlesongs; all the while, Saecsen Berserkers howled and slapped each other until their flesh was red and insensitive to pain. Everywhere I looked I saw wild gyrating barbarians, screaming and gnashing their teeth, dashing into the water now and again, taunting, always taunting.

Some few among the High King's warriors had never seen Saecsens before, and were as unprepared for the unholy sight as for the horrendous sound beating in their brains. This display is calculated to unnerve those who must face it, and it accomplishes its aim admirably. If not for the steadying influence of the battle-seasoned in our ranks, I fear many would have broken and run long before the first blow was struck. As it was, we waited, growing impatient and fearful.

It is never good to keep men waiting to go into battle: doubt gnaws holes in even the strongest resolve, and courage leaks away. But there was no help for it — Uther needed time to take up his new position. So, we waited.

Uther's force had disappeared into the brush at the river's edge to the north. This manoeuvre had not gone unnoticed by Hengist, who had moved a portion of his host upriver to meet them. There we stood, face to face with the enemy, neither one of us wanting to cross the stream and thereby give the other an advantage.

It occurred to me to wonder how Uther would cross the water since there was, as far as I knew, only the one fording place along this section of the river. I leaned close to Aurelius, but before I had time to put words to this misgiving there came a cry from the opposite shore. 'Here they come!' cried Aurelius. 'God in Heaven, help us!'

Hengist, having time to assess his position, had decided that Uther's absence more than made up for the disadvantage of fighting with his back to the water, and had signalled the attack — though with the hideous din, how any of them could have heard the signal I will never know.

They came in a swarm: chaos in motion. The sight of the churning mass rolling towards us caused the front rank to draw back involuntarily. 'Steady!' called Aurelius to his chieftains; his command was repeated along the line.

The first enemy reached the shallows to be met by the surge of our own troops. So determined was the foremost rank that the Saecsen should not come ashore, that they halted the enemy rush and forced it back upon itself. The enemy screamed in rage.

From the first blow the battle was hot — so much pent-up fury, nursed through the long summer, kindled it to white heat instantly. Men stood in water to their thighs and hewed at one another with axe and sword. The world was filled with the shattering sound of steel on steel. The Nene swirled around the combatants, its sluggish grey-silted waters blushing crimson.

Only determination kept our smaller force from being overwhelmed outright. That, and the horses, which the barbarians feared — and with good reason, since a good horse is as much a warrior on the field as his rider, and with fearsome weapons of its own.

Nevertheless, little by little, the superior numbers of the foe began to tell. Once the first wind of battle passed and the combatants settled into fighting rhythm, Hengist succeeded in pushing out around our flanks and Aurelius was forced to steal men from the centre to keep the enemy from closing behind and surrounding us entirely.

'Uther must join us soon, or come to bury us,' the High

King said grimly, drawing his sword from its sheath. 'We cannot hold the centre much longer without the aid of his horsemen.'

My sword was already in my hand. I lofted it, saying, 'My king, the day is ours! Let us go and wrest it from that heathen prince, and teach him the sting of British wrath.'

Aurelius smiled. 'I believe you mean it, Merlin.'

'Only a fool jests on a field of battle.'

'Then let us begin the lesson,' replied Aurelius, spurring his mount into the fray.

As I say, the centre had been thinned and was in danger of caving in under the barbarian onslaught. So that is where Aurelius struck first, heedless of his own safety.

Uther would have been furious with him, for Uther had taken to protecting his brother, striving to keep Aurelius out of all but the most necessary conflict, saying, 'I have fought too many battles to make him High King for him to get himself killed now.'

You see, Aurelius had no sense of danger. He could not weigh one risk against another; and this caused him to do things in battle which, counted as courageous in certain situations, became foolhardy in others. Uther knew this about his brother and protected him from it as much as he could.

But Uther was not there and Aurelius saw the need and instinctively went to it, throwing himself into the breach. I have never seen a man so gloriously innocent in battle. It was a joy to watch him fight. And a terror.

A terror, for it fell to me to protect him, and this was no easy task. Aurelius risked enough for two men, and I had my hands full just trying to keep up with him. I did not fear for myself; that never occurred to me. I did fear for Aurelius, however; because, as Uther had suggested, we had endured hardship enough to make Aurelius High King, and I was not about to have him throw it all away in a foolish act — no matter how glorious!

So we fought side by side, my king and I. We were like men joined shoulder to shoulder at birth, matching bladestroke for bladestroke. The enemy fell before us, and our own warriors, seeing their king wading into the thick of the fight, drew courage from the sight and redoubled their efforts. Even so, we could not help giving ground to the barbarian.

With every push, the enemy gained and we lost. We were the shore and they were the storm wave battering against us, dragging us grain by grain and stone by stone into the foaming maelstrom. I felt each successive blast in my bones. And I waited for the shock of the fight to send me into the curiously distorted frenzy that had become familiar to me in battle.

But it did not happen.

It came to me that I had not entered into this heightened state, this *battle awen*, since Goddeu. I had taken no great part in the battles for Aurelius' kingship. In truth, I had not unsheathed my blade until this day; there had been no need.

I needed it now, however, and now I fought as any other warrior and I found myself wishing for my old sword, against which all other blades shattered as if made of glass — the great sword of Avallach which Charis had given me years ago. What had happened to it?

Had it, like so much else, been lost at Goddeu?

Fool! I had no time to dwell on these things. Keeping myself and Aurelius alive occupied my mind and skill — all the more since the High King would take no thought for himself.

We were now pushed far back from the river — it was either give ground or allow Hengist to surround us — and each blow of the enemy drove us further back. The fight had been carried away from the Nene, although Angle, Jute, Pict, and Irish still swarmed across. Incredibly, the main body of Hengist's host still remained on the other side!

We would soon be crushed by the weight of their numbers alone.

Where was Uther?

Great Light, I prayed with every breath, if you mean to save us today, let it be now!

We fought, grimly hacking at the foe before us. Not a man among us could swing his blade without wounding an enemy. Yet we were losing ground quickly now, as more and more of the barbarians pushed across the river. One band and then another, and another, and still more succeeded in getting round our flanks. We were now almost surrounded, and were being forced into a circle: the death circle, warriors call it, for once adopted there is only one outcome of this manoeuvre.

Where was Uther?

The Saecsen horde, seeing us apparently deserted by our allies, screamed their blood lust to their loathsome gods, calling on Woden and Tiw and Thunor, to maim and slay and destroy. Eager to make British blood the sacrifice, they leapt slavering to the fight.

I slashed at every bit of exposed barbarian flesh that offered itself. I worked as the harvester labours before the lowering storm. I reaped a vast harvest, but took no pleasure in my mowing. Men fell beneath my streaming blade, or beneath my mount's brain-spattered hooves. I saw men contemplating severed limbs; I saw brave warriors weeping into their death-wounds. I saw faces, sun-bronzed and fair, with eyes the colour of winter ice, once whole and handsome, now twisted in unreasoning agony, or broken and bloody in death.

But no matter how many I slew, more crowded in. Clutching, thrusting, grappling, hewing with notched and ragged blades. One great chieftain loosed an ear-splitting scream and leaped onto the neck of my horse; he clung there with one arm, flailing at me with his war axe.

I flung myself backward in the saddle. His blood-stained blade sliced the air where my head had been and I thrust with the point of my sword, catching him just under the line of his ribs. He roared and dropped his axe, then grabbed the sword with his hands and held it as he fell, seeking to pull me from the saddle with him. My sword was dragged down by his weight and one of his comrades, crazy for the kill, lofted his axe to cleave my skull.

I saw the blade hover in the air. Then the wrist spouted blood and the axe spun awkwardly away. Pelleas, ever alert to my danger, had reached me; and it was not the first time his sword had delivered me. 'Stay with the king!' I shouted, jerking my sword free at last. Pelleas turned and darted after Aurelius, who was charging on ahead, bodies toppling behind him.

The Britons strove mightily against the foe. Never were men more courageous in going to their doom. . . but there was nothing we could do. Though we slew one, four more arose to take the place of the one; though we slew a thousand, five thousand more remained. Meanwhile, our brave companions were falling beneath the relentless slaughter.

We were completely surrounded now. Aurelius sounded the call to circle the troops. This is the beginning of the end for any army. Knowing this, hating it, we rallied. I do not know where the strength came from but, with prayers and curses, and broken weapons in our hands, we forced the screaming Berserkers back once more.

This angered Hengist, who committed the rest of his vast war host against us — all save his House Carles, his own personal bodyguard made up of the strongest, most formidable of all the Saecsen warriors. Aside from these, every last warrior was pressed into the fight. He intended destroying us utterly.

Across the river they came, streaming towards us, their faces tight with the ecstasy of hatred. We were slowly being crushed by the steady advance of the enemy. The heads of our countrymen now adorned the long spears of the foemen. Smoke from burning corpses began to drift into the air. So Hengist reckoned that he had won already.

But he reckoned falsely, for the battle was not over yet.

Aurelius saw it first. 'Uther!' he cried. 'Uther has taken Hengist!'

How he saw this, busy as we both were, I cannot say. But I lifted my eyes and scanned the hillside opposite — the tide of battle had carried us back up the hill where we had begun — and I saw a force of mounted men surrounding Hengist's horsetail standard, and the fight there seemed over. The rest of Uther's force was galloping across the river to cut off the enemy rushing to their leader's aid.

I do not know when Hengist realized his mistake, but it must have struck him like a cold blade between the ribs when he turned defenceless to see Uther swooping down on him from behind.

For our part, we sensed the sudden shift in the battle, just as the enemy was about to overwhelm us. We braced for the final thrust, and then, inexplicably, fell forward as the enemy melted away.

Just like that, all at once, the weight of the battle fell from us like a wall crumbling inward upon itself after leaning outward for so long. Aurelius wasted not a moment. He wheeled his horse, snatching up the royal standard, and, waving the proud Eagle above his head, he mounted the attack.

Great Light, we are saved!

Aurelius retaliated quickly and without mercy. Instantly, the remaining horsemen gathered to him and they rode down the enemy from behind.

There is no honour in slaughtering a fleeing foe — only grim expedience. It had to be done.

Caught between the two forces, the barbarians found themselves waist-deep in the Nene, unable to advance or fall back. Confusion seized them and shook them like a dog shaking a rat. Chaos closed its fist round them and they gave in to it. Hengist was securely held; those of his bodyguard still alive, were bound, as he was, and disarmed.

It is a curious thing with the barbarian, but capture a war leader and the fight quickly goes out of them. Let him be killed and they will go on fighting for the honour of accompanying their lord into Valhalla; let their battlechief fall prisoner and they become confounded and dismayed and are easily overcome.

It is as if theirs is a single mind, a single will — that of their leader. And without him they fall instantly into panic and despair.

Therefore, despite superior numbers, despite the awful fact that our main force was well and truly beaten, once Uther held the blade to Hengist's throat, the Briton had prevailed.

The battle continued only in isolated enclaves, mostly Pict and Irish whose chieftains still lived to lead them. These were quickly put down. Would that the Saecsen had behaved that way, for now Uther was left with the odious task of dealing with the prisoners.

Of course, Aurelius had not intended that there should be any prisoners, but that the fight should have been fought to the death. Had the Saecsen won, it would have been. Though a warrior might kill in the heat of battle, slaying time and again without hesitation, among civilized men there are not many who can slaughter defenceless human creatures as they stand mute and passive before him.

I say this because, when the fighting was done, there remained several thousand Saecsen still alive and it was simply not possible to run the spear through them all. If we had, we should have been worse barbarians than those we fought!

'Well?' I asked Uther. He was still in the saddle, his bloody sword across his thigh. 'What will you do?' Aurelius had sent me ahead to Uther while he saw the smaller fights ended and organized aid for our wounded.

Uther scowled darkly, as if it were somehow my fault that this decision had fallen to him. He sought to put off the question by asking, 'What says Aurelius?'

'The High King says you are war leader; it is your decision.'

He groaned. Uther was no murderer. 'What do *you* say, Exalted Ambrosius?'

'I agree with Aurelius. You must decide — and quickly, if you will not lose the trust and respect of your men.'

'I know that! But what am I to do? If I kill the prisoners I am a butcher, and I lose respect; let them live and I am soft-hearted, and I lose even more.'

I sympathized. 'In war there is no easy course.'

'Tell me something I do not already know.' His words were harsh, but his eyes pleaded.

'I will tell you what I would do if it were my decision.'

'Tell me then, O Wisdom Incarnate. What would you do?'

'I would do the only thing I could do and still call myself a human being.'

'Which is?'

'Let them go,' I told him. 'There is no other choice.'

'Every one I release today will come back. And he will father sons that will come back. Every life I spare today will be a life spent later — the life of a countryman.'

'Perhaps,' I allowed. 'That is the way of it.'

'Have you nothing else to say, Mighty Prophet?' he mocked, his face twisted with distaste.

'I say only what is, Uther. It is for you to decide: kill them all and you may save a future life, and prove us more detestable in the sight of God than these poor wretches who do not know him. But, if you let them go, you will prove the true nobility of the British spirit. You will truly exalt yourself far above those you have defeated.'

He saw this but he did not like it. 'I could obtain blood oaths and hostages.'

'That can be done, but I advise against it. These men are not to be trusted to keep an oath made to one they despise.'

'I have to do *something*!'

'Very well,' I relented, 'but choose the youngest of them for your hostages.'

'And I will not spare Hengist.'

'Uther, think! He is beaten and disgraced. If you kill him he will become a leader whose life must be avenged. Let him go; Hengist will trouble us no more.'

Jesu help me, my own heart was not in it. Perhaps I might have made Uther believe if I had believed myself.

'And I say he will not go free from this battle.' Uther had made up his mind.

Hengist was brought forward, tightly bound, his broad face snarling in silent defiance. Those of his bodyguard who still lived, were brought forth, too, and made to stand behind him. The rest of the Saecsen host, disarmed, the fight gone completely out of them, stood a little way away, up on the hillside, heads lowered in defeat, watching in sullen silence.

Gorlas, hot from the fight, galloped in quickly and threw himself from his horse. He ran up and, before anyone could stop him, seized Hengist by the arms and spat in his face. The Saecsen leader regarded Gorlas impassively, spittle glistening on his cheeks. The prisoners murmured ominously.

It was a stupid thing to do. I wanted to shake Gorlas by the shoulders and make him see what he had done. 'Stay, Gorlas!'

The voice was Aurelius', who now joined us. He strode slowly towards the captives, stopped, and stood regarding Hengist casually. After a moment he turned and spoke to Uther. 'Well, Duke of Britain, what is it to be?'

'Death for Hengist and his chieftains,' Uther replied evenly. 'The rest will go free —' he shot a quick glance at me. 'They will be escorted to the coast and put on ships, never to return to this land again under pain of death.'

'Very well,' said Aurelius, 'so be it.'

Gorlas, hanging back, now thrust himself forward. 'If Hengist is to be killed, Lord Aurelius, let it be by my hand.'

Aurelius looked at him shrewdly. 'Why, Lord Gorlas, should you be his executioner?'

'It is a matter of honour between us, lord,' Gorlas confessed. 'My brother was murdered in the Massacre of the Knives, when Vortigern was king. I have made an oath that if ever I were to meet Hengist, I would kill him. I had hoped to meet him in battle.'

Aurelius considered this. He glanced at Uther, 'I have no objections.'

'Someone must do the deed,' muttered Uther.

The High King turned to me. 'What say you, Wise Counsellor?'

'The taking of life in revenge is hateful to me. But if his life is forfeit for the wrong he has done, let him be killed quickly and quietly — but alone and away from here.'

A strange light glinted in Gorlas' eyes. He threw back his head and laughed hideously. 'Kill him quietly?' he hooted. 'We have just slaughtered ten thousand of these motherless bastards! Here is the Chief Bastard himself — if any deserve to die, he does!'

'We killed today because we had no choice,' I spat. 'We killed to save ourselves and our people. But now we have a choice, and I tell you that killing for revenge is murder, and has no place among civilized men.'

'My Lord Aurelius,' shouted Gorlas, angry now. 'Let Hengist be killed here and now, before all his people. I would have them see and remember how we punish treachery.'

Many others agreed with Gorlas, and loudly, so Aurelius gave his assent, and Gorlas wasted no time about it. He picked up a long spear and shoved it into the Saecsen's belly. Hengist groaned but did not fall. Gorlas withdrew the spear and stabbed Hengist with it again. Blood gushed out onto the ground and the barbarian leader crashed to his knees, doubled over his wound. Still, he did not cry out.

Gorlas stepped quickly to his victim's side, drew his sword, raised it, and struck off Hengist's head. The body pitched forward into the dust. Gorlas raised his grisly trophy in triumph.

Then, seized by the frenzy of his vengeance, Gorlas turned and fell on the corpse, chopping and chopping with his sword. He hacked the body into pieces and, when he was finished, scattered the pieces in the dust.

All the while the men. . . the men, Holy Father forgive us all, cheered him.

SIX

When the cheering was over, an awful silence descended upon the battlefield; a silence instantly shattered by a heart-rending shriek. A youth thrust himself forward from the mass of captives: tall, thin — he had not yet attained his manly growth — his fair hair hung in long braids from his temples, and, beneath the dirt, his face, now distorted in grief, bore the same proud aspect as his father. There was no question whose offspring it was.

The boy threw himself upon the severed head of his father and hugged it to his breast. Gorlas, breathless and sweating from his exertion, whirled on the youth and raised his sword to strike.

'Gorlas! Hold!' Uther swung down from the saddle and strode to where they were. 'It is done. Put your sword away.'

'Not while the wolf's whelp lives,' said Gorlas, thickly. 'Let me kill him and make an end.'

'Do we kill children now, Gorlas? Look at him, he is only a boy.' The youth had not so much as glanced at the danger looming over him; he continued to wail, rocking back and forth piteously, cradling the bloody head in his arms.

'Lleu blind me, he is Hengist's son! Kill him now or he returns to lead another murdering wolf pack when he is grown.'

'There has been enough killing for one day,' replied Uther. 'Put your sword away, Gorlas. I tell you, there is no shame in it.'

Muttering dark oaths, Gorlas sheathed the blade and contented himself with a sharp kick at the boy before him. Then he stomped off to rejoin his war band.

Uther raised the boy to his feet where he stood sullenly, his dirty face streaked with his tears. 'What is your name, boy?' Uther asked.

The youth understood him well enough and answered, 'Octa.'

'I give you the gift of your life, Octa. If you or your people ever return here again, I will take back my gift. Do you understand?'

The boy said nothing. Uther took the youth's naked arm in his glove, turned him and pushed him gently back to his place among the other captives. Aurelius, who had kept himself apart, now came forth and, placing his hands on his brother's shoulders, kissed him, and embraced him. 'Hail Uther! Duke of Britain! The victory is yours! To you belongs the triumph and the spoil!'

There was little enough spoil, and much of it of British origin. Most of what we collected from the captives and their camp had been stolen earlier in the summer by the Saecsens. But there were some handsome armbands and bracelets of red gold, and jewelled knives, all of which Uther divided among his battlechiefs, keeping nothing for himself.

When the wounded had been tended and the dead buried — or, in the case of the enemy, heaped onto impromptu pyres and set alight — the Saecsen captives were escorted to the coast: back across fields they had destroyed, back through settlements they had decimated on their way to the place of battle. At each place, the survivors came out to rail against them, pelting them with stones and dirt.

Many wanted blood for the blood the Saecsens had spilled: wives for the husbands they had lost; husbands for their dead women and children. But Uther would not be swayed. He did not allow any harm to come to the enemy under his care, though his soul writhed within him. In this, he showed the grace of an angel.

'In truth, Merlin,' he told me when it was finished, 'if I had seen what they had done, I would never have let a single Saecsen escape. I would have made them face the justice of those they had wronged, and there would not be a barbarian drawing breath in all this land tonight, I can tell you.' He paused and dashed down the rest of his wine and then slammed the cup down on the board. 'It is over, and that is something at least.'

Aurelius sympathized. 'Showing mercy to an enemy is battle's most difficult charge. But you have acquitted yourself well, Uther. For your deed this day, you have covered

333

yourself in honour. I drink to you, brother. Hail Uther, Merciful Conqueror!'

It was the night of the day following the battle and Uther was exhausted to the point of collapse. He swayed on his feet — wine and fatigue vying to claim him — his smile thin and uncertain.

'Go to bed, Uther,' I said, holding out a cloak to him. 'Come, I will take you to your tent.'

He allowed himself to be led to his tent where he fell face first onto his pallet. His steward, a west-country youth named Ulfin, was there to help him, but I loosened his boots and belt, and covered him with the cloak. 'Douse the light,' I told Ulfin. 'Your lord will not need it tonight.'

I left Uther asleep in the dark and returned to Aurelius' tent. He was yawning while his steward unbuckled his leather breastplate. 'Well,' he said, 'it looks as if I will be High King after all.'

'You will, my lord Aurelie. There is no avoiding it.'

The steward removed the armour and Aurelius scratched himself. 'A last drink, Merlin?' he asked, gesturing towards the pitcher on the board.

'It is late and I am tired. Another night we will drink together. Still, I will pour one for you, if you like.'

'No. . . ' He shook his head, and the dark curls bobbed. 'Another night it is.' He looked at me pensively. 'Merlin, tell me — did I do right to let them go? Was it the best thing?'

'You did right, my lord. Was it the best thing? No, Aurelius, I fear it was not.'

'Gorlas was right then: they will come back.'

'Oh yes, they will come back. Trust in it,' I replied, adding, 'But they will return in any case and nothing you can do will prevent that.'

'But if I had ordered them put to the sword —'

'Do not let men like Gorlas deceive you, Aurelius, and do not deceive yourself. The barbarians were beaten yesterday, but not defeated. Killing the captives would have changed nothing — save burdening your soul with everlasting shame.'

He dragged a hand through his hair. 'Am I to live with a sword in my hand all my days?'

'Yes,' I told him gently. 'You will rule with the sword as

long as you live, my king, for the man has not been born who will hold this land in peace.'

Aurelius considered this, and true to the spirit in him did not shrink from it. 'Well,' he said slowly, 'will I see him?'

I told him the truth. 'No, Aurelius, you will not.' This was harsh to him, so I sought to soften it. 'But he will know you, Aurelius, and he will revere you and win great honour in your name.'

Aurelius smiled, and yawned again. 'That, as Uther says, is something at least.'

I went to my tent through the sleeping camp. How many fewer we were tonight! The men lying on the ground around low-burning campfires might have been dead, so soundly did they sleep. Yes, all the realm slept soundly this night, thanks to these brave warriors and their comrades who now slept under the gravemounds.

In my tent, I fell on my knees to pray, saying, 'My Lord Jesu, Great Giver, Redeemer and Friend, King of Heaven, Beginning and End, hear my lament:

'Three times three hundred warriors, bright was their hope, fierce their grip on life — three times three hundred we were, but no more, for death has claimed the hero's portion from the blood of good men.

'Three times three hundred, light of life shining full and without wavering, warm was their breath, quick their eyes — three times three hundred but no more, for tonight our sword brothers lie in silent turf-halls, cold and abandoned by their own who cannot follow where they go.

'Three times three hundred, bold in action, keen in battle, steadfast companions when the fire of battle raged — three times three hundred we were, but no more, for the raven croaks over the fields where grief has sown her seeds and watered them with women's tears.

'Merciful Jesu, Great of Might, whose name is Light and Life, be light and life to these your fallen servants. As you delight in forgiveness, forgive them; do not count their sins, rather consider this their virtue: that when the call came to defend their homeland they took no thought for themselves, but roused courage and went forth to do battle, knowing death awaited them.

'Hear me, Lord Jesu, gather our friends to your hall; seat them in your palace in Paradise, and you will not want for finer companions.'

The next day the High King struck camp and rode for Londinium, where his father had been made king, and where his own kingmaking would take place. Pelleas and I rode west to Dyfed, to find Bishop Dafyd. I had it in mind that Dafyd should officiate at Aurelius' accession — *if* he was as hale as Pelleas indicated, and agreeable to the journey.

Londinium had a bishop, a priest named Urbanus, who, from what I had heard in camp, was a devout if slightly ambitious young man. I had nothing against Urbanus, but Dafyd's attendance would, I thought, further strengthen Aurelius' bond with the kings of the west. Also, I had not seen Dafyd since my return from my long vigil in Celyddon, and this weighed heavily on my heart. Now that I had time to myself once more I desperately wanted to see him.

Pelleas and I rode through a land that seemed to have passed from under the shadow of a preying bird. Everywhere men breathed more freely; we were welcomed in settlements, we met traders on the road, gates and doors were opened — all this, and yet word of the Saecsen defeat could not have travelled from the battlefield. How did the people know?

I believe people living close to the land know these things instinctively; they sense fluctuations in the fortunes of men, as they sense minute changes in the weather. They see a red sunglow at dusk and know it will rain on the morrow; they taste the wind and know that frost will cover the ground when they wake. They apprehend the subtle ripples that great events cause in the atmosphere of the spirit. Thus, they knew without having to be told that some great good had come to them and they did not have to be afraid any more.

They knew, and yet they were glad to have news of the battle from us. This they would repeat to one another for many days until all — toddling child and bent-backed crone alike — could repeat it, word for word, just as it had come from my mouth.

We did not linger on the way, but sped with all haste to Llandaff, which was what men had begun calling the place where Dafyd had built his church: a sturdy rectangular structure of timber on a high stone foundation, surrounded by the smaller huts of the monks. Llandaff was a monastery like the others springing up like mushrooms all over the west country — not a few of them owing directly to Dafyd's tireless work.

As we approached the tiny settlement we could see the good brothers going about their chores. The younger men wore homespun robes of undyed wool; their elders' garments were light brown. The women among them, for many of the monks were married, wore the same simple garb, or more traditional clothing. All were busy about some task or other — toting firewood, building, thatching, tending the fields, feeding pigs, teaching the children of the nearby settlements and holdings — and all with the same jovial zeal. The place fairly hummed with earnest contentment.

We stopped to take this in, then dismounted and entered the compound on foot. I was greeted courteously, and addressed as a king — owing to my torc. 'How may we help you, lord?' the priest asked, taking us in with frank appraisal.

'I am a friend of the bishop here. I wish to see him.'

The monk smiled pleasantly. 'Of course. As you are his friend, you will understand that will be difficult. Our bishop is very old and he is resting at this time of day, as is his custom. . . ' He spread his hands as if to imply that the matter was beyond his influence, as no doubt it was. 'And then there is his sermon.'

'Thank you,' I told him. 'I would not think of disturbing him. And yet I know he will wish to see me.'

Two more monks had come to greet us and stood looking on, whispering to one another behind their hands. 'Then wait if you will,' replied the monk, 'and I will see to it that your request receives due consideration.'

I thanked him again and asked whether there was a superior I might speak to while I waited. 'That would be Brother Gwythelyn.'

'I was thinking of Salach.'

'Salach? But. . . ' he searched my face, questioningly, 'our dear brother Salach died years ago.'

I felt the pang of sorrow I usually feel upon receiving such news. In truth, I had forgotten how old he must be. 'Gwythelyn, then. Tell him that Myrddin ap Taliesin is here.'

At the sound of my name the two looking on murmured in surprise. '*Myrddin* is here! Here!' They gaped at me and then dashed away to tell the others.

'Lord Myrddin,' said the monk, inclining his head towards me. 'Allow me to lead you to Brother Gwythelyn.'

Gwythelyn was the image of his uncle, Maelwys — as happens in dynasties of strong blood lines, the family resemblance was correspondingly strong. I hesitated as he turned from the manuscript on his table to greet me. 'Is something wrong?' he asked.

'No, nothing. It is just that you remind me of someone else.'

'My grandfather, no doubt. You knew Pendaran Gleddyvrudd?' He appraised me closely. 'May I know your name?'

The monk who had led us to Gwythelyn's cell had, in his excitement, forgotten to give my name. 'Yes, I knew Red Sword well. I am Myrddin ap Taliesin,' I said simply.

Gwythelyn's eyes grew round. 'Forgive me, Myrddin,' he said, taking my hands and squeezing them in his own. They were hands made to hold a sword, and contrary to my expectation they were not soft; long days of rough labour had made them strong and hard. 'Forgive me, I should have known you.'

'How so? We have never met.'

'No, but from the day of my birth I have heard about you. Until this moment, I confess, I thought I should know you as I knew myself.'

'And I confess that when you turned round just now I thought I was seeing Maelwys in the flesh once more.'

He smiled, enjoying the compliment. 'If I can become half the man he was I will die content.' His smile broadened. 'But Myrddin ap Taliesin ap Elphin ap Gwyddno Garanhir — you see, we all know your illustrious lineage — I had always hoped to meet you one day, and now you are here. It is true, you are a marvel to behold. But tell me, what great event brings you to Llandaff? Will you stay? We have room for you.'

'Your welcome is most heartening, Gwythelyn; worthy of your generous uncle. I can stay but a short while — a day or two, and then I must go on to Londinium.' I went on to tell him about the new High King who would be crowned very soon.

'My brother —' he interrupted, 'Tewdrig, is he. . ?'

'He is well and will return as soon as the High King has taken the throne. And this is why I have come: I would like Bishop Dafyd to officiate.'

Gwythelyn considered this and then replied slowly, 'It is true that Dafyd has not stepped a dozen paces outside Llandaff in as many years — but. . . well, we will ask him and see what he says.'

'I would not disturb his rest. I am content to wait until he has awakened.'

'Very well, he is accustomed to taking refreshment after his sleep. We will go to him then. I know he will wish to see you. Until then, perhaps you would not refuse refreshment yourself?'

We did not have long to wait, for no sooner had Pelleas and I finished eating than a young man came, saying, 'Bishop is waking, Brother Gwythelyn. I thought you would like to know.' He addressed his superior, but his eyes never left me.

'Thank you, Natyn. We will come along at once.'

Dafyd's room was a clean-swept cubicle, bare of all furniture save his bed and one chair. I recognized the chair: it had once sat in Pendaran's hall; likely, Maelwys had given it to him. There was a tiny window covered with an oiled skin, through which light poured like honey, thick and golden. His bed was a straw pallet on a raised wooden frame and covered with fleeces.

On this bed sat a man who appeared to have been carved from fine alabaster. His white hair, ablaze in the light, surrounded his head like a nimbus, a halo of bright flame. On his face, so calm and serene, lingered still the beauty of his dreams. His dark eyes radiated peace to his simple world.

It was Dafyd. Much changed, much aged. Yet there was no mistaking him. He was leaner to be sure, but his flesh was firm and his teeth were good. Despite his advanced age — which must have been well past ninety, I realized with a shock — he looked robust and vital, a man in whom the fires of life burned with energy and passion and zeal.

In short, he appeared a man in whom holiness had nearly completed its transforming work.

As we entered the cell, his gaze shifted and he half rose to receive us. Then he saw me. He stopped. His mouth opened

339

to speak, but his tongue gave no utterance. Emotions played across his features like cloud-shadows chasing over the slopes of a hill. Tears welled up in his eyes — and in mine as well.

I went to him, raised him and clasped him to my breast.

'Myrddin, Myrddin,' he murmured at last, speaking my name as he would one of his holy texts. 'Myrddin, my soul, you are alive. To see you after all these years — alive and well. Oh, but you have not altered a whit. You are the same as my memory of you. Look at you now!'

His hands patted my shoulders and arms, as if he would be reassured that I was indeed flesh and bone before him. 'Oh, Myrddin, to see you is joy itself. Sit. Can you stay? Are you hungry? Gwythelyn! This is Myrddin, of whom I have often spoken. He is here! He has returned!'

Gwythelyn smiled. 'So he has. I will leave you to speak to one another until dinner.' He closed the door silently and left us to our reunion.

'Dafyd, I wanted to come sooner — so many times I thought of you and wanted to come to you. . .'

'Shh, it is nothing. We are together at last. My prayer is answered. Ever I have prayed for you, Myrddin, that I might see you again before I die. And now you are here. God is good.'

'You look well, Dafyd. I had not hoped —'

'To see me alive? Oh, aye, I am quite alive — much to the chagrin of the younger monks. I am something of a terror to them.' He winked slyly at me. 'They believe God keeps me alive just to torment them, and they may be right.'

'Latin a torment? Surely not.'

He nodded innocently. 'The mother tongue, language of scholars — a torment. But you know what students are. They complain incessantly. "Better a heart broken in love, than a head broken on Latin," they say. So, I tell them, "Fill your heads with Latin, and let God fill your hearts with love — then neither one can be broken."'

'Was it ever any different?'

'No, perhaps not,' he sighed. 'At least you never gave me such trouble.'

'I gave you more,' I laughed.

Dafyd laughed too. 'You did! You are right, you did. Oh, when I think of the hours we spent tangled in it!' He fell silent, nodding to himself, remembering. In a moment, he shook himself, as if waking from a dream. 'Ah, well, we were young then, eh, Myrddin?'

He cupped a hand to my face in a fatherly gesture. 'But you, my golden-eyed wonder — you are young still. Look at you, a young man's face and frame. Not a grey hair on your head. You are the flower of your race, Myrddin. Praise God, my son, for your long life. He has blessed you among men.'

'What good is a blessing I cannot share?' I asked, seriously. 'I would share what I have with you, Dafyd. You are far more deserving than I.'

'Have I not been blessed also? I am well content in years, Myrddin, never fear. I am satisfied. Do not be sorry for me — and do not denigrate the gift you have been given. The Lord High God has made you as you are for a purpose. Be thankful you are knit with such strong stuff.'

'I will try.'

'You do that.' He turned and indicated his chair. 'Now sit you down and tell me all that has passed with you since last we met.'

I laughed. 'That will take as many years as we have been parted!'

'Then you had better begin at once.' He settled himself on the edge of his bed and folded his hands in his lap.

So I began to tell him about Ganieda's death and all that followed from it — the hole in my life, that hideous waste, the years of loss and lament. And the square of honied light slipped lightly across the floor and up the opposite wall as I spoke. I told him about Vortigern — much of which he knew already — and about Aurelius, the new High King, and Uther, his brother, the war leader.

He drank in every word, like a child listening to a terrible, fascinating story. And no doubt he would have gone on sitting in awed attention on the edge of his bed had not Gwythelyn come and rapped gently on the door, to break Dafyd's reverie and rouse us to our supper. 'Dinner is being laid,' he informed us. 'I have had a special table set up for you.'

'I will hear more later,' Dafyd said, rising slowly. 'They will be waiting for me to bless the meal. Come, let us go and eat. Although my appetite is not what it was, tonight I am hungry. See? Just beholding you once more quickens me.'

'It cheers me to hear you say that,' I replied, taking his arm. But he did not need my assistance, for where I expected bone and sagging flesh, there was firm muscle beneath my grip. He did not shuffle as old men do, but walked upright and with vigour.

He ate with vigour, too, enjoying his food, remarking once and again that my coming was a balm to him. Clearly, he enjoyed himself and enjoyed the attention I was getting. 'You cannot blame them for staring, Myrddin. They have never seen one of the Fair Folk, Myrddin, but they have all heard of you. Everyone has heard of the great Emrys. And son, you are the equal of your legend. You have the look of greatness on you.'

Gwythelyn served us with his own hand — so that he could be near to hear what we said, I suppose. Pelleas sat with us, but spoke not a word the whole time, not wishing to intrude on our conversation. When the meal was finished, Dafyd rose and, taking the holy text one of the brothers handed him, began to read out the passage. The monks, still sitting at the board, listened with bowed heads.

'Praise the Lord,

Praise the Lord from the high places,
    praise him in the Halls of Light.
Praise him, all his angels,
    praise him, all you hosts of heaven.
Praise him, sun and moon,
    praise him, all you shining stars.
Praise him, you in the sky realms
    and you waters above the skies.
Let them all praise the name of the Lord,
    for he spoke forthrightly and they were created.
He established them in place for ever and ever;
    he uttered a decree that will never pass away.

Praise the Lord from the earth,
    you dragons, and all sea deeps,
lightning and hail, snow and clouds,
    stormy winds that do his bidding,
you great mountains and all fair hills,
    fruit trees and cedars,

wild beasts and all cattle,
creeping things and flying birds,
kings of the earth and all nations,
you chieftains and all rulers on earth,
young men and maidens,
old men and children.

Let them all praise the name of the Lord,
for his name alone is exalted;
his splendour is above the earth and the heavens.
He has raised up for his people a king,
the praise of all his saints. . . '

Dafyd paused, and, turning the pages, read again:

'But the father said to his servants, "Hurry! Bring forth the best robe and put it on him; and put a ring on his finger, and shoes on his feet. And bring the fattened calf, and kill it, and let us eat and celebrate. . . "

Here he stopped and closed the book reverently. Gazing at me, he finished the text: ' "For this my son was dead and now is alive again; he was lost and now is found." So, they began to celebrate.'

He raised the holy book to his lips and kissed it, saying, 'May God bless the reading of his word.'

'May God bless the hearing of his word among us,' the monks answered.

'I am happy tonight because my friend, long absent from me, has returned.' He turned and placed a hand on my shoulder. 'My son, my soul, has returned. Great is my rejoicing, great the blessing in my heart.' He lifted an admonishing hand to those before him. 'Tonight, before you close your eyes to sleep, I would have you contemplate the mystery of human love as a reflection of divine love.'

He blessed them then and sent them to their rest. The brothers trooped out of the hall and each wandered off by himself to find a lonely place to pray, as was their custom. Bishop Dafyd and I remained in the hall; chairs had been placed before the hearth for us, for the night had turned chill. Hot mulled wine in wooden cups was brought as we settled before the fire.

'Well, Myrddin, what has brought you?' Dafyd asked, when we had sipped from our drinks.

'Need it be anything more than a wish to see my friend?'

'No, it need not — with ordinary men. But you, Myrddin Emrys, are far from ordinary. Your life is not your own, you know; you serve the kingdom and its needs are yours.'

He looked at me over his cup, eyes shining like a mischievous child's in the firelight. 'Do you wonder that I say this to you? I will tell you something else: you will never rest until this realm is united and at peace.'

'That is a hard prophecy,' I told him, for I foresaw the troubled years stretching out ahead of me.

He smiled. 'Well, perhaps the Lord Jesu will bring his peace to this land with all speed.' He drank again and waited for me to speak.

I took a last draught and set the cup on the hearth. 'You ask what has brought me. Two matters, both urgent. For the first, I simply wanted to see you. It is true that I serve the Island of the Mighty and my life is not my own — Jesu knows I wear that duty like a harness — but as soon as I had a moment to myself I came straight here.'

'I did not say that for you to chide yourself. It was on my heart, that is all.'

'No doubt it was a word I needed to hear,' I assured him. 'But it brings me to the second reason for my visit: the High King.'

'Yes, the High King. Is he a worthy man?'

'He is; and the more I know of him, the more I feel that he is sent of God.'

'As you were.' Dafyd leaned back in his chair. The firelight playing over his features made him appear insubstantial, as if he were made of some finer, yet more ephemeral material; a momentary being. I realized he would not long remain in the world of men.

I must have been staring at him, for he said, 'The Champion, oh yes. Why do you look at me so? Hafgan always maintained as much.'

The memory came in a rush: Hafgan standing beside this trembling boy, and calling to the Learned Brotherhood to bear witness, saying, *Before you stands the one whose coming we have long awaited, the Champion who will lead the war host against the Darkness*. . .

'Ah, Hafgan,' Dafyd was saying. 'His name has not passed

344

my lips in many years. That man possessed a soul, Myrddin; a very great soul indeed. The discussions we had! Jesu bless him. What a reunion it will be!'

The good bishop made it sound as if he were merely going on a day's journey to visit his friend. Perhaps that was how he saw it.

'What do you know of the Champion?' I asked gently. 'What can you tell me?'

'What can I tell you about the Champion?' he continued. 'That he will be a man to save the Britons, that he will come when we most have need of him, that his will be a rule of righteousness and justice.' He paused and eyed me sharply. 'Are you suggesting that Hafgan was mistaken?'

I sighed and shook my head. 'I cannot say. Hafgan believed; it could be he saw in me what he wanted to see. Or perhaps he saw through me to another.'

'Myrddin,' Dafyd's voice was soft and comforting as a crooning mother's, 'have you lost your way?'

I pondered this. The fire crackled in the hearth as the pine knots popped and scattered sparks at our feet. Had I lost my way? Was this the source of my confusion? Until just now I had never doubted. . .

'No,' I answered at length, 'I have not lost my way — it is just that so many ways open before me that sometimes I hardly know which way to choose. To decide for one is to decide against another. I never imagined it would be this hard.'

'Now you know,' Dafyd said gently. 'The higher a man's call and vision, the more choices are given him. This is our work in creation: to decide. And what we decide is woven into the thread of time and being for ever. Choose wisely, then, but you must choose.'

Great Light, help me! I am blind without you.

'Well, I have said enough,' Dafyd said, settling back once more. 'You were telling me about the High King.'

'Aurelius, yes; he is High King, although he has yet to take the throne. I do not know how Vortigern received his kingship, but in elder times the chieftain would be blessed by the clan's druid, and I thought. . .'

'You wish me to consecrate this king as I consecrated you?' Dafyd saw the implications of this at once, and the idea delighted him. 'Myrddin, you are a far-thinking man,' he said approvingly. 'Of course, I will be your druid. Although you could do it yourself just as well. When will he come here?'

'He is going to Londinium,' I replied. 'It is where his father was crowned.'

'There is a church in Londinium, and a bishop — Urbanus, I know him well, a zealous servant of our Lord.'

'He will serve most admirably, no doubt,' I said lamely.

He read my expression. 'But as Aurelius will require the continued support of the western kings, it might help to bolster that support with well-placed pride. Tewdrig would feel better if his own bishop consecrated this new king.'

'And not Tewdrig only.'

'Yes, I see that and I agree. Very well, we will go to him and do what we can to give him a proper kingmaking. Is Aurelius a Christian?'

'He is willing.'

'That is half the battle. As Jesu himself said, "He who is not against us, is for us." Eh? If Aurelius is not against us, we will go to him. And I will enjoy the journey. Urbanus will not mind my coming; he will take account of my years and yield this favour to me.'

'Thank you, Dafyd.'

He rose slowly and came to me. He placed his hands on my head. 'In my heart I have long carried you, most beloved son. But the time is soon coming when you must go your way alone. Be strong, Myrddin. Be the hope of our hope. The people will look to you, they will believe and follow you — though I fear the church will not love you for it. But remember the church is only men, and men can become jealous of another's favour. Do not hate them for it.'

He took my hands and raised me from my chair. 'Kneel,' he said, 'and let an old man give you his blessing.'

I knelt before him on the hearth, and Dafyd, Bishop of Llandaff, renewed the blessing he had given me long ago.

346

SEVEN

Londinium had changed much with the years. Never more than a wide space on the Thamesis River, a scattering of mud and wattle huts and cattle enclosures, it was nevertheless chosen by the Romans for their principal city, for the simple fact that the river was deep enough to allow their troop ships to come inland, yet shallow enough to cross without undue difficulty. For generations Londinium's greatest glory remained the enormous docks built by the Roman engineers and maintained, with greater or lesser zeal, ever since.

Though the troop ships eventually ceased, the city remained the centre of Imperial power in the island, in time acquiring not only a fortress, which was all of Londinium in the early years, but a governor's residence, a stadium, baths, temples, markets, warehouses, public buildings of various types, an arena, and a theatre — in addition to its massive docks. In later years a stone wall was put up round the whole, but by then the city was a sprawling, brawling monstrosity of crowded streets and close-built houses, inns, and tradesmen's shops.

The governor's residence became a palace, a forum was added and a basilica, and the future of Londinium was secure. Henceforth, any Briton wishing to impress Mother Rome had first to win Londinium in one way or another. In short, Londinium, to the Britons, *was* Rome. Certainly, it was as close to Rome as many a Celtic citizen ever came. And for this reason, if for no other, Londinium, despite the filth and noise and squalor, basked in the golden sunset that was Rome and remained ever glorious.

To Londinium Constantine had come as Emperor of the West, first High King of the Britons. Therefore, to Londinium Aurelius had come to receive the crown of his father, identifying himself with his father — and, through Constantine, with Rome.

This was wise as it was necessary: there were still many men of position and influence who considered allegiance to and membership in the Empire essential for the proper ruling of Britain. That raw circumstance had far outstripped this archaic requisite could never have occurred to these men. They were cast of an older mould: civilized, refined, urbane. That Rome itself had become little more than a provincial backwater, its once-proud residences slums, its noble Colosseum a charnal house, its stately Senate a gathering place of jackals, its imperial palace a brothel — all this made not a whisker of a difference.

As I have said, the men who believed this way were powerful men and any High King who would own the title along with the crown had to be recognized by the staunch sophisticates of Londinium — or for ever be considered a usurper, or worse, and thus be denied Londinium's considerable resources.

Aurelius understood this; Vortigern never had. More's the pity. For if Vortigern had won Londinium he might never have been forced to the awful exigency of embracing Hengist and his horde. But Vortigern was proud. He vainly supposed that he could rule without Londinium's blessing.

True, Londinium considered itself above the petty affairs of Britain. Or, put another way, the concerns of Londinium were the only legitimate concerns of Britain. Flawed as this outlook was, Vortigern ignored it to his peril, and to the ultimate peril of Britain.

Fools! Drowning in their folly. Raving on about *Empire* and *Pax Romana* while the tattered remnants of that Empire crumbled around them, and peace became a hollow word. Empty-headed men playing at politics, while the world rushed headlong to its ruin.

Be that as it may, Aurelius had no intention of repeating Vortigern's mistake. He would proceed with the formalities; he would woo the pride-bound citizens of vain-glorious Londinium. In return, he would receive its blessing, and then he could get on with the work of saving the realm.

Sympathy held with Vortigern, but intelligence recognized Aurelius.

So it was that Dafyd, Gwythelyn, Pelleas and I, along with a small escort of monks, came to Londinium. Our trip was speedy and uneventful — which is to say we travelled unmolested through a countryside quickly forgetting terror in its need to gather in the harvest. It was a beautiful harvest time — sun-warmed days and crisp nights. In the morning we awoke to steaming streams and heavy dew; at night we sat before crackling fires with the scent of burning leaves in our nostrils.

Dafyd continued in good health. Though it had been, by Gwythelyn's estimation, a good few years since the bishop had sat a horse, Dafyd gave no indication of discomfort. He rode when we rode and rested when we rested and did not complain. Although I was careful not to overtax him, he seemed wholly unaffected by the journey, remarking often how he enjoyed viewing the wider landscape once more.

We sang, we talked, we discussed and debated — and the distance between Llandaff and Londinium shrank by happy degrees.

It was nearing midday, on a day that had begun overcast with grey clouds of mist that had burned off in time to a bright white haze. Londinium, or Caer Lundein as some now called it, lay squalid before us in its shallow bowl beside the snaking river. A pall of turbid smoke hung grey and drab over the vast expanse, and even from a distance we could smell the fetid reek of the place. Too many people, too many competing desires. My spirit recoiled within me.

'There is a church here,' Dafyd reminded me. 'And many good Christians. Where there is great Darkness, the need for the Light is greater also, remember.'

Well, Londinium had need of its church and bishop. Nevertheless, we all took a last deep breath before riding on. At the massive iron gate to the city we were challenged. For no good reason, it seemed to me. The dolts manning the gate could see we were not Saecsen marauders!

But it is a mark of the arrogance of the place that it deemed all men suspect who were not already within its walls. In the end, we were admitted and allowed to proceed about our business.

The streets were thronged with people and livestock — apparently wandering at will through the city. The din was horrific. Tradesmen hawked their wares in a most unbecoming manner, cattle bawled, dogs barked, beggars chanted, painted women offered themselves for our pleasure. On every hand

349

were men wrangling, shouting, fighting, and contending in any of a thousand different ways in stone-paved streets befouled with garbage and dung.

'If I lived in this place,' remarked Pelleas loudly, 'I should be deaf before winter.'

'If you were not dead first!' Gwythelyn added grimly, speaking my thoughts also.

The place was unspeakable, but possessed of a perverse energy which did not fail to arouse. Londinium was a realm unto itself, and I began to sense something of its deadly allure. Weak men would succumb without struggle to its charms and enchantments; stronger men would be won by the grand and imposing prospect of power. Even wary souls might stumble and fall to their ruin — not for lack of vigilance perhaps, but for lack of fortitude. The Enemy possessed so many wiles and weapons here that all but the most powerful must eventually be overwhelmed in one way or another.

As yet, I saw no evidence of the Light Dafyd proclaimed, and wondered whether he was mistaken after all — even though I know the Light is ever found in the most unlikely places.

Dafyd alone did not seem to mind the stink and noise. He turned a beatific countenance on one and all, passing with the peculiar grace of a saint moving through a shadow-bound world that neither recognizes nor comprehends its true masters.

Perhaps it was myself who did not recognize or comprehend. I admit I have never loved cities — living most of my life, as it happens, close to sun and wind, rock and water, leaf and branch, earth and sky and sea and hill. It was difficult for me to apprehend the subtle expressions of goodness that Dafyd seemed to find. Or maybe I lacked the generosity of forgiveness that he possessed.

We rode directly to the governor's palace — an imposing edifice rising above the tallest rooftops of the city in columned splendour, albeit a splendour now much faded. There we hoped to find Aurelius.

Instead we found a mob.

If the confusion we had thus far encountered was set all on one side, it would not equal the chaos that met us as we rode into the inner courtyard of the palace: a red-tiled square choked with angry men. Many were dressed in an archaic way, affecting Roman garb and appearance. They were calling for the governor to come out into the courtyard to speak to them about some matter, the nature of which we could not discern.

A balcony overlooked the courtyard, and it was to this that the mob addressed itself. But the balcony was empty and the door leading to it remained closed. Aurelius was nowhere to be seen, of course, nor any trace of his army.

'What shall we do, lord?' asked Pelleas. 'I believe there will be a riot here soon. My lord. . .?'

I heard Pelleas, but I could make no answer. My limbs stiffened as if with sudden and inexplicable cold. The looming violence of the mob held me fast and their cries bound me fast. I could not move or speak, for a powerful *awen* had seized me.

The bawl of the mob rang in the enclosed courtyard, and their voices became a single voice; a great universal voice sounding a single word: Arthur! . . . Arthur! . . . *ARTHUR!*

I turned my eyes to the sky and saw an enormous purple cloud spreading over the city — it seemed to me an imperial cloak rippling in the wind of an oncoming storm, a cloak much worn and ragged.

When I looked again the people were gone and the courtyard was empty. Dry leaves blew across the weed-grown spaces. The roof of the palace had collapsed and its tiles lay broken and scattered on the ground. The wind whispered in the forsaken places. . . Arthur. . . Arthur. . .

A woman appeared, wearing a long, white garment of the kind highborn ladies are often buried in. Her skin had the pallor of death, and her eyes were sunken and red-rimmed, as if from sickness or mourning.

But she came purposefully towards me over the cracked pavement, the wind whipping her long garment against her legs, blowing her black tresses before her face. She raised her arms to me and I saw she held something in her hands — a magnificent sword, broken now, sundered by a mighty stroke. The ruined weapon dripped blood.

The raven-haired woman approached and held the broken blade to me. 'Save us, Merlin,' she whispered, her voice raw with sorrow. 'Heal us.'

I reached for the sword, but she let it fall from her hands and it clattered on the tiles. I saw in its pommel the Imperial jewel — the eagle-carved amethyst of Magnus Maximus.

The *awen* passed. I felt a touch on my arm and found that I could move once more. I turned. Pelleas was staring at me, his brow wrinkled in concern. 'Lord Myrddin?'

I passed a hand before my eyes. 'What is it, Pelleas?'

'Are you well? I said that I think there will be a riot here soon.'

'Nothing we do will prevent that,' I said, glancing quickly around. The mob still stood before us and their shouts were growing louder and more angry. 'I think that if we hope to find Aurelius, we must search elsewhere.'

'If not the palace,' Dafyd said, 'then the church.'

'Let us go there in any case,' Gwythelyn urged. The monks with us voiced their approval. Although they were holy men, most were trained warriors and could handle themselves in a fight if it came to that. Naturally, they preferred to avoid confrontation in any but the most needful circumstance, hence they were eager to leave the governor's palace for the quiet of the church.

'Very well,' I agreed. 'If he is not there, at least we may have some word of him.'

The church was not far from the palace as it turned out, but we had to ask several passers-by where it was before we found it, for no one seemed to know. It was not a large structure, but large enough to serve, and surrounded by a goodly-sized plot of ground which was planted with trees — plum and apple, mostly, and a few pear. The mud-and-timber building was washed white with lime, so that it fairly sparkled in the sun. An inviting place, but much at odds with its surroundings, which crowded in as if lusting after its comely green plot. The church appeared distinctly out of place.

As much out of place were the ranks of horses, and the warriors lolling beneath the fruit trees. They jumped to their feet as we rode up; someone sang out as if in warning, 'Lord Myrddin is here! Lord Emrys!'

Clearly, our arrival was anticipated. Several warriors came running up; we left the horses in their care and gladly dropped from the saddle. Dafyd and Gwythelyn started at once for the church, Pelleas and I following, the monks staying behind to speak to the soldiers, some of whom, I gathered, were kinsmen.

The interior of the church was larger than it appeared from outside, owing to the fact that its floor had been excavated and lowered. We walked down several stone steps to the richly tessellated floor. There were candles burning on candle trees all round the large, dark room — a cool place of refuge from the hot, bright day. Yet it had something of the feel of a tomb.

We were met by Urbanus himself, who was obviously expecting us. He made a quick bow to Dafyd, and the two bishops greeted one another with a holy kiss and exchanged brief words about the journey, while Pelleas and I looked on. But as soon as the pleasantries of protocol were finished, Urbanus turned to me and gripped me by the hands.

He was a man above medium height with a scholar's oblong head — high-domed and covered with dark hair growing thin on top. His skin was sallow, as marks a man who spends his days away from the sun. His long fingers were smudged with ink.

'Lord Merlinus,' he said, affecting the Latin form of my name. 'I am indeed happy you have come.' He did not appear especially happy; he appeared relieved. 'Aurelianus will be most pleased to see you.'

'Is the High King here?'

'No, not at present. But he hopes to return soon. If you will await him here —' the churchman faltered.

'Yes?'

'He has asked me to make you comfortable until he returns.'

'Where is Aurelius? What is wrong?'

Urbanus glanced at Dafyd, as if hoping his spiritual superior would answer for him. But Dafyd only gazed benignly back. 'I hardly know where to begin,' Urbanus sighed.

Obviously, he had little experience with trouble; merely speaking about it fairly undid him. I did not choose to make it easier for him. 'Tell us at once.'

'I do not understand all of it,' he admitted to his credit, 'and no doubt the warriors outside can tell you more, but evidently some problem has arisen with Aurelianus' — ah, coronation. He went to the governor, you understand, and was received with all cordiality, I believe. He stayed in the palace a day and a night and then rode out of the city once more to make provision for his troops. When he returned, and his kings with him, the governor would not see him.'

'Aurelius turned away?' wondered Dafyd.

'Why?' echoed Gwythelyn.

Urbanus shook his head in bewilderment. 'I cannot say. I do not know if Aurelianus can say. He came here in a rage, livid. Uther was with him, they talked to one another in my cell — the men with him waited outside. When they came out Uther asked if he might leave some of their men here. Of course, I had no objection. Aurelianus told me that, should you come while he was away, I was to ask you to await him here and that he would return soon — as I have told you.'

'When did this take place?' I asked.

'The day before yesterday,' Urbanus replied, and added, 'I do not know what has happened, but the mood of the city has grown ugly since he arrived.'

'We have seen the mob at the governor's palace,' Gwythelyn said. He went on to describe what we had seen, and he and Dafyd and Urbanus fell to discussing it.

Pelleas turned to me. 'I do not like the sound of this. What does it mean?'

'Between the time Aurelius left the city and the time he returned, something happened to poison the governor's favour against him. I do not know what it was, but likely that does not matter overmuch. Aurelius has gone to gather his kings, I think, and will return with a show of power.'

'Will there be a fight?'

'Unless we can prevent it,' I told him. 'I think it will not serve to have our High King begin his reign with the slaughter of the citizens of Londinium.'

EIGHT

Among the warriors lolling outside, we found one who had spoken to Uther just before he and Aurelius had departed. 'Where has Lord Aurelius gone?' I asked, as I came to stand over him. The soldier, pointed out by one of his comrades, jumped to his feet and removed the blade of grass from between his teeth.

'Lord Emrys,' he said quickly, 'I was just —'

I saved him his explanation. 'No matter. Where is Aurelius?'

'He has left the city.'

'That much is obvious.'

'My Lord the Duke said to wait here for them to return. If there was to be trouble he wanted men inside the walls. That is what he said. We were to wait here, and —'

I was rapidly losing patience. 'Where was he going?'

'He did not say, my lord.'

'Perhaps not. But you have an opinion, do you not? Think! It is important.'

'Well,' he replied slowly, 'it was in my mind that they were riding back to the camp — we camped the war host half-a-day from Londinium, as the king did not wish to overwhelm the city.'

'Yes, and he met with the governor. What happened?'

'Nothing that I could tell. We stayed in the palace for a day and then returned to camp.'

'Was all well in camp?'

'Not as well as may be,' the soldier allowed. 'Several of the lords had gone and taken their warbands with them.'

'And in the city? What happened on Aurelius' return?'

The warrior shrugged. 'Nothing that I know of.'

'Nothing — and yet the governor's temper turned against Aurelius.'

'It did, Lord Emrys. For a fact it did.'

At last, I began to understand what had happened: Aurelius, exuberant and fresh from the saving of the realm, nevertheless refrains from marching into Londinium in triumph. Adopting a humbler demeanour, he arrives in the city and presents himself to the governor in order to determine how he will be received in the city. Reassured, he returns to his lords, thinking perhaps to enter in force with the governor's blessing. However, things begin to go wrong. He arrives in camp to find that several lords have deserted him — that's how he would see it, whether they intended a slight or not.

In the meantime, a few of the wealthy and influential of Londinium have had time to make up their minds about Aurelius, and apparently what they have decided is not flattering: *he calls himself High King, but where is his war band? Where are his lords and battlechiefs? He is no king at all!* Something like that.

They spread this slander about and incite the people, who come to the governor with their petition against this impertinent youth. And the governor, owing no allegiance to Aurelius, instantly withdraws his support.

Poor Aurelius, by rights deserving a hero's welcome, returns to discover himself *persona non grata*. Outraged, he rides to gather his lords once more and march on the city, thinking to take it by force if need be. Needless to say, the citizens, fearful of this young warlord's anger, descend upon the governor, demanding safety, demanding protection, demanding action be taken against this upstart High King.

Well, that was the way of it, or near enough.

The warrior still stood before me, watching, and I realized that I would have no more from him; Aurelius had confided nothing to him. I obtained the location of the camp, thanked him and left him to his duty. I went to Gwythelyn and told him to wait with Dafyd, warning him that for their own safety they must stay at the church with the warriors. There was no telling what the citizens of Londinium might do if roused to it.

Then Pelleas and I rode out to find Aurelius.

Having come by a more northerly route, we had not encountered the camp on our way to Londinium; but the warrior's directions proved themselves and we came upon the camp as the sun stretched our shadows long behind us.

I saw at once the reason for Aurelius' fury, and I did not blame him. For, of the great warhost he had commanded, now only a few bands and their lords remained — among them Tewdrig, to be sure, and Ceredigawn, one of Cunnedda's sons, was still there, and Custennin's band with their lord's battlechief.

I went to Tewdrig directly.

He was not happy with the situation and let me know it at once. 'I tried to stop them,' he insisted. 'But they had it in their heads to leave as soon as Aurelius rode to Londinium. "We fought his war for him," they said, "let him win the city for himself!" That is what they said.'

'And they said they'd had enough of High Kings!' remarked Ceredigawn, striding up. 'And I am beginning to agree with them. Are we to wait here like shavelings while the grown men divide the spoils?' He had seen me ride into camp and came to add his own opinion.

'Who voiced these things among you?' I asked him.

'Gorlas of Cerniu, mostly,' Ceredigawn replied. 'And some others.'

'Friends of Gorlas,' Tewdrig informed me. 'I might have gone myself —'

'I am glad you stayed,' I told him quickly. 'I think you will not be disappointed for your loyalty.'

'How so?' Tewdrig asked.

Before answering, I bade Pelleas bring the other lords and battlechiefs to me and, when they had gathered, I sat them down and addressed them, saying, 'My lords and sword brothers, I have just returned from Londinium and I have a fair idea what happened there.'

'Tell us, then, if you will,' said one of the chieftains, 'for unless you do, I am leaving at once. There is a harvest to bring in at home, and I have had enough of waiting.'

His ultimatum was greeted with grunts of approval from several of the others. I had arrived none too soon — they were all on the point of leaving.

I took a deep breath and began, 'I do not know if what I have to say will make any difference to you, but I tell you the truth: it appears that to keep from making one blunder, our young king has made an even bigger blunder.'

'Oh, aye,' agreed someone. 'He forgot who his friends are.'

'Perhaps,' I allowed, 'but that was never his intention. He did not march with you into Londinium because —'

'He was ashamed!' shouted one of the battlechiefs of the north. 'We were good enough to fight for him, but not to be seen in his great city!' The man spat in the dirt to add emphasis to his words. 'Mithras kill me if I lift a blade for Aurelius again!'

I understood then how it was with them. 'Let Lord Emrys speak!' shouted Tewdrig. 'I would hear him out.'

'Aurelius declined to march with you into Londinium, not because he was ashamed — never believe that! — but because he did not wish to appear arrogant in the eyes of the citizens.'

'Citizens!' spat the battlechief once more, showing what he thought of the word.

'Aurelius,' I continued, 'feared that marching into the city in force would appear arrogant and would turn opinion against him. Worse, it might have been seen as an attack, and there would have been bloodshed. So he bade you wait for him and he went on alone. But deeming him a man of little account, Londinium turned against him anyway.'

'What does he need with Londinium?' demanded Ceredigawn. 'They have no king, and no war band.'

'No, but they have wealth and power. Anyone who will be High King in this land must be recognized by Londinium.'

'Vortigern never was!' someone called out. How quickly they forget!

'Yes, and look where Vortigern has led us!' I answered. 'That is the mistake Aurelius did not wish to make. He thought to win Londinium with meekness after Vortigern's arrogance. Still, they turned against him. So be it. When next he marches into the city, he will want you at his side.'

The gathering remained silent, thinking it over. Finally, Tewdrig rose from his place and proclaimed, 'I have always wanted to see this wonder of a city and, as I am so close, I would not be turned back now. Let us go with Aurelius and see that our High King receives proper respect from the stiff-necked rabble of Londinium.'

It was what the others needed to hear. They all stood up with a shout, adding their voices to Tewdrig's, and an uneasy peace settled over the camp once more.

So it was that when Aurelius returned late that night, there was still a camp and men to return to.

'Gorlas, blast his bones!' He paced his tent in agitation, still sweating from his ride. 'I swear he planned this as revenge on me for letting Octa go free.'

'Calm yourself, Aurelie,' said Uther, '*I* was the one that let Octa go free. Gorlas is difficult and that is the end of it. This was his way of making himself important.'

Uther had a way of reading men simply and directly. He had struck the truth of Gorlas. 'Listen to your brother,' I said, 'if you will not listen to me. Gorlas is not the only one who mistook your reasons for not marching into Londinium like a hero.'

'I would have received no hero's welcome in Londinium!' Aurelius growled.

I turned on my heel and started from the tent. Aurelius saw this and cried after me. 'So you desert me, too, eh, Myrddin? Go then! Leave me! Get out all of you!'

'Myrddin, wait!' Uther came after me. 'Please, we have been in the saddle since before sunrise, and then we did not so much as catch a glimpse of Gorlas — or any of the others. Do not be angry with him.'

'I am not angry,' I said, turning to meet him in the moonlight. 'But I will not waste my time talking just to hear myself speak.'

'Let him rest. He will be ready to listen in the morning.'

I did not go to my tent, but went instead to a nearby alder grove to think. I sat down among the slim, moon-silvered trunks and listened to the water ripple in the little stream. It was peaceful there and I had much need of peace. Much need of respite from men and their self-important schemes — all desire and ambition, no thought, no restraint or compassion, no understanding.

The last few days, coming after the benevolent company of Dafyd and his monks, seemed diabolic in contrast: the jealousy, the grudging animosity, the petty spite. . . My spirit recoiled from it as from a fanged serpent.

Great Light, deliver me from the enmity of small-minded men!

Or, if I may not be delivered, give me the strength to overcome, or if not to overcome, simply to endure. I would settle for that.

Then, sitting there in the moonlight, I felt the confusion of the past days dissolve like hard dirt clods in the rain. I breathed deep of the tranquillity of the sleeping world and began to see the way ahead more clearly.

Aurelius must be established as High King and must be recognized by all as supreme king of all Britons. His claim must remain unchallenged and all lesser kings must be seen to give him fealty. This was of foremost importance. If it could be accomplished without increasing ill will and contention, so much the better.

By the time the moon dipped below the far horizon, a plan had begun to take shape in my mind. I went to my bed at last, satisfied that I had found a solution. It seemed that I had just stretched myself out when Pelleas woke me saying, 'Lord Myrddin, the king is asking for you.'

I rose with a yawn, dashed water in my face from the basin in Pelleas' hands and went to see the king. He was seated at his board, his dark curls wild on his head, a loaf of bread in his hands. It did not appear that his night's rest had soothed him. He half-rose when I came in, remembered himself, sat again, and extended half the loaf to me. Uther sat at the end of the board, looking out of sorts; he too had been dragged from his bed.

'Well, Wise Counsellor,' Aurelius said, 'give me the benefit of your wisdom. Am I to be High King, or hermit? What am I to do?'

'You will be High King,' I reassured him. 'But not yet.'

'No?' His eyebrows rose. 'How long must I wait?'

'Until the time redeems itself.'

'Speak plainly, Prophet. How long?'

So I told him my plan, and ended by saying, 'Thus, send the rest of the kings back to their realms. Tell them to ready their tribute to you and await your summons — which will come when you are ready.'

'When will that be?' A sly smile wreathed his lips, for he understood the implications of my words.

'At the Christ Mass.'

'Yes!' He rose with a shout. 'Well done, Myrddin!'

Uther nodded vaguely. 'It is all very well for the kings to pay tribute to Aurelius, but why must he wait until the dead of winter to be crowned? The throne is his, he should take it.'

Aurelius was on his feet now, excited. 'Do you not see it, brother? Londinium will have time to misdoubt its treatment of me. The citizens will wait for me to act, and they will grow fearful in waiting. They will fear my wrath, they will fear the worst. And then, when I come, they will seek to soothe me; they will throw open the gates, they will lavish gifts upon me. In short, they will welcome me in all meekness, glad in their hearts that I did not destroy them as they deserved. Am I right, Myrddin?'

'That is the meat of it.'

'And the other kings — by letting them go now, I rescue my dignity.'

'Essentially.'

Uther still appeared in a fog. 'I do not see that at all.'

'Half of the kings have left me,' Aurelius said, 'and the other half *wish* they had.' He was overstating it, but not by much. 'Very well, let them *all* go. I will send word to them to attend me at Christ Mass in Londinium. They will come, and the people will see me attended by the kings of Britain in all their finery. Oh, it will be a splendid spectacle!'

'They will think you weak if you do not act now.'

'No, brother, it is by choosing *not* to act that I show my strength. He is truly strong who withholds his hand when he could strike.'

It was not as simple as that, I knew, but if it was what Aurelius believed, and he did, it might amount to the same thing in the end. I prayed that it would. Besides, I did not think he would lose anything by waiting — and letting the lords think better of their oaths of fealty. Also, the troublesome lords like Gorlas and his friends, Morcant, Coledac, and Dunaut would be more easily dealt with singly; alone, without support of other dissenters, they could be brought into compliance.

Uther remained sceptical. 'What do we do while we wait? Where will we go? Need I remind you, brother, we have not so much as a rooftile to call our own?'

'It is not so long to wait,' I said quickly. 'And you have no lack of hearth places where you will be welcome. We could return to Dyfed, or —'

'No,' replied Aurelius firmly, 'it must not be at the hospitality of any of my kings. It must be somewhere else.'

'Just where might that be?' wondered Uther. 'Not Londinium, surely.'

'Leave it to me,' I said. 'I know a place where you will be received in all luxury, and accorded the dignity of your rank.'

Uther rose. He was happy with the plan; or at least happy to let the matter rest until he had properly broken fast. He took his leave of us and returned to his tent; I got to my feet as well. 'Merlin,' said Aurelius. He stood and came to place his hands on my shoulders. 'I am stubborn and impatient, but you forbear me. Thank you for your indulgence, my friend. And thank you for the benefit of your wisdom.'

The High King embraced me like a brother, and then went out to tell his lords that they were to return home to their harvests, and that he would send word for them to meet him in Londinium at the Mass of Christ, when he would take the crown.

'The Christ Mass,' wondered Ceredigawn. 'When is that?'

'At the midwinter solstice,' answered Aurelius.

'And where will you go now, my lord?' asked Tewdrig. 'What will you do?'

'I am going away with my Wise Counsellor,' Aurelius answered, and with a conspirator's smile turned towards me. 'I will hold vigil in prayer and holy instruction until I be made High King.'

This pronouncement caused as much sensation as if Aurelius had announced that he would forsake the throne altogether and become a monk. The lords turned to one another and remarked that such a thing had never been heard of before. Aurelius left them floundering in their surprise. 'I will summon you when the season draws near, that you may make ready to attend me in all courtesy.' Saying this, he returned to his tent, leaving his lords staring after him.

A more kingly act he could not have conceived.

NINE

I should have seen more clearly. I should have known where events were leading. I should have recognized what shape the future would take. My vision was clear enough: I should have known to protect Aurelius. Above all, I should have recognized the hand of Morgian working unseen to shape the world to her will. So much I should have seen and known.

Should have. . . Empty, useless words. How they cleave bitterly to the tongue. To utter them is to taste bile and ashes in the mouth. Well, I am to blame.

Aurelius was so happy, so confident. And I was so pleased to sojourn a season in Avallach's house, and to see Charis again, that I did not think further ahead than the day at hand. Feeling no threat, I let time take its course. That was my mistake.

In truth, I feared Morgian and that was my failing.

Upon leaving Londinium, we rode to Ynys Avallach, the mysterious Glass Isle of old, to Avallach's palace. We stopped along the way and were received with great acclaim; word of Hengist's defeat had permeated the landscape itself, and we were everywhere made welcome.

Gwythelyn and the monks parted company with us at Aquae Sulis, but I induced Dafyd to continue on with us, and to undertake Aurelius' tutelage. Not that he needed much coaxing; the happy prospect of seeing Charis and Avallach once more cheered him greatly.

Oh, it was a glad reunion. They fell into one another's arms, tears of happiness shining on their cheeks. I do not think they ever hoped to see one another again, so many years had passed. But like all good friendships the passage of time did little to alter their love for one another, and within the space of a few heartbeats it was as if they had never been apart.

After the hardships of a season of almost continual fighting, it was good to let the tranquillity of the Glass Isle seep into our battle-weary souls. False summer faded and autumn progressed apace, bringing wind and rain to the Summerlands. The sea rose to flood the lowlands around the palace and Ynys Avallach became a true island once again. Though the days grew shorter and the world colder, our hearts remained light and we luxuriated in the warmth of one another's company.

Dafyd taught in the great hall by day. Most of Avallach's household gathered to hear the wise bishop expound the teachings of God's Holy Son, Jesu, Lord and Saviour of Men, and the hall was filled with love and light and learning. Aurelius, true to his word, spent his days in instruction and prayer at Dafyd's feet. I watched him grow in grace and faith, and I rejoiced in my heart that Britain should have such a High King.

Great is the king who loves the Most High God. Before the first snows of winter fell, Aurelius consecrated himself to God, and took the sign of the Saviour Son, the cross of Christ, as his emblem.

Pelleas grew restless, and one day I found him on the rampart, staring southward towards Llyonesse. 'Do you miss it?' I asked him.

'I did not think so until now,' he answered, without taking his eyes from the southern hills.

'Then why not go back?'

He turned to me, pain and hope mingled in his face. But he did not answer.

'Not to stay. But I can spare you yet a while; go back to your people. How long has it been since you have seen them? Go to them.'

'I do not know if I would be welcome,' he replied, and turned back to stare into the grey distance.

'You will never find out standing here,' I told him. 'Go; there is time. You could rejoin us in Londinium at the Christ Mass.'

'If you think I might. . . '

'I would not have said it if I did not think so. Besides, it would be good to have some word of happenings in Llyonesse.'

'Then I will go,' he said resolutely. He turned and, with the air of a man going to his doom, strode from the rampart and across the courtyard. In a little while, I saw him ride along the causeway; I watched until he disappeared from sight along the hilltrack.

For my part, I spent much time with my mother, talking, playing chess, playing my harp and singing for her. It was good to sit with her beside the hearth, the scent of oak and elm hazy in the air, wrapped in our woollen cloaks, listening to the icy rain spatter on the courtyard stones, and the small ticking of the fire before us.

Charis told me of her life as a bull dancer in Atlantis, the cataclysm that claimed her homeland, their coming to Ynys Prydein, and the difficulties of those first hopeless, tragic years — all the old stories. But I heard them in a way I had never heard them before, and I understood. Hearing with understanding is, perhaps, the better part of wisdom. I learned much in listening to my mother speak about her life and came to see her in a new way.

One morning I asked about the sword — Avallach's sword, the one she had given me when I became king. Pelleas had told me that he found it on the battlefield when I fled, and that he had carried it back to Ynys Avallach, along with word of my disappearance, that first winter when the weather forced him to give up searching for me.

'Do you wish to have it back?' she asked. 'I have kept it for you. But when you did not ask for it on your return, I thought. . . But, of course, I will get it for you.'

'No, please; I only ask about it. I told you once that sword was not for me. I held it for a time, but I think it is meant for another hand.'

'It is yours. Give it to whomsoever you wish.'

I would have given much to remain in Avallach's house, but it was not to be. Too soon the time came to leave. One day Aurelius sent out his messengers to his lords, as he had said he would, summoning them to his kingmaking. Then, a few days later, we started out.

In the cold heart of a mid-winter morning we mounted our horses and began the journey to Londinium. Aurelius was in high spirits and eager to seize his crown. He had embraced Dafyd's instruction, and now owned the Holy Jesu as his Lord. Upon his taking the crown, he meant to be baptized, as a sign to all his people where his allegiance lay.

Uther distrusted the church. I do not know why. He would speak of his misgivings to no one. He allowed the good in men like Dafyd and the good their lives and teaching produced, even acknowledged its source, but could not bring himself to embrace the truth they proclaimed, nor make it his own. But, as I have said, he loved his brother, and whatever Aurelius chose, Uther at least tolerated.

Nevertheless, Uther's sojourn at the Glass Isle, although restful, had something of captivity in it. So the day of our leavetaking was a day of liberation for Uther and he breathed deep of it. He was the first into the saddle, and he sat jerking the reins back and forth impatiently as the rest of us made our farewells.

'Mother, pray for me,' I whispered as I stepped close to embrace her.

'Like my love, my prayers have never ceased. Go in God's peace, my Hawk.'

So, wrapping ourselves in our cloaks and furs against the cold, we started down the snaking trail to the causeway, and across the frozen meres to the snow-dusted hills beyond. The cold brought colour to our cheeks, and keenness to our appetites. We travelled with all speed over the hard winter ground, making the most of the too-short daylight hours, stopping only when it became too dark to see the road ahead. At night, we huddled close to the fire of our night's host — chieftain or magistrate or village elder — and listened to the winter-starved wolves howl.

Nevertheless we rode through a land silent and at rest, and arrived in Londinium a day sooner than we had planned. This time Aurelius did not go to the governor's palace, but went straight to the church. Urbanus received us cordially and made us comfortable in his quarters — the lower floor of a plain but spacious house adjacent to the church.

While we warmed ourselves over the brazier and sipped hot mulled wine, he told us how the church might be prepared for the coronation. He declared enthusiasm for the coronation to take place in his church, but confessed, 'I still do not understand why you wish to be made king here.'

'I am a Christian,' Aurelius explained. 'Where would you have me go? Governor Melatus is not my superior that I should receive my crown from his hand. But Jesu is my Lord, therefore I will take up my kingship in his holy presence. And I will receive my crown from the hand of his true servant Bishop Dafyd.'

It was as I had always intended it to be, of course, but hearing the confirmation from Aurelius' own lips thrilled me. Only such a king would be fit for the Kingdom of Summer; and Aurelius had the grace and the strength; he had the faith. He could rule this worlds-realm island, and it would flourish like a meadow in midsummer.

Though the land lay barren in the cold grip of winter, I saw summer's cloak falling over her like the mantle of a bride. And I rejoiced to see it.

Great Light, let my vision prove false! Let Aurelius live to do his work.

The next day the first of Aurelius' kings arrived in Londinium: Coledac and Morcant, neither of whom had far to travel, came into the city with their lords and advisers, a small band of warriors each, and, to my surprise, their wives and children. Dunaut and Tewdrig arrived the next day, and Custennin and Ceredigawn the day following. And there was a scramble to find places for them all — for each had brought a large retinue to attend the ceremony.

Others arrived: Morganwg of Dumnonia, with the princes Cato and Maglos; Eldof of Eboracum; Ogryvan of Dollgellau and his chieftains and druids; Rhain, prince of Gwynedd, Ceredigawn's cousin; Antorius and his brother king, Regulus, of Canti in Lloegres; Owen Vinddu of Rheged; Hoel of Armorica, braving the winter seas, with his sons, Ban and Bors.

Still others came, and not lords and chieftains only, but holy men as well: Samson, most reverent priest of Goddodin in the north; the renowned Bishop Teilo, and abbots Ffili and Asaph, noble churchmen of Lloegres; and Kentigern, the much loved priest of Mon; Bishop Trimoriun and Dubricius, both learned and respected priests of the church at Caer Legionis; and, of course, Gwythelyn with all the monks of Dafyd's monastery at Llandaff.

Kings and lords and churchmen from all the realms of the Island of the Mighty came to uphold Aurelius as High King. And each had brought gifts: objects of gold and silver, swords, fine horses and hunting hounds, good cloth, ash bows and steel-tipped arrows, hides and skins and furs of finest quality, silver-rimmed drinking horns, casks of mead and dark beer, and more.

All brought gifts according to their wealth and rank, and I realized that they had been long anticipating this event and awaiting it with eagerness — even as I had predicted. Time had worked its wonder in their hearts, magnifying Aurelius in their eyes. They came to Londinium to make a High King, and they would see him crowned with all honour and esteem.

Did I say all? There was one whose absence fairly shouted: Gorlas. He alone risked the High King's wrath with his defiance. With the Christ Mass but one day away, there was still no word or sign from Gorlas. This weighed more heavily on me and on Uther than it did on Aurelius, who was so busy receiving the gifts and honour of his lords that he did not appear to notice Gorlas' slight.

But Uther noticed. As the days dwindled and preparations for the Feast of the Mass of Christ hurried apace, he stormed the upper rooms of Urbanus' house, angry, shouting, pounding tables and doorposts with his fists.

'Give me twenty men and I will bring back Gorlas' head for the High King's crowntaking, by Lleu and Jesu I would!'

I answered, 'Calm yourself, Uther. Lleu might approve of your gift, but I heartily doubt Jesu would find favour in it.'

'Well, am I to stand by and do nothing while that whore's whelp thumbs his nose at Aurelius? Tell me, Merlin, what am I to do? Mind, I will not suffer Gorlas' impudence lightly.'

'I say that it is Aurelius' affair, Uther, not yours. If the High King wishes to overlook Gorlas' insult, so be it. No doubt your brother will deal with it at a more opportune time.'

Uther subsided, but he was not appeased. He continued to grumble and growl, snarling at all who approached him, making himself so unpleasant that I finally sent him out to look for Pelleas, who had not yet arrived. For I knew Pelleas would have come by now unless prevented, and I had begun to be anxious over him.

I could have studied the fire for some sign of him, but I will tell you the truth, that since my healing and release from Celyddon, reading the embers, or gazing into the seeing bowl had become distasteful to me. Perhaps I feared that in walking the paths of the future I might meet Morgian — that occurred to me and the prospect chilled my heart. Or perhaps I was restrained by something else. In any event, I did not care to satisfy my curiosity with the fire or bowl, and I would not unless need were great.

So, Uther, glad to have something to do, ordered his horse to be saddled, and gathered a small band of companions and rode out from the city at midday. I was free to go about my own affairs, which included visiting Custennin and Tewdrig.

This kept me occupied well into the night, for the noblemen came to Aurelius one after another without cease, drinking his health, giving gifts, and pledging themselves and their heirs to his service. On the eve of the Christ Mass, the High King was awash in a floodtide of fealty and well-wishing. I spoke to this one and that, gathering information and knowledge, learning what I could from the lords about whose realms I was ignorant.

Dawn was but a whisper away when I finally made my way to my bedchamber — only to realize that Uther had not yet returned. Notwithstanding my reluctance, I was tempted to stir up the embers and see what had befallen him. But instead I donned my cloak and went to find my horse. The monk whose charge was the stable lay sleeping in his corner on a pallet of fresh straw, snoring. Loth to wake him, I saddled my mount and rode out into cold, silent streets.

The gatekeeper was nowhere to be seen, but the gate was not locked so I opened the gate myself and hastened out. Gusts of wind hissed through frost-stiffened foliage along the road outside the walls. The heavens were heavy with unshed snow, and shone like molten lead in the rising sun. I turned west with the road, knowing Uther would have ridden that way in search of Pelleas.

I rode, letting my horse have his head, glad to be out in the countryside once more and free of the too-close company of men. My thoughts turned to Pelleas. Perhaps I had not acted wisely in urging him to return to his home in Llyonesse. I knew nothing of affairs there. King Belyn might not have been pleased to see his bastard son; Pelleas might have come to harm.

Even now I did not think it likely and the thought would not have occurred to me at all, if not for the obvious fact of Pelleas' absence. Of course, he might have had trouble on the road — always possible, although it was hard to imagine what kind of trouble a seasoned warrior might encounter that could not easily be discharged by the quick stroke of his blade.

Or might it be something else entirely?

The empty road passed beneath my horse's hooves and my danger sense sharpened with each step. At every moment I expected to see Pelleas cresting the hill ahead. But I reached it first and he was not to be seen.

I rode until midday and then stopped. I must turn back if I was to return to Londinium in time for the Mass and Aurelius' crowntaking. I stopped and waited a moment on a tree-crowned hilltop, gazing into the distance all around, then, reluctantly, started back.

I had not ridden far, however, when I heard a shout.

'*Mer-r-lin-n!*'

The call came from some distance away, but was distinct in the crisp winter air. Instantly, I halted and whirled in the saddle. There, a long way off, a lone rider galloped towards me: Pelleas.

I waited and he reached me a few moments later, exhausted, out of breath, his horse lathered from a hard ride. 'I am sorry, my lord —' he began, but I dismissed his apology with a gesture.

'Are you well?'

'I am well, my lord.'

'Have you seen Uther?'

'Yes,' Pelleas answered with a nod, gasping for breath. 'We met him on the road —'

'We? Who was with you?'

'Gorlas,' Pelleas wheezed. 'I would have come sooner, but in the circumstance, I thought best —'

'No doubt you did right. Now tell me what has happened.'

'One day ago, on the road, Gorlas and his party were attacked. He travelled with but a small escort, and we were forced to fight for our lives; we held them off for a good while nevertheless. Uther came upon us when it appeared that we would fail. Our attackers fled; the Duke gave chase, but was eluded.' Pelleas paused, gulping air. 'Upon his return Uther sent me on ahead. He rides with Gorlas now.'

'How far behind?'

Pelleas shook his head. 'I cannot say for certain. I have been riding all night.'

I scanned the road behind, hoping to see some sign of Uther and Gorlas; there was none. 'Well, there is nothing we can do now. We will return to Londinium and await them there.'

Owing to Pelleas' fatigue, we were late in reaching the city. But we hurried to Urbanus' house and washed ourselves, before going to the church. By the time we arrived, the church was already full; the yard was thronged with the lords' retinues and curious citizens. We forced our way through the press at the doors and made our way among the crowd inside, finding places beside a pillar near the front.

The interior of the great room was a blaze of candlelight; shining, white gold, like the light of heaven after a violent storm. Blue-misted vapours of incense ascended to the roof-beams in sweet-scented clouds, to waft above our heads like the prayers of saints. The church buzzed with excitement. Here was a thing that had never happened before: a king crowned in a church, receiving his kingship from the hand of a holy man!

We had only just taken our places when the inner doors were thrown wide open and a robed monk swinging a censer came forth down the central aisle. Behind him came another, carrying a carved wooden cross before him. Urbanus followed, wearing a dark robe and a huge cross of gold upon his chest.

Dafyd walked behind him dressed in his robes, face shining in the candleglow. I stared at him as all the others stared, for he was a man transformed. Splendid in humility, radiant in simple holiness, Dafyd appeared a heavenly messenger come down to bless the proceedings with his presence. No one who saw him could have mistaken his kindly smile for anything but the rapture of one close to the living source of all love and light. Just to see him was to bow the knee to the God he served; it was to draw near true majesty with meekness and submission.

Behind Dafyd walked Aurelius, carrying his sword — the Sword of Britain — blade across palms, dressed in a white tunic and trousers with a wide belt of silver discs. His dark hair was oiled and combed back, bound at the nape with a thong. He walked easily, his expression at once serious and joyful.

Gwythelyn came after him, bearing a narrow circlet of gold on a cloth of white linen. Four more monks followed with a cloak of imperial purple, each holding a corner in his hand.

All these made their way to the altar, which was raised on a stepped marble dias. Urbanus and Dafyd approached the altar and turned to face Aurelius, who knelt down before them on the steps.

No sooner had this taken place than a chorus of monks, lining the perimeter of the church, began shouting:

GLORIA! GLORIA!

GLORIA IN EXCELSIS DEO! GLORIA IN EXCELSIS DEO!

'Glory to God in the High Realms!' they shouted, and their shout became a chant. Others joined in and soon everyone was chanting; the church reverberated with it, the sound lifting the heart and spiralling up and ever upward through the night-dark sky to the first twinkling stars, to the very throne of heaven.

When the chant had reached its crescendo, Dafyd stepped forth with arms outspread and the room fell silent at once. 'It is right to pay homage to the Great Good God,' he said, then he turned to the altar, knelt, and began to pray aloud.

'Great of Might, High King of Heaven, we honour you!

Light of sun,
Radiance of moon,
Splendour of fire.
Speed of lightning,
Swiftness of wind,
Depth of sea,
Stability of earth,
Firmness of rock,
Bear witness:

We pray this day for Aurelius, our king;
For God's strength to steady him,
God's might to uphold him,
God's eye to look before him,
God's ear to hear him,
God's word to speak for him,
God's hand to guard him,
God's shield to protect him,
God's host to save him

372

From the snares of devils,
From temptation of vices,
From everyone who shall wish him ill.

We do summon all these powers between him
    and these evils:
Against every cruel power that may oppose him;
Against incantations of false druids,
Against black arts of barbarians,
Against wiles of idol-keepers,
Against enchantments great and small,
Against every foul thing that corrupts body and soul.

Jesu with him, before him, behind him,
Jesu in him, beneath him, above him,
Jesu on his right, Jesu on his left,
Jesu when he sleeps, Jesu when he wakes,
Jesu in the heart of everyone who thinks of him,
Jesu in the mouth of everyone who speaks of him,
Jesu in the eye of everyone who sees him.

We uphold him today, through a mighty strength,
the invocation of the Three in One,
Through belief in God,
Through confession of the Holy Spirit,
Through trust in the Christ,
Creator of all Creation.

So be it.

When he had finished, Dafyd turned to the monk with
the cross and lifted the wooden symbol before Aurelius.
'Aurelianus, son of Constantine, who would be High King over
us, do you acknowledge the Lord Jesu as your High King and
swear him fealty?'

'I do so acknowledge him,' answered Aurelius. 'I swear
fealty to no other Lord.'

'And do you promise to serve him through all things, as you
would be served, even to the last of your strength?'

'I do so promise to serve him through all things, as I am
served, even to the last of my strength.'

'And will you worship the Christ freely, honour him gladly,

revere him nobly, hold for him your truest faith and greatest love, all the days that you shall live in this worlds-realm?'

'I will worship the Christ most freely, honour him most gladly, revere him most nobly, and hold for him my truest faith and greatest love, all the days that I shall live in this worlds-realm.'

'And will you uphold justice, dispense mercy, and seek truth through all things, dealing with your people in compassion and love?'

'I will uphold justice, dispense mercy, and seek truth through all things, dealing with my people in compassion and love, even as I am dealt with by God.'

All that Dafyd asked, Aurelius answered without hesitation and with a loud voice, so that even the crowd outside the doors could hear. Pelleas leaned near and whispered, 'All gathered in this church this night, Christian and pagan alike, will know what it is to worship the Most High God.'

'So be it,' I answered. 'May such knowledge increase.'

Urbanus came forward with a vial of holy oil and, dipping his fingers, anointed Aurelius' forehead with the sign of the cross. Then he nodded to the monks holding the cloak; the monks lifted the cloak and wrapped it round Aurelius' shoulders. Urbanus fastened it with a silver brooch.

Dafyd had turned to Gwythelyn, holding the circlet. He now took up the narrow golden band and held it above Aurelius' head. 'Arise, Aurelianus,' he said, 'wear your crown.' Aurelius rose up slowly and, at the same time, Dafyd lowered the circlet upon his brow.

The holy man kissed Aurelius on the cheek and, turning him to face his people, cried out, 'Lords of Britain, here is your High King! I charge you to love him, honour him, follow him, pledge yourselves to him as he has pledged himself to the High King of Heaven.'

At this the assembled lords broke out with a mighty cheer — one voice of acclaim, one spirit of good will, one heart of love for their new king. Aurelius smiled and spread his arms as if he would embrace all the world. And I know that in that moment he did — as few men ever do.

When the cheering ended, Aurelius knelt once more for the bishops' blessing. Both Dafyd and Urbanus laid their hands upon him and gave him the blessing of the church, saying,

'Go in peace, Aurelianus, to serve God, the realm, and your people; and to lead them in holiness and righteousness to the end of your strength and life.'

The people knelt as he passed, but not one could take his eyes from the king. He reached the centre of the church and someone cried out, 'Ave! Ave, Imperator!'

Another answered, 'Hail, Emperor Aurelius!'

All at once every man was on his feet again, raising the new cry. 'Emperor Aurelius! Ave Imperator! Hail, Aurelius, Emperor of the West!'

Not since Maximus had British men raised an emperor. Him they gave a name, Macsen Weldig, to make a Briton of him, but he marched off to Rome with the best of the British troops and never returned. Aurelius had a Roman name, but a British heart. He knew nothing of Rome; this emperor was a Briton.

They proclaimed Aurelius emperor and, doing so, though they little understood, proclaimed the beginning of a new age for Ynys Prydein, Island of the Mighty.

TEN

Aurelius left the church and the throng pushed after him, spilling into the yard, cheering still. Torches lit the night, and from somewhere, above the wild celebration, there came a song. Slowly, softly, gaining strength as men and women took up the melody; the song, an old Briton battle song, became a hymn to the new High King. And Aurelius stood ringed by his lords in the torchlight, his crown gleaming as if with captured stars, arms outstretched, turning and turning as the song flowed upward, spreading in rings like a fountain in a pool.

They sang:

> 'Rise up, bold warriors,
>   take steel in your strong hands,
>   the foeman stands below, loudly shouting.
> Sound the horn and iron, gather spear and shield;
>   the day is bright for battle,
>   and glory for the taking.
> Mount up, brave warband, the battlechief is fearless;
>   bold leader, keen in victory,
>   he will win the hero's portion,
>   and the bards laud his name in song-making.

Voices echoing down the narrow streets, the crowd followed Aurelius to the governor's palace. Given time, the governor too had changed his mind about Aurelius. For upon his return Aurelius found Governor Melatus of a much-changed disposition. Fearful of offending such a powerful ally, Melatus had extended every hospitality of the city — which was heavily taxed finding places for all the kings and lords attending Aurelius. So it was to the governor's palace that Aurelius went now, to celebrate the Feast of Christ Mass with his lords.

376

The palace glowed beacon-bright in the winter night with candletrees and torches and fires in the courtyard. Large as it was, not everyone could be accommodated in the governor's hall that night. But it made no difference, for the doors were opened wide and the celebration filled the courtyard.

Oh, it was a gladsome time — a feast of love and light for winter's ending. I was uneasy in one detail only: Uther and Gorlas had not arrived.

What could be keeping them, I wondered? They should have reached Londinium long ago.

Aurelius seemed not to notice their absence. He was too much occupied with drinking the health of his lords and receiving their pledges of fealty. But I noticed. And as the feasting began and continued, Uther's and Gorlas' absence weighed on me.

'Pelleas, are you certain they were coming after you?' I had pulled Pelleas aside to ask him.

'Assuredly, my lord.'

'What can be preventing them?'

Pelleas frowned. 'More trouble, do you think?'

'Perhaps.'

'What would you have me do, lord?'

'Nothing for now; stay here. I may leave for a little while to see if I can discover what has become of Uther.' So saying, I left the hall and made my way through the courtyard. The citizens of Londinium, drawn by the noise and light, flocked to the celebration, and the courtyard revelry now overflowed into the streets. More people were joining all the time.

I entertained no hope of reaching the stable to get a horse, so, pulling my cloak around me, I pushed through the streaming throng and made my way to the western gates, which, as I expected, were closed and barred for the night. Also as I expected, the gatesmen were nowhere to be found; doubtless they had abandoned their duty at first opportunity.

Thinking only to take a look on the other side, I climbed the steps to the wall walk and gazed down upon the road. To my surprise, there was Uther, sword in hand, fuming and furious, standing in the dark, cursing the gate. He had been banging on the wooden door with the pommel of his sword, but of course no one had heard him.

'Uther!' I shouted.

He glanced up, but could not see me. 'Who is it? Open this gate at once or, by my life, I will burn it down.'

'It is Myrddin,' I answered.

'Merlin!' He stepped towards me. 'What do you here? Open the gate.'

'Where are the others?'

'I have sent them to find another way in. Gorlas waits on the road. This is embarrassing, Merlin, let us in.'

'Gladly, if I could. The gate is barred and the gatesmen are gone. Everyone has joined the feast at the governor's palace.'

'Well, do something. It is cold and we are tired.'

'I will see what can be done. Go and bring Gorlas here, and one way or another I will see that these gates are opened.'

As Uther mounted his horse and rode to fetch Gorlas, I hurried back down, and, taking a torch from the wall beside the gatesman's hut, I went to the gate. The wooden beam was secured by a crosswise iron bar that held it in place. The iron could not be withdrawn for it was clamped, and the clamp fastened with a lock. It began to appear as if Uther would have to burn down the gate after all — unless. . .

Now I had scarcely thought of the lore I had learned with the Hill Folk those many years ago, and certainly I had rarely used their art. But what is a gate but wood and iron, after all? There was no one around, so I quickly drew my knife and scratched a circle in the wood around the lock. Then I uttered the words in the Old Tongue, amazed that I had not forgotten.

At a touch, the lock simply fell off, and the wooden beam slid easily beneath my hand. With a finger I pushed and the huge gate swung open on groaning hinges.

Soon I heard horses on the road ahead; I lifted the torch and held it high. Uther appeared and Gorlas with him. But there was another, riding between them; and, as they came within the circle of light created by my torch, I saw that it was a woman. Young, beautiful, wrapped in furs to her chin, a silver circlet on her fair brow. Gorlas' queen?

'I did not know Gorlas had taken a queen,' I whispered to Uther as Lord Gorlas and his escort passed through the gate. He sat his saddle and watched the lord and lady ride on.

'She is Ygerna, his daughter,' Uther informed me. 'A rare flower of womanhood, is she not?'

I stared up at the man. I had never heard Uther utter such a sentiment. 'She is fair indeed,' I allowed. 'But Aurelius is waiting. What has detained you?'

Uther shrugged, and replied, as if it explained all, 'A woman was with us.'

A woman. She was little more than a maid. And although she was beautiful, she did not appear frail or debilitated in any way. Indeed, the bloom of youth was on her and, to my eye, she seemed to have endured the rigours of her journey most commendably.

'Pelleas told me about the attack.'

'The attack?' Uther asked, then nodded absently. 'Oh, that. It was nothing.'

'Well, Aurelius is waiting. You have missed the crowning.'

Uther accepted this amiably. 'I would have been here if I could. Is he angry?'

'In truth,' I replied, 'I do not think he has noticed your absence yet. If you hurry now, he may not.'

'We will make haste then,' said Uther placidly. 'But, Merlin, have you ever seen a woman so fair? Have you ever seen such eyes as hers?'

The last of Gorlas' men had passed through the gate. 'Go on with you, I will wait here until your men return.' I do not know if Uther even heard me, for without a word he turned his horse and trotted after Gorlas.

As it happened, I did not have long to wait. One of Uther's men approached the gate almost at once. I gave him instructions to wait for the others and bar the gates again when all had passed through.

Flying back along the streets, I returned to the governor's palace where the celebration continued. Uther was engaged in ordering stablehands to attend the horses. Gorlas and Ygerna stood a little way off, looking on at the roister around them. The fires leapt high in the courtyard and the governor's beer flowed freely to match the high spirits and liberal good will for the new High King.

Her face illumined by the fireglow, I had a moment to assess this beauty that had so bewitted Uther. She was, perhaps, all of fifteen years. Tall, slender, her finely-formed head borne gracefully on an elegant neck, she lacked the awkward girlishness of her age and appeared far more mature. Nor was

379

appearance deceiving: Gorlas' wife had died when the girl was still a babe and she had been raised from childhood to be the lady of the realm.

This I learned later. At the time, I saw only a comely girl with soft-woven brown hair and large dark eyes, in whose pretty smile a man might gladly lose himself.

'Will you be announced?' I asked Gorlas.

'Are we not expected?' he answered hotly, then turned to me. 'Oh! it is you, Merlin. . . ' My name was spoken like an oath. He worked his mouth silently, and at last forced out, 'As you think best.'

No, Gorlas wasted no love on me. But he respected me, and no doubt feared me a little — as any lord fears the man closest to his ruler's ear. 'We will go in together then, since —' I began.

'I will see to it,' Uther said, shoving between us. He turned Gorlas by the arm and led him off across the courtyard. I watched the three of them walking between the leaping flames of two fires and I saw Ygerna step lightly between Uther and Gorlas. Everything froze in my sight, all sound and motion ceased, vision narrowed as in that instant a deathly foreboding awakened within me. Nothing else existed but the terrible vision before me:

Ygerna between two kings.

Here was the nameless danger I had felt earlier in the day, redoubled in force. *Ygerna!* Oh, fair daughter, in your hands rests the future of the realm. Tonight you are destiny's handmaiden. Do you realize that?

No, of course she could have no idea. There was virtue as well as nobility in her rearing. Her natural innocence prevented her from using her beauty as a less scrupulous woman would have. Another year or two older, and I might have been seeing the end of the world stepping so lightly between the coronation fires.

I made my way after them, stumbling, numb, coming into the hall as they approached the High King. Uther worked to his brother's side. Aurelius welcomed him, clapped him on the back — I think that until this moment the High King had not a thought to spare for his brother — and thrust a drinking cup into Uther's hand. Uther took the cup, drank, and passed it to Gorlas, who proclaimed his loyalty to the

High Kingship.

Then Aurelius' eyes fell upon Ygerna. I saw him smile. I saw the change in his nature as he beheld her. Perhaps it was the giddiness of celebration, or the play of light upon her face, or youth calling to youth, or merely the wine running strong in Aurelius' veins. Perhaps it was something more. . . But I saw love kindled in that first brief glance.

Alas, I was not the only one to see it!

Uther stiffened. Had he been a porcupine he would have bristled. His grin froze on his face and the light died in his eyes. He seemed to grow visibly smaller as he stood in his brother's shadow.

Oblivious, Aurelius made a gentle remark. Ygerna lowered her eyes and laughed, shaking her head in response. Gorlas placed his hand on his daughter's shoulder and drew her forward. A minute gesture, imperceptible perhaps to anyone else, but I saw it and read well its meaning. Whether he knew it or not — I do not say that he did — Gorlas was offering his daughter to the High King.

And Aurelius, dear blind Aurelius, unaware of his brother, accepted her with the whole of his heart. He offered Ygerna the cup and his fingers lingered at her hand. Ygerna glanced meekly at Uther.

That look might have saved much, but Uther did not see it. He stared ahead dumbly — a man whose head has been severed from his body in a single stroke and knows for certain that he is dead and now must fall.

Then Aurelius bent near and whispered something to Ygerna. She smiled shyly and Aurelius threw back his head and laughed. This could not be endured; Uther turned on his heel and flew from them, disappearing into the roister. Ygerna looked uncertainly after him; her hand fluttered out to where he had been. But Uther was already gone and Aurelius was speaking again and Gorlas, holding his cup high, was beaming with delight.

I felt as if I had been kicked in the stomach by my horse, as if the floor had become unsteady beneath my feet, as if I had drunk a very powerful draught that confused the senses. The room spun and all became sharp noise and sharper light. Pelleas was suddenly there beside me. 'Master, what is wrong? Are you ill?'

'Take me from here,' I whispered. 'I cannot breathe.'

A moment later we were standing outside in the crisp, cold air. My head cleared and sense returned, but I was left with the sick feeling of deepest dread. What had been lost? More to the point, what could be saved?

I marvelled at the speed with which it had happened. How could I have foreseen it? Oh, but I should have known. I had been warned — out on the road my danger sense had been aroused, but I had not looked for the cause. Come to that, I had been amply warned in Celyddon. Nevertheless, my only thought had been to get the crown securely on Aurelius' head. I had looked no further than that.

It is strange that when a man spends all his time fighting one enemy, he fails to recognize another, greater foe. I knew him now, but it was too late. The damage was done. The Saecsen battles of last summer would dim in men's memory before I finished righting the destruction of this night.

Great Light, we are not equal to the fight!

Pelleas held me by the arm. 'Lord and master, are you well?' The concern in his voice was like a slap. 'What has happened?'

I drew a deep, unsteady breath. 'The world has tilted from its course, Pelleas.'

He stared — not in disbelief, but in sympathy. 'What is to be done?'

'That I cannot say. But we will be long repairing the breach, I fear.'

He turned his head and looked back into the feast hall, where the High King stood with his lords. Gorlas and Ygerna had moved away to find their places at the board. The food was being served now and it would have been sweet delight to have forgotten, if only for a moment, that what happened had ever taken place.

But that is not how the world is made. Once spoken, a word cannot be called back; once loosed, an arrow cannot return to the bow. What happens, for good or ill, happens for ever and that is the way of it.

The feast proceeded, but I had no appetite for it. I left Pelleas to watch for Uther, knowing he would not be found, and slipped away to my room. There was nothing to be done.

I did not sleep well and rose with a throbbing head and a bitter taste in my mouth. The sun was rising on a grey, rain-swept day. Londinium lay strangely quiet; most of its citizens must have found their rest but late and were still abed. From the church nearby I heard the light tolling of a bell. The brothers were telling Prime and would soon be at prayer.

I rose, threw my cloak over my shoulder and went down, slipping through the silent house, and across the wet yard to the church. I pushed open the door and entered. A number of monks were kneeling before the altar and I started towards them.

'Merlinus!' The whisper echoed in the room. Several of the monks turned round to look at me. I stopped and Urbanus hurried forward, his sandals slapping the stones at his feet. 'I did not think to find you here. I was about to send for you.'

I heard the note of strain in his voice. 'I am here. What is it?'

'It is Dafyd,' he said. 'Come with me; I will take you to him.'

Urbanus led me out across the inner court to the cells. Monks had gathered outside one of the doors. They parted when we came up, and Urbanus ushered me into the room. Dafyd lay on a pallet of fresh straw in a room illumined by a candle tree brought from the altar. He smiled as I came in and lifted a hand in greeting. Gwythelyn was with him, kneeling beside him, praying; he turned to me and I understood from his grave expression that Dafyd was dying.

'Ah, Myrddin, you have come. That is good. I hoped to see you here.'

I sank down beside Gwythelyn, my heart a bruise in my chest. 'Dafyd, I — ' I began and faltered. Where were the words?

'Shhh,' Dafyd hushed me. 'It was in my mind to thank you.'

'Thank me?' I shook my head.

'For letting me see the future, lad.' We were once again master and pupil in his mind, ending as we had begun. 'I had a dream last night, wondrous and terrible: I saw Aurelius striving mightily against a black and raging storm. He was beaten down and his cloak torn in rags from his shoulders. But, when it seemed that he must be ground into the dust, his hand closed upon a sword. He grasped it and it was his strength. Up he rose, holding the sword before him. Oh, the lightning flashed and the thunder rent the heavens. But Aurelius — I knew him for I saw his golden torc shining at his throat — raised his great sword and would not be moved.'

'Truly, it is a dream of great significance,' I told him, taking his hand.

'Oh, aye!' Dafyd's eyes shone with the wonder of it. He bore no pain, and rested comfortably. But I could feel his life slipping away from him. 'It was a fine kingmaking, was it not? I would not like to have missed it.'

'Rest you now,' urged Gwythelyn, fingering a small wooden cross.

'Son,' Dafyd replied lightly, 'I have rested, and soon must begin my journey hence. Have no fear for me, neither grieve. For I go to join my Lord and take my place in his retinue. Look! Here is Michael himself come to escort me!' He pointed towards the door. I saw no one, but did not doubt him. His face shone with the light of his vision.

Tears started into my eyes; I raised his hand to my lips and kissed it. 'Farewell, Dafyd, most noble friend. Greet Ganieda for me, and Taliesin.'

'That I will do,' he replied, his voice a whisper between his teeth. 'Farewell, Myrddin Bach. Farewell, Gwythelyn.' He raised an admonitory hand to us, saying, 'Grow strong in faith, and mighty in love, my friends. Be bold in goodness, for the angels stand ready to aid you. Farewell. . . '

The smile lingered on his face, even as his spirit departed. He died as he had lived: peacefully, gently, lovingly.

My heart split in two and I cried — not for grief, but because a great soul had gone out of the world and men would know it no more.

Gwythelyn bent his head and prayed quietly, then took Dafyd's hands and folded them upon his still breast. 'I will take him home now,' he said. 'He wished to be buried beside his church.'

'That would be best,' I replied.

'You bear no blame in this, Myrddin,' Gwythelyn said unexpectedly. I looked up. 'It was his desire to come here. He told me last night that crowning Aurelius was one of the chief acts of his life. He was glad you asked him to do it.'

I gazed at Dafyd's face, which seemed now to have taken on something of its former youthful appearance. And I remembered when he had held the crown above my head. There were few alive who would remember that, except perhaps as a tale told by a grandfather to his grandchildren. But, remembering, I bent and kissed Dafyd's cheek.

'Farewell, good friend,' I murmured, then rose abruptly and left — not for lack of feeling or respect — but because Dafyd had gone, and I had seen him on his way. And now I must be about this world's affairs, if I was to salvage anything from the ruin of last night.

ELEVEN

Tell me what I could have done? You who see all things so clearly, tell me now, I invite you: give me your infallible counsel. You who cover yourselves in everlasting ignorance and display it like a priceless cloak, who embrace blindness and count it a virtue, whose hearts quail with fear and call it prudence, I ask you plainly: what would you have done?

Great Light, deliver me from the venom of small-souled men!

The Enemy is subtlety itself, keen, vigilant, tireless, and infinite in resource. Ah, but evil ever overreaches itself, and very great evil overreaches itself greatly. And Lord Jesu, High King of Heaven, bends all purposes to his own, labouring through all things to turn all ends to the One. That is worth remembering.

But in the thin grey light of that cheerless morning, I despaired. The small kings would soon hear of the rift between the brothers. There are always those who will seize even the most unlikely weapons and use them most effectively. And some of the lords needed little enough encouragement. They would use Ygerna as a wedge between Aurelius and Uther, to divide them. Once divided, they would rebel against Aurelius and advance Uther — only to throw off Uther as soon as Aurelius was put down.

Then the kingdom would split once more into a wild scattering of fractious, warring, self-obsessed clans and kingdoms. And the Island of the Mighty would go down into the dark.

Well, Aurelius loved Ygerna and would have her. Knowing nothing of Uther's love, he wooed her with passion. Gorlas approved, indeed he encouraged the match, doing all he might to further it. To have his daughter, treasure that she was, married to the High King increased his own status immeasurably. In any event, Gorlas would never have assented to Uther.

And Uther, too stubborn to utter a word of his desire to his brother, and too proud to press his claim, endured his agony in bitter silence.

So, recognizing the hopelessness of Uther's position, I supported Aurelius. Uther resented this, but would say nothing directly. He loved Ygerna, but he loved his brother more. Bound by three strong coils — duty, honour, and blood — he was forced to stand by and watch his brother steal the light from his life.

Naturally, no one thought to ask Ygerna her thoughts on the matter. She would obey her father in any event, and it was abundantly clear where Gorlas' sentiments lay. Once he saw his opportunity, he wasted not a moment in arranging the marriage.

Accordingly, Aurelius and Ygerna were betrothed and planned the celebration of their union at the Feast of Pentecost.

I will not tell of their wedding; you can hear that tale from any of the itinerant harpers wandering the land, much embroidered and exalted, to be sure. But that is how men wish to remember it.

In truth, Aurelius very nearly was not married at all. He was busy in the months following his crowntaking: organizing the kingdom's defences; building and rebuilding in Londinium and Eboracum and elsewhere; creating churches where there was need. In all, binding his lords to his kingship in a hundred different ways.

To lead the new churches, he made new bishops — and one to replace Dafyd at Llandaff; he chose Gwythelyn for that, and rightly. The others were Dubricius at Caer Legionis, and Samson at Eboracum. Good and holy men each one.

Uther brooded and stormed through the wet end of winter. And spring brought him no joy. He grew gaunt and ill-tempered — like a dog long chained and denied the comfort of his master's hearth. He snarled at all who approached him and he drank too much, seeking to numb his heart's wound with strong wine — which only increased his misery. A more doleful, disagreeable man would be hard to imagine.

The attack on Gorlas during the previous winter was not forgotten. And with spring opening the land other attacks began taking place in the middle kingdoms and in the west. It was soon learned that Pascent, Vortigern's last living son, was responsible. Inflamed by the notion of avenging the blood debt of his father, he had sought and won the support of one, Guilomar, a minor Irish king ever eager to increase his fortunes through plunder.

Evidently, Gorlas had surprised Pascent on the road as the young man was making good his return to the island. Pascent, waiting with his few followers for Guilomar's warband, attacked out of fear lest his war be finished before it was begun. Aurelius deemed Pascent no great threat — save that the rebellious lords might find it in their interest to throw in with Vortigern's son. Therefore the High King was anxious that Pascent and Guilomar be dealt with firmly and finally, before anyone else could become involved.

So it was that spring found Aurelius preparing for his wedding and for war. The wedding could wait perhaps, but the war could not. This is where I made the decision which has earned me such scorn and contempt, although at the time it was the only wise course.

In order to help ease Uther's pain at his brother wedding the woman he loved, I suggested to the High King that Uther should lead the warband out to deal with Pascent and Guilomar. Aurelius, much preoccupied with his various works, readily agreed and gave the order, saying, 'Go with him, Merlin, for I worry after him. He has become contrary and keeps to himself. I fear these long months away from sword and saddle weigh too heavily on him.'

And Uther, glad for any excuse to quit Londinium, where life had grown so distasteful to him, became the image of a man afire. After hasty preparations we left the city a few days before Aurelius' and Ygerna's wedding. Uther could not have endured that; nor was he greatly cheered to have me with him.

Although he was too proud to say as much, he blamed me for not taking his part with Ygerna, forgetting that his lady had a father who would in no wise see his daughter married to him. As long as Gorlas lived, Aurelius was the only choice for his daughter.

Men will tell you that the war with Pascent was bloody and brief, and that Uther, in his smouldering rage, swept all before him. I wish it had been like that. Deeply, deeply, I wish it.

In truth, the campaign was a maddening chase across most of the kingdom, for the simple fact that Pascent would not fight. Instead, the coward would strike any undefended holding or settlement farm, plunder the stores and valuables and set fire to the buildings, killing any brave enough to oppose him. In this, he was no better than the worst Saecsen. Worse, in fact, for at least the barbarians do not slaughter their own kinsmen.

But as soon as Uther appeared, Pascent vanished. Oh, the rogue was shrewd, and quite skilful in choosing his targets and evading confrontation. Time and again we glimpsed the black smudge of smoke on the horizon, whipped our horses into a lather in our mad flight. . . only to find the grain burned, the blood soaking the ground, and Pascent long gone when we arrived.

Spring passed and summer settled full on the land, and still we chased, no nearer to catching Pascent than when we left Londinium.

'Why do you sit there doing nothing?' the Duke demanded of me one evening. We had lost Pascent's trail yet again that day in the hills of Gwynedd, and Uther was in a dangerous mood. 'Why do you refuse to help me?' An empty wineskin lay on the board next to his cup.

'I have never refused you aid, Uther.'

'Then where is this famed sight of yours?' He leapt to his feet and began stalking the tent, beating the air with clenched fists. 'Where are your visions and voices now when we need them?'

'It is not so simple as you think. The fire, the water — they reveal what they will. Like the bard's *awen*, the sight comes as it comes.'

'Were you a true druid, by the Raven, you would help me!' he cried.

'I am not a druid, nor have ever claimed to be.'

'Bah! Not a druid, not a bard, not a king — not this and not that! Well, what are you, Merlin Ambrosius?'

'I am a man and I will be treated so. If I have been summoned to suffer your insults, you must find someone else to abuse.' I rose to take my leave of him, but he was far from finished.

'I will tell you what you are. You are whatever you want to be — everything and nothing. You come to us, smooth as a serpent on a sunwarmed rock, speaking your subtle words, stealing Aurelius from me . . . turning him against me.' Uther was shaking now. He had worked himself up to it and gave vent to the fury pent inside him. Blaming me was easier than facing the true source of his misery.

I turned and walked from the tent, but he followed me outside, still shouting. 'I tell you, Merlin, I know you for what you are: schemer, deceiver, manipulater, false friend!'

It was his anger speaking and I did not listen.

'Answer me! Why do you refuse to answer me?' He grabbed me roughly by the arm and pulled me round to face him. 'Ha! You are afraid! That is it! I have spoken the truth and you are afraid of me now!' Stinking sweat dripped from him and he swayed on his feet.

Some of the warband standing near turned and gawked at us. 'Uther, have a care,' I snapped. 'You are embarrassing yourself before your men.'

'I am exposing a fool!' he gloated. His grin was grotesque.

'Please, Uther, say no more. The only fool you have exposed is yourself. Go back into your tent and go to sleep.' I made to turn away again, but he held me fast.

'I defy you!' he screamed, his face darkening in drunken rage. 'I defy you to prove yourself before us all. Give me a prophecy!'

I glowered hard at him. Were he and I alone I might have ignored him or found a way to calm him. But not with his men looking on — and not his alone, for, since we were in Gwynedd, Ceredigawn had supplied men, too. Uther had forced the matter too far to abandon; it was a matter of honour to him now. 'Very well, Uther,' I answered, loud enough for all to hear, 'I will do as you demand.'

He smiled in stupid triumph.

'I will do it,' I continued, 'but I will not answer for the consequence. For good or ill, the responsibility is yours.'

I said this not because I feared what might happen and wished to evade the consequence, but because I wanted Uther to know that it was not child's play, or a trick to impress the ignorant.

'What do you mean?' he demanded, suspicion flattening his tone.

I answered directly. 'It is not like deciphering scribbles from a book. It is a strange and unsettling thing, fraught with many dangers and uncertainties. I do not control it any more than you control the wind that blows through your hair, or the flames of your fire.'

'If you are trying to warn me off, save your breath.' Some of the men voiced agreement. They did not like to see their lord bested in anything.

'What I do will be done in the sight of all, so that you all may know the truth,' I told them. 'You there,' I pointed to the men close to the fire. 'Stir up the flames, put on more logs! I want live embers, not cold ash.'

This was not strictly necessary, I suppose, but I wanted time to compose myself and allow Uther's temper to cool. In any event, it worked, for Uther shouted, 'Well? You heard him. Do as he says and be quick about it.'

While the men heaped oak branches onto the fire, I went to my tent to get my cloak and staff. Neither were these necessary, but it would make a better show, I thought, and impress those looking on with the seriousness of what I did. The art should never appear too easy or people will not respect it.

Pelleas did not like what was happening. 'Lord, what will you do?'

'I will do what Uther has asked me to do.'

'But, Lord Myrddin —'

'He must learn!' I snapped, then softened. 'You are right to be concerned, Pelleas. Pray, my friend. Pray that we do not loose on the world a danger greater than we can safely contain.'

A steward came to me a little while later saying that the fire was ready. I wrapped myself in my cloak and took up my staff. Pelleas, praying silently, rose solemnly to his feet and joined me. Night was full upon the land when we emerged from the tent. We walked to the fire, which had burned down to a heap of fireshot coals, white-hot with crimson and orange flames. As good a bed for birthing the future as any.

The moon shone pale, its light tangled in the branches of trees whose trunks blushed red in the fireglow. The warband had assembled and stood round the pit, eyes glittering, silent now that I was come, almost reverent. Uther had moved his camp chair outside and sat before his tent — the image of a homeless king holding court in the wilderness.

He drew breath to speak when he saw me, but thought better of it and closed his mouth again and merely nodded towards the firepit, as if to say, 'There it is, do your work.'

I had half hoped he might have cooled to the idea and would release me from my promise. But, having fastened onto a thing, Uther was not a man to let go easily. Come what may, he would see it through.

So, gathering my cloak about me, I began walking in sunwise circles around the fire, holding my staff high. In the Old Tongue, the secret tongue of the Learned Brotherhood, I uttered the ancient words of power that would part the veil between this world and the Otherworld. At the same time I prayed Lord Jesu to give me wisdom to discern aright the things I saw.

I stopped walking and turned to the fire, opening my eyes to search among the glowing coals. I saw the heat shimmer, the deep hot crimson. . . the images:

A woman standing on the wall of a fortress on a high promontory, her hair flying in auburn streams as the wind lifts her unbound tresses, and gulls flying shrieking above her while the sea beats restlessly below. . .

A milk-white horse cantering along a river ford, riderless, the high-backed, heavy saddle empty, the reins dangling, dangling. . .

Yellow clouds lowering over a dusky hillside where a warhost lies slaughtered, spears bristling like a grove of young ash trees, while ravens gorge on the meat of dead men. . .

A bride weeping in a shadowed place, alone. . .

Bishops and holy men bound in fetters of iron and marched through the ruins of a desolated city. . .

A huge man sitting in a small boat on a reed-fringed lake, the sun glinting in his golden hair, eyes lightly closed, his empty hands folded upon his knees. . .

A Saecsen war axe hacking at the roots of an ancient oak. . .

Men with torches bearing a burden up a hill to a great burial mound set within an enormous stone circle. . .

Black hounds baying at a white winter moon. . .

Starving wolves tearing one of their own to pieces in the snow. . .

A man in a monk's woollen tunic skulking along a deserted street, glancing backward over his shoulder, sweating with fear, his hands clutching a vial such as priests carry for anointing. . .

The cross of Christus burning above a blood-spattered altar. . .

A babe lying in the long grass of a hidden forest glade, crying lustily, a red serpent coiled about his tiny arm. . .

The images spun so fast as to become confused and disjointed. I closed my eyes and raised my head. I had seen nothing of Pascent, nor anything that would help Uther directly. Nevertheless, when I opened my eyes again I saw a strange thing:

A new-born star, brighter than any of its brothers, shining like a heavenly beacon high in the western sky.

In the same moment, my *awen* descended over me. 'Behold, Uther!' I cried, my voice loud with authority. 'Look you to the west and see a marvel: a newmade star flares in God's heaven tonight, the herald of tidings both dire and wonderful. Pay heed if you would learn what is to befall this realm.'

Men exclaimed around me as they found the star. Some prayed, others cursed and made the sign against evil. But I watched only the star, gathering brightness, growing, soon shining as if to rival the sun itself. It cast shadows upon the land, and its rays stretched forth to the east and the west, and it seemed to me that it was the fiery maw of a fierce, invincible dragon.

Uther stood up from his chair, his face bathed in the unnatural light. 'Merlin!' he shouted. 'What is this? What does it mean?'

At his words my body began to tremble and shake. I staggered dizzily and leaned on my staff, overswept by a sudden onrushing of sorrow which pierced me to the heart. For I understood the meaning of the things I had seen. 'Great Light, why?' I cried aloud. 'Why am I born to such sorrow?' So saying, I sank to my knees and wept.

Uther came and knelt beside me. He put his hand on my shoulder and whispered softly. 'Merlin, Merlin, what has happened? What have you seen? Tell me, I will bear it.'

When at last I could speak, I raised my head and peered into his anxious face. 'Uther, are you there? Uther, prepare yourself,' I sobbed. 'Woe and grief to us all: your brother is dead.'

This revelation caused a sensation. Men cried out in disbelief and anguish. 'Aurelius dead! Impossible!. . . Did you hear what he said?. . . What? The High King dead? How?'

Uther stared in astonished disbelief. 'It cannot be. Do you hear, Merlin? It cannot be.' He turned his gaze to the star. 'There must be some other meaning. Look again and tell me.'

I shook my head. 'Great is the grief in this land tonight and for many nights to come. Aurelius has been killed by Vortigern's son. While we chased Pascent throughout the realm, he has dealt in treachery, sending a kinsman to murder the High King in his own chamber with poison.'

Uther groaned and fell forward, stretching himself full length upon the ground. There he wept without shame, like an orphaned child. The warband looked on, tears shining in more than one pair of eyes, for there was not a man among them who would not have gladly traded life for life with his beloved Aurelie.

When at last Uther raised himself up, I said, 'There is more, Uther, that is betokened. You are a warrior without peer in all this land. In seven days' time you will be made king, and great shall be your renown among the people of Britain. You will reign in all strength and authority.'

Uther nodded unhappily, not much consoled by these words.

'This also I have seen: the star that shines with the fire of a dragon is you, Uther; and the beam cast out from its mouth is a son born of your noble lineage, a mighty prince who will be king after you. A greater king will never be known in the Island of the Mighty until the Day of Judgement.

'Therefore, arm the warband at once and march boldly with the star to light your path, for at sunrise tomorrow in the place where three hills meet you shall put an end to Pascent and Guilomar. Then let you return to Londinium, there to take up the crown of your dead brother.'

Finished, my *awen* left me and I slumped back, suddenly weak with exhaustion. Sleep rolled in dark waves over me, drowning all senses. Pelleas lifted me to my feet and guided me to my tent where I fell asleep at once.

Well, it was a night for dreams. Though my body slumbered, my mind was filled with restless images that fought in my fevered brain. I remember I saw much of blood and fire, and men whose lives in this worlds-realm had not yet begun.

I saw the swarming darkness massing for war, and the land trembling under a vast, impenetrable shadow. I saw children growing up who had never known a day's peace. I saw women whose wombs were barren from fear, and men who knew no craft or trade, but battle. I saw ships fleeing the shores of Britain, and others hastening towards the Island of the Mighty. I saw disease and death and kingdoms wasted by war.

And, dread of all dreads, I saw Morgian.

She, who I most feared to see in the flesh, met me in a dream. And though it chills the marrow in my bones to tell it, she appeared most happy to see me. She welcomed me — as if I were a traveller come to her door — saying, 'Ah, Merlin, Lord of the Fair Folk, Maker of Kings, I am glad to see you. I was beginning to think you had died.'

She was formidable; she was beautiful as dawn, and deadly as venom. Morgian was hate in human form, but she was not human any more: the last of her humanity she had given over to the Enemy in exchange for power. And she was powerful beyond imagining.

But even her power did not extend to harming men through their dreams. She might frighten, she might insinuate, she might persuade, but she could not destroy. 'Why do you not speak, my love? Does fear bind your tongue?'

In my dream, I answered forthrightly. 'You are right when you speak of fear, Morgian, for I do fear you full well. But I know your weakness, and I have learned the strength of the Lord I serve. I will live to see you destroyed.'

She laughed charmingly and darkness leapt up around her. 'Dear nephew, what must you think of me? Have I ever done you harm? Come, you have no reason to speak so to me. But, as you profess an interest in the future, I would speak to you.'

'We have nothing to say to one another.'

'Nevertheless, I will speak and you will listen: your unreasoning hatred of the Old Way, of your own past, cannot continue. It will not be tolerated, Merlin. If you persist, you will be sacrificed. And that would be such sorrow to me.'

'Who has told you to tell me this?' I already knew, but I wanted her to say.

'Fear not him who has the power to destroy the body, rather fear him with the power to destroy the soul — is that not what poor, blind Dafyd taught?'

'Name your lord, Morgian!' I challenged her.

'You have had your warning. If not for me, you would have been killed long ago, but I interceded for you. See? You owe me a debt, Merlin. Do you understand? When next we meet, I will be repaid.'

'Oh, you shall indeed have your reward, Princess of Lies,' I told her boldly — much more boldly than I felt. 'Now get you away from me.'

She did not laugh this time, but her icy smile could have stopped the warm heart beating in the breast. 'Farewell, Merlin. I will wait for you in the Otherworld.'

While I slept, Uther heeded the counsel I had given him. He ordered the warband to be armed and, when the horses were saddled, they made their way to the place I had indicated: Penmachno, a high valley formed by the convergence of three hills, well known from ancient times as a gathering-place.

They travelled all night, the strange star lighting their way, and arrived at Penmachno as a sullen dawn coloured the sky in the east. There, just as I had said, lay Pascent and Guilomar encamped. At the sight of the elusive foe, all fatigue left the warriors and, lashing their horses to speed, they fell like silent death upon the unsuspecting enemy.

The battle proved a bloody and brutal affair. Guilomar, naked from his bed, led his warriors to the fight and was run through by the very first spear thrust. Seeing their king fall in the foremost rank, the Irish voiced a great shout of anguish and determined to avenge their chieftain.

Pascent, on the other hand, had not the stomach for a fair fight and immediately sought how best to make his escape. He pulled an old cloak over himself, caught the reins of a horse, and galloped from the battlefield. Uther saw him fleeing and gave chase, crying, 'Stay, Pascent! We have a debt to settle!'

Uther caught the coward and struck him with the flat of his sword; Pascent fell from the saddle and sprawled on his back on the ground, squealing with fear and pleading for his life.

'As you would have your father's portion,' Uther said, dismounting, his sword lowered, 'come, I will give you your desire.' With that he thrust the sword through Pascent's mouth so that the point went deep into the earth. Pascent died, writhing like a snake. 'There, dwell you now with Guilomar, your trusted companion, and possess the land together.'

Leaderless and unmanned, the Irish made a poor fight as Uther's warriors, frustrated by the long and futile campaign, exacted revenge for their dead countrymen.

The fight was over by the time Pelleas and I reached the battlefield. We sat our horses in a yellow dawn on the crest of one of the hills overlooking Penmachno and saw what I had foreseen in the embers: warriors lying dead upon a hillside thick with spears like an ash grove. Carrion birds croaked, flocking to their morbid feast, their gleaming black beaks worrying the flesh from the corpses in bloody strips.

Uther allowed the warband to plunder the Irish camp and then remounted them and turned back towards Londinium. Five days later we were met on the road by some of Lord Morcant's chieftains. 'Hail, Uther,' they called as they joined us. 'We bear grievous tidings from Governor Melatus. The High King is dead of poison by one called Appas, a kinsman of Vortigern.'

Uther nodded, his mouth tight, and glanced at me. 'How was this accomplished?'

'By stealth and trickery, lord,' the foremost rider answered bitterly. 'The craven clothed himself after one of Urbanus' kind and gained Aurelius' confidence. Thus he won his way to the High King's chamber and gave him to drink of a draught he had made — to celebrate the king's wedding, he said.' The rider paused, distaste twisting his mouth. 'The High King drank and slept. He awoke in the night screaming with the fever and died before morning.'

'What of Ygerna?' asked Uther, his voice betraying no emotion. 'Did she drink as well?'

'No, lord. The queen had returned with her father to Tintagel for her dower and was to join the king at Uintan Caestir.'

Uther appeared thoughtful. 'What of this Appas?'

'He could not be found in the governor's palace. Nor was he to be found in all the city, lord.'

'Yet, I say that he *will* be found,' uttered Uther softly. The cold menace in his voice cut like a blade of ice. 'All gods bear witness, on the day that he is discovered he shall share in his friends' reward which he has won by his own hand.' Then he straightened in his saddle and asked aloud, 'Where have they laid my brother?'

'By his own wish, and by Urbanus' order, the High King has been buried at the place of the hanging stones, called the Giant's Ring.' The rider hesitated, then said, 'It was also his wish that you hold the realm after him.'

'Very well, we will turn aside there and pay him honour,' replied Uther simply. 'Then let us ride to Caer Uintan where I will have my kingmaking. I tell you the truth, Londinium has grown abhorrent to me and I will never again enter that odious city while I draw breath.'

That was one vow Uther held all his remaining days.

TWELVE

When the false-hearted Lord Dunaut heard of Aurelius' death he called his advisers together and rode to Lord Gorlas' holding in Tintagel to discuss how they might best profit by this sudden and unexpected turn of events. He also sent word to Coledac, Morcant, and Ceredigawn to join them. It did not take the Sight to see what they intended.

To his credit, Gorlas, although he welcomed Dunaut and extended the hospitality of hall and hearth to him, refused to participate in any talk of rebellion. Even later, when Coledac and Morcant arrived, Gorlas kept faith with Aurelius, out of respect for the High Kingship and for his daughter's sake.

'But Aurelius is dead,' Dunaut argued. 'Your oath returns now to you. And until you give it again, you are free.'

'You yourself might be High King,' put in Coledac, believing no such thing. 'Then you would not be breaking faith at all.'

'I have more honour than that!' protested Gorlas. 'Yours is a trick of words and has no substance.'

'It makes no sense to me,' Morcant complained. 'You speak of honour and trickery in the same breath — as if we had no thought at all for the good of the realm. We need a strong king to hold the land. Aurelius is gone and since from death there is no return, we must do what we can to honour him by keeping the peace of this land.'

'I will honour him by keeping my oath.' Gorlas would not be moved.

Although he loved Aurelius and wished with all his heart to honour him, he loved his daughter most dearly. And, in the end, it was his love for Ygerna that proved his undoing.

Uther, of course, could not abide this insult to his kingship, and it angered him that he was not unanimously acclaimed as High King — all the more since before his death Aurelius had ordained that Uther should follow him and complete the good works he had begun. Also, he loathed the prospect of having to fight old battles over again, battles he had himself won the first time.

Nor was that all that laboured in Uther's heart, to be sure.

Therefore, when Ceredigawn, whose lands Uther had saved by vanquishing Pascent and Guilomar, sent word that the kings were meeting in secret in Gorlas' rockbound stronghold in the west country, Uther delayed not a moment, but gathered such warriors as he commanded and any who could be summoned at once, and off they rode to Tintagel.

It was high summer, with days bright as new-burnished blades and nights mellow as honeyed mead, and, our work finished, Pelleas and I had returned to Ynys Avallach.

My pact had been with Aurelius, not with Uther. And, despite all I had done for him, Uther made it abundantly clear to me after his crowning that he did not require my services as counsellor. So be it. In truth, I was glad for a rest.

Thus, knowledge of the events at Tintagel reached me slowly and very late. By then the deeds were accomplished and the seeds well and truly sown.

It is a curious thing, I am thinking, that I, who have so often stood at the centre of world-shaping events I could not prevent, should so often be absent from those I could have done something about. When I think of the wounds I could have prevented, the bloodshed I could have saved. . . well, it makes my heart ache.

Great Light, you do not make it easy on a man!

Yet I sojourned with the Fair Folk a goodly while, and allowed the serenity of Avallach's excellent isle to mend my troubled spirit. I had nursed such hopes for Aurelius; he possessed such high promise. His death could not be lightly borne. Still, I remembered the prophecy given me, which I had spoken to Uther, that a son of his noble line should be born who would surpass even Aurelius. In this I took comfort, though I little knew or guessed how or when this should come about.

As I have said, the illumining spirit, like the wind, goes where it will, and sheds a light that all-too-often obscures as much as it reveals.

Charis was pleased to have me with her again. She had

learned to treasure our times together — she always did that, yes — without yearning for them to be something more. There is a love which suffocates, just as there is a love which quenches the flame that gives it light and life. These loves are false, and Charis had long ago learned the difference between false love and true.

She now spent her days in healing works; she had learned much of medicines and their properties, and how to cure various wounds and diseases. She traded knowledge with the monks of the Holy Shrine — as well as with those of the Hill Folk she came in rare contact with — and practised her art at the nearby monastery where those suffering from illness or hurt came seeking aid.

We spent many happy days together, and I would have remained content on the Tor indefinitely if not for Uther's urgent summons. Two riders appeared one evening looking for me at the church below the Hill Shrine. The monks told them where to find me and, although the sky still held daylight enough, they waited until the next day to come — fearing to approach the Tor after sunset.

But, when the sun rose again the next morning, they crossed the causeway and climbed the Tor to Avallach's palace. 'We have come searching for the Emrys,' they announced, after being admitted to the courtyard.

'And you have found him,' I answered. 'What do you want with me?'

'We are from the High King, and bring our lord's greetings,' answered the messenger with rough courtesy. 'He bids you to join him at Gorlas' stronghold at Tintagel. We are sworn to take you there.'

'What if I choose not to go with you?' I did not know these men and they obviously did not know me.

The man did not hesitate. 'Then we are instructed to bind you hand and foot and drag you there.'

That was Uther, rope and knot. 'Do you think,' I laughed, 'that anyone could take me anywhere I did not wish to go?'

This worried them. The two men glanced at one another nervously. 'The Pendragon says —' began the first.

'Pendragon?' I mused. 'Chief Dragon — is that what Uther calls himself now?'

'Yes, lord, ever since the night of the Dragon Star when he became king,' the man answered.

So, Uther, you did heed me after all. Yes, it was fitting for him: Uther Pendragon. Well and good, my difficult friend. What else did you learn that night?

The two were peering round anxiously. 'Come, break your fast with me,' I offered. 'And you can tell me more of your errand.'

The messengers eyed me suspiciously. 'You fear for nothing,' I scolded them. 'Be gracious enough to accept hospitality when it is offered you.'

'Well, we are hungry,' admitted one of the men.

'Then come and eat.' I turned and they followed me reluctantly into the hall. Fair Folk always amaze other races, which has its uses. 'Why does he seek me?' I asked as we ate bread and cheese together.

'We do not know, lord.'

'You must know something of your lord's affairs. Why did he send you?'

'We were only told to find you — there are many others searching as well,' the man answered, as if this proved the truth of his words.

I looked at the other rider, who had not spoken. 'What do you know of this? Tell me quickly, for I will not go with you unless I have some better reason to do so than I have heard yet. Speak!'

'Uther requires your aid with his marriage,' the man blurted out, surprising himself completely. It was a secret he had not meant to tell.

Ygerna, of course! But what was I to do? Ygerna was free to marry, and Uther did not need my approval. Yet Uther would not have sent for me if he did not badly need my help. Of that I could be certain.

'What is the trouble?' I asked my abashed accomplice. 'Go on, tell me. No harm will come of telling — though some may if you withhold.'

'It is Gorlas and the others — Dunaut, Morcant, and Coledac — they are holding vigil at Tintagel. Uther surprised them there and challenged them. Between them there was only Gorlas' warband and a few others. To fight Uther would be to invite slaughter upon themselves, so they refused.'

'They wait up there in Gorlas' stronghold,' put in the other messenger. Now that the stream had begun to trickle it might as well be a flood. 'Uther cannot go in to them, and they will not come out.'

I understood. Uther had indeed surprised the kings. He had ridden hard and arrived while they were still plotting their treason. Since they had not planned on an attack, the kings had brought only an escort and were caught without men and weapons enough to oppose Uther outright.

This unwelcome circumstance placed Gorlas in an imposs-ible position. A man of Gorlas' stamp would not turn traitor on his friends by helping Uther, and in any event no force on earth would cause that stubborn west country chieftain to bring dishonour to his own name by withdrawing the hospitality he had extended. At the same time, however, protecting the rebel lords meant defying the High King, who owned his oath of fealty.

I could well imagine Gorlas must be writhing with the pain of his predicament. And Uther, growing more furious with each passing moment, would hold Gorlas to blame.

Yet, Uther was prevented from storming the gates. What held him back? Ygerna. His lady love was also shut up in the caer. He could not bring himself to make war on his future bride's father and risk losing her affection. Nor could he withdraw and leave the traitors to go free.

So, in his dilemma, not knowing anything else to do, he summoned me. Well, Uther, my headstrong young prince, so hot-tempered; they do well to call you Chief Dragon.

I suppose I should have felt vindicated somehow, knowing that Uther could not do without me. In truth, I just felt tired. For it seemed to me that all my work with Aurelius had been wasted, and that time spent helping Uther would come to naught as well.

Uther, I had long ago decided, was not what I needed in a High King. Certainly, he was not the ruler to help bring the Kingdom of Summer into existence. For that, I must look elsewhere.

Be that as it may, he was the High King, and despite what power-mad petty potentates like Dunaut and Morcant might think — if it ever occurred to them to do so — Uther was neither stupid nor inept. He possessed a keen military mind and knew how to command men. This Britain desperately needed. At the very least, he should have been accorded the dignity of his rank.

Consequently, I foresaw a messy end to this affair. I must, of course, side with Uther. Of that there was never a moment's doubt. Still, I would go and see what might be done to save whatever might be saved, though I did not think much of my chances.

Pelleas was even more dubious than I. 'Why not let Uther tear them to little pieces and be done with it?' he asked as we made our way hastily to Tintagel. Neither was there any doubt in his mind who would emerge victorious. 'It seems Dunaut and his friends have brought this on themselves. Let them pay for their treachery.'

'You are forgetting Ygerna,' I replied. 'I am certain that Uther is not.'

No, Uther was not forgetting Ygerna. Indeed, he was thinking of very little else.

By the time we joined him, encamped in the narrow cleft of valley below Gorlas' stronghold, Uther wore a scowl that would have cowed snarling dogs. His advisers and chieftains stood off away from him; no one dared come near for fear of a lashing or worse.

At my appearance, a murmur of excitement fluttered among the warriors, who, bored with the stalemate and fearful of their lord's displeasure, viewed my arrival with some relief. 'Something will be done now,' the whispers said. 'Merlin is here! The Enchanter is come.'

Oh yes, it would take strong enchantment to save this situation. It would take a miracle.

'I am here, Uther.' I announced myself, as his steward feared going in to him. He sat listlessly in his camp chair in the tent, unshaven, his red hair wild on his head.

He raised his eyes. 'It took you long enough,' he snarled. 'Come to gnaw at the carcass?'

I ignored the compliment and poured myself some wine from the jar into the king's cup. 'What is the trouble?'

'What is it not?' he countered sullenly.

'If you want my help, you must tell me now. I have ridden far in great haste to be here, but I will leave just as quickly if you do not sit up and speak to me as a man.'

'My loyal lords lie up there,' he gestured impatiently in the direction of the caer, 'plotting my destruction. Is that trouble enough for you?'

'Yes, but I would have thought you most able to deal with that kind of trouble, Uther. Yet, you sit here in the dark, moaning and whimpering like a maid who has lost her best bobble.'

'Oh, aye, rub salt in the wound. Get you gone if this is the help you bring.' He leapt from his chair, as if it had suddenly become too hot to sit in any longer. 'By the Raven, you are no better than that pack of yapping hounds out there. Go and join them. Shall I throw you all a bone?'

'This is not worthy of you, Uther,' I told him flatly. 'You still have not told me what ails you.'

He turned, a dog-bitten bear finally at bay. 'I cannot attack the caer with Ygerna inside!'

At the saying of her name his aspect changed and my purpose was fulfilled. No longer surly and unreasoning, Uther spread his hands and smiled ruefully. 'Now you know, Meddler. So tell me, what am I to do?'

'What can I say to you that your advisers have not already said?'

He rolled his eyes and puffed out his cheeks. 'Please!'

'Your mood has blinded you, Uther, or you would see your way clearly.'

He made no reply, but stood with his head down and his hands hanging at his sides. 'Oh, for the light of Lleu,' I sputtered, 'you are not the first man to love a woman. Stop behaving like a wounded bear and let us discover what might be done.'

'We cannot attack the caer,' he sighed, then added more forcefully, eyeing me peculiarly. 'At least, not while she is there.'

'No,' I replied, shaking my head. 'Do not think it.'

'But *you*, Merlin. . . You could go up there. Gorlas would let you in. You could see her; you could get her out.'

'Perhaps, I could — but what then?'

'I would clean out that viper's nest once and for all.'

'A bold plan, Uther. And do you think she would so easily marry the man who murdered her father?'

'Murder?'

'That is how she would see it.'

'But — but — they are traitors!'

'Not in her eyes.'

'There! You see? It is hopeless!' He smashed his fist against the board. 'Any way I turn, I am undone.'

'Retreat then.'

Anger sprang up in his eyes. 'Never!'

I turned and strode from the tent. He followed me a few moments later and came to join me where I stood on a rock mound looking up at the black, gleaming stone walls of Gorlas' fortress. It was an impressive structure, and probably impenetrable, for it squatted on a great, high, jutting headland crag thrust out into the sea. The headland was joined to the main by the narrowest causeway, which ran through a single, easily defended gate, the only landward entrance.

'I do not mean run from the field. But remove yourself from this place,' I said softly.

'To what purpose?'

'You can do nothing as long as you remain here. Just as they can do nothing against you.' I lifted a hand towards the fortress, black and immense above us. 'In the game of chess this is called stalemate, and no one can win in such a position. Therefore, since they cannot move, you must.'

'I will not,' he growled through clenched teeth. 'By all the gods of heaven and earth, I will not.'

'Swear no oaths, Uther, until you have heard all.'

He let air hiss through his teeth. 'Oh, do go on then.'

'I do not suggest you drag yourself back to Caer Uintan; just behind the line of hills to the east will suffice. Then wait there while I go and speak to them.' He considered this and nodded. 'Very well. Now, what terms will you offer?'

'Terms?' He rubbed his jaw. 'I have given no thought to terms.'

'Well, which do you desire more: their lives or their loyalty?'

The High King hesitated, then showed what he was made of. 'Their loyalty — if that is possible after this.'

'It is possible, if you will allow it.'

'Allow it? I will welcome it.'

'Then I will see if they will listen to reason.'

'By the god you pray to, Merlin, if you can secure their loyalty without undue bloodshed, and save Ygerna, I will give you anything you ask, even to the half of my kingdom.'

I shrugged. 'Never have I asked anything for myself, nor will I.'

As I spoke, I saw a vision: Gorlas lying dead on a hillside, his blood blackening the soil. And I heard, as from the Otherworld, the cry of a babe amidst the howl of wolves on a cold winter's night. My heart felt heavy in my chest, and I tasted salt and sour sweat on my tongue.

Words came to my tongue unbidden. 'Yet my service exacts a price. One day soon I will demand my reward and bitter will be the granting. Let this be your comfort: what I shall demand will be for the good of Britain. Remember that, in the day of reckoning, Uther Pendragon. And refuse me at your peril.'

Uther stared, but accepted my pronouncement. 'Let it be as you say, Merlin. I am content. Do what you will.'

Although it was late in the day, orders were given to strike camp and depart. I knew this activity would draw the attention of those in the caer, so Pelleas and I climbed into a coracle and paddled round the headland to see if there was another way into the fortress.

There was, of course, as I knew there must be; but it could be used only at low tide — for only when the water was low could a boat be landed on the hard shingle below the fortress. Any other time the tunnel mouth was flooded and the waves thrashing around the tumbled rocks were too dangerous to navigate.

Unless I wished to make entrance in the dead of night, the mainland causeway remained my best choice. I held no great hope that Gorlas would welcome me as a brother, but he would receive me and bear my presence for at least as long as it took me to say what was in my mind. He respected me that much, I considered. He *owed* me that much for that day on the battlefield when we had fought Hengist together.

By dusk, Uther had decamped and withdrawn beyond the hills. Pelleas and I, our survey of the headland completed, mounted our ponies and made our way up the narrow, slate-paved spine of a causeway to the great dome of rock upon which Gorlas had built his caer. The sea washed ceaselessly on one side, and a freshet tumbled noisily on the other — a sheer drop to a sudden and certain death on either hand.

We waited outside the timber gate while the guards fetched their lord, who appeared in a moment — as I said, they had been watching. 'What do you here, Emrys?' Gorlas demanded. The question was a challenge.

'I have come to speak to you, Gorlas.'

'I have no business with Uther.'

'Perhaps not,' I allowed, 'but he has business with you or, more precisely, those who shelter beneath your roof and claim your hospitality.'

'What of that?' the Cornovii chieftain sneered. 'I withhold hospitality from no man who asks it. Those you seek are welcome here as long as they care to stay.'

'If that is the way of it,' I replied easily, 'then I claim the same hospitality for myself and my steward. It is getting dark and night is upon us. We have nowhere else to go.'

To be trapped with his own words made Gorlas furious; that it was so easily done did not improve his disposition. I began to think he would not let us in after all, but honour went deep in Gorlas and he relented in spite of himself.

He unbarred the gate and opened it himself, his face frozen in a grimace of mingled rage and humiliation. 'Enter, my friends,' he muttered through clenched teeth, each word a curse, 'you are welcome here.'

'Our thanks to you, Gorlas,' I replied sincerely, leading my pony through the gate. 'You do yourself no wrong.'

'That remains to be seen,' he huffed, and impatiently ordered the gate closed, lest Uther himself appear to claim hospitality from him.

Tintagel's rock formed a mighty foundation for a sprawling fortress of timber and stone — more stone than timber, since the black rock of the region lay ready to hand, and the timber must be cut and dragged in from forests a fair distance away. This gave the place a cold, harsh appearance; the solid house of a hard man, unused to small comforts, strong of will and principle, and slow to bend.

Tintagel could be a sanctuary, or a prison — its gate keeping in as easily as keeping out. I wondered if Uther understood this.

The high-arched hall rose from the centre of an aimless scattering of smaller buildings: cook houses, granaries, larders and hoardings of various types, smaller sleeping quarters and round houses of stone. Between these buildings a narrow paving of dressed and channelled stone had been put down so that in wet weather — which, so close to the sea, was continual — men and beasts need not flounder in fields of mud.

In all, Tintagel proved a simple, yet impressive, fortress: a fitting seat of power for the king of the Cornovii. Nor was I the first to think so, for the settlement had been occupied for many generations, and, I had no doubt, would continue to serve for many, many more.

'Supper will be laid soon.' Gorlas came puffing up the track behind us as we dismounted. 'Your horses will be cared for.'

He led us into a hall bright with torchlight and a huge fire on the hearth. Dogs and children played in the corners, and a cluster of women occupied the far end of the hall, talking quietly, heads together. I did not see Ygerna among them. Morcant, Dunaut, and Coledac, and their retinues, lolled carelessly at Gorlas' board. Heads turned as we entered and laughter ceased.

Then Morcant was on his feet. 'Look you, my friends, here is that craven Uther's lap dog! Well, Merlin Embries, have you come to sniff after us and run back to your master with the tale?'

'The insult is beneath you, Lord Morcant. I require no respect from you, but at least do not endanger yourself further by speaking ill of the High King.'

'High King?' sneered Morcant. 'High Coward, more like.' Dunaut and Coledac laughed loudly at this.

'You call him coward because he ignores your treason and extends his hands in friendship?'

'Extends his hands in fright!' snorted Coledac, who convulsed himself with laughter. Gorlas, embarrassed by his guests' rudeness, called loudly for the supper to be brought. Servants scurried at his sharp command, and in a few moments baskets and platters of food appeared.

The three lords had been guzzling Gorlas' mead and were not inclined to stop. No doubt their relief at Uther's withdrawal from the field had put them in a celebratory mood, and drink had made them bold. But it was a fool's courage that abetted them.

'There will be trouble,' Pelleas warned, as we took our places at the board. 'Drink will make them surly and they will pick a fight.'

'If it comes to that we will not disappoint them,' I replied. 'They must learn respect for their king. Now is as good a time as any for the teaching.'

'I believe I could think of a better time.' Pelleas scanned the hall, mostly filled now with the lords' escorts — each with a knife in his belt and a sword on his hip. 'If they begin, I do not think even Gorlas could stop it.'

The meal proceeded uneventfully. The three, having turned to their meat, promptly forgot about us. We ate in peace, and were nearly finished when the hide that covered the inner entrance to the hall was pulled aside and Ygerna entered with a few of her women.

She did not look at us — in fact, kept her eyes averted — although she must have known we were there. I think she did not wish to notice me for fear that her secret might be betrayed. But, to me, her distraction spoke with some force.

My heart went out to her. Such a lovely young woman — a bride still, really; I could not see her as a widow, though widow she was — she carried her nobility in every line of her slender form. How rough Gorlas came by a daughter so refined and regal was a mystery.

The meal concluded and Gorlas, keen to avoid trouble, called for his harper. An old man stumbled forward with a well-worn harp and proceeded to sing a long, all-but-unintelligible song about the change of seasons or some such thing. I pitied him. More, I pitied his listeners who likely had never heard a true bard and never would.

At his lord's bidding, the singer began another song, and as all attention was on him, I made opportunity to speak to Ygerna. She was abashed that I should approach her, but, thinking quickly, she jumped up and pulled me to a shadowed corner.

'Please, Lord Emrys,' she cautioned, 'if my father —'

'He will not see us here,' I reassured her, then asked: 'Why? Do you fear him?'

410

She bit her lower lip and lowered her head shyly. An utterly feminine gesture of uncertainty and innocence. I loved her for it, remembering another girl long ago. 'No, no —' she began, hesitated, then said, 'but he watches me so closely. . . . Please, I cannot say more.'

'You were a married woman,' I reminded her. 'You need remain under your father's roof no longer.'

'The High King is dead. Where would I go?' She spoke without guile, and without sorrow. She did not grieve for Aurelius, nor did she pretend to. She had not loved him. In truth, she hardly knew him! She had married him only to please her father.

'There is one, I am thinking, who might be persuaded to take you in.'

She knew well enough who I meant, for she had been thinking of it, too — often and with great anxiety. 'Oh, but I dare not!' she gasped.

'Why?'

'My father would never allow it. Now, please, I must go.' But she made no move to leave. Instead, she turned her eyes to where her father sat with the other lords, listening to the harper drone on.

'If you were to leave here freely, would you go to Uther?' I asked it bluntly, for I had to know and time grew short.

She dropped her head once more, then, looking up shyly, murmured, 'If he would have me.'

'Would and will,' I replied. 'I know that he would have laid fire to the gates long before now if it were not for you, Ygerna.' She said nothing, but nodded slightly. 'So. You already guessed as much. Very well, I will see what may be done. If I come for you, will you go with me?'

Her eyes went wide, but she answered with a steady voice. 'If it must be done that way, yes. I will go with you.'

'Good, then gather your things and wait. Pelleas or I will come for you tonight.'

She cast a quick backward glance over the hall — as one looking her last upon a place that held only unhappy memories. Then, placing a hand on my sleeve, she squeezed my arm and quickly disappeared into the shadows.

Why did I do this? Why was it so important to bring Uther and Ygerna together?

411

Perhaps it was for Uther's sake: to redress the wrong he had suffered. In any event, it was clear he could not be king without her. Perhaps it was for Ygerna: she looked so unhappy in that cold place. Perhaps it was the Lord's Spirit working to redeem the time. To tell the truth, I cannot say.

But that night, I acted as events led me. It happens like this sometimes — and all the plans, all the reasons, all desires and possibilities fade to nothing. And all that remains is the single unwilled act.

What have I done? I wondered, aghast, as I crept back unnoticed to my place. What has been done through me?

Still, even now, I wonder.

THIRTEEN

In the time between times, when the world awaits the renewing light of day, a life is sometimes required for a life. This is what the Wise Men of the Oak, the druids of another age, believed and taught. I am not persuaded that they were wrong.

Ygerna led me down through the secret passage to the rock shingle below Tintagel on the sea side. Well she knew the way: she had often sought sanctuary on the brittle little beach out of her father's sight. Lightning flickered out to sea, and thunder grumbled far off. The wind blew wild, whipping the water, and we listened to the hollow drum of the waves breaking against the stone roots of the headland as we descended the narrow steps made treacherous with sea spray. One mis-step and we would have plummeted to our graves.

'There is a cave in the rock beneath the caer,' she told me, her words torn from her lips by the wind as she spoke them. 'We can wait there until the boat comes. It will not be dry, I fear.'

'We will not have long to wait,' I reassured her, peering into the moaning darkness. Wind and water, everything was slippery wet; wind-flung foam spattered our faces and fouled our cloaks.

The moon had set and it was the darkest part of the night. The few stars that shone through the flying tatters of cloud gave but fitful light, and that dim. It was a stupid plan, and I berated myself for suggesting it.

However — and this you must understand — when the Unseen Hand leads you in its grasp, you follow. Or, turn back, and live in eternal regret.

Of course, there is no certainty in following, either. That is what makes faith. Follow or turn back — there is no middle way.

That night, I chose to follow. It was my decision; I chose

freely. And I bear responsibility for the consequences. That is the price of freedom. Oh, but I felt alive that tempest-tossed night with the rumble of waves and thunder in my ears, the sting of salt in my eyes, and the smell of moss and wet rock in my nostrils. And that warm, trusting girl by my side. I was alive, and I gloried in the living.

Ygerna showed surprising strength; she was borne up by love. I do not know precisely what she felt, or whether she understood all that her decision meant. She was going to meet her lover; that's all she knew. She trusted me for the rest.

And I trusted Pelleas. Our lives were in his hands; he must reach the place where we had left the boat and then bring it round the headland to the shore where we waited — before the tide came in again, drowning the shingle and filling the cave.

So, we waited: shivering with clammy cold, hardly daring to think what we were doing. We waited, not knowing if Pelleas had even found his way free of the caer. It was a frail enough ruse to be committing our lives to: he was to leave the hall unobserved, and tell the gateman that I required an important token from Uther, which he had been sent to fetch. Once outside the walls he was to make his way with all haste to the boat and come round — in a sour wind and heavy seas! — to rescue us from the rising water.

I have thought many and many a time what I might have done had I stayed at Tintagel and seen my task through. How might things have turned out differently?

As it happens, I do not now believe I could have accomplished what I came there to do — although I did believe it then, for I considered most men reasonable in the face of reason. This, I have learned since, is pure folly. Unreasonable men are ever unreasonable, and only become more so when threatened. Truth always threatens the false-hearted.

The contrary kings wanted no reconciliation; they would have denied their misdeeds, and resisted all attempts to forge a lasting peace; they would have reviled any offer of clemency; they would have despised appeasement as weakness!

Well, and there would have been a fight after all. Many good men would have been killed and that is a fact. But perhaps Gorlas would still be alive.

How ironic that the one who above all things tried to remain loyal to the High King should suffer for the disloyalty of others. Yet Gorlas chose his own course, as every man must; no one pressed the sword into his hand.

My thoughts, I see, are as confused as the events of that wild night. Let me make some order. I will say it thus:

Ygerna and I waited on the shingle for Pelleas. Gorlas discovered his daughter's absence, then mine, and, enraged, alerted his warband and flew out of the caer in pursuit, outracing his escort. He saw a light on a hill and made for it. Thinking he had found me, he attacked. In fact, he encountered two of Uther's sentries. Swords crossed. Gorlas fell before his men could reach him.

That is what happened. There is no glory in it, because there is no dignity in killing. Insane waste.

As dawn coloured the slate-dark sky in the east, Pelleas appeared — and none too soon, for the seawater seethed around our shins and we clung to one another, shivering. Ygerna and I clambered into the boat and Pelleas, praying our forgiveness, pulled on the oars and took us out to sea and away from the rocks.

All of us were too exhausted to speak, and too discouraged. Our plan, splendid as a dream in the night, showed itself a tawdry, contemptible thing in the ragged light of day. I was disgusted with myself for my part — and yet. . . and yet. . .

In the time between times, when the world awaits the renewing light of day, a life is sometimes required for a life.

They were still gathered on the hill when we arrived later — Gorlas' escort and Uther's men, standing mute and shamefaced in dawn's light. Uther himself had only just arrived and was giving the order for the body to be taken back to the fortress. He did not see Ygerna at first, and she did not see him. She saw only her father's corpse lying face up on the heath.

Curiously, she gave no appearance of surprise. She did not shriek or whimper, but simply knelt and put her hand on her father's head and brushed the hair back from his forehead. Then she straightened his cloak, arranging it to cover the ugly gash in his side. The only sound was the sea breeze sighing through the gorse and heather, and a lark somewhere high above, singing a lonely hymn to the new day.

Nor were there any tears in her eyes when she rose a few moments later and, gazing steadily at Uther, stepped round Gorlas' body to stand beside him. Uther put his arm around her shoulders and drew her to him. They turned together and walked back down the hill to the High King's camp. Not a word had been spoken between them.

Uther did not return to Caer Uintan, but occupied the caer and stayed on through the summer at Tintagel. Why not? It was a fine stronghold and well situated to keep an eye on his contrary lords.

Shocked into contrition by Gorlas' death, they renounced their treason and, in the end, accepted Uther's terms, pledging the king tribute for their misdeeds and making hostages of their best warriors, which he immediately placed in his warband.

No longer needed — indeed, the High King was embarrassed to have me near him, for the rumours that he had plotted Gorlas' death from the beginning and had sent me to accomplish it — I returned to Ynys Avallach. Gorlas was buried and Uther married on the same day, I am told.

But then, men tell many tales about this affair. I have even heard it said that Ygerna was Gorlas' wife — imagine that! — and I, by deep enchantments, transformed Uther into Gorlas' likeness and led him to her bed. Or that I gave Ygerna a draught that made her believe Uther to be Aurelius, her husband, come back from the grave. Or, stranger yet, that Aurelius himself actually returned from the Otherworld to lie with her.

People will believe anything!

FOURTEEN

If it had not been for the babe, I would not have seen Uther alive again. I very nearly did not go anyway: Pelleas and I had just returned to Ynys Avallach after visiting some of the humbler places in the realm — the smaller settlements and holdings where men speak their minds and misgivings forthrightly. Upon our return, I sent Pelleas to Llyonesse to discern how matters stood there. I was anxious to discover how Morgian's influence, which seemed to be stronger there, affected Belyn's court. The last thing I desired was a long ride back to Tintagel alone.

But Uther must be stopped from carrying out that hideous scheme of his, and there was no one else to do it. No one else knew.

I saw it all in a vision.

Tired from a day's fishing and riding with Avallach and Charis, we had eaten a simple supper of stew and bread, and I had fallen asleep early in my chair by the fire. A sound — a dog barking outside, I think — awakened me. I stirred and opened my eyes. The fire had burned low on the hearth before me and I saw in the glowing embers a newborn babe, a manchild, hanging by its heel in the grasp of someone pressing the cold steel of a sword against the soft pink flesh. A terrified woman stood in the shadow, her white hands over her face.

I recognized the blade: Uther's great war weapon, the Imperial sword of Maximus.

'What is it, my Hawk?' asked Charis. She eyed me closely from where she sat across the hearth, a bookroll in her lap. Her healing work had sent her back to the old books for remedies and medicines, and she often spent her evenings reading from among the texts she had saved from Atlantis. 'You look as if you have seen your death.'

I shook my head slowly, sick to my stomach with dread. 'Not my death,' I replied. 'Another's.'

'Oh, Merlin. . . I did not mean to —'

'No,' I tried to smile, 'it has not taken place. I may yet prevent it.'

'Then you must try,' she said.

Oh, there was never any question. If not for the sake of the babe, then for Uther's, to prevent him from making a most grievous mistake. Nevertheless, it was not without some reluctance that I made my way back to Tintagel — clothed simply as a wandering harper for I did not wish my journey to attract unnecessary attention. My affairs were becoming common knowledge from one end of the island to the other and, as there were enough eyes spying out my every move, I did not need more speculation about this visit. The less known about this sordid matter, the better for everyone.

The Island of the Mighty in late summer — what place on earth can compare to it? The hills flame with heather and copper-coloured bracken; the valleys shimmer golden with grain; all the fruits of the year's labours are ripening wealth beneath shining skies so high and clean and blue; the days are still warm and the nights soft and full of light. It is a time that makes a man glad to be alive.

It is the time of Lugnasadh, the day of First Fruits, when harvest begins. A most ancient and sacred celebration, to be sure, and one that even the church observes, for it is a high and holy day of thanksgiving to the Gifting God for his largesse. Great fires flare from every hilltop, and every stone ring becomes, once again, a sacred circle: a centre of power where, on this night, the veil between the Otherworld and this worlds-realm grows thin and allows the initiated a glimpse at what was, or will be.

And now that the old Roman towns are falling into ruin and the people are moving back into the countryside, I believe there are more Lugnasadh celebrations than ever. Men look to the old ways more often these days, seeking what comfort they can find in the beliefs of a simpler time.

I travelled lightly, unhindered by the weather, arriving at Tintagel a few days after Lugnasadh. The gateman took one look at my harp and threw the gate open. At least my arrival cheered someone, even if it did not exactly lift Uther to the heights of song.

He was suspicious and closed from the beginning, and I saw that it would be heavy going. In the end, there was no hope for it but to confront him bluntly.

'We are friends, you and I,' yes, he required that reminder, 'and I know you, Uther. There is no use denying that there is a child and that you plan to kill it when it is born.' I did not expect him to admit it to me, but I wanted him to know that lying to me was useless.

Ygerna stood a little way off, watching me, worrying her mantle into knots, her expression mingling relief and apprehension. I think in her secret heart she had hoped that something like this would happen and Uther would be diverted from his plan.

'Do you think me mad?' he cried, defensively it seemed to me. 'The child could be male. It could well be my heir we are talking about!'

Damned from his own mouth. Still, he did not realize what he had said. For if he entertained so much as the merest suspicion that the child was his none of this would be taking place. No, the seed growing in Ygerna's womb was Aurelius' and he knew it. Uther had, typically, spoken what lay closest to his heart: his heir.

'Doubtless the child is your heir,' I replied. Whether Uther's or Aurelius', the babe would be recognized as a legitimate heir to the High Kingship. Whether he would *be* king was another matter entirely.

'You know what I mean, Meddler.' Uther dismissed my comment with an impatient gesture. 'In all events, I am not a murderer — despite what they are telling of me.'

This was a reference to the baseless rumours that he had killed Gorlas outright so that he could marry Ygerna. 'I did not come here to call you murderer,' I soothed. 'My only concern is for the child.'

'At least we agree on something, then,' he said, his eyes flicking to Ygerna and back to me. 'What do you propose?'

'Need I propose anything?'

'You mean to tell me that you came all this way just to see if I meant to kill an infant?' He laughed guiltily; a less mirthful sound I could not imagine.

'It would not be the first time a king decided to clean up

an untidy problem with the sharp edge of his sword. But I am glad to hear that my fears were groundless.'

'Not entirely so, I should think.' He twisted the red-gold bracelet on his arm — a dragon, his emblem from now on. 'There are, I am thinking,' he said slowly, speaking low as if he feared someone overhearing him, 'many who would dearly pay to see this child removed.'

Ygerna gave a little cry.

'True enough,' I replied. 'But a king can always protect his own. Besides, it happens so rarely that —'

'Not as rarely as you think,' Uther insisted. 'Are you forgetting what happened to Aurelius? These are dangerous times we live in.' He allowed himself a shrewd smile. 'Dangerous men abound.'

'Come to the point. What are you getting at?'

'It would not be safe for the child to remain here.'

'Where would be safer?'

'You would know, Merlin. You could find a place.'

I will give him his due. When pressed to it, Uther could think on his feet with the best of them. Ygerna saw where the king's line of reasoning was leading and stepped forward. 'He is right, Myrddin Emrys, you could find a place.'

I wondered at this, but I suppose it was only natural, in a way. In her mind, if Uther did not kill the child, someone else would. Even if that could be avoided, the child would surely stand between her and her husband — which was worse. She was only choosing the best of several alternatives, all of them bad.

Better to give the child up to a safe obscurity than keep it near her and live in constant fear for its life, and resent it for living.

And Uther was right. If Aurelius could so easily be murdered, how much more easily might a defenceless infant be killed? While it was true that the child would be in constant danger from ambitious, proud, and powermad fools like Dunaut and Morcant and Coledac — and there would be others like them, always, Heaven help us! — that was not all Uther was thinking. I understood his mind: *let this child be put aside in favour of my own son*.

I saw merit in the plan, too; though for a different reason. For, if something should happen and Uther fail to get an heir for one reason or another, Aurelius' son would still be alive to step forward. I did not mention this at the time, however.

Ygerna stepped close and laid a hand on my arm. 'Please, Myrddin Emrys, find a good place, a safe place for my baby. I could not do this if it were not for you.'

She looked at me with those big, dark eyes, so full of hope and apprehension — it would have been a cruelty to refuse her. It was for the best in any event. 'I will do what I can, my lady. But,' I raised my finger in warning, 'it must be as I say. And once agreed there can be no going back. Think about it; there is time, you do not have to decide now.'

'No,' she said, 'it must be now. I have already decided. I will trust you, Myrddin Emrys. Do what must be done.'

'Yes, I trust you, too, Merlin. Whatever you say, we will do.'

Uther could be quite magnanimous when he wished. Why not? He had, so he reckoned, solved his problem and saved his name all in the same brilliant stroke. He was pleased, and proud of himself. There would be more sons, after all. And, having once made up his mind, he would be resolved to the end.

We talked some more and it was agreed that I would come and receive the babe upon its birth — Ygerna did not believe she could part with it otherwise — and take it to be raised in a place that only I would know.

Fair enough. But what seemed a simple matter at the time — the fostering of an unwanted child — very soon developed into a tangled and thorny affair for all involved. For this was no ordinary infant.

I returned then to Ynys Avallach to await the birth. Pelleas had returned from Llyonesse with distressing news: Belyn was deathly ill and would not last the winter. A new king would be chosen upon his death, of course, but as Belyn left no legitimate heirs the kingship would pass to Avallach's line: the sons of Charis or Morgian. And, since Charis stood in direct line of inheritance from Avallach, more than likely the choice would fall to the first of Morgian's sons.

The old Atlantean custom of inheritance, developed and refined over countless ages and bound by tradition, was as far removed from the straightforward, simple observances of the Britons as the Isle of the Everliving from the Island of the Mighty. But Avallach gravely confirmed Pelleas' assessment that one of Morgian's offspring would very soon come to power.

'That my brother should die saddens me greatly,' the Fisher King said. 'But that Morgian and her spawn should benefit grieves me more.' He said nothing more about it, brooding in silence for two full days before announcing, 'I will go to Llyonesse, and I will ask the brothers of the Shrine to accompany me. Perhaps, if we may not ease his suffering in this life, we might at least prevent it in the life to come.'

Charis offered to go with him, as did I, but he replied, 'It is better that I go alone. There is much between us that must be spoken — no, I know you would not intrude — but we will speak more freely if we are left alone to do it. The monks will attend to all else we require.'

He did not speak the fear central to his thinking — that Morgian would appear while he was there. If so, Avallach intended to face her and did not want Charis or me anywhere near when that happened.

The Fisher King left the Tor as soon as arrangements could be made and provisions gathered. He took only two stewards as escort, and six brothers from the monastery below the Shrine — although the good brothers were educated in swordthrust and spearthrow as well as Latin and the Gospels. Indeed, more than a few monks across the land had worn steel before donning the undyed wool, and it was not accounted a shameful thing at all.

The days turned cool. Pelleas and I hunted for the winter table, riding the hills and wooded vales surrounding the Tor through days crisp as new apples. We watched and waited, and sought the signs that would tell us how Avallach fared. But there were none, neither was there any word from Uther.

In the absence of signs we turned to our own affairs: finding a place for Uther's son to live. We were determined to find the safest home possible, but one after another our choices were quickly reduced and we were left with three: Tewdrig in Dyfed, Custennin in Goddeu, and Hoel in Armorica.

I did not seriously entertain the idea of raising the child at Ynys Avallach, although the thought did occur to me. The boy would not benefit from an upbringing that did not fit him for the world in which he must live. 'Life on the Tor,' Pelleas pointed out, 'has more in common with life in the Otherworld than it does with life in this worlds-realm.'

'It suited me,' I replied.

'Certainly, but I do not think it would suit another.' Pelleas thus confirmed my own misgivings.

'So, we must look to one of the three,' I mused.

'Two,' Pelleas suggested. 'Hoel is willing, and though he is getting old, he is a strong and able lord yet. But he is too far away.'

'There is safety in distance,' I remarked.

'Safety from the casual assassin perhaps,' Pelleas agreed, 'but not from the most determined. Besides, anyone murderbent would think of looking there first since Hoel fostered Aurelius and Uther.'

'That leaves only Tewdrig and Custennin,' I mused. 'Tewdrig is strong and loyal enough, but Dyfed is surrounded by prying eyes. Morcant and Dunaut are near, and will certainly discover that the child raised in Tewdrig's care is Uther's heir.

'While Custennin's stronghold in the north is far enough away to be free of spies, by the same token it is too far to the north to remain as secure as Tewdrig's.' I held my hands palm up, level, indicating that the balance was even between them. 'Which, then, will you choose?'

Pelleas' brow furrowed in a thoughtful frown. 'Why must we choose between them at all?' He brightened as the idea took hold inside him. 'Why not let the child be reared in both places depending on time and need?'

'Why not, indeed?'

A sound idea, that. Let the child receive the benefit of both hearths; let him learn the ways of two very different lords and kings. It was inspired.

That decided, I put the matter from me; there was nothing more to be done until the birth. I did not wish to risk sending a messenger to either king; and I could not go myself now, lest at some time in the future my visit would be remembered for what it was — the High King's counsellor arranging fosterage for his heir.

For I had no hope that Uther would succeed in keeping the birth secret. Sooner or later, word, like water in an oaken bucket, would leak out. And across the land ambitious men would begin searching for the child.

Nevertheless, satisfied with my plan, I reckoned I need make no further arrangements — until the birth of the babe called me forth in the dead of winter. So, since there was nothing more to be done at the moment, I promptly put the matter from my mind and concerned myself with other affairs.

I will tell you the truth: I did not in those days regard the child in any special way. Despite the hints I had received — the warnings one might say — he was merely an infant that required protection. He was the son of my dead friend, true. But that was all. Other matters were more pressing, or seemed so.

I turned to these and promptly forgot all about the child.

FIFTEEN

In the black month, the bleak month, when cold winds blow snow from the ice-bound north, the month of privation and death in which winter itself dies in the Christ Mass, the babe was born. Birth from death: it is the ancient and holy way of the earth. I consulted the oaken bowl, and stayed up five nights together to view the winter-clean sky. In this way I learned that the time was near.

Pelleas and I travelled to Tintagel and waited a little way off in the woods of the deep glen for the birth. I did not like to go up to the caer itself, for my coming would be noticed and discussed.

For three days we sat wrapped in our cloaks and furs before our small fire of oak twigs and pine cones, waiting. At midnight of the third night, as we sat watching, a strange thing happened: an enormous black bear came out of the woods, padded softly round the fire, snuffling at us warily, and ambled up the trail leading to the caer.

'Let us follow,' I whispered. 'Perhaps that fellow knows something that we should also learn.'

We followed and found the bear standing on its hind legs at the edge of the wood, its blackness sharp against the moon-bright snow. The beast's nose sniffed the seawind and its great head swung towards us as we approached, but the creature did not move. It remained for some little time, standing, looking up at Uther's fortress, and then, as if making up its own slow mind, lumbered on.

'Hunger has driven it from its lair,' remarked Pelleas. 'It goes to find food.'

'No, Pelleas, it goes to honour a birth.' I still remember the look Pelleas gave me, his face white in the moonlight. 'Come, it is time.'

By the time we reached the gates, the great bear, by some

means — animal strength perhaps — had gained entrance into the caer. The gateman, no doubt asleep at his watch when the beast appeared, had run away to raise the alarm, leaving the gate unattended. Men with torches dashed here and there in confusion while the dogs barked wildly at the ends of their leashes, working themselves into a killing frenzy.

No one saw us slip through the gates and we made our way directly to the hall, and through it to the king's chamber. Ygerna lay in the room above, her women and a midwife or two gathered with her. But Uther remained below, alone, awaiting the birth.

The sword of Maximus lay unsheathed across his knee.

Uther glanced up as we entered: guilt writ large upon his features for all to see. I had caught him and he knew it.

'Oh, Merlin, you are here. I thought you would be.' He contrived to sound relieved. The sound of the chaos outside had entered with us, and Uther seized on this to aid him. 'By the Raven, what is that commotion?'

'A bear has entered your stronghold, Uther,' I told him.

'A bear.' He appeared to ponder this as if the thing bore deep significance for him, then said, 'My wife is not delivered of the child. You may as well sit — it will likely be some time yet.'

I motioned for Pelleas to find us some food and drink, and he disappeared behind the hanging hides into the hall. I sat down in Gorlas' big chair — Uther preferred his camp chair even in chamber — and studied the High King as he sat before me.

'I am disappointed, Uther,' I told him flatly. 'Why have you gone back on your word?'

'When did I promise anything?' he flung back angrily. 'You accuse me falsely.'

'Tell me I am mistaken then. Tell me that the sword across your knee is not for the babe. Tell me you did not intend to kill it.'

Uther frowned and turned his face away. 'By God, Merlin, you hound a man!'

'Well? My apology only awaits your denial.'

'I have nothing to deny! I do not answer to you, Meddler.'

'Does Ygerna know what you intend?'

'What would you have me do?' He jumped up and threw the sword on the table.

'Honour our agreement.' I told him, thinking of many other things I could have said. I was trying to make it easy for him.

Still the High King resisted. As I say, once Uther fastened on a thing, he was loth to give it up. And he had had a long time to work himself up to this. He stalked around the room, glaring at me. 'I agreed to nothing. It was all your idea — I never agreed.'

'That is untrue, Uther. It was *your* idea for me to take the child.'

'Well, I have thought better of it then,' he growled. 'What have you to do with this anyway? What is your interest?'

'Only this: that the son of Aurelius, and a blood descendant of Constantine, should not suffer death before he has tasted of life. Uther,' I said gently, 'he is your kin. By all laws of heaven and earth it would be a grievous crime to kill the child. The deed is not worthy of you, Uther — you, who let Octa, the son of your enemy, live. How will you justify killing the son of your brother, whom you loved most dearly?'

Uther snarled. 'You twist things!'

'I say only what is, Uther. Give it up! If not for the child's sake, then for your own. Do not think to enter God's rest with this black deed on your soul.'

The High King stood unmoved, feet apart, glaring balefully, his mouth a firm line. Oh, he could be difficult.

'What is the use, Uther? Where is your gain?'

He had no answer, and made none. Neither did he give in.

'Very well,' I sighed. 'I had hoped to persuade you, but you leave me no choice.'

'What will you do?'

'I claim the promise you gave me, Uther. And I bind you with your honour to grant it.'

'What promise?' he asked warily.

'On the night I brought Ygerna out of the fortress, you promised me anything I desired. "Even to the half of my kingdom," you said, if I would deliver her to you. I fulfilled my half of the bargain, and asked nothing for myself at the time. Well, I make my claim now.'

'The child?' Uther was incredulous. Until this moment he had forgotten that promise. He remembered it full well now.

'The child, yes. I claim the child as my reward.'

Uther was beaten and he knew it. But he was not about to give up so easily. 'You are a cunning hound,' he faced me squarely. 'What if I refuse?'

'Refuse me now and lose all honour and self-respect. Your name will become a curse. You will never command a man with authority again. Consider, Uther, and answer: is killing a helpless babe worth that?'

'All right!' He fairly burst with exasperation. 'Take it! Take the child and let there be an end to it!'

Presently, Pelleas returned with a jar of mead, cups, bread and cheese. He put these on the table and began pouring the cups. 'I could find no meat,' he said. 'The kitchens were empty.'

'This is enough, Pelleas, thank you.' I turned to Uther and handed him a cup. 'I accept my reward, Uther,' I said lightly. 'Let us part as friends.'

The High King said nothing, but accepted the cup in one hand and a bit of bread in the other. We drank and ate together, and Uther calmed somewhat. But as his guilt and anger seeped away, he was left with the shame. He slumped in his chair and became despondent.

To shift his attention to something else, I said, 'What has become of that bear, I wonder? Perhaps we should go and see.'

We walked back through the empty hall and outside. The dogs had stopped barking and I thought by this that the bear must be killed. But no; it lived. The men had it cornered by the fortress wall, where, surrounded by torches and spears, the beast stood reared on its hind legs, its forepaws outspread, pelt bristling, claws extended, fangs bared. The yard was strangely quiet.

A magnificent beast, its dark eyes glinting in the ruddy torchlight. It was cornered but unconquered.

Uther looked upon the bear, and his aspect changed. He stopped and stared. What he saw, I cannot say. But when he moved again, it was as one in a dream: walking lightly, languidly, he made his way to the ring of men, stepping among them on his way to the animal.

'Lord King! No! Stay back!' shouted one of his chieftains. He threw down his spear and made to lay hold of the High

King and pull him back.

'Silence!' I hissed. 'Let him go!'

My senses prickled to the presence of the Otherworld. I saw everything in sharp relief: the risen moon, the bear, the men holding the torches, Uther, the glinting points of the spears, the stars, Pelleas, the dark hardness of the wall, the stones at my feet, the silent dogs. . .

It was a dream, and more than a dream. The dream had become real — or reality had become a dream. These times are rare; who is to say where the truth lies? Afterwards, men shake their heads in wonder and endure the scoffing of those who were not present. For it cannot be explained, only experienced. But this is what happened:

Uther boldly approached the bear and the animal lowered its head and dropped onto its forefeet. The High King held out his hand to the beast, and the bear, like a hound recognizing its master, pushed his muzzle into the High King's palm. With his other hand, Uther stroked the bear's huge head.

Men stared in astonishment: their lord and a wild bear, greeting one another as old friends. Perhaps, in some inexplicable way, they were.

I will never know what Uther thought he was doing, for he could never remember it clearly. But the two stood this way for the space of a few heartbeats, then Uther lowered his hand and turned away. One of the dogs growled and lunged forward, pulling its leash free from the slack hand of its holder. The bear reared as the dog leaped, and gave a sideways swipe with its great paw. The dog tumbled away, howling with pain, its back broken.

The dream ended then in the yelps of a dying dog. The other dogs were at the bear in an instant. The chieftain grabbed Uther by the arm and pulled him back to safety. Then the warriors loosed their spears.

The bear snarled and clawed the air, breaking spearshafts as if they were reeds; but the wounds were made and the blood was already flowing. Roaring with pain and rage, the great beast fell and the dogs tore out its throat.

'Take them off!' shouted Uther. 'Put the dogs away!'

The dogs were pulled away and all was silent once more. The bear was dead, its blood pooling black and thick on the stones beneath the immense body. This worlds-realm had reasserted itself — as it always will — in stark, unforgiving brutality.

Ah, but for a moment — if only for the briefest moment, those standing in the courtyard knew something of Otherworldly grace and peace.

There are those who say that it was Gorlas come to pay homage to the birth of his grandson that night. Or that the spirit of that great bear, poured out onto the stones in sacrifice at the moment of the babe's birth, found its way into the child that was born that night.

For it is true that when we reached the door of the hall once more, we heard the babe, squawling lustily at the top of its lungs. A hearty cry at the moment of birth is a good sign. Uther shook himself like one awakening, and turned to me. 'It is —' he paused, 'a boy.'

'A son,' he had been about to say.

'Wait here, I will have the babe brought out. It is best if Ygerna does not see you.'

'As you wish, Uther.' I signalled to Pelleas to go back to the wood and fetch our horses.

He hurried off down the track to the gate and I waited at the door. People, roused by the noise in the courtyard, passed by on their way to see the bear, which the men were already skinning where it lay. Indeed, it was a giant among bears.

Pelleas came with the horses. We had planned to take the babe without being seen. But the bear had changed that. People knew we were there now, and would know that we had taken the child. There was nothing to be done about that any more; we would have to trust the Guiding Hand and proceed boldly.

We waited and watched the men work over the bear. When the skin was free, they quartered the animal and fed the heart and liver to the dogs. The rest of the meat would be roasted, or made into stew for the feast.

Yes, I had forgotten: the Christ Mass. I turned and looked to the east and saw that dawn stood not far off. Already the sky lightened at the horizon; grey going to pink and rust. I heard footsteps behind me and Uther approached, carrying a fur-wrapped bundle, his face impassive. A woman walked behind him.

'Here,' he said curtly. 'Take it.' Then softly — possibly the only softness I had ever witnessed in Uther Pendragon — he lifted the edge of the fur and brushed the tiny head with his lips. 'Farewell, nephew,' he said, then looked up at me. I thought he would ask me where I took the child — surely it was in his mind — but he merely tucked the wrap and said, 'Go now.'

'He will be well cared for, Uther. Never fear.'

'Ygerna is asleep,' he said. 'I am going to wait with her.' He turned, saw the woman standing there, and remembered. 'I am sending this woman with you; she will suckle the child. A horse will be made ready for her.' He made to leave, but something held him. He hesitated, his eyes resting on the bundle in my arms. 'Is there anything else you require?'

The men came towards us, carrying the skin of the bear into the hall. 'Yes, Uther,' I answered, 'the bearskin.'

He eyed me curiously, but ordered the raw skin to be rolled up and tied behind my saddle. While this was being done a stablehand arrived leading a horse for the woman. When she had mounted, I handed the child to her; and, taking the reins of her horse into my hand, led my horse and hers out through the gate and down the narrow causeway. Several caer-dwellers watched us from outside the walls, but nothing was said and no one followed.

As daylight struggled into the sky, staining the eastern clouds and snow-covered hills crimson and gold, we rode back through the clefted valley and into the smooth, empty hills beyond Tintagel. And seagulls wheeled above us, keening in the cold winter air.

I did not like the idea of a winter sea voyage. But we must reach Dyfed as quickly as possible. The road is no place for a newborn, and in winter even those who make the road their home stay inside. Crossing Mor Hafren was necessary, though the prospect was far from welcome. Enough men lose their lives in winter seas that most boatmen refuse all commerce in that treacherous season.

Be that as it may, there are those who can always be bought. A flash of gold and they will go against all natural inclination, risking life and limb to an enterprise they would not consider otherwise. Consequently, we had little trouble

431

finding a boat to take us across. Still and all, we waited four days for calm weather.

I was uneasy the whole time. But, if anyone marked our passing, we learned nothing of it, for we saw no one else on the road, nor did the boatman take an interest in us. Once the price was settled, he asked no questions and went about his business with silent efficiency.

If he thought anything, he no doubt supposed the woman to be my wife and Pelleas to be my servant. I helped this impression as much as possible, hovering over the lady and the baby with protective authority, seeing to their comfort. The woman, an unfortunate whose husband had been killed when his horse stumbled on Tintagel's murderous causeway, and whose own babe had taken the wasting fever and died only days before, was not as old as I first thought.

As the journey went on, such beauty as she possessed, ravaged by grief and care, began returning to her. She smiled more often when she held the child, and thanked Pelleas and me for the small kindnesses performed for her. The woman, Enid by name, suckled the child readily, and cradled it as lovingly as any natural mother would. And I surmised that the closeness of the babe, its helplessness and dependence, had begun healing the wound in her heart.

The day of crossing came at last. It was wet and cold — the kind of wet cold that goes to the bones and stays long — the wind gusty and dagger-sharp. But the wind did not raise the seas against us, so we made good time and landed safely. I paid the boatman double his price, and was glad to do it.

Upon crossing Mor Hafren, we quickly entered Tewdrig's realm, sheltering the first night at the little seaside abbey at Llanteilo where the renowned Bishop Teilo had built his church and monastery. The next day, frosty cold but with a sky clear and high and bright as a flame, we rode the remaining distance to Caer Myrddin.

The sun sets early that time of year. Dusk was well upon us and the first winter stars already in the sky by the time we reached Tewdrig's stronghold. The market town stood a sad reminder of another age, abandoned now — perhaps for ever.

We urged our horses through the ruin and turned up the hill trail to the caer. Silvery smoke from many hearth fires drifted into the still night air, and the aroma of roasting meat reached us as we neared. Our arrival was foreseen, of course, and we were met at the gates by a young man with a sparse brown beard. 'Greetings, friends,' he called to us, taking up a place in the centre of the path. 'What business brings you to Tewdrig's house this cold winter's night?'

'Greetings, Meurig,' I told him, for it was Tewdrig's eldest son who confronted us. Others were gathering round, watching us with polite, but undisguised curiosity. 'You have become a man I see.'

At my use of his name, Meurig stepped closer. 'I am at your service, sir. How do you know me?'

'How should I not know the son of my friend, Lord Tewdrig?'

He cocked his head to one side. I think that my escort — a woman with a babe in arms — confused him. But one of the onlookers recognized me, for someone whispered, 'The Emrys is come!'

Meurig heard the name; his head whipped round and, laying a hand on my bridle, he said, 'Forgive me, Lord Emrys. I did not know it was you —'

I cut short his apology with a wave of my hand. 'There is nothing to forgive. But now, if we may go in — it is getting dark and the child will be getting cold.'

'At once, my lord.' He motioned some of the others forward to take our horses as we dismounted. Another ran to the hall to announce our arrival, so that Tewdrig himself met us as we crossed the yard.

'Your son has become a fine man,' I told Tewdrig when, after our greetings and after Enid and the child had been seen to, we were settled before the hearth with a steaming bowl of mulled wine in our hands. 'I did not remember him so well grown.'

'Oh, he has grown indeed, that one.' He smiled, pleased with the compliment. 'He was married a year ago and will have a babe of his own before spring.' He laughed suddenly. 'But I did not know *you* had taken a wife.'

'Alas, I have been too busy.'

'That I can easily imagine. So tell me, what is happening in the Island of the Mighty that I should know about?'

'You will have heard of Gorlas' death,' I replied.

'A bad thing that, very bad. I was sorry to hear of it. He was a strong battlechief.'

'Then you are also aware of the High King's marriage. As for the rest, you will know more than I — I have been at Ynys Avallach these many months.'

'Not with the Pendragon?' Tewdrig raised his eyebrows at this.

'Uther has his own advisers,' I explained simply.

'Perhaps, but you are —'

'No, it is better this way. I have Uther's ear when I need it, and he has mine. I am content.'

We sipped our sweet wine for a moment, feeling the warming draught thaw the cold places within. And Tewdrig waited for me to tell him why I had come. 'As it happens,' I began, setting my cup aside, 'I have come on an errand for the High King.'

Tewdrig leaned forward. 'So?'

'A matter of some importance, Lord Tewdrig. Your confidence is enjoined.'

'Whatever can be done, that I will do. For you, Myrddin Emrys, as much as for the High King. Of that you may be certain.'

'Thank you, my friend. But the thing I have come to ask will not be easily granted, and I would have you consider it carefully — perhaps discuss it with your counsellors before agreeing.'

'If that is what you wish. Although, if you deem it a virtue to come to me, I can tell you that I will refuse nothing you ask. For it is in my mind that if I could not help, you would not have come to me.'

Had he already guessed why I had come? Tewdrig was shrewd; his next words confirmed my suspicion.

'It is about the child, yes?'

I nodded. 'It is.'

'Whose child is it?'

'Aurelius' and Ygerna's,' I told him.

'I thought as much,' Tewdrig mused. 'Not Uther's flesh, yet the same noble blood in his veins. So, the Pendragon did not care to have the poor babe in his house reminding him that his own brats stood no closer to the throne.'

'That is the pith of it,' I agreed. 'Yet the babe must be kept safe, for —'

Tewdrig nodded gravely. 'For he will surely be the next Pendragon of Britain!'

I assure you I can be as blind as the next man. And here is the proof: until Tewdrig said those words, I had never seriously considered that likely. Nor did I believe it now. To me, the child was merely that: an infant who must be protected from the overweening ambition of others, *not* the future king. My blindness was complete.

The deeds and doings of the present, I confess, occupied me more than that one little life. I saw no further. That is the simple truth, and there is no pleasure in the telling of it.

Tewdrig continued: 'Oh, I see the problem. Let Dunaut or Morcant or any of that stripe know that Aurelius has an heir, and the lad's life would not be worth a nettle.'

'He will be a danger to himself, to be sure — and perhaps to those around him as well.

'Bah! Let them try to harm that child! Just let them try and they will soon learn to fear righteous wrath.'

It was not an idle boast, for Tewdrig was no braggart. But I needed more than his loyal indignation. 'I know I need have no fear there, Tewdrig. Your strength and wisdom, and that of your people, will be most important. For the child must not only be protected, he must be nurtured and taught.'

'Gwythelyn is nearby at Llandaff. The boy will be well taught, never fear.' Tewdrig sipped his wine and smiled expansively. 'The son of Aurelius in my house. This is an honour.'

'It is an honour that must remain unsung. He cannot be Aurelius' son any more. From this day, he is merely a child fostered at your hearth.'

'I understand. Your secret is safe with me, Myrddin Emrys.'

'It is *our* secret now, Tewdrig,' I reminded him. 'And we will speak of it no more.'

'No more,' agreed Tewdrig, 'except to say me what is the name of the child? What is he to be called?'

Shameful to tell, I had not thought to call the infant anything. Neither Uther nor Ygerna had bestowed a name, and I had been too preoccupied with its safety to give it any consideration. But the babe must have a name. . .

A word is given when a word is required. And at this time, like so many others, the name came unbidden to my tongue: 'Arthur.'

Instantly, upon uttering the word, I heard again the voice of my vision: the throng in Londinium clamouring, 'Arthur! Arthur! Hail Arthur!'

Tewdrig was watching me closely, his brows knotted in concern. 'Is something amiss?'

'No,' I reassured him. 'The infant — let him be called Arthur.'

Tewdrig tried the name. 'Arthur. . . very well. An unusual name, though. What does it mean?'

'I believe he will have to make its meaning for himself.'

'Then we must make certain he lives long enough to do so,' replied Tewdrig. He retrieved his cup, raised it, 'To Arthur! Health and long life, wisdom and strength! May he win the hero's portion at the feast of his fathers.'

SIXTEEN

We stayed a while at Caer Myrddin, and would have been content to remain there longer but, when the weather broke, Pelleas and I made our way back to Ynys Avallach. The journey was uneventful — indeed, we met no one at all on the road. But a day out from Dyfed a deep melancholy settled on me. A nameless longing, sharp and poignant as grief.

Into my mind came all the losses I had known. And, one by one, I saw forms and faces of those who had touched my life and now were gone to dust in the ground:

Ganieda, fairest daughter, wife and lover; her clear gaze and ringing laughter; shining hair, long and dark; her sly smile when she hid a secret; the sweetness of her mouth when we kissed. . .

Hafgan, Druid Chief, watching the world from the lofty elevation of his vast wisdom; welcoming the curiosity of a child; instilling dignity in the humblest gesture; standing firm for the Light. . .

Dafyd, goodness embodied, kindness with a soul; diligent searcher, defender, and warrior for the Truth; ready believer who did not condemn the unbelief of others; sower of the Good Seed in the soil of men's hearts. . .

Gwendolau, stout companion; fierce in battle and in friendship; first to raise the cup and last to set it down; drinking deep of life; knowing no pain or hardship for the sake of a sword brother. . .

Blaise, last of the true bards; keen of perception and understanding; unwavering in devotion, steadfast in virtue; a burning brand touched to the dry tinder of the Old Way. . .

And others: Elphin. . . Rhonwyn. . . Maelwys. . . Cuall . . . Aurelius. . .

This heavyheartedness lasted with me into the spring and summer. I found myself turning more and more to thoughts of my father, wondering what sort of man Taliesin had been, regretting that I had not known him, weeping for the sound of his voice in song. The regret, at first merely sorrowful, festered and grew into black hatred for Morgian who caused his death.

That she lived and breathed the air of this world — when Taliesin, and so many other good people had gone out of it — infuriated me.

It came into my mind to kill her.

I even planned how this deed might be accomplished. And, before spring was over, I had conceived every aspect of her death — indeed, I had murdered her many times over in my heart.

Nor did I fear carrying out my plan. I believe, if left to myself, I would have found her and slain her. However, we are rarely left to ourselves. Jesu, who watches over the affairs of all men, is not content that any should fall from his hand or long remain beyond his touch. If not for that, I am certain I would have joined Morgian in the stinking pit of hell.

What happened was this:

A woman came to Shrine Hill, suffering from an ailment of her bones which caused them to become brittle as sticks, quickly broken and slow to mend. In the least, the slightest blow would cause a bruise that would swell painfully and last for many days. She had suffered long with this affliction, always in the sorest agony, labouring with her arm in a sling, or hobbling on a crutch — the small bones in her hands and feet snapped so easily.

But she prevailed upon some kinsmen to bring her to the Shrine, for she had heard of the healing work the brothers practised there. In truth, she had heard of the wonders Charis had performed with her healing art. So she came with simple faith to be healed.

Charis had marked — with alarm, I should think — my growing bitterness and depression. She had spoken to me about it, but I was beyond listening. So the day she went to minister to the woman she took me with her. It was a day of darkness for me and, not caring where I was or what I did, I accompanied her to the Shrine.

The woman, neither old nor young, was dressed in a well-patched green mantle, ragged at hem and sleeves, but clean as she could make it. She smiled as Charis came into the room the brothers set aside for treatment of the sick. There were others gathered there — other sick, and a few brothers in their grey robes moving among them. The sound of Psalm-singing came down to us like sweet rain from the hilltop Shrine above.

'What is your name?' asked Charis gently, settling on a stool beside the woman's pallet.

'Uisna,' she replied, her smile tight with pain.

'May I see your hands, Uisna?' Charis took the woman's hands in her own. They were delicate, with fine long fingers, but hideous blue-brown bruises discoloured them and made them ugly. The woman winced as Charis gently, gently probed the bruises, and I saw that it hurt her even to have them touched.

Her feet and legs were the same: beauty made grotesque by the grossness of the malady. One leg had been broken in the past and poorly set; it was crooked and misshapen. I had to look away.

'Can you help me?' Uisna asked softly. It was a plea, a prayer. 'It hurts me much.'

To my amazement Charis answered, 'Yes, I can help you.'

How could this be? If I had not known her better, I would have thought my mother callous or unthinking for promising the impossible. But she added, 'The God of this place helps all who call upon his name.'

'Then tell me the name, please, that I may call upon him.'

Looking directly into the woman's pain-filled eyes, Charis replied, 'His name is Jesus, King of Love and Light, Great of Might, Lord of Heaven. He is the Son of the Good God, the Everliving.'

No one expected what happened next. For no sooner had Charis uttered the name, the woman's head snapped back and a scream of utter torment tore from her throat. Her body became rigid, the cords of her neck and arms standing out against the skin. She fell back on the pallet, writhing.

Charis jumped to her feet and I dashed forward. She extended a hand to keep me away, saying, 'No, do not come nearer. There is an evil spirit in her.'

The body thrashing on the pallet began to laugh — a sickening, hateful sound. 'You cannot help this bitch whore!'

the woman screamed in a rough, raucous voice. 'She is mine! I will kill her if you touch her!'

The brothers hurried to Charis' side and conferred quickly. One of them dashed from the room and returned a few moments later with a wooden cross and a vial of anointing oil. Meanwhile, the poor woman thrashed and flung her limbs around so wildly that I feared she would break them off — screaming continually with that dreadful, demented laughter.

The monk approached with the cross and oil, but Charis went to him saying, 'I will do it, but I will need help. Go and tell the brothers at the Shrine to uphold us in prayer.'

The man raced away again, and Charis nodded to several of the other brothers, who stood near. 'Hold her so that she does no hurt to herself,' she said. The monks knelt beside the pallet and gently but firmly laid hold of the woman's flailing limbs. Charis, holding the cross and vial, knelt down by the pallet.

'In the name of Jesu the Christ, who is the living Son of God, I abjure you unclean spirit, and demand that you come out of this woman.'

The woman, poor wretch, was instantly beset with violent tremors, convulsions that seized every part of her body, flinging her back against the straw bed again and again, despite the brothers' best efforts. At the same time, the hideous laughter came forth, bubbling up from her throat as from a very great distance.

'JES-S-S-S-U-U-U!' she hissed with wicked glee, and uttered an unspeakable oath against that sacred name.

The monks fell back in horror. But Charis did not so much as cringe. She held out the cross in her hand. 'Silence!' she commanded. 'You will not blaspheme the holy name!'

The spirit twisted the woman's face in a ghastly grin. 'Oh, oh, please, be not angry with me,' the thing whined. 'Please, fine lady, be not angry with me.'

'In the name of Jesu, I command you to silence!' Charis insisted.

The woman convulsed, her stomach swelled and foul gas broke from her bowels. She spat, and her spittle ran yellow with puss. She laughed and spread her discoloured legs, breaking her foul wind.

Abbot Elfodd appeared, crossed himself and entered the room. 'Brother Birinus told me to come straight away,' he whispered, coming to stand beside Charis. 'What is to be done?'

'I have commanded it to silence,' Charis replied. 'But it is a stubborn thing. Exorcizing it will be difficult.'

'I will do it, sister,' Elfodd offered.

'No,' Charis smiled and gripped his hand, 'I have begun; I will finish. She is in my care.'

'Very well. But I will stand with you.' He nodded to the monks, who took up places across the room; they knelt and began singing a prayer.

The woman lay still, panting like a winded dog. At the sight of the abbot her eyes grew round, she shrieked and spat more of the vile poison. Her hands became claws and she reached for him to scratch him — all the while mouthing silent obscenities.

Charis knelt down, holding the cross before her. I marvelled at her composure: she was so calm, so self-assured. 'Uisna,' she said softly. 'I am going to help you now.' She smiled gently, a smile of such hope and beauty, I believe the smile alone could have healed any malady. 'Rejoice! It is God's good pleasure to heal you today, daughter.'

Poor Uisna's eyes rolled up into her head and she spewed forth more puss and bile, and began choking on it.

The abbot bent over her and lifted her head. Her arm whipped up and struck Elfodd on the side of the face with such a blow that he was flung back against the wall. The monks prayed louder.

'I am unharmed,' said Elfodd; rubbing his jaw, he returned to his place. 'Continue.'

'In the name of the Most High God, Lord and Creator of all that is, seen and unseen, and in the name of his Holy Son, Jesu, Beloved Friend and Saviour of men, I renounce you, Evil One. I command you to come out of this woman and trouble her no more.' Charis held the cross before the woman's face; Uisna shrank from it, expressions of terror and triumph rippling over her features.

'In the name of the Christ, be gone!' Charis shouted.

At once, the woman gave out a tortured scream. It seemed as if the sunlight dimmed and the room became cold, and that a rushing wind filled the room. This unseen wind whirled once, twice, again; then, lifting the thatch of the roof, raced out into the clear blue sky above.

Uisna lay as one dead: limp, grey-faced, no breath left in her body. But Charis placed the wooden cross on her breast and, taking the woman's discoloured hands in her own, began rubbing them gently. Abbot Elfodd lifted the vial of oil, offered a blessing, and, dipping his finger, anointed Uisna's head.

Both Charis and Elfodd prayed over the woman then, asking Jesu to forgive her sins, and heal her body and soul, and receive her into the Holy Kingdom. It was simply done and, when they finished, Elfodd said, 'Awake, dear sister, you have been healed.'

Uisna's eyes fluttered open. She looked up at the two bending over her, puzzled. 'Am I. . ? What has happened?'

'You have been saved,' Abbot Elfodd replied. 'And you have been healed.'

Uisna sat up slowly. She raised her hands, and her mouth fell open in awe. The grotesque bruises had vanished, and her flesh was smooth and white. She lifted the hem of her mantle: her feet and legs were no longer discoloured; the flesh was firm and healthy, the once-broken leg straight.

'Oh!. . . Oh!. . . ' Uisna cried, throwing her arms around Charis. Tears streamed down her face.

The monks exclaimed in praises to God. Abbot Elfodd embraced the woman and, as if it could no longer remain silent, the bell at the Shrine began ringing out wildly. Moments later monks began crowding into the room to share in the joy of the miracle.

'You must continue in faith, sister,' warned Elfodd gently. 'Renounce sin, Uisna, take Jesu for your Saviour, and trust only in him. Be filled with God and his Holy Spirit so that the evil spirit cannot return again — or it surely will return sevenfold.'

And I — suddenly, I felt as if the room was closing in around me, suffocating me. I could not stand to be there any longer. With the sound of thanksgiving and praise songs ringing in my ears, I fled the place, my breath coming in raking gasps.

Charis found me later, where I sat among the reeds below the Tor with my feet in the water. The sun was lowering in the afternoon sky and she came to me and quietly sat down beside me on the bank, laying a hand on my shoulder.

'I saw you run from the sickroom,' she said softly.

I shook my head sorrowfully. 'I am sorry, Mother, but I could not stay any longer — I had to get away from there.'

'What is wrong, my Hawk?'

I turned to peer at her through a mist of tears. 'I have been afraid,' I sobbed, tears running freely now. 'I have been afraid. . . and oh, oh Mother, I have failed. . . I have failed. . . '

Tenderly, Charis gathered me into her arms. She held me for a long time, rocking slowly, gently. 'Tell me, my son, how have you failed?' she said at last.

'There was so much,' I answered finally, 'so much I meant to do. And I have done nothing. I have betrayed the trust of my birthright. I have strayed; I have wandered far, Mother; and I have wasted myself in empty pursuits — because I was afraid.'

'What did you fear?'

I could scarcely bring myself to say the word. But, squeezing my eyes shut, I forced it out: 'Morgian.'

Charis said nothing for a long time. She was quiet so long, I turned to look at her and saw that her eyes were closed, shedding silent tears beneath her lashes.

'Mother?'

She smiled bravely. 'I had thought myself free of her. Now I know I never will be. But her power belongs only to this world.'

'I know that — at least I was reminded of it today. . . that poor woman — '

'Uisna is healed, Merlin. God has made her whole.'

'Are there many like her?'

'Yes,' Charis sighed, gazing across the lake to the Tor, 'and more all the time. She is the third since winter. Abbot Elfodd tells me that it is the same in other places. He has spoken to the bishop about it — there is talk of a plague.'

I winced. 'A plague of evil spirits?'

'Bishop Teilo says that it is to be expected. For when God's kingdom increases, Satan is roused to wrath. The Evil One seeks always to keep us from the knowledge of God, for then we are defenceless before him.' She smiled again. 'But, as you have seen today, we are far from defenceless.'

I remembered that day on the mountain-top in Celyddon, and I shuddered. A plague of evil spirits — a ghastly thought. Yet, it was true, our Lord was more powerful in his simple goodness than the Enemy in all his vast evil.

That is what I had seen this day at the Shrine, and I had been admonished — indeed, I had been rebuked — and sternly reminded that I feared for nothing. Morgian could be faced, and Morgian could be defeated. This truth, like so many, was bitter to me, for it brought me to my knees beneath the weight of all my failings.

Oh, yes. So many failures, so much wasted time and effort. The barbarian still threatened, the petty kings still strove with one another for power, the blessings of civilization were fading from memory. . . The Kingdom of Summer was no nearer to becoming reality.

Could this be blamed on Morgian?

Only in part.

It was Morgian, and the lord who ruled her. It was my own short-sightedness — or lack of faith, it amounts to the same thing sometimes. Time and again, I had been given opportunities and I had wasted them. Time and again, I had held back when I might have acted more swiftly, more forcefully. Why? Why had I done this?

The heart of a man remains a mystery for ever beyond his reckoning. What of that? I did not have to continue in my ignorance and disgrace. I could change. Knowing the difference, I could choose the higher way.

'What are you thinking, Merlin?' Charis asked after a while.

'I am thinking that this is my battle. I have run from it long enough.'

'What will you do?'

I shook my head. 'I cannot say. But I will be shown soon enough. And, while I wait, I will make myself ready. I will stay here at Ynys Avallach and I will strengthen myself with prayer and meditation on the Holy Christ.'

Charis hugged me again, and kissed my forehead. 'My Hawk, forgive yourself as you have been forgiven. Your failings are not unique to you alone.'

That was all she said; she left me soon after that. But I felt forgiven. I prayed: 'Great Light, thank you for waking me from my long, selfish sleep. Lead me, my King. I am ready to follow.'

The next day but one Avallach returned from Llyonesse. The news he brought was mixed. Belyn had improved, though would not recover, and did not expect to see Samhain. Nonetheless, he seemed content, and welcomed Avallach's visit. Consequently, the brothers had effected a reconciliation. And Avallach had gleaned what he could from Belyn regarding Morgian.

'There is little enough to tell,' Avallach informed me, 'but that little is disturbing. King Loth is dead, and Morgian has left the Orcades. Where she has gone is not known. Belyn expected her to return to Llyonesse in the spring, but there has been no sign or word from her.'

'Loth dead?' I mused. 'Then there are *two* thrones that will fall to her.'

Belyn's and Loth's, I was thinking: both would see one of Morgian's offspring made king. Two realms had fallen to the Queen of Air and Darkness — which was what the people of Ynysoedd Erch, the Islands of Fear, had taken to calling Morgian. Two kingdoms — one in the north, one in the south — under her power. But Morgian's influence extended much further than that — as I was soon to discover.

Three days later word came to Ynys Avallach that Uther was dead.

SEVENTEEN

Strange to tell, two years had passed me in the Fisher King's hall. So given to hate and despair was I, that I had noticed nothing of the wider world — the silent turnings of the seasons, the long, slow swing of the Earth through her measured course.

Now Uther was dead.

I pondered this. The Imperial line of Constantine was never ordained to flourish. Each of noble Constantine's sons had been king, and each in his turn had been, like his father, cut down before his time.

Poison, again, it was said: one of Gorlas' loyal stewards who blamed Uther for his master's death and sought to even the blood debt. Many believed this, although there was also vague talk of a mysterious malady; it seemed Uther had suffered a lingering illness through the winter. I gathered my things together and prepared to leave the Tor.

'Farewell, my Hawk!' called Charis as she waved me away. 'We will uphold you in your battle.'

She was right, of course. My battle, so long avoided, was finally beginning.

I sent Pelleas ahead to Londinium and made my way to Tintagel in all haste, hoping I was not too late. But it was not Uther I was concerned with now. I wanted to see Ygerna, and to collect Uther's sword. For word had gone out: the kings of Britain were gathering in Londinium to choose a new High King from among their number. I must be there when this took place.

Ygerna received me gladly. She had borne her loss bravely, but was tired and wanted someone to share her grief. Indeed, Uther was not much mourned; he was not the High King to inspire the love and sympathy of the people. What he had accomplished for Britain — his fierce battles, his brilliant victories — these were already forgotten. The only thing people remembered was that Uther had killed Gorlas to marry Ygerna. That is all they remembered, and that little a lie.

I found the twice-widowed queen standing on the rampart of the wall, gazing out at the sea, her hair streaming in the sea breeze. In the falling light she appeared at once frail and wonderfully strong — fragile as sorrow, potent as love. She turned lightly when I approached, smiled, and held out her hands to me. 'Myrddin, you have come. Welcome, dear friend.'

'I came as soon as I received word, my queen.' I said, taking her hands. Her fingers were cold, although the late afternoon sun was warm on the wall. Then, hesitantly, she stepped nearer and embraced me chastely, brushing my cheek with cool lips. I held her for a long moment, very much aware that she was a young woman who needed the comfort of a reassuring touch.

'Will you sit with me a while?' she asked, stepping back, a queen once more.

'If you wish.' We walked along the wall to a block of grey stone which jutted out from the rampart. She settled herself on it and indicated that I should sit beside her.

'It happened so quickly,' she said abruptly, her voice sad and low. 'He had been out hunting and returned feeling unwell — it had been a bad spring for him so I did not remark upon it. He went to bed and awoke in the night with a fever. He remained in bed the next day which was most unlike him. I saw him twice, but he complained of nothing. I expected him at supper, but when he did not come I went to his room.'

She squeezed my hand tightly. 'Oh, Myrddin, he was sitting in his chair. . . his flesh was cold, and he was dead. . . '

'I am sorry, Ygerna.'

She seemed not to hear. 'The odd thing was — he had his shield beside him, and his standard; he wore his leather breastplate. His sword lay across his lap. It was as if he expected to fight an enemy.' The queen lowered her head and sighed. 'I did not speak to him again. I did not tell him I loved him — I wanted so much to tell him, and then it was too late. Myrddin, why does everything always come too late?'

The wash of the sea around the roots of the headland and the cry of the soaring gulls carried an inexpressible sadness to me. I put my arm round Ygerna and we sat together in the sun, listening to the gulls and the waves, feeling the comfort of two hearts grieving.

The sun went behind a cloud and the day turned suddenly cool. 'Where has he been buried?' I asked as we rose and made our way back inside.

She did not answer at once. When she spoke there was triumph in her voice. 'Beside Aurelius.'

Jesu bless her, she had done what she could for Uther's memory. It was right that they should be buried together in any case, but Ygerna wanted their names for ever linked in renown and respect. She had buried the husband she loved next to the one the people loved.

As we came near the hall, she turned to me, and, laying a hand on my arm, said, 'I carry Uther's child.'

'Does anyone know?'

'My serving maid. She is sworn to silence.'

'See that she keeps it.'

Ygerna nodded. She understood. 'Will there be fighting?'

'Possibly. Yes, it is likely.'

'I see,' she said absently; there was something else on her mind I could tell. She was weighing her words carefully. I waited for her to come out with it in her own time.

The sea crashed below us, restless as Ygerna's heart. I could sense her unease. Still, I waited.

'Myrddin,' she said at last, her voice tight. 'Now that Uther is dead. . .' Words failed her; she could not make them say what she felt. 'Now that the king is gone, perhaps it would not be. . .'

'Yes?'

She pressed my hand and gazed earnestly at me — as if I held power to grant or withhold her heart's desire. 'The child — my son. Please, Myrddin, where is he? Is he safe? May I send for him?'

'It cannot be, Ygerna.'

'But surely now — now that Uther. . .'

I shook my head gently. 'The danger has not diminished; in fact, with Uther's death it has increased. Until you have delivered Uther's child, Aurelius' son remains the only heir.'

Ygerna dropped her head. The babe had been much on her mind and in her heart, as it would with any mother. 'May I go to him?'

'That would not be wise, I fear,' I told her. 'I am sorry. I wish it could be otherwise.'

'Please, just to see him —'

'Very well,' I relented, 'that may be arranged. But it will take time. Arthur must be —'

'*Arthur. . .* ' she whispered, 'so that is what you named him.'

'Yes. Please understand, I would have acted differently but Uther told me no name to give him. I hope you approve.'

'It is a good name. A strong name, I think.' She smiled wistfully, repeating the word to herself. 'You have done well. I thank you.'

'I have taken your child from you, my lady, and you thank me. Indeed, you are a remarkable woman, Ygerna.'

She searched my face with her eyes, and apparently found what she was seeking. 'You are good, Myrddin. You, above all men, have treated me as an equal. I will do whatever you tell me to do.'

'You need do nothing for the moment. Later, when the High Kingship is decided — well, we will leave tomorrow's worries for tomorrow.'

Her smile showed the relief she felt. We entered the hall and fell to talking of other things. We dined most pleasantly, and retired early. The next morning I asked for the sword and one of the dragon standards Uther had devised as the symbol of the High Kingship.

Ygerna gave them to me, saying, 'Dunaut was here and wanted the sword. I would not let him have it. I told him Uther was buried with it.' She paused and smiled guiltily. 'I am not sorry I lied.'

'It was well you did not give him the sword,' I told her. 'We would have a hard time getting it back from him, I think. Indeed, we will have a difficult enough time keeping his hands off it as it is.'

'Farewell, Myrddin Emrys. Send word, if you think of it — I should like to know what happens at the king choosing.'

'Farewell, Ygerna. I will bring word myself, if I can, when it is over.'

A few days later, I turned aside at the plain above Sorviodunum and the Giant's Dance: that great and ancient circle of stones the folk of the region call the Hanging Stones,

449

for the way those enormous rock lintels seemed, in certain light, to float above the ground.

The circle stood by itself on the crest of a wide, smooth hill. No one was about, nor did I expect otherwise. Cold, immense, mysterious, men left the Ring alone for the most part. It reminded them that there were secrets in the earth which they would never know, that the wonders of a previous age remained for ever beyond their ken, that a superior race had lived where they lived now and that they, too, would one day vanish as the ring-builders and the mound-builders before them had vanished, that life in this worlds-realm was furtive and short.

A small herd of cattle grazed in the area, and a few sheep wandered bleating in the ditch around the stones. I rode in among the standing stones to the inner ring and dismounted. The twin grave mounds — one new made, the other covered with short-cropped grass — lay side by side.

The wind moaned among the Hanging Stones, and the bleating sheep sounded like the disembodied voices of those buried in the earthen chambers that stood a way off from the great circle. Above, black crows sailed on silent wings in a white, empty sky. And it did seem, as the Hill Folk believed, that the Ring marked the place where two worlds touched.

Appropriate then that here, where the worlds met, were the brother kings united: together for ever. Uther would never have to leave his brother's side, and Aurelius would never lack his brother's care. Neither would be separated from the other any more.

At the sight of the bare-earthed mound, I sank to my knees. And I sang:

> I passed time at dawn, I slept in a purple shadow;
> I was a rampart beneath bold emperors,
> A cloak folded on the shoulders of two kings,
> The shining arc of two lusty spears thrown down from heaven.
> In Annwfn they will sharpen the battle,
> With golden deeds they will rout the everlasting Enemy;
> Seven-score hundred have bowed in death before them,
> Seven-score thousand will uphold them in victory.
> Brave kings and true, their blood is cold,
> Their song is ended.

Oh, Uther, deeply do I regret your death. We were wary friends at best, but we understood one another, I think. May it go well with you, my king, on your journey to the Otherworld. Great of Might, accept this wayward soul into your company and you will not want for a more loyal companion. For I declare to you most solemnly, King of Heaven, Uther lived by the light that was in him.

May all men alive claim as much.

By the time I reached Londinium, the chase was already well along — which is to say that the crown-lusting hounds had the scent of the High Kingship in their nostrils and were hot on the trail. Dunaut, of course, with his friends Morcant and Coledac, led the pack. But there were others close behind them: Ceredigawn with the support of his kinsman Rhain of Gwynedd; Morganwg of Dumnonia and his sons; Antorius and Regulus of the south Cantii; and Ogryvan of Dollgellau.

There would have been more — in fact, there would *be* more when those whose realms lay farther away arrived. As it was, the sparring was merely boasting and posturing, the swagger of combatants before the contest. The actual fight had not yet begun.

Bishop Urbanus, beside himself with indecision, welcomed me distractedly. 'Merlinus, I am glad you have come. I tell you the truth when I say that I am at my wits' end keeping peace between the lords. The things they say to one another,' he complained, adopting a shocked demeanour, 'and in a church!'

'It will get worse before it gets better,' I warned.

'Then I do not know how it will be settled without bloodshed.' He shook his head gravely. 'Still, I think it proper to conduct such important matters on consecrated ground.'

Urbanus was not as troubled as he pretended. In his heart he was pleased to have a hand in the king choosing — if only in providing a roof under which it could take place. Make no mistake, that this king choosing should take place in a church was no small thing. For it meant that the lords accepted Aurelius' precedent; they felt comfortable with the church and were willing to allow it a place in supporting their affairs.

451

Although I entertained no illusions that most of those sheltering under Urbanus' roof would just as well have gathered in a stable or a mud hut if that had been offered. Their eyes were on the crown, not the cross.

'And I do not mind telling you,' the bishop continued, 'this has happened at a most inopportune time. If you have not guessed already, we are enlarging the edifice. When the masons are finished, we will have an apse joined to the basilica, and a larger transept. And there will be a proper narthex with an arched entrance like the larger churches of Gaul.'

I had noticed the building work, of course. There were piles of rubble stone scattered around the church; masons worked on wooden scaffolds and cutters trimmed the huge blocks lying in the yard. I guessed the work had been paid for by Aurelius — for a certainty, Uther would never have given money for such a venture.

It was clear Urbanus' fortunes were rising in the world, and he relished the ascent. Very well, allow him his big church; there was no harm in it — so long as he managed to keep a true heart and humble spirit.

The kings were not the only ones with an interest in the High Kingship. Governor Melatus had summoned some of the more powerful magistrates as well. What they thought to do, I cannot say. No doubt they saw in the gathering of the kings a chance to reclaim some small part of their dwindling power. Roman government survived only, if it survived at all, in old men's memories and the Latin titles they wore.

Pelleas found us a place to stay — the house of a wealthy merchant named Gradlon, who traded in wine, salt, and lead, among other things, and who owned the ships that carried his goods. Gradlon was a friend of Governor Melatus and an influential man in the affairs of Londinium. I suspect that Melatus had requested that his friends make free their houses to anyone attending the king choosing, so that he could be informed as events took shape.

Gradlon, however, was a genuine host and made no secret of his allegiances, saying, 'A merchant pays tribute to the man who keeps his business healthy. If it is a king, I bow the knee; if an emperor, I kiss the hem. Either way I pay taxes.' He held a chubby finger in the air for emphasis. 'But I pay them gladly as long as the roads and sea routes remain open.'

The governor and magistrates held council in the governor's palace with the intention of drafting an ultimatum to lay at the feet of Emperor Aetius: send the troops, or lose Britain's good will.

Britain — in the greatest good will or vilest temper — had never been worth the Empire's sweat in maintaining it. Well, for a few generations the tin and lead and corn the Britons paid had been some value to the Empire, I suppose. But this little island had cost Rome far more than it ever returned.

Now, when the rest of the Empire bled under the relentless blows of the barbarian axe, the concerns of little Britanniarum were no concern of the Emperor at all. The small agonies of a flea-bitten hound in the Emperor's stable might elicit more sympathy, I considered, but could expect no more relief.

I pitied the governor and his magistrates for not realizing this.

Our future was as Britain, not Britanniarum. To think otherwise was folly. Perhaps dangerous folly at that. Reality can be most severe; it has a way of punishing those who ignore it too long.

The kings, on the other hand, were not much better. They believed, apparently, that the barbarian threat could be checked by personal aggrandizement: the greater the king, the more the Saecsen trembled.

I need not tell you what I think of such beliefs.

Well, and this is how the council of kings began: deadlocked over the question of who was qualified to decide among those who fancied themselves capable of wielding Macsen Wledig's sword. The question of how to settle that question added another stratum of animosity to the proceedings.

The only voices of reason were those of Tewdrig and Custennin. But by the time they arrived, the others were too far withdrawn behind the walls in their indefensible positions to hear. Reason, as I have said, does not avail in these situations anyway.

Each day when the kings gathered in the church to begin their debate, I went with them, biding my time. I did not speak, and no one asked me. I waited, thinking I might yet find an opportunity to help. Certainly I could expect no more than that. One chance only. I must make it count.

While I waited, I sat in my place and watched all. I searched among them, noting each one carefully — the tone of his voice, his command, wisdom, strength. I weighed all and found none the measure of Aurelius, or Uther either, for that matter. Lord help us, I would have settled for a Vortigern!

The most able among them was Custennin. But his kingdom was small and he was a northerner. That is to say, he lacked the near inexhaustible wealth of the southern kings which he would need if he were to try maintaining two, or possibly three, courts and field a warband large enough to keep order in the land. And then, living so far in the north made him dubious in the south. Northerners, it was widely thought, were savages and brutes, lacking all refinement and civility. Men would never follow a king they considered little better than the barbarian.

Tewdrig, I thought, might be more likely. He possessed great wealth, enough to command the respect of the southern kings. But the Demetae and Silures, among the oldest tribes of Britons, were also the most independent. It was doubtful that other kings would hold to Tewdrig when already they complained of Dyfed's indifference and insularity. Also, I suspected that the High Kingship meant little to Tewdrig; it might mean more to his son, Meurig, but he was still an untried leader.

Of the others, Ceredigawn showed some promise. That his great grandfather was Irish might be overcome, for he was a forceful and upright ruler. But the fact that his family gained their realm by virtue of the unpopular Roman practice of planting rulers in troubled regions, over the protests of those who must live with them, was a lasting embarrassment. As a consequence, his people had never troubled themselves with forming alliances with other ruling houses and so Ceredigawn, however able, was not well liked.

As the days dragged on — days of insane posturing, absurd threats, and breathtaking arrogance — it became clear to me that there could be no harmony of opinion reached among them. Lord Dunaut, of the wealthy Brigantes, succeeded in thwarting all reasonable discussion with his ludicrous demand that the next High King should support the entire warhost out of his private treasury.

Rather than maintain the warhost of Britain from a warchest into which all the lords contributed equally, Dunaut and his friends insisted that the freedom of Britain depended upon the freedom of the High King to rule the warhost without let or hindrance from the petty kings. Otherwise, the small kings would be tempted to influence affairs by withholding tribute needed to support the warhost. 'The High King will only be free,' Dunaut declared, 'if he rules from his own treasury!'

This infuriated men like Eldof and Ogryvan and Ceredigawn — able leaders who nevertheless had trouble enough maintaining even their own modest warbands, simply because their lands were not so well suited to the growing of grain, or the mining of gold and silver.

While it did appeal to the vanity of men like Morganwg of Dumnonia, also very wealthy and very proud, who saw in the proposition the flash of imperial purple, it did not sit well with others who might have been persuaded, but recognized and resented Dunaut's vaunting ambition for what it was. The thought of Dunaut as High King over them, free to do as he pleased because he ruled the warhost unopposed could not be stomached, let alone seriously supported.

Time and again the debate foundered on this point; and, until it was settled, Dunaut and his supporters would allow no other to be raised. Other voices, other issues, battered down, ignored, discouraged in a hundred different ways, fell by the way.

Resentment grew, hardened; animosity spread; hostility flourished. It began to appear as if Bishop Urbanus' worst fears would come to bloody fruition: the next High King of Britain would only be chosen by the sharp edge of the sword.

Then something unforeseen happened. Two unsuspected allies appeared to forestall the rush to bloodshed: Ygerna, and Lot of Orcady; two whose sudden and unannounced emergence fairly startled the assembly, preoccupied as it was with thinking itself the centre of all creation.

Lot ap Loth, of the tiny island fastness of the Orcades in the far north, with his black braided locks and armbands of enamelled gold, the blue, woad-stained clan marks on his cheeks, and his crimson-and-black checked cloak, seemed a visitor from the Otherworld. He arrived with all the frost of a northern winter, unconcerned with the stir his coming provoked: young, high-spirited, but with such calm command that his glance unsettled kings twice his age.

The council had just reconciled itself to Lot's presence when Ygerna appeared. With an escort of Uther's chieftains — those who were still with her — she strode purposefully into the church, looking stern and strong and beautiful. Arrayed regally and simply, Ygerna wore a dove-grey cloak over a white mantle edged in silver; a slim golden torc encircled her throat. Every line of her body spoke eloquently of authority and reserve. Her grace and poise served a rebuke to the fatuous posing of the petty kings.

That these two should arrive so suddenly, and on the heels of one another, was perhaps more than coincidence. It was certainly uncanny in the effect it had on the council. For suddenly the mood of the assembly changed, as the lords evaluated the newcomers and calculated how best to make use of these unknown quantities. No one, I am quite convinced, had given a thought to either of them, or considered that they might have a part in the proceedings.

Indeed, in my own dealings with Ygerna I had completely overlooked the fact that, as Uther's widow, she maintained the right of sitting in council. And now that she was here I experienced the momentary fear that her presence would cause the gathered kings to remember something else: Aurelius' son. But apparently no one knew or remembered, for nothing was said. Perhaps the secret was safe after all.

As for Lot, because he lived on the rim of the world, everyone else apparently assumed that he would have no interest in the affairs of the rest of the realm. So no one had summoned him. Nevertheless, he had heard and he had come.

I confess that I did not welcome his arrival — but for reasons other than the threat of whatever claim he might make to the High Kingship. No, it was his bloodline that concerned me. Lot was the son of Loth, of course; and Loth had been the husband of Morgian.

That Morgian's son should appear as out of the north-island mist alarmed me more than a little. What did it mean? Was Morgian behind it? Need I even wonder?

No doubt Morgian saw in the king choosing an opportunity for gaining power of a kind different from what she already possessed. But why send the boy? Why not come herself? Where was Lot's father?

These things concerned me in no small measure. As I

stared at Lot across the council ring, I tried to discern what kind of man he was. But, aside from the obvious fact that he, like many in the bleak north, loved his colour bright and his manner ostentatious, I could discover nothing.

At one point in the proceedings Lot caught me watching him. His reaction puzzled me: he gazed back for a moment, then slowly smiled and touched the back of his hand to his forehead in the ancient acknowledgment of lordship. Then, as if dismissing me from his mind, he turned his attention back to the assembly.

When, much later that day, the council finished, I waited for Ygerna in the yard outside the church, watching the builders. The masons were making use of the day's last light to move the huge keystone of the great arch. The ropes they used were too small for the task and their levers were too short. For all their labour, and their energetic cursing, they could shift the enormous stone but a few paces.

As soon as Ygerna entered the yard she saw me and hurried to me, two of her chiefs following at a respectful distance behind. 'Do not be angry with me, Myrddin,' she began at once. 'I know what you are thinking.'

'Do you indeed?'

'You are thinking that I have no place here, that I should have stayed in Tintagel, that I will only make things worse for my presence.'

I grinned with pleasure; she was not so purposeful and self-assured as she seemed. 'Ygerna, I am glad you have come; you have as much right here as any of the others. And you could not make matters worse than they already are, if that were your sole ambition. So, you see, you have no cause to feel unwelcome.'

She smiled, the corners of her mouth bending down. 'Well, you may not think so when I ask you what I have in my mind to ask.'

'Ask then, but do not think anything you ask will change my mind.'

Glancing quickly round — a kitchen girl about to speak a guilty secret — Ygerna said softly, 'I must ask you to return Uther's sword to me.'

I considered this for a moment.

'You see?' the queen remarked sulkily. 'You *are* angry now.'

'Please, I am not angry. But why the sword?'

'I have seen what is happening here. They treat me well enough, but I am ignored. If they will not recognize me, perhaps they will recognize the sword.'

It is not the first time a woman's heart read the matter truly, and far more quickly than any man might arrive at the same conclusion. After only one day in council, she had discerned the crux of the thing: without any power of her own, she would be ignored — politely perhaps, but ignored all the same.

'Well? May I have it back?'

'Of course, my lady. But what do you plan to do with it?'

She shook her head. 'That will come to me when it comes. I will send Kadan to fetch it tonight.'

'I will have it ready for him.'

That settled, she turned to pleasantries. 'It was a most enjoyable journey — not like the last time. . . ' She paused, remembering when she had come with Gorlas and Uther. 'And yet, I shall never forget that journey. It was the first time I saw Uther — the first time for so many things it seems.'

We walked together along the narrow street to a near-by house, where she had lodging. 'Dine with me tonight, Myrddin,' she offered. 'Unless you have made better plans.'

'I have no other plans,' I replied. 'And certainly none better. I would be honoured to dine with you, Ygerna. And I will bring the sword.'

She smiled winningly. 'In truth, you are not angry?'

'Who am I to be angry with you?'

She shrugged. 'I just thought you might be.'

I returned to Gradlon's house, where Pelleas was waiting outside the door. 'He came here with his men. There was nothing I could do.'

I observed five thick-necked, stout-legged horses tied to the rings in the side of the wall. 'Who has come, Pelleas?'

'Lot.' His brow creased unhappily. 'He said he would speak with you.'

Well, there was nothing for it but to meet him. I entered the house and found it crowded with north-country strangers. Lot stood at Gradlon's hearth, back to the door, one foot on a firedog, his hands wrapped in the iron chain suspended there.

At my entry, the men fell silent. Lot turned. His eyes were the colour of snow shadow — grey-blue and cold as winter ice. I stood in the doorway and he regarded me casually, confidently.

For the space of three heartbeats I paused, then stepped into a room bristling with hidden knives and unseen spears.

EIGHTEEN

'Well, Merlin Ambrosius — Myrddin Emrys,' Lot said, finally. 'I am honoured.'

'Lord Lot, I did not expect you.'

'No, I suppose not. It seems no one expected me in Londinium.' His smile was sudden and sly. 'But I much prefer it that way.'

Uneasy silence reclaimed the room. I broke it at last, saying, 'Will you drink with me? Gradlon's wine is excellent.'

'I do not drink wine,' he said coolly. 'That is a luxury we do not allow ourselves in Orcady. And I have never developed the taste for southern vices.'

'Mead?' I offered. 'I am certain our host will oblige.'

'Beer,' he said, spreading his hands in a gesture of helplessness. 'As you see, I am a man of simple pleasures.'

The mocking emphasis he gave the words suggested a wildly voracious appetite and brought to my mind images of unspeakable perversion. Yet he smiled as if it were a point of honour with him. He was his mother's son, and no doubt. I resisted the impulse to flee the room. The only reason I suffered him at all was to discover why he had come.

I motioned to Pelleas, standing protectively beside me, to bring the beer. Lot gestured to one of his men, who silently followed Pelleas from the room.

I saw no reason to prolong the pointless. 'Why have you come?' I asked. The bluntness of my question amused him.

'And the beer not even in the cups,' he chided good-naturedly. 'Why, cousin, since you ask, I will tell you. There is only one reason to venture so far from the balmy borders of my sun-favoured realm. Surely you can guess.'

'The others are here to win the High Kingship, but I cannot think you hope to gain that for yourself.'

'Do you think me unworthy?'

'I think you unknown.'

'Your tact is celebrated.' Lot tossed back his head and laughed. Pelleas, shadow looming, entered with the cups. He offered the guest cup to Lot, who took it and splashed a few drops over the rim for the god of the hearth. He drank deeply and with zeal.

Then, handing the cup to the first of his men, he wiped his mouth with his fingertips and fixed me with a fierce gaze. 'My mother warned me you would be difficult. I wondered if you had lost your will to cross blades.'

'You have not answered my question, Lot.'

He shrugged. 'All my life I have heard of Londinium. So, fancying a sea-voyage, I said to my chieftains, "Let us go and see this wonder for ourselves. If we like it, perhaps we will stay." Imagine our surprise when we discovered a king choosing taking place.'

His whole demeanour was mockery. But I detected a thread of truth in his answer: he did not know about the king choosing when he set out from Orcady. He had come for an altogether different reason and had learned of the council somewhere along the way — perhaps, as he said, only upon his arrival. Still, I reflected, he had not answered the question I asked.

I sipped from my cup and then passed it on. 'Now that you are here, what will you do?'

'That, unless I am far wrong, will very much depend upon how I am treated.'

'I find that I am generally treated as well as I treat others.'

'Oh, but it is not so simple for some of us as that, dear cousin. Would that it were.' He sniffed unhappily. 'Ah, but you would know little of the adversity lesser mortals must endure.'

Was he trying to provoke me? I thought it likely, though could perceive no reason for it. 'Is your life so burdensome to you?' I asked, not expecting any particular reaction. But, as if I had fingered a very raw and painful wound, Lot winced. His eyes narrowed and his smile grew tight.

'Burdensome is not the word I would choose,' he replied stiffly. 'Where is that cup?' He reached for it and took it from the hand of one of his men, tossing back the remaining draught. 'Empty so soon? Then we must leave,' he said, and walked to the door.

Reaching the doorway, he paused, saying, 'You know, Myrddin, I had hoped our first meeting would be different.' He turned abruptly and started away.

I can, when I choose to, make my command almost irresistible. I made it so now. 'Do not leave!' I called after him. Lot halted. He stood for a moment and then turned round slowly, as if expecting a swordpoint against his throat.

The uncertainty of that gesture argued eloquently for him. He was an untried boy playing bravely at being a king, and I was moved with compassion for him. 'We should not part like this,' I told him.

His grey-blue eyes searched mine for any hint of deception — I think he was a master of discerning it — but found none in me. 'How would you have us part?' His tone was wary, testing.

'As friends.'

'I have no friends in this place.' It was an unthinking response; nevertheless, I know he believed it.

'You can hold to that,' I replied, 'or accept my friendship and prove yourself wrong.'

'I am not often proved wrong, Emrys. Farewell.' His men followed him and in a moment I heard the clatter of hooves in the street and they were gone.

Pelleas closed the door, and then turned to me. 'He is a dangerous man, my lord Myrddin. The more so because he is confused.'

I knew Pelleas to possess no mean ability in weighing out the character of a man. 'Confused, there is no doubt. But I do not think he intends me harm. I am not certain he knows what he intends.'

My companion shook his head slowly. 'The man who does not know his own heart is a man to be feared. Have nothing to do with him, my lord.' Then he spoke my own misgivings. 'Who can say how Morgian has twisted the youth?'

If my meeting with Lot was disconcerting, my dinner with Ygerna was all delight. She had dressed in her finest clothes, and, in the glimmering, golden sheen of light from a hundred candles — light that Ygerna herself seemed to radiate — she appeared more lovely than I had ever seen her.

She kissed me as I entered the room where a table had

been set up, and took my hands and led me to a chair. 'Myrddin, I was afraid you would not come tonight and I would be disappointed.'

'How so, my lady? Had you eaten as many suppers cold by the side of the lonely road as I have, you would never let pass an opportunity to dine in comfort. And were you a man, you would never disappoint a lady as beautiful as I see before me, my queen.'

She blushed with the innocent pride of a maid. 'Dear Myrddin,' she murmured, then stopped suddenly. 'You have not brought the sword?' Ygerna looked at my hands as if expecting to see it there.

'I have not forgotten,' I replied. 'Pelleas will bring it later. I thought it best not to be seen carrying it with me. Someone might notice.'

'A wise thought.' Sitting me in my chair, she turned to the table and poured wine into two silver cups. She knelt beside my chair and offered one to me; it was the formal gesture of a servant to a lord. I made a movement of protest, but she held out the cup, saying, 'Allow me to serve you tonight. Please, it is small enough repayment for the kindness in all you have done for me.'

I shook my head gently. 'All I have done? My lady, you honour me too highly. I have done nothing to warrant such affection.'

'Indeed? Then I will tell you, shall I? When everyone else thought me a foolish girl, you treated me as a woman and the equal of any man. You have ever been my true friend, Myrddin. And true friendship, for a woman, is difficult to find in this world.' She pressed the cup into my hand with her cool fingers. 'Let us drink together in friendship.'

We drank, and then she rose and began setting the meal on the board. I allowed her ministrations to me and it made her happy. It saddens me now to admit that the kindness she referred to had been extended to her not because she was Ygerna, and therefore worthy of such consideration: no, it was that she was Aurelius' bride, or Uther's wife. In truth, I had given her no particular consideration as a fellow human being; but so barren was her life on that seabound rock that my small courtesies loomed large with her. I thought of this and my shame overwhelmed me.

Great Light, we are blind men all of us; slay us and be done with it!

Oh, Ygerna, trusting heart, if you only knew. That she loved where she should rightly despise was her glory. I think I did not taste a single bite of the meal she laid before me. But I know I have seldom enjoyed a repast more. Ygerna fairly shone in her beauty and happiness.

In this, I should have had my warning of what she was planning. Although it is likely that Ygerna herself did not yet know. I believe that she acted out of the pureness of her heart and there was no other motive.

Pelleas was mistaken; one who did not know what he intended might be turned to the light as easily as the darkness. Good is always possible, and redemption is never more distant than the next breath. Somehow, Ygerna reminded me of this.

All the same, when Pelleas arrived with Uther's sword and I realized how quickly the evening had passed, I bade Ygerna good night and stepped out into a star-filled night without the slightest suspicion of what would take place on the morrow.

The next morning the kings assembled in the church once more. And once more, as at all the other times, Dunaut and Morcant devised to hobble the proceedings with insulting and outrageous demands. If they could not realize their ambitions in council, at least they might provoke the others to arms and win in that way. It was all the same to them.

But from the beginning that day's events took shape differently. Ygerna and Lot were present and the others were forced to take account of them. As Dunaut was warming to his long harangue, Ygerna simply rose from the chair that had been added to the circle for her, and stood.

She stood until Dunaut, distracted by her quiet presence, stopped and acknowledged her. 'My lords,' he sneered, 'it appears that Queen Ygerna wishes to speak. Perhaps she does not understand the proper observances of this assembly.'

'Oh, indeed,' she replied. 'I have observed much in the short time since I have joined this noble assembly. It appears to me that the only way to be heard is to shout at the top of one's lungs while impugning the characters of those present. That, I think, would avail me little, so I stand and wait to be recognized.'

'Lady,' said Dunaut in an exasperated tone, 'I yield to you.'

Coolly, but politely, she dismissed him. 'Thank you, Lord Dunaut.'

It must have taken all her strength of will to appear so calm and self-possessed. But there was no trace of fear or hesitancy in her manner; indeed, anyone would have thought dealing with power-mad kings was all her world. 'I am Uther's widow,' she began, speaking slowly and forcefully, 'and before that I was Aurelius' widow. No other woman, I think, has shared meat and bed with two High Kings.'

Some of the kings laughed nervously. But, though she smiled, Ygerna did not allow them to make light of her. For, she continued, 'No other woman can claim to be twice High Queen of Britain. . . and no other woman knows what I know.'

That stopped them. The lords had not considered that Uther and Aurelius might have confided their secrets to her. They surely considered it now; I could almost hear them grunting under the strain of guessing what she might know.

'We are at war here, my lords. We do battle here among ourselves while the Saecsen send out the husting.' This revelation, spoken by one so fair and self-assured, sobered them. 'Oh, yes, it is true. Or did you think that when news of Uther's death reached them they would lay down their weapons and weep?

'I tell you, they weep for joy to hear it. They gather the warhost and soon they will come.' She paused, gathering every eye to herself. 'But this you already know, my lords. I have not come here to tell you that which you already know.'

Blessed girl, she had them like fish in a net. What would she say next?

She raised a hand and Kadan, her adviser, came to her holding a cloth-wrapped bundle. He placed the bundle in her hands and then took his stand behind her. Ygerna stepped to the centre of the floor, and held the bundle well up, so all could see. Then she began unwinding the cloth.

Gold and silver flashed beneath the wrappings and all at once the cloth fell away to reveal what I knew to be hidden there: the Sword of Britain.

'This,' she said, lifting the sword, 'was Uther's sword, as it was Aurelius' sword; but once, long ago, it belonged to the first

High King in the Island of the Mighty. And each High King has held it since, save one —' she meant Vortigern, of course, ' — for this is the sword of Maximus the Great, Emperor of Britain and Gaul.'

She turned slowly, so that all could see that it was, without doubt, the Emperor's famed blade. Light from the narrow, high-cut windows fell in long, slanting rays, catching the blade and setting fire to the great eagle-carved amethyst.

Oh yes, they recognized it: the lust glinting sharp in their eyes told all. Dunaut's right hand actually fondled the hilt at his side, as he imagined what it must be to wear the Imperial weapon as his own. Other hands twitched, too, and eyes narrowed to see the play of light along that cold, tapering length of polished steel.

The sanctuary fell silent as Ygerna raised the sword in both hands above her head. 'My lords, this is the Sword of Britain and it is shameful to fight over it like hounds over a gristlebone!'

Then, lowering the sword, point first to the floor, she folded her hands over the hilt, slowly knelt and bowed her head.

I do not know what she prayed. No one does. But, whatever the words, there could have been few more heartfelt prayers uttered in that church before or since.

I see her still, kneeling there in the ring of kings. Her blue cloak is folded upon her shoulder; her torc glints at her slender throat; her long fingers are interlaced around the golden hilt; the great jewel touches her fair brow. The light falling around her enfolds her in a holy embrace.

If the kings were embarrassed by her words, they were mortified by her example. Heartless indeed was the man among them who could look upon that innocent sight and not feel remorse and shame. Guilt made them dumb.

At last, her prayer finished, she rose and, holding the sword before her, began walking slowly round the ring.

'Lords of Britain,' she called, her voice loud and sure, 'this sword belongs to the one who has never sought to advance himself over any other, the one in whom the vision of our realm burns most brightly, whose wisdom has been valued by high and low alike, whose strength as a leader and prowess in battle is sung in timber halls and wattle huts from one end of this world's-realm to the other. . . '

Ygerna had stopped before me.

'My lords, I give it now into his hand. Let those among you who would take it wrest it from him!'

So saying, she put the sword into my hand and held it there with both of hers. 'There,' she whispered, 'let them try to undo that.'

'Why?' My voice was harsh with astonishment.

'You would never have spoken for yourself.'

She turned to the assembly and called, 'Who will join me in swearing fealty to our High King?'

Ygerna knelt down and stretched her hands forth to touch my feet in the age-old gesture. The lords looked on, but no one made a move to join her.

Time slid away and it began to appear as if Ygerna's noble gesture would be reviled. Standing or seated, they stubbornly held their places. The silence turned stone-hard with defiance.

Poor Ygerna, made to look a fool by their haughty refusal to acknowledge me. I could have wept for the beautiful futility of it.

But, then, just as it seemed as if she must withdraw, across the floor someone stirred. I looked up. Lot rose slowly to his feet. He stood for a moment and then walked to me, his eyes on mine as he came. 'I will swear fealty,' he announced, his voice echoing full in the vaulted room. He sank to his knees beside Ygerna.

Lot's example amazed the kings even more than Ygerna's. They stared in disbelief — as I did myself. However, two against all the rest is not enough to make a man High King.

But Custennin had stepped forward, too. 'I will swear him fealty,' he called in a loud voice. And the next voice to break silence was Tewdrig's. Both men knelt before me, and were joined by their chieftains. Eldof of Eboracum and Rhain of Gwynedd came next with their advisers, and all swore fealty and knelt. Ceredigawn and his men did likewise.

Had it been another time, or another man, it might have gone differently. Though, I believe that what happened that bright morning was ordained from the beginning.

Dunaut and Morcant, and their contentious ilk, were strong. They would never bring themselves to bend the knee to me, and I knew it. As it was, the kings were divided in their support of me, and more were against me than for me.

I could not be High King. And no, no, I did not desire it. Nevertheless, I had the support of good men. Now, at least, I had leave to act.

'Lords and Kings of Britain,' I said, taking up the sword. 'Many among you have proclaimed me High King —'

'Many others have not!' cried Dunaut. 'Everyone knows you have not lifted so much as a knifeblade in years.'

I ignored him. ' — And though I could persist in furthering my claim, I will not.'

This stunned nearly everyone, and emboldened Dunaut, who called, 'I say we must choose one who is not afraid to raise the sword in battle.'

I did not let this go unchallenged. 'Do you think me afraid? Does anyone think Myrddin Emrys afraid to use this weapon as it was intended? If that is what you believe step forth and we will put your faith to the test!'

No one was foolish enough to accept my challenge.

'So, it is as I thought,' I told them, 'you believe otherwise. You know it is not for fear that I have refrained from taking up the sword, but because I learned the lessons of war long ago: that a man can kill only so many enemies — so many Saecsens, so many Picti, so many Irish.

'And then there are more Saecsens, more Picti, more Irish and I tell you that though rivers run red with the blood of the foeman and skies blacken with the smoke of their burning corpses they cannot all be killed.'

I felt a stirring in my blood. Words began to burn in my breast.

'This sword is Britain,' I declared, lofting it. 'My claim is no less worthy than any other lord's, and better than some. Yet I am not the man to hold it. He who holds this sword will hold Britain, and he must hold it in a firm and unfaltering grasp.

'Therefore, from this day I will put away the sword, that I may serve and strengthen him who must wield it.

'But I tell you the truth, this sword will not be won by vanity. It will not be gained by arrogance or stiff-necked pride. And it will not be won by one man advancing himself over the bodies of his friends.

'The Imperial Sword of Britain will be won by the one king among you who will bend his back to lift other men; it will be gained by the king who puts off pride and arrogance, who puts off vanity and puffed-up ambition, and takes to himself the humility of the lowest stable hand; it will be earned by the man who is master of himself and servant of all.'

These words were not my own; the bard's *awen* was on me now and, like a fountain pouring forth its gifts unbidden, my tongue gave utterance of its own volition. I spoke and my voice rang out like sounding iron, like a harp struck by an unseen hand.

'Bear witness, all you kings, these are the marks of the man who will make this sword his own:

'He will be a man such as other men will die for; he will love justice, uphold righteousness, do mercy. To the haughty he will be bold, but tender to the meek and downcast. He will be a king such as has never been in this worlds-realm: the least man in his camp shall be a lord, and his chieftains shall be kings of great renown. Chief Dragon of Britain, he shall stand head and shoulders above the rulers of this world in kindness, no less than in valour; in compassion, no less than in prowess. For he will carry the True Light of God in his heart.

'From his eyes will fly fiery embers; each finger on his hand will be as a strong steel band, and his sword-arm judgment's lightning. All men alive in the Island of the Mighty will bow the knee to him. Bards will feast on his deeds, become drunk on his virtue, and sing out unending praises that the knowledge of his reign will reach all lands.

'As long as earth and sky endure, his glory will be in the mouths of men who love honour and peace and goodness. As long as this world lasts, his name will live, and as long as eternity his spirit will endure.

'I, Myrddin Emrys, prophesy this.'

For the space of a dozen heartbeats no one dared speak against me. But the moment passed; the *awen* moved on. A shout snapped the silence.

'Empty words!' cried Dunaut. 'I demand a sign!'

Coledac and others, too, joined in: 'How will we know this king? There must be a sign.'

I suppose it was only the grasping of drowning men after straws. But it angered me. I could not abide them even a moment longer. Seeing nothing, knowing nothing but the blood-red cast of rage, I fled the church, the sword still in my hand. They all ran after me, their voices bleating in my ears. I did not listen and I did not turn back.

There in the yard before the doorway, where the masons were at work on the arch, lay the enormous keystone. Taking the hilt in my fist, I raised the sword over my head.

'No!' screamed Dunaut wildly. 'Stop him!'

But no one could stop me. I thrust the Sword of Britain down towards that unyielding stone. . .

The astonishment on their faces made me look as well. The sword had not broken: it stood upright, quivering, buried nearly to the hilt and stuck fast in the stone.

EPILOGUE

Some claim a hand appeared to grasp the naked blade and guide it into the stone; others say a flash of light blinded them for a moment and that when they looked the sword stood in the stone. However it was, all agree the sharp stench of burning stone filled the air and stung their eyes.

'You ask for a sign,' I shouted. 'Here it is: whosoever raises the sword from this stone shall be the true-born king of all Britain. Until that day the land will endure such strife as never known in the Island of the Mighty to this time, and Britain shall have no king.'

So saying, I turned at once and made my way through the shock-silenced crowd. No one called after me this time. I returned to Gradlon's house and gathered my things, while Pelleas saddled the horses.

But a short time later, Pelleas and I rode alone through the narrow streets of Londinium. We reached the gate, passed beneath the wall, and turned onto the road.

The day was far gone; the sun burned yellow-gold in a fading sky. We paused on a hilltop to see our shadows stretched long behind us, reaching back towards the city. But it was not in me to turn back. No, let them do what they would; the future, our salvation, lay elsewhere.

So, setting my face to the west, I rode out in search of Arthur.

Other novels by Stephen Lawhead
published as Lion paperbacks

THE DRAGON KING TRILOGY
1984 C.S Lewis Medal Honor Books

Book 1: In the Hall of the Dragon King

Quentin, a young acolyte serving in the temple of Ariel, is
thrust into the centre of a conflict in which the life of the
king and the future of the realm of Mensandor hang in the
balance. Drawn into the web of intrigue spawned by the
Necromancer Nimrood, Quentin, with the aid of friends
loyal to the Dragon King, embarks on a dangerous quest.

ISBN 0 85648 859 3

Book 2: The Warlords of Nin

Mensandor is once more in desperate straits. The Wolf
Star grows nightly greater and more threatening as the
power of Nin increases and black terror reigns. It is
Quentin, once again, who holds the kingdom's destiny in
his hands. Hope lies in the forging of a sword –
Zhaligkeer, the Shining One. But the secret source of
lanathil, the living metal from which it must be made, is
long since lost.

ISBN 0 85648 874 7

Book 3: The Sword and the Flame

Quentin now reigns as the Dragon King, and is faced with the bitterest onslaught of all – the insidious attack of evil from within himself. As a young acolyte in the temple of Ariel he set out gladly on a journey which was to take him away from the old gods to a life-giving encounter with the Most High. Now it is not simply his own life, or the kingdom, which hangs in the balance. Nimrood holds Quentin's son hostage. The Dragon King has lost his sword – Zhaligkeer, the Shining One – and he has lost his way. Will he also betray his vow to the Most High?

ISBN 0 85648 875 5

THE PENDRAGON CYCLE
Book 1: Taliesin

'I will weep no more for the lost, asleep in their water graves. The voices of the departed speak: Tell our story, they say. It is worthy to be told. And so I take my pen and write . . .'

So begins the tragedy of lost Atlantis, extinguished for ever in a hideous paroxysm of earth and sea. Out of the holocaust, three crippled ships emerge to bear King Avallach and his daughter to the cloud-bound isle of Ynys Prydein.

Here is another world, where Celtic chieftains struggle for survival in the twilight of Rome's power. One heroic figure towers over all, the Prince Taliesin, in whom is the sum of human greatness — grandeur and grace, meekness and majesty, beauty and truth.

This is a tale that spans two worlds, a vision that sings in the heart, and a love that creates the miracle of Merlin . . . Arthur . . . and a destiny that is more than a kingdom.

ISBN 0 7459 1309 1

THE PENDRAGON CYCLE
Book 3: Arthur

'Arthur is no fit king. Merlin's pawn, he is lowborn and a fool. He is wanton and petty and cruel — a sullen, ignorant brute.

'All these things and more men say of Arthur. Let them.

'When all the words are spoken and the arguments fall exhausted into silence, this single fact remains: we would follow Arthur to the very gates of Hell and beyond if he asked it. Show me another who can claim such loyalty.

' "Cymbrogi," he calls us: companions of the heart.

'Cymbrogi! We are his strong arm, his shield and spear, his blade and helm.

'Cymbrogi! We are earth and sky to him. And Arthur is all these things to us and more.

'Ponder this. Think long on it. Only then, perhaps, will you begin to understand the tale I shall tell you...'

ISBN 0 7459 1311 3

THE PENDRAGON CYCLE
Book 4: Pendragon

'I, Myrddin Emrys, was with Arthur from the beginning. I stood beside him on his darkest day. A day unlike any other in the long history of our race – a day of deceit, and dread, and great glory. For on that day Arthur won the name he treasured above all others: Pendragon. That is a tale worth telling.'

When the Black Boar, Twrch Trwyth, leads his Vandali hordes into the Island of the Mighty, can Arthur, the Bear of Britain, stem the tide of destruction? Even with the wise bard Myrddin Emrys, Llenlleawg the champion and dauntless Queen Gwenhwyvar at his side, can Arthur defeat the invader and become Pendragon of Britain? Or will he die in the attempt?

ISBN 0 7459 2763 7

THE PENDRAGON CYCLE
Book 5: Grail

War, drought and plague have brought Britain to the brink of destruction. Then, in the great battle which finally brings peace to his tormented land, Arthur is mortally wounded. But at Ynys Avallach he is miraculously healed by a sacred and secret relic, the Holy Grail. Determined to establish his long dreamed of Summer Realm, Arthur decrees that a shrine shall be built to house the Grail, so that all his subjects may share its healing powers.

But evil in a more beguiling and subtle form attacks Arthur's grand plans, and his most loyal champion is seduced into committing a most hideous betrayal. The Grail and Arthur's beloved queen vanish into the dark unknown. Soon chaos and fear are once more abroad in the land.

In pursuit, Arthur and his faithful Dragon Flight – helped by the bard Myrddin Emrys, known to the world as the sage, Merlin – confront fearsome spirits and magic in a battle to the death for the soul of the nation and the future of the Island of the Mighty.

ISBN 0 7459 3882 5 (hardback)

All Lion books are available from your local bookshop, or can be ordered direct from Lion Publishing. For a free catalogue, showing the complete list of titles available, please contact:

Customer Services Department
Lion Publishing plc
Peter's Way
Sandy Lane West
Oxford OX4 5HG

Tel: (01865) 747550
Fax: (01865) 715152